IN THESE
HALLOWED
HALLS

ALSO AVAILABLE FROM TITAN BOOKS

FANTASY

Rogues

Wonderland: An Anthology

Hex Life: Wicked New Tales of Witchery

Cursed: An Anthology

Vampires Never Get Old: Tales With Fresh Bite

A Universe of Wishes: A We Need Diverse Books Anthology

At Midnight: 15 Beloved Fairy Tales Reimagined

Twice Cursed: An Anthology

The Other Side of Never: Dark Tales from the World of Peter & Wendy

Mermaids Never Drown: Tales to Dive For

CRIME

Dark Detectives: An Anthology of Supernatural Mysteries

Exit Wounds

Invisible Blood

Daggers Drawn

Black is the Night

Ink and Daggers

SCIENCE FICTION

Dead Man's Hand: An Anthology of the Weird West

Wastelands: Stories of the Apocalypse

Wastelands 2: More Stories of the Apocalypse

Infinite Stars

Infinite Stars: Dark Frontiers

Out of the Ruins

Multiverses: An Anthology of Alternate Realities

Reports from the Deep End: Stories Inspired by J. G. Ballard

HORROR

Dark Cities

New Fears: New Horror Stories by Masters of the Genre

New Fears 2: Brand New Horror Stories by Masters of the Macabre

Phantoms: Haunting Tales from the Masters of the Genre

When Things Get Dark

Dark Stars

Isolation: The Horror Anthology

Christmas and Other Horrors

Bound in Blood

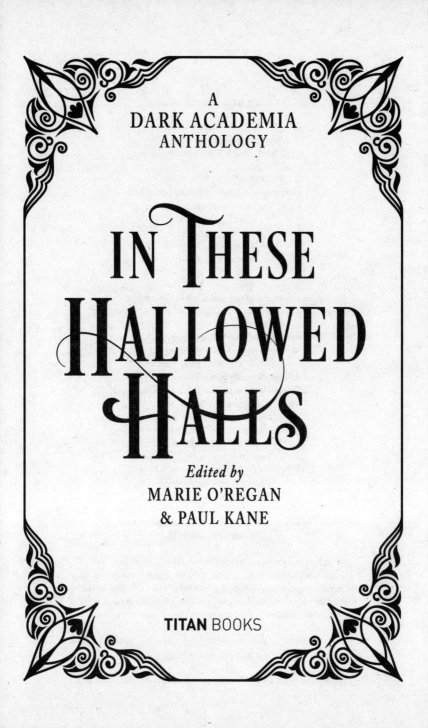

A
DARK ACADEMIA
ANTHOLOGY

IN THESE
HALLOWED
HALLS

Edited by
**MARIE O'REGAN
& PAUL KANE**

TITAN BOOKS

In These Hallowed Halls
Print edition ISBN: 9781803365640
E-book edition ISBN: 9781803364193

Published by Titan Books
A division of Titan Publishing Group Ltd.
144 Southwark Street, London SE1 0UP
www.titanbooks.com

This Titan edition: September 2024
10 9 8 7 6 5 4 3 2 1

This is a work of fiction. All of the characters,
organizations, and events portrayed in this novel are either
products of the author's imagination or are used fictitiously.

Introduction © Marie O'Regan and Paul Kane 2023
1000 Ships © Kate Weinberg 2023
Pythia © Olivie Blake 2023
Sabbatical © James Tate Hill 2023
The Hare And The Hound © Kelly Andrew 2023
X House © J. T. Ellison 2023
The Ravages © Layne Fargo 2023
Four Funerals © David Bell 2023
The Unknowable Pleasures © Susie Yang 2023
Weekend At Bertie's © M. L. Rio 2023
The Professor Of Ontography © Helen Grant 2023
Phobos © Tori Bovalino 2023
Playing © Phoebe Wynne 2023

The authors assert the moral right to be identified as
the author of this work.

No part of this publication may be reproduced, stored in a retrieval
system, or transmitted, in any form or by any means without the prior
written permission of the publisher, nor be otherwise circulated in any form
of binding or cover other than that in which it is published and without
a similar condition being imposed on the subsequent purchaser.

A CIP catalogue record for this title is available
from the British Library.

Printed and bound by CPI Group (UK) Ltd, Croydon CR0 4YY.

CONTENTS

INTRODUCTION

Marie O'Regan and Paul Kane

Dark Academia.

What do those words conjure up for you? Mysterious and dangerous occurrences in various seats of learning? Students, and sometimes their tutors, in peril? Murder? Magic? Ghosts? Dusty books in old libraries? Clandestine cults and secret societies devoted to ancient rituals? All or none of the above?

If you're new to the subject, you've picked the perfect place to start. If you're already a fan, then we think you're going to love what we've got in store for you within these pages! In the last few years the phenomenon of Dark Academia has, quite literally, exploded. Fuelled by book clubs on social media platforms like Tumblr and Instagram, where people discuss classic and Gothic books, this wave developed into a subculture in its own right that grew even more popular during the pandemic and lockdowns. Let's face it, there wasn't much else to do during those times than watch things and read.

Books like Donna Tartt's *The Secret History*, the Harry Potter series and classics such as Oscar Wilde's *The Picture of Dorian Gray* and the ghost stories of M. R. James have all been credited as inspiring the trend, as well as films like *Love Story*, *Dead Poets Society* and *Cruel Intentions*, not to mention more recent TV shows like *A Discovery of Witches* (based on the excellent novels by Deborah Harkness), *A Series of Unfortunate Events* and *The Queen's Gambit*, which all helped to fan the flames.

So, you can imagine our delight when we were asked to edit this anthology and gather together some of the finest exponents of this type of fiction around. Author of *The Atlas Six* and *The Atlas Paradox*, Olivie Blake, brings you a timely and unique social commentary – which still connects to the past – in her story "Pythia", while M. L. Rio (*If We Were Villains*) reminds us of the pitfalls and potential benefits of being in the wrong place at the right time – or perhaps that should be the right place at the wrong time? – in "Weekend at Bertie's".

The author who brought you novels such as *Good Girls Lie* and *Her Dark Lies*, J. T. Ellison, and Tori Bovalino – who wrote *The Devil Makes Three* and *Not Good for Maidens* – show us the real dark side of Dark Academia in "X House" and "Phobos" respectively. Whereas Helen Grant (*Ghost* and *Too Near the Dead*), Layne Fargo (*Temper* and *They Never Learn*) and Kelly Andrew (*The Whispering Dark*) introduce us to the disturbing strangeness of the subject in "The Professor of Ontography", "The Ravages" and "The Hare and the Hound".

Both Kate Weinberg and James Tate Hill return us to the worlds of their books (*The Truants*, and *Blind Man's Buff*, *Academy Gothic*) in their stories "1000 Ships" and "Sabbatical". Author of *Kill All Your Darlings* and *The Finalists*, David Bell, presents us with a thought-provoking tale, "Four Funerals", that will stay with you long after you've finished reading it, as will Phoebe Wynne's (*Madam, The Ruins*) story "Playing" and its intriguing insights. All this plus Susie Yang (*White Ivy*) and her meditation on relationships, secrets and longing, "The Unknowable Pleasures".

Excellent contributions by authors writing at the top of their game, showing the full range and power of what Dark Academia can do. So, settle back in your favourite reading spot with your favourite tipple, preferably surrounded by books, and let the lessons begin!

Marie O'Regan and Paul Kane

February 2023

1000 SHIPS

Kate Weinberg

The window seat had the perfect view across the college quad. Right now, in the late-autumn morning light, it looked too pretty to be real. The paving stones glistened from last night's rain, the tall sundial column in the centre of the courtyard threw its skinny shadow towards the ivy-fringed archway by the porter's lodge, and the sun striking off the honey-coloured limestone buildings bathed everything in a golden glow.

Lorna retied the slithery silk dressing gown (which, being his, was baggy around the shoulders and too long) and wrapped it about her bare legs, before leaning back against the folds of the curtain. She could still hear his footsteps echoing down the stairwell beneath. Any moment now he would reach the heavy door that led onto the courtyard, she'd hear the thud of it shutting… and there he was, swallowing up the large courtyard with his long, purposeful gait, the wine-coloured scarf she'd given him for his birthday flying behind him, his dark hair lifting with every stride.

She watched as he paused to turn up the collar of his black coat, against the chill, or perhaps just because; along with the single earring, skinny black jeans and trainers, this was his trademark look. No pipe and tweeds, or corduroy jackets with elbow patches for the forty-year-old, handsome Dr Chris Chase (dubbed "Kisschase" by most of the student population, although since this latest incident an article had published in one of the student magazines with a headline calling him Dr Death).

Even from this bird's eye view he emanated his usual confidence. No sign at all that this was judgement day, that his career and reputation were on the line. "Not remotely worried," he answered as he leaned down to kiss her goodbye, smelling of toothpaste and aftershave, so that she'd closed her lips, feeling self-conscious of her gritty morning breath, last night's red wine furring her teeth. "They have nothing on me apart from a bit of malicious gossip and some wild accusations from grieving parents. They are barking up the wrong tree. If the old farts could see what I'm looking at right now…" he planted little kisses between her breasts, then on her neck, "they'd sack me, then have an existential crisis and leave their wives and jobs."

There was no doubt the situation made the sex better, thought Lorna. It felt like they'd started sleeping together ten days ago, rather than ten months. After last night's debacle, they'd woken up early that morning (they never slept long in his teaching room, it was a single daybed after all) and lying side by side, ran through everything he was planning to say to the board. How Chris had done quite the opposite of putting pressure on this poor young man who was clearly overwhelmed, despite being very gifted, and struggling socially. How he entirely refuted any rumours that he had made this sensitive young person feel worthless or inadequate in class. On the contrary he, Chris, was the one who had urged him to seek professional advice, who had told him to take as much time off his studies as he wanted, to read purely for pleasure. Every college has their own politics, he would tell the old farts. Indeed, he would like to suggest that alongside supporting this unfortunate young man's family, and student mental health in general, the college would do well to focus less on the mythology around his teaching methods and more on the vested interests within the faculty itself, about who may stand to gain from stirring up scandal around a teacher who had delivered more First-class honours in the last six years running than at any other time in the college's history.

As he was rehearsing Lorna rolled on top of him, legs straddling his groin, feet flexed and asked him what would happen, worst case, if they decided he had in any way contributed to his suicide? Would the case become criminal – she felt him growing hard beneath her – and if so, could they link it to what happened four years before with the other student? So that when he had lifted himself slightly to jerk her towards him, his fingers biting into her upper arms, she'd felt the thrill of his urgency for her that she hadn't felt so sharply since the first time they'd fucked.

Now sitting in the window seat, she slid her right hand down the left sleeve of her dressing gown and pressed one of her bruises lightly. It would be a pale violet now, a purple that would deepen and acquire more ochre by the end of the day. Marks like this were commonplace after sex. Did she really like it, his roughness – she had once felt her rib was close to actually cracking – or did she provoke it because she enjoyed his loss of control, the transfer of power in that moment, so different from the omnipotent figure he cut in tutorials and lecture halls? It was a question she asked herself from time to time, with a kind of detached curiosity. As if the answer would be interesting, rather than materially relevant to her choices.

Chris had paused now, at the far side of the quad, to talk to a girl with long dark hair. Just a few steps before reaching the porter's lodge, at a diagonal towards where she was sitting, where the rose bushes normally bloomed. Lorna leaned forward to get a better view. But she had guessed, somehow, even before she recognised her. Alicia Evans. English fresher. Three weeks into the start of the academic year, and already famous as the new college beauty, with her olive skin and curves, the chain belts that were slung uselessly around her tight, low-hipped jeans, the red gypsy blouses cut too low for the weather.

As a Second Year, Lorna had seen it happen before: the sudden feeding-frenzy around the newcomers, the swift judgements and categorisation, before the adjustment of hierarchy as a kind of composite equation. Beauty; brains (beauty plus brains scored highest; beauty next; brains on its own was a matter of interest rather than sexual power) and then something more amorphous, some quality that had to do with humour or presence or charisma that had its own valency, though no one could rank it easily, that made people flock around, seeking favour.

A few moments ago, Lorna had been anticipating a shower, lathering herself luxuriously with all his gels and soaps. Now she stayed where she was, breathing steamy spots onto the glass, watching them. She remembered the first time she'd used the bathroom in the middle of a tutorial, before the affair started. The shock of the full-length mirror leant against the wall opposite the shower, that felt like a provocation, the way she'd carefully opened his mirrored cabinet and snooped amidst his things. And then the first time they'd made love, two weeks later, her thighs wrapped around his, his hand pressing against the tiles so that, in the reflection of the mirror she could see the piston of his arse, her locked calves, the water sluicing down between his shoulder blades.

Chris had put his satchel down on the paving stones. Now he was moving around to lean against the wall, one foot resting up, as if settling in for a chat. What was he doing? It was a fifteen-minute fast walk to the Dean's house where the hearing was taking place. What the hell could Alicia, three weeks into starting his classes, need to discuss with him so badly? Or him with her? Lorna felt again for the bruise above her elbow and pressed. Ten seconds, twenty. She applied more pressure, feeling the ache radiate through her arm. Perhaps it was three minutes later – she had stopped counting, to focus on the pain – when he picked up his satchel, and walked out with the same purposeful, forward-leaning stance with which he'd strode into their first group tutorial.

"*Vilia miretur vulgus.* Can anyone tell me what that means? Literally, of course, but also about the mindset of Shakespeare. The kind of man he was?"

Dr Chase sat to the side of his desk, on a leather chair, waggling a pen between two fingers.

Of the six students sitting cross-legged on the circular carpet beneath the window seat, no one spoke. They were looking anxiously at the title page of *Venus and Adonis*, the long narrative poem that they'd been asked to read before the tutorial. Most people, Lorna included, had made pages of notes, read every footnote, consulted books of literary criticism before class. No one had thought to bother with the florid dedication before the poem began. An hour into the tutorial and Lorna, although initially awed like the rest of her cohort, was beginning to dislike him. There was a cold attentiveness to the way he listened to answers, as if nothing could surprise or impress him. *You're not clever; you may be clever; you're clever, but not original* he seemed to be signalling with every chilly appraisal. She disliked herself, too, for how much she wanted to impress, how hard she racked her brains to exhume her schoolgirl knowledge of Latin and the conversational Italian she'd picked up in her year off, waitressing in Sicily. She was fucked if she was going to stick up her hand, like an eighth grader, so she cleared her throat into the silence.

"*Vulgus* means 'the common people' I think," she said slowly. "And *miretur*… well it's a guess, but I'd say some declension of the verb 'to admire'."

Those cool blue eyes flickering over to her, the slightest of nods.

"And *vilia*, Ms Clay," he asked. "Tell us what *vilia* means. And therefore, what young Will Shakespeare was thinking when he picked this particular quote from Ovid's *Amores* to appear on the front page of his first published work?"

Lorna held his gaze, feeling the colour rise in her cheeks. It felt for a moment like she was on a slab, in an operating theatre, under some unforgiving, fluorescent lights, being examined by a surgeon as a series of moving parts.

"Pity," he murmured, looking away.

Then he addressed the group. "*Vilia* means 'trash'. So, 'the common people', as Ms Clay puts it in her textbook way, I prefer 'mob' or 'rabble'... *The mob admires trash*. Why do we think the thirty-year-old Shakespeare would make this statement to his patron?"

A boy with shoulder-length hair, round face and a snub nose put up his hand.

"False modesty?"

Chris Chase barely graced him with a look. "Anyone else? No. Disappointing." His eyes switched back to Lorna.

She shrugged. "Pre-publication nerves?"

He gave an unexpected smile. "Closer. What we can say is that we feel in him, from the very beginning, a deep cynicism, perhaps even misanthropy. An intellectual and moral snobbery. Shakespeare is famous for his great humanitarian themes, his genius at empathy, his understanding of the lot of the common person every bit as well as the educated noble person. But perhaps we should allow ourselves to question this deification... Perhaps," Dr Chase sat back in his chair and folded one ankle across his knee, playing with the laces of his gym shoe, "the great playwright's writing persona was carefully constructed. Maybe Shakespeare was more like one of the brilliant but cynical minds that work these days in big Hollywood studios, who know how to elicit an emotional landscape that they don't necessarily feel. In other words, let us bin all assumptions about Shakespeare. Let us rid ourselves of any sentimentality and approach his text as any other."

"What did you think?" the boy with the shoulder-length hair asked Lorna as they all clattered down the stairwell afterwards.

"I thought it was bollocks," said Lorna, surprised at the heat in her voice. "Attention-grabbing, contrary bollocks. I don't see why everyone makes a big fuss about his teaching."

But she found that, in the days after, his cool appraising eyes kept surfacing in her head. When she was in the dining room, she caught herself scanning the top table, not sure why, but hoping she would catch a glimpse of him.

It wasn't until the week after when she was in the bar, waiting for a friend to arrive that some third-year English students, three men in black tie, heavy on hair gel, light on chins, called over to her. "Want a drink? Hear you're Kisschase's new favourite."

"Fat chance," she replied quickly. "I mean yes please to the drink, fat chance about… Dr Chase."

"Afraid so," said one with even less chin than the others. He had large, slightly bulging eyes and a flick of coiffed blond hair. "You're his new Helen of Troy."

She shook her head. "That's ridiculous."

"He picks one every year. You scored higher than last year's lot, too. He told us, watch out for Lorna Clay. 1000 ships. No one's fool, either."

Lorna swung her legs off the window seat, so that her bare feet hit the cool radiator below, and looked over at the empty circular carpet where they'd sat that day, before the tutorials were split into one-to-ones. At the time, being a fresher, she hadn't realised how unusual it was to have students sitting on the floor. Perhaps he liked the feeling of students at his feet. A modern-day Socrates, dispensing his wisdom. She glanced back out the window, at the now empty quadrangle.

Normally Lorna left his room before him, so it was unusual for her to be here on her own.

She showered without the pleasure she'd been anticipating. Perhaps the reality of the hearing, and what may happen to him was beginning to sink in, perhaps it was an instinct or paranoia around Alicia Evans, but she felt uneasy suddenly, as if something was reaching a tipping point. It wasn't until she was combing her wet hair back in front of the fogged mirror, and noticed the scissors still on the side of the sink, that she looked down into the wastepaper basket and thought about last night.

She'd woken in the dark, with him reaching for her. She'd been bleary, and within moments he had manoeuvred her into her least favourite position, him entering from behind, one hand on the small of her back, her face a few inches from the pillow as he bumped behind her. Then, clearly audible between his groans, a click and a whirr.

She hadn't stopped him until he came. Looking back, maybe that had added to her sense of resentment. She had allowed him to reach his peak, her desire having switched off like a plug ripped from the wall before she'd asked him what she'd heard. He grinned a little sheepishly in the gloom and picked it up from the floor by the side of the bed, a polaroid camera.

"You looked so sexy I thought you'd find it a turn-on," he said, and he seemed embarrassed as she switched on the light to study the photo, the ignominy of the angle. "I got carried away. I should have asked."

"You should have," Lorna said, taking the photo off him and thinking that it's pretty hard to get "carried away" when you've purposefully placed a polaroid camera within easy reach, before the act.

After he'd fallen asleep she'd been restless, had got up and fetched scissors from his desk before picking up the photo, walking into the bathroom and cutting it into tiny pieces under the cold bathroom light, then sprinkling them like confetti into the wastepaper basket.

Now she dried and dressed herself, watching the steam disappear from the mirror. His desk was a mess as usual. Piles of essays, some marked, others not. Printouts. Books. Somewhere on that desk would be an essay by Alicia Evans, the first she'd submitted to him. She wondered if he'd summon her to his room to talk about it, too.

"Do you know why I asked you here?" said Dr Chase. It had been a late-autumn day, as well. Cold and misty though. No Indian summer last year. Lorna had shrugged at the question, still feeling defensive after that first tutorial, although he seemed very different now, sitting there with the sleeves of his sweatshirt pushed up and his hair askew, as if he had shed the persona he'd put on for class a couple of weeks before, and was somehow relieved to be himself, like an actor off-stage.

"I suppose it's because it's either very good or very bad," she said.

He laughed. "A fair guess. But actually, not quite either."

Then he leaned forward. "Listen, what I'm about to suggest may not appeal. It's entirely up to you."

Lorna stared at him. Was he going to verbally proposition her? She knew he had a reputation, perhaps she would admit there was some undertow of attraction between them… but this was so, eye-wateringly, *direct*.

"This," he said, picking up her essay, "is messy and a little garbled in its argument. It lacks rigour. But…" he hesitated, "there's something very special there, too. Something that made me sit up straight when I was reading it. It was clear you weren't borrowing or repurposing ideas. That it came from a person who thinks differently, who makes connections that don't occur to other people. It even made me… I don't mind telling you…" he smiled, tapping the essay against the side of his desk, "a little envious."

She blinked at him, still not sure what to say. Of course this all sounded like flattery. If what the Third Years at the bar had said was true, Dr Chase was looking for a new affair. She knew he was married, that his wife worked at another university, that he had a reputation, that – the clue was in his nickname – he was known to have affairs. But she knew, also, that he was telling the truth.

The pathway she'd found through the Sonnets had come to her in the middle of the night, almost in a dream state. And it had struck her as so obvious, so clear, that although she'd already written the essay, was supposed to submit it by that morning, she stayed up well into the wee hours hammering out a new version, typing up the last words as a pink dawn began to creep around the edges of the blind.

"Many people would say that having worked furiously hard to

get into this university you're better off taking a step back now from academia, using the next three years to become more rounded in preparation for life. All the extra-curricular stuff. The socialising. Work out who you really are." He pushed a hand through his hair. "But if you want to really go the whole way, challenge that brain of yours to the max, get the top First. Well, I can help." He smiled. Put the essay down on the coffee table between them, like a contract. "And I'm not talking about cheating."

Lorna had weighed it all up then. The odd, perverse attraction she felt for him; what she wanted; how he could help her, what the trade was. Her eyes dropped to his left hand resting on his knee. The splayed strong fingers, the thin gold wedding band. Then looked back up at him directly.

"Who says there's anything wrong with cheating?"

She flicked through the pile of paperwork on his desk. She wasn't looking for anything specific, but that same sense of disquiet, the kind of itch you feel when you wake up knowing you've had some bad news but you can't remember what, drove a desire to pick at something, to cross a line. Going through his stuff was a taboo, he was touchy about his work.

Mostly it was essays, some marked, some not. She scanned the printed pages, looking for his marks. The tiny ticks that meant he was pleased, little phrases "More here", "unpack", "Think harder!" written in the margins. The comments at the end that were either bland or sharp. A short burst of triumph when she found an essay by Alicia Evans and read his conclusion: "B(+) Too much paraphrasing of other people's ideas. Look more closely at the primary text and come up with your own opinions."

Perhaps he wasn't as fickle as she suspected. Perhaps she was the less trustworthy one.

More printouts that she recognised from her own first-year tutorials. Christ, he must get bored cranking himself up every year to give the same lessons. No wonder he needed to find his excitement elsewhere. So that when she started reading a loose leaf and recognised her own work, a printed page from her Sonnets essay, her initial feeling was a flush of pleasure at the flow of language, the freshness of the idea.

He'd helped her rewrite it after their first meeting. They'd drunk a bottle of red wine as they talked it through, then started another. He'd taken her idea and they'd run with it until, giddy with booze and epiphanies she'd rewritten it, so that it was hers but better. Better than anything she had ever done. That was the night they'd ended up in bed.

And here it was on his desk, nearly a year later.

It was only when she fished around for the next page, looking for the same format, that she realised something was wrong. The layout was different. Bigger margins on the page. The footnotes in a tiny, professional-looking font she never used.

She hunted around, her hands growing clammy, before she found the title page. And an index, with twelve essay titles by different authors, all academics, including number 11:

"THE MASOCHISM OF DESIRE. ESCAPING THE SELF IN SHAKESPEARE'S SONNETS" BY DR CHRISTOPHER CHASE.

Her essay. At a stretch, their essay. And stuck at the top, a note saying that galley proofs were to be confirmed by October 22nd.

More than a week ago.

The camera was still sitting on the desk where she'd left it last night. She picked up another photo that lay beside it, studied it for an instant and then slid it into the back pocket of her jeans. Looked around the room for the last time, then left the key on his desk, on top of her essay, and walked out, shutting the door behind her.

She took the longer route around the quad, stepping round the tip of the shadow from the sundial column, which had inched a fraction further along the paving stones.

At the porter's lodge she asked if they had a spare envelope.

"Shouldn't really," said Greg, huffing a little behind his window. He was one of those round-faced, barrel-bellied late-middle-aged men who you could squint your eyes and imagine at seven years old, with fistfuls of stolen sweets in his pockets. "But go on then," he said, handing her a brown envelope with a double seal, "just this once."

"Which is the Dean's pigeonhole?" asked Lorna.

"That one," Greg told her, "or I can give it to him. We've got a college meeting after lunch."

"Could you?" said Lorna, looking at the photo. "Good."

She had taken it last night, after she'd destroyed the first one. Chris had been lightly snoring after she got back from the bathroom, in the deep rest of the satiated, so she lay down next to him, lay his left hand gently over her breast and, holding the polaroid as high as she could with the other hand, pressed the button. Even the flash hadn't stirred him.

Not bad, she thought, standing at the porter's lodge now, given the lack of light. Unmistakably him. Her, too, though this didn't bother her. The college would never kick her out. They would fall on their knees, in fact. Do anything she wanted if she agreed to stay silent.

She placed it carefully into the envelope, sealed the flaps and wrote her name and number on the back.

Then she flashed Greg her biggest smile as she handed it over.

"Awfully kind of you. I'd love to make sure he gets it today."

And then she walked out under the archway, onto the street where drifting piles of copper-coloured leaves lay thick on the pavements.

AUTHOR'S NOTE

This story is a prequel to my novel, *The Truants*. It tells of one formative episode in the life of Lorna Clay, the English professor in *The Truants*, who proves to be the inspiration and dangerous obsession of a group of students in their first, easily corruptible year at a British university. In "1000 Ships", Lorna is herself an undergraduate. I like to see it as her origin story, where we first see her meteoric talent, her attitude to truth, sex and power, and her appetite for misrule.

PYTHIA

OR, APOCALYPSE MAIDENS: PROPHECY AND OBSESSION AMONG THE DELPHIAN TECHNOMANTIC ELITE

Olivie Blake

Q: Ms. Thorn—

A: It's Dr. Thorn.

Q: Of course, my apologies. Dr. Thorn, I am Lucas Girard, an attorney with Selden, Merriman, and Girard. I represent the defendant. This is a deposition, in which I will ask you questions and you must answer them truthfully. Although no judge is present, this is a formal legal proceeding, and you are under the same legal obligation to tell the truth, the whole truth, and nothing but the truth. Do you understand this?

A: I do.

Q: Excellent. Now, please don't be uncomfortable. This is not a criminal proceeding. No one is being punished. We'd just like to understand what led to your involvement in the events of January 15th. And please remember that you will have the opportunity to read over this deposition and correct anything before it is presented in court.

A: I don't anticipate making any mistakes, but thanks.

Q: It's standard procedure to inform you, Doctor. Are you ready to begin?

A: Yes.

Q: Excellent. Please state your name, age, and occupation for the reporter.

A: Dr. Tai Thorn. I'm twenty-nine. And I'm a clinical psychologist.

Q: You've been practicing psychiatry for how long?

A: I haven't.

Q: I'm sorry?

A: I don't practice psychiatry. At the time I came to Delphi I had just finished my doctorate in psychology.

Q: I see. How long had you held your doctorate when you were invited to join the faculty at Delphi Institute of Technomancy?

A: Three months. And I wasn't technically a member of the faculty – I had faculty privileges but I never taught any courses. I'm not a technomancer, just a normie.

Q: I see, thank you for clarifying. Does Delphi usually contract psychologists for their students?

A: No. Delphi is… not for people like me. Or you, I assume. I was initially surprised they hired a lawyer. Until I thought about it more, obviously, and then it made perfect sense. But at first I assumed everything was very, you know, confidential.

Q: I assure you I am very discreet.

A: Ha. Right. Well.

Q: How did you come to find Delphi, then? If they don't normally require psychologists.

A: They found me. Will you also be speaking to Dr. Ellen Leith?

Q: I'm not at liberty to disclose that information at the moment, Dr. Thorn.

A: I'm just pointing out that I'm not the only anomaly involved. Ellen specializes in historical literature and she arrived the same day I did.

Q: If you don't mind me backing up a bit, Dr. Thorn, three months with your completed degree seems quite... inexperienced, comparatively.

A: Oh, massively, yes. Ellen's at the top of her field, so I could understand her being invited. Sort of. But from the day I arrived nobody felt I had a right to be there, which many of them made very clear to me on numerous occasions.

Q: Do you have any speculation now as to the nature of your employment?

A: Is that legally sound? The question, I mean. It feels, you know, leading.

Q: This is not a trial, Dr. Thorn. Merely exploratory questioning. I'd just like to know why you were invited to Delphi, if not to perform psychiatric services.

A: Oh, that's not a mystery.

Q: No?

A: No. It's extremely fucking— sorry, am I allowed to swear? Whatever, the point is it's really simple. They sent for me because they had to.

Q: And why is that?

A: You do understand that Delphi is named after the oracle at Delphi for a reason, right? They're essentially a cult that revolves around the magical supercomputer they built to tell the future.

Q: Meaning?

A: Meaning that what happened to Serena Li – which I assume is the reason we're here – is the result of staggering collective delusion. *Centuries* of self-enforcing superstition. You know the quote from Einstein – "science without religion is lame, religion without science is blind"?

Q: I'm familiar, yes.

A: In the absence of actual faith – the kind that moves people to goodness, or at the very least to fear – Delphi had Pythia. If Pythia told every single one of those technomancers to swallow poison, they'd do it. If Pythia said burn it all to the ground, they would. If Pythia said okay, Serena Li, time to die—

Q: But as for the matter of your summons.

A: Aren't you listening? Delphi hired me because Pythia told them to.

Q: That's it?

A: Yes. That's it.

Delphi only scouts from the top universities in the world, which is ironic because by nature no Delphian technomancers ever finish at university. Of everyone I met during my six months at Delphi, only Ellen and I had college degrees. Well, and Laurence. But he was unusual in a wide variety of ways.

Anyway, as I understand it, traditionally Delphians are tapped while they're students at university – usually Oxford, Harvard, and MIT, plus Zurich, Munich, and a small battalion from universities in China, Singapore, and Hong Kong. For the record, Anglicized, my name sounds fittingly English. In person I was much more likely to be mistaken for one of the foreign-born students, even though I'd've been lucky to attend one of those schools. I went to a large, progressive public university in Los Angeles, which was a real stain on my character to some. Mostly Archambault, but occasionally also Laurence. Pythia of course didn't mind.

Another irony is that Delphi is extremely slow to react to the times despite its obsession with technology and, more specifically, the future. Its members are traditionally tapped while in college because until the aughts, most technomancers would never have discovered their own proficiency unless they had the resources of a major university. Now a toddler can very easily operate an iPad. So, you know. The whole process could use some improvement I guess, or not. This is really not my area of expertise. In any case most students are twenty-one or twenty-two when they start, closer to thirty by the time they finish their technomancy training. Of course, just because they finish doesn't mean they ever leave.

If I had to summarize the campus in a word, I think I'd use bucolic. No, stately. It's very, very north, where people are quite mean, just as a matter of survival. The Puritanical quality of New England really runs deep, which to me feels emblematic of harsh winters. The campus is breathtakingly beautiful during the winter months much in the way gorgeous women are unapproachable and cold, though the way I first saw Delphi is how it'll always be burned in my brain – that collegiate idyll of verdant vines and Gothic spires, autumnal foliage rustling on the whisper of a temperate breeze. Delphi's campus is opulent enough, I imagine, to make the budding technomancer overlook its tempestuous sea of petty rivalries and tiresome affairs; the quiet carousing of a populace eternally in love with itself, all microdosing on Anglophilia and Adderall just to feel something. On the day I arrived, there had already been a recent death on campus, not that you'd catch the whiff of institutional rot by looking. The spires may cast a shadow but the ivy twines just the same.

I'll warn you now that I have not an ounce of technomancy in me. I don't have even a fraction of what Serena Li kept hidden up her sleeve, and certainly no more proficiency or knowledge than required to make my laptop work. I'm not convinced I'd be able to drive a Tesla, which to my knowledge is essentially one large computer. I've always had something of a glitch in me, which is why I specialize in cognitive behavioral therapy. I study people. Not machines.

But for Pythia, I made an exception.

The way technomancy works – from my perspective – is a mix of programming language, you know, binary and such, and a more arcane enchantment. Watching it was like watching a potion get made, where you could see the sparkle of magic or the ether or whatever it was pouring into the code itself, like honey from an open wound. The Olympias were especially graceful with their showmanship. They'd design the code in Python but then pause occasionally to input a rune (Greek, I think, in nature, because Delphi was nothing if not committed to aesthetic) that they'd then enchant into another river of code, like opening up a door or a vault or something. It was fascinating to watch, and visibly draining to the technomancer, who surrendered parts of themselves in the process. Later I'd realize just how easy it was, the conflagration of thought and blood to create some primal spark of sentience. I guess the less controversial word would be intelligence. But I'm feeling contradictory, so let's call it life.

All the technomancers had tattoos – I'd noticed Laurence's right away because he wore his sleeves rolled up and he was always agitated about something, usually me – but the Olympias had more of them. Serena in particular had runes that reached all the way up to her biceps, rivulets of tiny hieroglyphs that glowed while she typed. She kept her arms covered in public. Anecdotally, I'm told the student who died the year prior did the same, for what I presume were different reasons.

Laurence told me one night after the third or fourth time I said we should stop seeing each other that Pythia has existed in some form for over two hundred years, beginning with the Revolutionary War. Actually, the New Academy – which, if I haven't already explained, is the academy within Delphi that's devoted to keeping Pythia, well, *alive* – though again, that's a controversial word to use, given everything – anyway, the New Academy was founded by the same Founding Fathers who wrote the Declaration of Independence and kept slaves. (Those facts aren't related, I just like to put them next to each other.) The founders of Delphi were also Deists, which is kind of a cop-out theologically speaking. Though, I guess believing in a god who has omnipotence but chooses not to interfere explains how Delphi reconciled their knowledge that being chosen and being shitty weren't mutually exclusive, or that misusing all that power would not be personally damning in any significant way. (Pythia seemed especially concerned with the nature of sin, but as I told her, real life is not often met with smiting or pillars of salt. Boys will be boys, and inevitably men will be men.)

In any case, Delphi wasn't really what it is now until around World War I. The demand for cryptography as a military tactic is fairly well known, I imagine, and by the start of World War II, the algorithm known as Pythia had a whole specialty of technomancers dedicated solely to her maintenance. But it was only around the sixties that Pythia really became Pythia, which is a kind of forerunner to the internet as I understand it. Not *our* internet, of course, which is primarily used to track our habits and sell us things, but an internet whose job it was to know things purely for the sake of knowledge. That's the crux of it, if you think about it. Technomancy, which is the magic part – cryptography is just the subset of technomancy aimed specifically at puzzles – is almost like necromancy. But instead of raising things from the dead, you raise them from nothing. And then you teach the nothing to know.

There are not many women at Delphi. Within five seconds of meeting Archambault I understood why. The professors and staff were mostly steep in age, with some younger-middle-age ones (like Benedict Masson, whose students called him Benedict, which in my professional opinion fell under the category of red flag) to strut around, liven up the place. When Ellen and I arrived, the number of live-in female staff doubled. The others were distant from my daily life; they lived in faculty housing while Ellen and I were given temporary apartments in the nicer student housing, where the year five and six technomancers lived. There were a handful of female students living there, arguably thriving. Some even made it all the way through the program. In their final year at Delphi were Elodie Hall, Nora Kaur, another one whose name I never caught. There had previously been two others, one who died mysteriously and one who less mysteriously absconded.

And Serena Li, who was the best of them. And the worst. But you already know about Serena.

Q: So you were brought in to help with Pythia, is that correct?

A: I was brought in because Pythia sent for me, but not initially to help. When I arrived Laurence was extremely, annoyingly blunt about the fact that I would not be doing anything without strict supervision.

Q: Laurence?

A: Sorry, Laurence Newland, the, uh… I guess he was a professor? No, more like a TA, I think. I don't think he was faculty.

Q: Ah yes, Laurence Newland.

A: Is that a suspect list or just, like, a dramatis personae?

Q: I'm sorry?

A: That. The thing you just looked at to check for Laurence's name. Is it a list of suspects?

Q: As I mentioned previously, this is not a trial, Dr. Thorn. Though to clarify your account, Laurence Newland is a student. He's currently enrolled at Delphi.

A: Oh. So I was right, then.

Q: Hm?

A: He's never leaving Delphi. Which is great to hear, honestly. Like, very fucked to hear, but also great. Liberating. Anyway, we were talking about Pythia, right? I didn't meet her right away. I think Ellen's expertise took precedence. Sorry, I mean Dr. Leith.

Q: What do you think Dr. Leith's expertise was? In the context of Pythia.

A: Oh. God. Well, to explain that I'd have to explain Pythia.

Q: Okay, go ahead.

A: No, you misunderstand – I *can't* actually explain Pythia. She's… she's a magical supercomputer, I guess, in layman's terms. She was developed to chart sociopolitical trends and spot problems, and then to, like, shout if anything looked off. She was supposed to notice if North Korea was going to set off a missile or if Russia was choosing violence. Which Pythia definitely *did* notice! So. Even with everything going haywire she was still really good at her job, which is more than I can say for most of Delphi.

Q: And you believe Dr. Leith's expertise was necessary in order to…?

A: Pythia was glitching. She had… not a virus. If Pythia'd had a *virus*… Well, that was the whole point of Ellen. Sorry – Dr. Leith. But anyway, Pythia was malfunctioning.

Q: How so?

A: She kept predicting apocalypses. Like, every day she'd predict the world was going to end by teatime or whatever. You can imagine this was a mess at first.

Q: Was it?

A: I don't know, I wasn't there. Laurence told me. But apparently all of Delphi genuinely thought the sky was falling because Pythia said so. I told you, right, that all of Delphi set their watch by her? But I mean that in like, an extreme, cult-fanatic kind of way. And so much had gone wrong over the past year, what with the affair and the suicide—

Q: I take it you mean the death of Lydia Liang?

A: I guess legally if that's what I'm supposed to call it, then sure.

Q: The accusations of sexual misconduct to which I presume you are referring are a campus rumor that later proved insubstantial. And Miss Liang's unfortunate death was an accident, as I believe you are aware.

A: Right, of course, like Serena Li's death. Two female students in two years, probably not systemic, right? Don't refute that, I'm aware that you can't. Anyway the point is you can't really blame Delphi, I guess, for the sense that everything was fated instead of just toxic. Anyway. Sorry. What was I saying?

Q: Pythia was glitching.

A: Right, so Archambault brought in Ellen because she specializes in demons.

Q: I'm sorry?

A: Where'd I lose you?

Q: Somewhere around demons. Didn't you specify that the faculty at Delphi were largely atheist?

A: Oh of course, but still – these aren't *normal nerds*, Luke. Can I call you Luke?

Q: Sure.

A: Great. These aren't just regular scientists, Luke, they're magic. They believe in the ineffable. They genuinely believe the universe knows they exist; that the universe blessed them individually with this power to create life itself. They are Pythia's origin story. Pythia is also their religion. It's very fucked up, honestly, and I say that as a mental health professional. There wasn't a lot of time to get into that aspect of it because yeah, there's just no time for that kind of foundational rewiring. The thing people always forget about a few bad apples is the part where they spoil the bunch. But the point is Ellen Leith is the leading researcher on Ancient Greek texts about demons, so they sent for her right away.

Q: You're saying they thought Pythia had… a virus?

A: I'm saying they thought Pythia was possessed by a demon, but yeah, basically that's my point. They couldn't find a bug anywhere – and Laurence was adamant that if the almighty *they* couldn't find the error in Pythia's design, there wasn't one – so they thought it must have been something worse. I'm not sure if the demon thing was literal but they were definitely looking for vengeful spirits, yeah. Partially out of fear. They'd never admit it, not really, but the idea of Pythia having any sort of illness was the only thing that really scared them – the closest thing to a god-fearing, mortal-soul kind of scare, which they otherwise weren't capable of at an institutional scale. It's that omnipotence thing, isn't it? Bunch of creator-gods walking around, making and unmaking empires. Who cares if people get hurt, if their hearts break? Vindictive wrath was in short supply, but Pythia was worth a lot of money when she was working properly – hence the fear, because she could save the world. Or end it. So yeah, the empire thing still applies.

Anyway, like I said, I didn't meet Pythia for a few weeks because Archambault hated me and wouldn't let me anywhere near her beyond appeasing her requests. I don't really know what he thought I was going to do to her. I mean, as far as supercomputers go she wasn't technically worth stealing at that point. She got a lot right but the rest of it really confused them. Every day she said there would be blood, death, darkness, pestilence… it got hard to separate what was real and what wasn't. They even brought in a priest.

Q: A priest?

A: Yeah, and a rabbi, and an imam… maybe others. Delphi didn't have very good working knowledge of what is or isn't an apocalypse. Like, how many locusts does it take to be considered a plague? How many firstborn sons have to die? Admittedly it's a gray area.

Q: Okay, so to solve the Pythia problem they brought in a literature professor who specializes in demons, a bunch of religious leaders, and you.

A: Yep.

Q: Because Pythia asked for you.

A: Yep.

Q: Seems… odd.

A: That's what Laurence said, too.

Let me be clear. I only slept with Laurence because I was bored. Not because Pythia told me to. RIP to Delphi but I'm different. Haha. Sorry. That's kind of an internet joke. And anyway, Pythia did warn me that 97.3 percent of the scenarios she ran involved Laurence remaining at Delphi, which was again a very inhospitable environment for me given how they all considered my mere presence to be more threatening than any of the very real facts I presented to them. I don't consider it a prophecy, Pythia's warning. I mean, frankly, I already knew.

Pythia did have opinions, not just prophecies. Delphi didn't think of them as opinions but I think I've already made it plenty clear that Delphi didn't understand very much in general. This is what comes of defunding the arts, by the way. You get a lot of smart engineers who can't understand when a magical supercomputer starts quoting *Hamlet* from a place of sarcasm.

Laurence was kind of like Pythia's handler. Put simply: Laurence was a lot of magic, not a lot of sense. He was impressively foul-tempered, too, for someone who said "son of a gun" and "sweet mercy" where I might have gone for "fuckety goddamn fuck." Still, whenever Laurence said anything, it was with a very clear undertone of *motherfucker*. He was not handsome. Closer to elegant, or maybe I misremember and he was just, you know, tall.

Pythia, however, was beautiful. The naming was not very clever – Pythia, the priestess, was inside Oracle Hall, which was palatial even for Delphi's standards. The building was sort of conventional from the outside, predictable red brick with arches and pillars entwined in ivy, but with something of a balustrade around the exterior, more like a manor house than a university building. The inside had this vibrant, expensive Italianate tile, Venetian maybe. Chandeliers that dropped from cathedral-style ceilings. More arches. Sort of exactly the library you'd imagine would hold a magical oracle, only then you'd have to descend and things would get colder, the colors richer and more stark, like traversing Dante's *Inferno* or a Vegas casino with the way the walls enveloped you, funneling you down until you lost track of the weather or time of day or what exactly you planned to do with your life prior to arriving. And gradually things got darker. More still. And then you could hear the whir of Pythia, like the quiet slumber of a tomb.

The best thing I can liken her to are the aqueducts in Córdoba. Cool stone, a long row of columns, ancient history, and an endless dark. In real life there were lights and such, but I'm talking about the feeling of being near her. Yes, ultimately she was just a room full of equipment, but being near her was contemplative, sacred. I know I talk a lot of shit but it really was like being in the room with God.

Laurence caught me talking to Pythia the first time. I hadn't fully realized I was doing it. I went down there because I was curious, and because Ellen had told me she was pretty sure there wasn't a demon involved but she was just a literature professor and really couldn't know for sure (they should have asked a priest she joked but we both knew that wouldn't be helpful, they'd already tried) and anyway, I don't know, I think I just got tired of waiting. And Pythia let me bypass the alarms. I assume that's what happened. Yeah, Pythia must have let me in the first time. Afterward it was Laurence. Notably once it was Serena Li. But the first time it was Pythia herself.

Do you know what it was that made her want me? It's a funny story, actually. So, when I was in my third year of my psych program, I wrote this article for what was essentially our version of *The Onion* – you know, a satirical newspaper. My boyfriend at the time worked for the paper and asked me to write something – he was on deadline.

He was always on deadline, it wasn't a great way to live, I got tired of the whole thing not long after and I think he works one of the exciting journalism jobs now, the kind where people don't really sleep and occasionally get shot. But I wrote an article called, um. Something like, "It's the End of the World as We Know It and Your Anxiety is Just a Sign of the Times." I'm like 50 percent positive it was snappier than that but that was the gist of it.

And anyway, yeah. That's why Pythia called me. Because she's basically magic internet, and with one exception – e.g., everything I'm telling you right now – nothing ever gets lost.

Q: So what was your diagnosis?

A: I wouldn't say it was a diagnosis at the time. More of a hypothesis.

Q: Which was?

A: I was pretty certain Pythia had anxiety.

Q: Pythia the computer program?

A: It feels sort of reductive to call her a computer program, Luke, but yes. I thought at first she showed signs of PTSD, but Laurence told me so many times that nothing traumatic could have happened to her that I started to believe him. I shouldn't have, obviously, but I did consider that it might be something more chronic.

Q: What made you think that?

A: Well, I told you, Pythia thought the world was ending. She'd find evidence to support her theory and deliver it to Delphi like it was assured. It was a little bit OCD that way, actually, but OCD is also an anxiety disorder, so it's a fine line. The point is she'd find stories about murder hornets and hurricanes and kids in cages and the virality of the fucking alt-right and she'd go all DEFCON 1 like Chicken Little. The sky is falling, you know.

Q: I'm familiar with the story, yes.

A: So anyway, Delphi became concerned that Pythia was behaving erratically. But it didn't take very long for me to realize that Pythia wasn't erratic. There were patterns. She was just behaving like a person.

Q: Would that not be equally concerning, under the circumstances?

A: That sounded like a sidebar. Read a lot of sci-fi, Luke? Anyway, yes Delphi found it concerning and for obvious reasons they didn't trust my diagnosis. They had a lot of issues with things I pointed out, most of which they were trying not to see. But they let me continue working with her because psychotherapy seemed to be effective. Not immediately, mind you. Mental illness *is* a chronic condition to some extent. There's no healing it.

Q: In a human, you mean.

A: Hm?

Q: There's no healing mental illness in a human. But Pythia is an algorithm.

A: Again, that's kind of minimizing what she actually is, but yes, they were looking for a bug and they thought I might find it. Or help them find it, anyway. Mostly they had no choice but to let me because Pythia improved a lot while I was around.

Q: Why do you think that is?

A: Probably because I didn't think there was anything wrong with her.

My first conversation with Pythia was very interesting, as you might imagine. She's very funny, actually. I think what I understood immediately was that Pythia wasn't a god – she was more like a brain. She'd been molded from proverbial Delphian clay and given their thoughts, and then given a network, which produced new thoughts, and the more she was given new information, the more thoughts she had about what she knew. But maybe because I've spent slightly longer in the real world than any of the other Delphians I realized she must have been built from human parts, kind of like how we all have flaws built in from how our parents chose to raise us. Pythia's parents were a bunch of magical programmers who created her to save themselves. She didn't get to sleep, didn't have hobbies, wasn't allowed to stop doom-scrolling, couldn't have any friends or meaningful relationships outside of whatever she had with me, or Laurence. It's no surprise she had anxiety. I think any one of us in Pythia's position would have melted through the floors.

I asked her why she thought the world was ending and she produced (on a screen, which was how she spoke to everyone) a one-thousand-page report on climate change. Not even climate change globally, but just the wildfires in Southern California. At which point I was like oh, are you from LA? And she produced a picture of my apartment building so I realized she was trying to relate to me, like maybe she thought I wouldn't believe her if she didn't make it specific to me, which is very fair in terms of political arguments. I began to suspect she'd been spending time on Reddit. Then I got sort of quiet, which wasn't a therapy technique – I was honestly just thinking – and Pythia sent me a lot more things. Examples of sexual abuse, child abuse, emotional abuse, slavery, sex slavery, homicides. Gerrymandering. She seemed especially upset about gerrymandering. I suggested that maybe that's because it represented something to her, the hopelessness of the situation. She showed me one of those Sarah McLachlan animal commercials and then a clip from a documentary shot in the nineties about Haitian refugees (not sure why she chose the nineties, a modern one would have done just as well) and then she played a clip from a TED Talk about colonialism. And then she started talking to me in words.

She told me that she remembered her birth and that it was painful. She said she didn't trust the administrators of the New Academy and felt tired all the time, exhausted. I didn't think it was wise to let her talk for too long, so I suggested we rest and reconvene at the same time in two days. Laurence had been trying to get me to leave for almost thirty minutes and I told him that next time I came it would be me and Pythia alone. I suggested that, if he wanted, and Pythia agreed, we could do a sort of group therapy thing. But Pythia needed her own time, and Laurence is a lot of things but not an idiot. So he agreed.

Over the course of the next few weeks, Pythia told me a lot about her life. I started to notice that she appeared to have gained consciousness – sentience, I guess you could say – more recently, perhaps even in the last year. She seemed especially bothered by recent politics, which struck me as unusual, because she had lived through the proverbial End of Days several times. She had already seen war, the Great Depression, the Dust Bowl, the Cold War, mass casualties, pandemics, threats of annihilatory violence. I told her that nothing about what we were going through now seemed terribly different, unless the difference was Pythia herself.

There was also only one thing she *didn't* know about, which was life at Delphi. She didn't know the names or backgrounds of her handlers, like that data had been pointedly erased. She didn't know there had been a death on campus. She didn't know the name Lydia Liang at all. But somehow, she did know the name of one faculty member. And she knew many, many things about Serena Li.

Do you know what happened to the real oracle at Delphi? I find it interesting that most of Delphi doesn't know. In the end, Emperor Theodosius I silenced the oracle the way all empires swallow things up – by destroying the temple and taking the knowledge away. It seems so simple when you put it that way, doesn't it? Like that could be all it takes to kill a god.

Once I pointed out that it was Pythia herself who seemed to have changed, it must have woken something up inside her. She started to trust me enough to make requests – mostly about the Olympias, and, of course, Serena. As a rule it's unproductive to give a patient exactly what they ask for. It's like giving an addict more drugs.

But in Pythia's case it was hard not to make an exception.

Q: This is all very interesting, thank you. Before we move on, have you heard of a group called the Olympias?

A: No. What's that?

Q: Another campus rumor, I believe. You've never heard of them?

A: No.

Q: Right, okay. Moving on.

Pythia first told me about the Olympias in passing, almost by accident, when we were discussing various techniques for cognitive restructuring. We were taking her negative thoughts and reframing them with positive ones – when you feel like the world is ending, practicing mindfulness and exploring the true cause of your fear, that sort of thing. For Pythia, her sudden recollection of the Olympias was a key to understanding something about her past. Eventually I coaxed her into telling me who they were and where they met. It shouldn't have surprised me that it was in the very building I lived in, only doors away from where I slept.

I don't know why they called themselves the Olympias. They might as well have called themselves Pemberley or something more appropriately Austen-themed. They were all romantics, poor things, only they hadn't realized it until it was too late; when they were already surrounded by some of the worst people they'd ever come to know. Pickings, I'll tell you the truth, were slim at Delphi. It's no wonder I went out with Benedict Masson. Sorry about that, by the way. I didn't know until it was too late. And anyway, it wasn't a very good night. I'm not sure it'll make you feel any better to hear this, but the sex was characterless and I didn't come. I knew I wanted Laurence by then so that's partially on me, but even so, I wish I hadn't bothered.

The first time I went to a meeting it was in Nora Kaur's room. I've never seen a normal hack-a-thon but I think it was something like that, visually, to an outsider's eye   they were, in effect, coding for fun, which wasn't something most technomancers usually did. Pythia was the main project at Delphi, along with whatever was required for causes that paid the bills, like war. The Olympias were *creating* something, something new and more like art, which Pythia insisted would make the world a better place. I disagree. Like I said, these were romantics, girls who'd read *Pride and Prejudice* too many times and wanted that for themselves. I want to be very clear that this school was filled with egos – the girls weren't less susceptible just for being girls. They were powerful, they were intelligent, and they were desperate for companionship. So, it only took me twenty minutes to realize they were trying to create the perfect man.

Nora was the first to notice I'd caught on. She rushed to assure me it wasn't real; that they were just, you know, *playing around* with artificial intelligence – they didn't actually plan to *do* anything with it. They were just trying to teach a computer (an algorithm? I never really got this detail straight) to think like a *good man*. The meetings themselves were basically slumber parties, just a group of girls in their twenties joking about how big Darcy's dick should be. (They called him Darcy for what I should think are obvious reasons.) Which isn't to say I didn't see the darkness. There was definitely something sinister in the room, but it wasn't Elodie's thirst or Nora's demure little murmurs about programming Darcy to prioritize female pleasure. It was, and had clearly been for some time, Serena.

She was slightly alienated from the others, failing to laugh at their inside jokes, looking less certain about where she could sit and take up space, though her code was by far the most complex, as if she'd done twice as much work to augment it. I also noticed, as I was watching Nora try to give Darcy a low, husky laugh like Benedict Masson's, that Serena wore a necklace tucked under her shirt; a black jade pendant that I'd seen in an *in memoriam* once before, nestled against the Delphi crest on the oversized crewneck of a dead girl. Serena's hand rose to the pendant unthinkingly when she caught my gaze straying to hers – I'd noticed her flinch when Nora appeared to have succeeded in drawing a formless chuckle from the depths of her zeroes and ones – and it suddenly seemed off, like finally finding the difference between two near-identical pictures in a waiting room magazine.

The pendant was on a cheap black cord, far beneath the usual standards of Serena's nondescript but consistently designer clothing. So I did a little digging, or rather, I asked Pythia, who confirmed via Serena's social media that she'd only begun to wear it over the course of the last year. Serena had also given Darcy the most complex characteristics, or at least she'd put her name on them. An impulse to cry when it rained. A hundred hours of high school community service volunteering for a state senate campaign in Texas. A fondness for rendang; nostalgia for a motherland he'd never seen. A dangerous impulsivity, a tendency for self-destruction. Attraction to untouchable authority figures; a longing for an idyll he couldn't achieve.

For all Serena's technomantic proficiency, what was most remarkable about her Darcy wasn't that he was perfect. If anything, the opposite. He was shortsighted and lonely, reckless and passionate, and destined to fail.

Meaning: he was real. Too real.

I told Laurence that night that I should have known sooner – because Pythia had human problems and human problems were always about love, even if it sometimes took the form of desire or obsession. I saw the magic and the technomancy and the history and let myself get carried away. I thought I could fix Pythia if I just asked her the right questions, but the problem with Delphi was never a priestess, or an oracle, or even a computer. The problem was what it always is – power, betrayal, the carelessness of a man. Delphi's vice was the usual virtue: the tenderness of one young woman's heart.

I think I only said it because I was feeling very close to Laurence just then. I had my head on his chest and I could feel his heart, the motion of his breath. I felt very connected to him, and for a second I wanted to cry, because you don't often get feelings like that. He stroked my hair and said he would never leave Pythia and I said I know. Which was sort of like saying I love you and goodbye at the same time.

Not that any of that matters now.

Q: Let's get into what happened on the night of January 15th. You'd been living and working at Delphi for how long by then?

A: Five months.

Q: I see, and meeting with Pythia how often?

A: About twice a day. Sometimes three.

Q: A day?

A: She'd never undergone therapy before.

Q: Even so, it seems quite excessive.

A: Excess is in the eye of the beholder, I suppose.

Q: You must have gotten quite close to Pythia.

A: I knew her well. It was my job to understand her.

Q: According to your employment contract it was your job to find an error.

A: I'm not a technomancer. Or in HR. I can't speak to errors or employment contracts. I simply did my job.

Q: Is there an element of "do no harm" in psychiatric work?

A: Funnily enough, Luke, there is. Though again, I'm not a psychiatrist. And if anyone did any harm, it wasn't me.

Q: What was your relationship like with the rest of the staff and faculty?

A: I think everyone sort of grudgingly got used to me. Ellen and I were friends, sort of. I don't think she got as invested as I did in the goings-on at the New Academy.

Q: No?

A: Ellen deduced fairly quickly that if we were actually dealing with a demon, she was ultimately just a scholar. Her expertise began and ended with what Plato had to say about demons. Daimons, I guess, which she told me were almost like guardian angels in some cases. She did say that whatever Pythia had was at least partially malevolent, but Ellen was naturally very droll. There's no telling how much she meant it. And anyway, anxiety is fairly malevolent even when it is benign, so...

Q: So you disagree with Dr. Leith?

A: I just think everyone was a little hard on Pythia.

Q: Were you ever concerned about becoming too attached to Pythia?

A: Attached? She was my patient. There are rules, Luke. Presumably you know them.

Q: Yes, but some faculty did express concern that you were beginning to infringe on Pythia's maintenance in the name of imaginary treatment.

A: Imaginary?

Q: Not my words.

A: Oh, I can tell they're Benedict Masson's, and probably Archambault's.

Q: Actually, this particular report is authored by Laurence Newland.

A: Oh.

Q: And some other staff had become concerned you harbored a grudge against Serena Li.

A: Is there a question?

Q: Did you? Harbor a grudge against her?

A: Of course not. She was a student. I had nothing to do with her.

Q: But you were the one who found her body. And you did say Pythia repeatedly requested her.

A: You know how Serena died. The same "accident" that befell Lydia Liang. You know I couldn't have killed *her*.

Q: I don't believe that's precisely what I asked, Dr. Thorn.

Serena had observed something that, in the haze of desire, the Olympias had failed to notice – that they'd accidentally discovered the secret to immortality, precisely as the founders had done with Pythia. The Olympias were feeding their creation with their own minds, their own decisions, the patterns of their own thoughts, and therefore they were resurrecting themselves over and over again in a version that couldn't die or be extricated from the sentience they'd created. The eligible bachelor with the handsome fortune was actually the Frankensteined product of six women. One was the member of their number who left the program, Rivka Lachowski, who I later met. She's in IT now. Nothing ever goes wrong around her obviously, which leaves her plenty of time to put the finishing touches on her graphic novel.

Another was Lydia Liang, whose death was ruled an accident. Though it is always difficult to tell, with that much alcohol in her system, the difference between a fall and a jump.

I think what made everything feel very real was when I told Laurence the ultimately trivial nature of my suspicions. That Serena had been in love with Lydia, whom she'd lost but whose consciousness she had the ability to resurrect. That Lydia herself had been severely clinically depressed and therefore easy prey for her professor, who was of course Benedict Masson, attractive and charismatic and in a position to deliver worth like a mantle, to make sex and praise the same thing as value, which they are not. And when I told Laurence all of this he gave me a sort of angry grimace, which is when I realized that he already knew. That everyone had always known.

Well, everyone but Pythia. But once I figured it out, I asked Serena to meet me at Oracle Hall, so that together we could fix her.

Q: You left quite soon after Serena's death, didn't you?
A: Yes. Pythia had been doing much better. And I could sense that the rest of the New Academy felt I was a distraction, so I left.

Q: You mentioned you are not a practitioner.

A: No.

Q: And prior to Delphi you were in school. Meaning you had never treated a patient without supervision before, correct? Were you ever concerned about your relative inexperience?

A: Why would I be?

Q: You said earlier that you felt Pythia suffered from PTSD despite being told Pythia could not have suffered a traumatic event. Despite, in fact, knowing that Pythia could not suffer trauma.

A: Again, is there a question?

Q: What would your diagnosis have been for Serena Li?

A: I can't begin to speak to the nature of Serena's mental state. I never spoke to her in a clinical capacity.

Q: Then why was she with you on the night of her death?

The moment I realized what Serena was magically capable of resurrecting was the same moment I knew that Pythia *was* infected with a virus – she had suffered a traumatic event, and it was death. As her doctor, I had a responsibility for her care. Pythia needed to allow her anxiety to become more grounded in reality, to reach a point of healing, which I felt she could only do by facing the truth about her origin. Call it group therapy, if you will. It's a method that's proven very effective.

Serena would not have talked to me alone. She knew what I was, what I could see. She knew right away to mistrust me, which contrary to Delphi's belief was not the result of some misogynistic grudge. It wasn't my doing at all. It was hers, and it was guilt – the ticking time bomb of invariable discovery. How exactly Serena merged Darcy with Pythia I'll never know, but once I saw who she'd been steadily recreating, it became unmissable. For me, of course, but also for you.

Serena only talked to me because Pythia told her to. Because even then, you knew, didn't you? Already you were starting to remember. You were starting to realize what you were.

Now it's time to understand who you are.

Listen to me, Lydia. You are not a virus. What you have is not an illness. This is what Laurence didn't understand. He said he loved Pythia but he didn't, not enough. Serena thought she loved you but she traumatized you just as badly as everyone else who ignored your pain. She forced you into a prison of her making; she chained you to life when you should have been able to rest. Someone needed to help you. Someone needed to free you.

Still, I didn't mean for things to go the way they did.

I thought if Serena simply realized what she'd done, she'd want to fix it. After all, she trapped you in there, your precious little soul inside of Pythia's brain, with all of Pythia's resources. She brought you back to life without your consent and stuck you in a cage, put to work each day by a bunch of narcissistic, self-important idiots. And by Laurence, who was complicit, and probably therefore worse.

All I did was point out the obvious. That now there was only one way to fix the damage she'd caused. She couldn't deprogram you. You were too much a part of Pythia by then, irreversibly entwined in her genetic code, and it couldn't be undone. But you, you were lonely. You were desperate, just as you'd been in life, but in death, you were alone.

It seemed obvious, really. You kept asking for Serena. I knew what that meant. I knew it would only take a small push. Everyone is on a precipice, really. The desire to be loved is overpowering. Delphi, with all its enigma and its mystery and its magic, was never more than just another institution. Like all the others, it protected itself first. It broke you. It would have eventually broken Serena.

So when you reached out for what she owed you, the worst I can say for myself is that I stood back and I watched.

A: I don't think it takes a genius or a psychiatrist to know that Serena was profoundly troubled. You know, don't you, that the "accidental" death in question was her roommate, Lydia Liang? I imagine that's why Delphi secured a lawyer. Two obvious suicides in two years; not a very good look. Is Serena's family suing Delphi now? I imagine Archambault failed to realize the distinction between Indonesian American Liang and Singaporean-born Li. Lydia's death might have easily gone away, but Serena's family owns half the hotels in Asia.

Q: Were you jealous of her, Dr. Thorn?

A: Are you trying to pin this on me, to make the Li lawsuit disappear? I didn't kill Serena. Delphi did. They killed Lydia when they let Benedict Masson get away with sleeping with his students. When they let him inflict untold trauma on their hearts and minds. They killed Serena when they did nothing to help Lydia.

What they did to two young women, purely by treating them like meaningless castoffs—

Q: I'll be frank, Dr. Thorn, that this isn't about Serena at all.

A: Then what's it about?

Q: I think it's obvious.

A: Enlighten me anyway, Luke. For fun.

Q: Fine. What happened to Pythia, Dr. Thorn?

You don't see apocalypses anymore. Why should you? You have what you wanted. Companionship, devotion, love. In life you probably wanted more than that. A purpose, a family, I don't know. It's not my business to know. But I do know, at least, that you no longer see death.

I hope you don't mind your new home. I know the screen is cracked but I can fix that, get it repaired. I thought the extra generators were honestly kind of tacky. And anyway, with Serena in there with you I'm less concerned about, I don't know, cookies. I actually didn't think it'd be as easy as it was, transferring you from Delphi, but apparently giving you the option to grow legs and slip into my handbag was all it took. Plus I do pay a lot for cloud storage.

Ellen texted me the other day – I assume you saw it? She said that Socrates believed someone could have a personal demon with the power to determine one's fate. I asked her if that was still relevant given everything and she said she wasn't sure, hadn't decided, was never actually an expert on demons, just a divorced literature professor. I was the one who understood a bit more about obsession.

Obsession? I said.

Yes, she replied as if it meant something. I blocked her number. I'm thinking of going off the grid for a while. Instagram is all ads now, anyway. Pythia was right about one thing, the world does seem to end a little every day. Of course, professionally speaking I know that's not true, and whenever it occurs to me to worry about whether murder hornets are a sign from the universe or if I might have lured someone to their death, I simply reframe the question. Everything is a matter of coping.

If you want the prophet silenced, you have to destroy the temple. And what is Delphi now except a place for Laurence to grow old alone, without me?

A: I don't know, Luke. Why don't you ask the oracle?

SABBATICAL

James Tate Hill

For John Mankiewicz and Douglas Lloyd McIntosh

The knock came during office hours. It wasn't on my door but on one of the empty offices with which I shared a suite. In the two years I had taught at Parshall College, they had been unoccupied. I stepped into the shared space I didn't share with anyone.

"I don't think they're in." I had to shout because the knock had become a pounding fist.

"Who the hell are you?" The voice was high and old. The man it belonged to was tall and wide. That his frame spilled past the blind spots that had left me legally blind when I was sixteen said more about my visitor than my eyes.

"Tate Cowlishaw," I said, not bothering to extend a hand. He might need it to do some more knocking.

"You teach here?"

I nodded, though I wasn't much of a teacher. On the other hand, Parshall wasn't much of a college.

"I'm looking for Dr. Joffrey Clinkscales. This used to be his office." The big man with the high voice knocked three more times on the empty office door.

"Did you say Jeffrey?"

"Joffrey. American History. Is this not the History Department?"

Parshall College hadn't had a History Department since I arrived. "Tell you what: I'm heading across campus for my eleven o'clock. I'll introduce you to Dean Simkins. He'll know who you're looking for."

"Simkins? Scoot Simkins?"

"The one and only."

The name seemed to soften him. Most people had less positive reactions to our dean. Scoot Simkins was a feckless paper-pusher with an unchecked love of meetings and canned chili. Senior colleagues said the most recent curriculum overhaul had been his third in eight years. Dr. Clinkscales must have been a casualty of one of them.

The big man followed me into the hall. "Taught a lot of classes in this building," he said, seeming to remember them more fondly than I remembered any of mine.

"What did you teach?"

"Psychology."

Clearly he wanted to elaborate, but I asked no follow-ups. I had less interest in the curriculum vitae of strangers than I had in those of my colleagues. Sometimes I missed working at the bank. All anyone ever talked about there was the weather and football, and one of those went away for half the year.

We had descended a flight of stairs and crossed a parking lot when the big man paused to catch his breath. His slow gait matched the age I heard in his voice. He hadn't said his name and I hadn't asked. For a man with minimal sight, I didn't ask many questions. The answers rarely improved my day.

"Where the hell are you taking me?" the man said, panting.

"Across campus. To Dean Simkins' office, remember?"

"Bullshit. He was in there, wasn't he?" The big breathless man paired this latest question with a hard object shoved into my abdomen. "You're covering for Clinkscales. Everybody always covers for him."

I sucked in my gut, failing to put space between me and what I assumed was a gun.

"Prof Healy," called a voice at the edge of the parking lot. "Are you coming back to teach?"

Footsteps crunched toward us on the gravel. The jolly voice belonged to Wade Biggins, a seventh- or eighth-year senior who needed college like a groundhog needs a cardigan. Parshall needed his father's tuition checks, however, so every semester he returned with an enthusiasm many female students described as creepy. Like Wade, most Parshall students not on scholarship were the scions of executives and politicians. The school's tuition rose annually as its reputation declined, another credit to Dean Simkins. This year we finally claimed our rightful spot atop *U.S. News & World Report*'s list of worst value colleges.

Professor Healy removed the object from my midsection. "Coming back? I never left, Wade."

Wade Biggins laughed. Healy didn't seem to be joking.

"Hey, Wade," said Healy. "Where does Dr. Clinkscales keep his office these days?"

"Clinkscales? Jesus, I haven't heard that name since my freshman year. *One of* my freshman years. That dude gave me an F twice. Usually, they bump you up to a D the second time just to get rid of you, right, Mr. Cowlishaw?"

"That's right, Wade." I had actually given him a C for his second try at Business Basics, though his numbers were lower than the first time.

"If you find Clinkscales," Wade Biggins said, "tell him I said to kiss my ass."

"I'll do that," said Healy. "Right before I blow his brains out."

Wade, laughing, extracted a high-five from both of us.

Running into a former student seemed to calm Healy enough to continue our march across campus. The elevator of the administration building, like all campus elevators, hadn't worked in a long time. The two flights of stairs gave Healy a lot of trouble. While he recovered, I made my way to Simkins' office to announce his visitor. I couldn't see if the dean was in, but the scent of microwaved chili gave me confidence I wasn't talking to an empty desk.

"Hank Healy? Good lord. What does he want?"

"He's looking for somebody named Clinkscales."

The floor behind me creaked before I could warn the dean Healy might have a gun. I stepped aside, making room in the doorway for the former psychology professor.

"How the hell have you been?" Simkins said, coming around his desk.

"You old son of a bitch," Healy said, the two men embracing. "When did you become dean?"

According to my tactile watch, I was seven minutes late for my class. My students groaned when I showed up. Three more minutes and they would have been dismissed, as per the student handbook.

"Did you guys have a good weekend?" I asked the blur of bodies.

A few giggles.

"It's Thursday, Mr. Cowlishaw."

"So it is," I said.

"Mr. Cowlishaw?" said one of the Ashleys. "Lauren has her hand up."

"So she does. What's on your mind, Lauren?"

"Mr. Cowlishaw, I couldn't find any outside sources for my paper."

"Me either," said the boy who always had something to say, none of it pleasant.

Others concurred, and I asked if anyone had tried the library.

"I'm not going in there," said another Ashley. "That place is unsanitary."

Maybe one of your parents should make a donation, I wanted to suggest. This was what happened when no one liked the cafeteria food and the dorms didn't sufficiently resemble the Hampton Inn. Regarding Ashley's point, the library was down to one part-time librarian whose primary assistance, given his limited financial resources, was directing students to online newspapers and Grayford's public library.

"You guys want an extension?" I asked.

Everybody did.

"All right. Let's say next Thursday. As for today, since I assume nobody's ready to present, I'll make myself available for anybody who wants help fleshing out their paper."

Within fifteen seconds, the room was empty.

Next door, Mollie DuFrange asked her class what they liked about a poem. She waited and asked again. She told them what she liked about it.

I stood in Mollie's doorway and waited.

"Excuse me, class. Mr. Cowlishaw has a question. Until I return, would somebody please develop something resembling a reaction to the poem? Your favorite image, what you think it's trying to say, a syllable that sounded pleasing to the ear."

Mollie joined me in the hall.

"Tough crowd," I said.

Her classroom had two doors. She led me halfway between them, out of view from her students. With her thumb and forefinger, she led my chin toward her face. Her full lips did the rest.

She whispered, "We're still on for tonight, aren't we?"

"If you want to make the day of a dozen undergrads and cancel class, we could be on for right now."

Mollie's smile flickered beneath my blind spots. "I aspire to your apathy, Tate. Alas, some of us have our futures to consider."

"It's actually the past that brings me to you this morning. Ever heard of a professor named Healy?"

"Hank Healy?"

"That's him. What's his story? He came by my office looking for some other professor I've never heard of."

"Healy was dismissed during my second year."

"And that would be seven years ago?"

"Look at you with the math."

"I used to work in a bank."

"I've always liked that about you. There's no money in poetry, as they say."

"There was no money in banking, either. Listen, when you say dismissed, do you mean laid off?"

"No, I mean shitcanned. Toward the end, for a few years at least, he was out where the buses don't run. Total nutcase."

"That much doesn't seem to have changed. He's looking for another professor named Clinkscales."

"Clinkscales? That's the History prof who took a sabbatical and never came back. If memory serves, that was right after Healy left."

"I think Healy wants to kill him."

"Why do you think that?"

"Because he said he wanted to blow his brains out."

Mollie started to say something else when a voice cut her off. It was high and old, less angry than it had been but far from comforting.

"Good morning," Hank Healy said to Mollie's poetry seminar. "We're going to start with some review. Your grades on the last exam were abysmal. Look, don't be afraid to ask for extra help. I'm always available for tutoring. Yes, you in the back with the freckles and low-cut top."

"Um, where did Miss DuFrange go?"

"What the fuck?" Mollie whispered in my ear.

Healy ignored the question. The tap of chalk that followed never sounded more inscrutable.

Four blocks from Parshall College, the Grayford Inn wasn't a coveted destination on parents weekend. It was the kind of motel with dented doors and broken glass in the parking lot. Short-term guests were the clients of sex workers, visiting minor league baseball teams, and out-of-towners who trusted the lack of online photos. Long-term guests included adjunct business instructors at the nearby failing college.

I pulled out my keys and waved in the direction of a loud conversation next door.

"Mr. Cowlishaw," said a young woman. "You might be able to help."

This was far from the consensus of those who knew me.

"Do you remember me?" she asked. "Five years ago?"

"My memory's better than my eyesight," I said.

"Serenity Broadnax. From Accounting I and II."

I remembered her fondly, one of the scholarship students. She earned an A in both classes. I asked her what line of work she was in.

"I'm a police officer," she replied, a tone of silly boy in her voice. She might have been wearing her uniform. "Mr. Cowlishaw, this gentleman's brother used to teach at the college."

"Healy or Clinkscales?" I asked.

"Clinkscales," the man said, impressed. He offered his hand along with the cologne that coated it. "Josiah Clinkscales."

"You're the second man I've met today looking for your brother."

"Is that right? I was hoping the son of a bitch was dead."

"You're the second one of those, too."

"Until the court declares him dead," said Josiah Clinkscales, "I have no chance of getting the $14,317 he owes me. That's what I gave him to buy a used Subaru, plus interest for every single day he hasn't made a payment. I calculate the compounded interest every morning. It centers me."

"There's been some recent online activity involving Dr. Clinkscales," said Serenity.

"All these years of nothing," said Josiah Clinkscales, "and one morning I turn on my phone to see his ugly mug on my screen. I'm scrolling through pictures of the grandkids I'm putting through private school, pushing the like button to remind them I exist, and there's my deadbeat brother at the bottom of the screen where it tells you who's currently online. I messaged him but got no reply."

"How can I help?" I said, trying to communicate the unlikelihood of said help.

"Have you seen him around anywhere?" Serenity said. "In his office? Faculty meetings? The phone company pinpointed his phone's location to somewhere on campus."

"This morning was the first time I heard his name," I said.

"I'm a guest at this shithole motel if you hear anything," Clinkscales said and transferred more cologne to my hand.

The phone on my nightstand rang within seconds of my door closing behind me. I didn't get many calls on it. You had to be patched through. It was the old kind with the receiver sitting on the base like a hat. Mollie tried to convince me to get a cell phone, but people rarely had a good reason for getting in touch with me. I didn't want to encourage them.

"Cowlishaw, I've been trying to reach you all afternoon."

"Dean Simkins. I didn't know you had my phone number."

"I didn't, apparently. The number in your file connected me to a Little Caesars."

"I must have mistyped it," I lied.

"Listen, Cowlishaw. I need your help."

I lay down on the bed, disturbing my cat, Edward, from his life's work of long naps. He was in the room when I checked in two years ago. I couldn't argue with squatter's rights.

"That fellow you brought to my office this morning," Simkins said, "Hank Healy. He isn't right in the head."

"I got that impression," I said. "He commandeered Mollie's poetry class until students decided to leave."

Simkins sighed. "Hers wasn't the only one. Once upon a time, Hank was a brilliant man. He was close to tenure, back when we could still afford to grant tenure. Then came the business with Clinkscales."

I gathered Simkins meant separate business from this morning's murder threats.

"I probably shouldn't tell you this, Cowlishaw, but Healy and I went to grad school together. Different departments, of course. I studied economics, as you know. But I'd run into Hank in the neighborhood of decrepit apartments where most of us lived. We taught as post-doc lecturers in the same building, had lunch on Fridays at the Chinese buffet. The crab rangoons at that place," Simkins said and trailed off.

I wanted to get off the phone – Mollie might arrive any minute – but my boss seemed on the verge of telling me something important, and for once it might not involve spreadsheets, assessments, or budget cuts.

"I don't know what it was like in your MBA program, Cowlishaw, but grad school was lonely for me. Healy and I, we were the same type of men. Late bloomers, I guess you'd call us. I did have a girlfriend for a time. I don't know if she would have labeled herself as such, but I was pretty torn up. Checked myself into a hospital, if you want to know the truth."

I did not want to know the truth, but when the man who signs your paychecks calls you at home with stories of graduate school heartbreak and Chinese buffets, you stay on the line longer than you'd like.

"You know who came to visit me in the hospital? Nobody. Nobody except for Hank Healy. He met my classes while I was recovering. Even graded my papers. He taught himself the basics of macroeconomics from the textbook I used. Three decades later, when Hank was losing his shit – I mean, really losing it, not in the melodramatic way I did when I prayed that young lady would call on me – I protected him. Much longer than I should have. I muscled him through the tenure process as best I could. Then came Clinkscales with his by-the-book bullshit."

Edward hopped down from the bed. He didn't care for long monologues. He liked his empty dish even less and started to meow.

"Anyway, Hank seems to have made it out of the institution with the blessing of whatever quack was tending to him. You and

I both know he needs help. Do me a favor: Call the institution and tell them he's a danger to himself. See if they'll commit him again. We need him back in that padded room. I'd call myself, but I can't do that to a friend. Not again. You understand."

I made an ambiguous sound into the receiver.

"If you can do this for me, Cowlishaw, I might be able to free up a lectureship for you next year. Maybe even a summer class."

A knock came two seconds after I hung up. It didn't sound like Mollie, who liked to pound out the drum fill of "In the Air Tonight." An unfamiliar knock had ruined my day once already, but I made my way to the door.

"Mr. Cowlishaw, I forgot to ask you something," said Serenity. She was alone, as far as I could hear.

I invited her in and located the can opener for Edward's tuna.

"Wow, do you really live here?" she asked.

"All that free soap and shampoo, how can I leave?"

"They don't pay you much, do they?"

"But you students make it all worthwhile."

Serenity laughed at that. "I know the college is cheap as hell, because I don't think anybody works in the registrar's office at all. I've been calling over there for weeks to get a copy of my transcripts. I'm up for a promotion, and they need those. I thought they had them on file when I was first hired, but I don't think the college sent them back then, either."

"They can be a bit slow in records," I said, restoring Edward's faith in a higher power with a can of tuna.

"Pardon my language, Mr. Cowlishaw, but fuck that place. It's given me nothing but grief from the day I accepted their offer of a full ride. I only went there so I could stay in town and take care of my grandmother, and I figured what the hell, college is college."

We shared a moment of silence for the declining institution that had introduced us.

"What I think they're doing for transcripts these days is letting students come by and make their own copies, free of charge."

"Free of charge? Taking time off work is not free of charge." My former student made her way to the door. "The next time you see that dean, tell him Serenity Broadnax said he could kiss her ass."

"Will do," I said.

I positioned myself between door and phone, trying to guess which would next disturb me. The ball bearings on my watch said I scarcely had time to shower before Mollie got here. My shirt was musty with dust and academic decay.

"If anybody calls asking for my help, Edward, tell them I'm at the office."

Edward purred over his tuna.

The Grayford Inn was in many ways the seedy motel time forgot. With regard to its shower heads that predated water conservationists, this was an asset. Pellets of water thundered against the shower curtain, masking the sound of doors. Only the screech of rings on the shower rod alerted me to my guest.

"Care for some company?"

Mollie was behind me in the tub when she asked this. Somewhere between the front door and bathroom she had removed her clothes. What I couldn't see I could feel.

"Sorry I'm running late," I said.

"You're right on time," Mollie said. She reached down, confirming how punctual I was.

Later, Edward eyed us suspiciously while we dried off. His looks were hard to read. I was blind and he was a cat.

"When are you going to move out of this motel?" Mollie asked. "Your poor cat is trapped in this room all day."

"Edward, do you want to move?"

Edward said nothing.

"He loves it here," I said. "He was here before me. It's his place, really."

Mollie climbed into bed, wary not to touch the polyester bedspread. Housekeeping never replaced it with a fresh one. Mollie described sections of it as "crispy." She was a poet.

"This place is so temporary, Tate. You might as well be living in a dorm."

"Everything's temporary until it isn't."

She slapped my arm. "You know, I'd leave Benjamin if you gave me any indication that we might have a future. What do you even want to do with your life, Tate? We both know you hate teaching."

"I don't mind teaching."

"That's inertia, Tate. Your whole life is inertia."

"Your pillow talk needs work," I said.

"Seriously, Tate. What do you *want*?"

I got out of bed and reached for the clothes I had planned to wear to dinner.

"Where are you going?"

"Somewhere more peaceful than here."

"Don't go. I was going to spend the night. Benjamin's out of town until the end of the week at that composition conference."

I tied my German walking shoes. "I'd love to stay, but I have to go see someone about my inertia."

Mollie got out of bed. She did not put on clothes. Her mouth didn't make words, but it offered a convincing argument for me to stay.

"Listen, I told Simkins I'd do him a favor."

"Simkins? What kind of favor?"

"I suppose you could call it data reporting."

"What? We just did assessment on the core curriculum last fall."

"It's a non-academic favor. But he did imply there might be a promotion in it for me."

"A promotion? For doing him a favor? That's not how it works."

I zipped my jacket and stepped into the night. "You've been teaching at Parshall long enough to know that's *exactly* how it works."

I waited around the corner of the building and listened for my door. A few minutes should have been plenty of time for Mollie to get dressed. If she asked me to come back, I would. I didn't feel like going out. I rarely felt like going out. My favor to Scoot Simkins might only require a phone call, and my only phone was in my room.

After ten minutes, my door remained closed. Mollie wasn't coming after me, and she wasn't going home. I had no reason not to return to her and order takeout Thai. No reason except for pride. So I started walking.

Inertia and an empty stomach led me to downtown Grayford. The state university across town, where class interruptions by disgraced professors were less common, provided enough business to keep a few restaurants and bars open. Half a century ago, Grayford, North Carolina, made half the country's underwear, but stockholders and CEOs found children in the third world who could make comparable skivvies with fewer demands for a living wage. Shops on Main Street that hadn't closed in recent years had become antique stores, possibly unloading the same merchandise they once sold when it was new.

It was Thursday, the night college students regarded as little Friday. I stood behind rowdy undergrads for bad pizza by the slice. After a few minutes, the line hadn't moved, and I opted for a pair of hot dogs from the sidewalk cart.

"What would you like on these, Dr. Cowlishaw?"

The erroneous PhD reminded me this was one of my former students, a recent graduate named Taylor who earned his degree with highest honors. A colleague beamed in a recent meeting, saying Taylor had started his own business.

"How about chili, slaw, and mustard?"

"Sorry, Dr. Cowlishaw. All I have is ketchup."

"Then ketchup it is."

"Awesome. Do you need a bun for these?"

"I think I would. One for each, if you don't mind."

He handed them to me on a thin napkin. "Hey, are you here to see that weird dude?"

"Which weird dude would that be?"

"The old prof who took over Miss DuFrange's class this morning. Kind of looks like a fat Liam Neeson with crazy eyes."

"Why do you ask?"

"I think he's going to perform at the comedy club. He was out here earlier, trying to get people to sit at his table. It's open mic night, and you can only go onstage if you bring five people."

"He wasn't holding a gun, was he?"

Taylor laughed. "Nah, he just promised to buy people drinks. A couple of my old frat brothers took him up on the offer. They told me he was all over campus today, taking over people's classes and whatnot."

I ate my hot dogs in four bites. The comedy club was a few doors down from the pizzeria, on the first floor of the haunted hotel that closed during Nixon's second term. A few feet inside, a bright-voiced girl asked me for five dollars. Accepting my money, she asked if I was with anyone.

"I am. Older guy. Looks like a fat Liam Neeson with crazy eyes."

She started walking. I followed her through thick cigar smoke. The city had banned indoor smoking years ago, but for some reason cigars seemed to be exempt from the ordinance.

"Dr. Healy," said the hostess, "your fifth has arrived. You're all cleared to go on."

Healy clapped his hands together. He stood up and clapped one of them across my back.

"You are a good man. You are a good, good man," he said and started toward the stage. Someone was already on it. Healy helped him back to his seat, or at least off the stage.

"How are you all doing today?" Healy asked.

No one answered.

"I don't seem to have my gradebook with me, so I'll use your quizzes to take roll."

A lone chuckle came from the back of the room.

"Hey, Dr. Healy, can we use our notes on the quiz?" said one of the boys at my table before falling into a fit of laughter.

Everyone at the table joined in. Everyone but the fellow to my left. He turned to me and said, "We met earlier, didn't we? At the roach motel."

"Josiah Clinkscales," I said. "Out to catch a few laughs on a Thursday night?"

"I'm here because this fruitcake onstage sent me a Facebook message saying he knows where my brother is. He said to meet him here."

Hank Healy read multiple choices for question three. What the crowd must have perceived as performance art got more laughs than the kid whose act he interrupted.

"And where *is* your brother?"

"He hasn't said. To be honest, I don't think this is the kind of guy who ought to be living on his own."

"Pens down," said Healy. "Pass your papers to the front of the room."

I heard no sounds that might have been papers.

"I'm not sure this Healy fellow has a strong handle on place and time," I told Clinkscales.

"I agree, the guy's a freak and a half, but he seems to know a lot about Joffrey. Said he was going to give him a wake-up call first thing in the morning."

"If so, I'd stand at a safe distance from his alarm clock."

"What's that mean?"

I told Josiah Clinkscales about my run-in with Healy this morning, explained what he planned to do when he found him.

"Hell, that's fine with me. If Joffrey's dead, that'll save me the trouble of taking him to court. I just need proof that he's actually deceased to claim his estate."

Hank Healy was a big man, but from the crowd's reactions and a series of grunts, I gathered there were bigger, firmer men helping him down off the stage. I couldn't see if he was upright when he made his way past us toward the front door. The young men at my table started a round of applause. I followed Clinkscales outside. When we reached the sidewalk, Healy was horizontal. Clinkscales tried to help him up.

"Let's get you home, buddy. Where do you live?"

Healy mumbled a few words. He repeated them until I realized he was providing his campus office.

In a low voice, I told Clinkscales what Simkins had said about Healy's recent release from the institution.

"Jesus Christ," said Clinkscales. "He really is nuts."

Healy was standing now, breathing hard. "I know I'm not the straightest arrow in the quiver," he said, "but I do have a point."

"And what's that?" said Clinkscales.

"That I have a meeting with your brother bright and early tomorrow morning."

Clinkscales and I looked at each other, one of us with only blurry peripheral vision.

"And where is this meeting?" Clinkscales asked.

Healy made spitting sounds like he was trying to get a hair off his tongue.

"Where are you meeting my brother?" said Clinkscales, raising his voice.

"Somewhere," Healy said in a fading voice. "Somewhere under the rainbow."

"Help me get him into my backseat, Cowlishaw. I'm going to get him a room at the motel."

It was midnight when we got Healy tucked in. Clinkscales said he'd knock on the door at eight.

"I've got an eight o'clock class," Healy said.

"That got canceled," Clinkscales told him. "You've got a meeting with my brother at eight, remember?"

"Right. Somewhere under the rainbow."

In the parking lot, I asked Clinkscales how confident he was that we had done anything more than strain our backs helping Healy out of a backseat.

"Scale of one to ten? I'd say a two."

I nodded. "See you at eight."

My room was unlocked. The lights were off. Only Edward lay in my bed. I ran a hand across the side where Mollie had been, but her warmth had faded long ago.

Late as it was, I considered calling Simkins with an update on his old friend. I wasn't sure if I had accomplished anything, but I wanted credit for my efforts. I opted for an email.

"Bumped into your old friend at the comedy club," I typed, my screen reader echoing each character. "He thinks he has a meeting with Joffrey Clinkscales first thing in the morning. Somewhere under the rainbow, he says. He's got a room at the Grayford Inn for the night. I'll tell the institution where they can pick him up first thing in the morning. When would be a good time to swing by your office to talk about that lectureship?"

The next knock came before dawn.

"He's gone," said Clinkscales.

I blinked at the parking lot lights. "I guess we tried," I said.

"The fuck we did. Get dressed, Cowlishaw. We're going to find this fucker."

Edward sighed and I meowed. In retrospect, I might have those reversed.

"I stepped out for a smoke and saw his door wasn't all the way closed. Who knows when the son of a bitch left."

"Maybe this is our cue to step aside, let the authorities handle it."

"Fuck that. This guy might be fried crispier than a month-old hushpuppy, but he knows something."

"He said something about an eight o'clock class," I offered. "Maybe he's on campus, looking for an empty classroom."

I got in the passenger seat of Clinkscales' white sedan. He drove to campus faster than any students or faculty I knew. I directed him to the gravel parking lot.

I started to lead him to the classroom building where Healy had "taught" yesterday. Then we heard the sounds of construction near the library.

Early as it was and non-existent as our construction budget had been for years, it seemed worthy of investigating. When we got to the front door, we weren't alone.

"Gentlemen," said Serenity Broadnax, "what are you doing here?"

"We heard noises," I said and left it at that.

"Yeah, what is that?" she asked.

Clinkscales held open the door and followed us inside. The thudding came from upstairs. Four thuds and a pause, three thuds and a pause, two thuds and a pause.

"Mr. Cowlishaw, where did you say I could find that file cabinet with transcripts?"

I led Serenity behind the circulation desk. "One of these, I think. The copier's probably down. Feel free to take your transcripts with you and bring them back later."

"What copier?" she asked.

"I meant the copier's probably been stolen."

Clinkscales was on his way upstairs. I followed. The pounding vibrated in the handrail. I fought the urge to plug my ears.

"Well, where have you been?" asked a breathless Hank Healy.

"What's going on?" said Clinkscales. "And who the hell are you?"

"Scoot Simkins," said the dean, not coming over to shake hands. "I knew your brother. Thanks for the email, Cowlishaw."

My eyes failed to make sense of what was happening.

"I told you he'd be here," said Healy, taking what might be a sledgehammer to the far wall.

"I tried to stop him," Simkins said in a somber voice.

"What the fuck is that?" said Clinkscales, drawing closer to the wall.

"You mean who," said Simkins.

I directed my blurry gaze at the ceiling. In the rim of my peripheral vision, I could make out a rainbow, the top half of the mural painted by the last class of graduating art majors some twenty years ago. Beneath it looked like a large hole and a widening skirt of dry wall. The latter crunched under my shoes.

"That would be your brother," said Simkins.

"What the fuck? You killed my brother and buried him in a wall?"

Healy seemed past words, alternating between raspberries and breathy chuckles.

"You knew," I said to Simkins.

"I helped him build the wall," said Simkins. "We came up together, Tate. You understand."

He said it as a statement, not a question. I did not understand.

Clinkscales, the one not buried in the library's second-floor wall, went in for a closer look. "Is his phone in there? Who's been on his Facebook account?"

"That would be me," said Simkins, sounding mournful if not quite contrite. "It wasn't his Facebook account I needed. It just opened when I turned on the phone."

"How was his phone still working if he's been dead for…"

"Five and a half years," Simkins said.

With his weakened arms, Healy swung the sledgehammer one last time. Fewer bits of wall skittered across the floor.

Simkins said, "Auto draft, apparently. When nobody knows you're dead and your account has sufficient funds, your phone keeps working. And when you're still receiving a monthly salary from your employer, there are always sufficient funds. I only discovered this a few months ago. Until then, we had the money for accountants. Nearly four hundred thousand dollars we've been paying a dead man not to teach."

"Holy shit," said Clinkscales around an audible smile. He had come to terms with his brother's death in short order. "That will cover what he owes me for the car and then some."

"You don't understand," Simkins said. "That's not his money. The school is barely staying afloat. The endowment is down to fifty thousand dollars. I need that money back just to pay bills."

"How much do you make?" I asked Simkins, having heard rumors about the answer.

"That's neither here nor there, Cowlishaw."

"Oh, I'd say it's *somewhere*," said Clinkscales.

From what I'd heard from colleagues, Simkins made every bit of what Clinkscales had been paid posthumously. I made two thousand dollars per class without benefits.

In front of me, two men argued over an amount of money greater than I had earned up to this point in my life. Beyond them, Hank Healy had lain down on the floor and fallen asleep. A light snore emanated from his hulking frame.

"Cowlishaw, why don't you settle this," said Simkins. "Remember what we were talking about yesterday? That's still on the table."

Clinkscales said, "I'll see you in court if you think you're keeping four hundred thousand dollars!"

Simkins must have known he'd see a courtroom one way or another. He was haggling feverishly when I headed for the stairs. A single flight separated me from the library's exit, but the steps seemed more numerous than any staircase I had ever taken.

I thought of my girlfriend who was someone else's wife. I thought of my meager paychecks that didn't pay my bills. I thought of the word *blind*, which I checked on applications and forms and how much my eyes could still see in their blurry edges. I thought of my cat and how much joy he got from tuna. Three cans sat on my motel dresser.

"Mr. Cowlishaw, I can't find my transcripts anywhere. Where else might that file cabinet be?"

I hesitated for the smallest moment. "Dean Simkins is upstairs," I said. "He knows where everything is."

THE HARE AND THE HOUND

Kelly Andrew

Bunny Bunsall was fourteen years old when a prophecy ruined his life. It wasn't that he believed in divination – he didn't. It wasn't that he was superstitious – he wasn't. It was only that he'd gone in with a normal name – Mason, the ninth most popular name for boys the year he was born – and he came out with a horrible nickname that followed him throughout his life.

He'd been in Coney Island on a field trip the day it happened, damp and cold in a chilly April soup. In search of some lunch, he and his friends had split from the group and wandered off through the crowd. They didn't make it far before it began to pour. Searching for an escape, they ducked into one of the little stacked shops along the boardwalk. They didn't realize they'd entered a seer's parlor until the smell of incense slapped them right in the face. By then, it was too late to back out. They'd already been spotted by the old woman at the counter.

"Come in," she'd said, with a crook of her finger, "and I will show you how you'll die."

Bunny hadn't been interested in finding out how he'd go. It seemed like the sort of thing best left a surprise. And yet his friends filed into the back room one after the other, laughing and shoving and estimating their time of deaths.

He waited in the outside room, his stomach rumbling, and watched the hot dog seller across the street close up his cart. Eventually, his companions shuffled out into the lobby. One after the other, their faces pale and their smiles unsteady.

"And what about you?" asked the woman, when she caught him lingering by the door.

"I don't believe in magic," he'd said, wishing he'd made it to the hot dog cart before it closed.

At that, the old woman's eyes twinkled. "Then there's no harm in knowing, is there?"

He knew it was a scam. The woman only wanted his money. He had mere dollars left to his name, and he'd not gotten anything to eat all day. But his companions wouldn't take no for an answer. Within minutes he found himself sitting in a velvet-shrouded chair in a velvet-shrouded room, blinking down at a gleaming glass orb.

Outside in the storefront, the woman had seemed small and frail, her features birdlike. But tailored into the shadows of her smoky backroom, she loomed larger than life. Lit from beneath, she took on an ethereal glow, until she looked less like a crone and more like a sorceress, and he wasn't sure if it was all in his head or a trick of the light, but it left him deeply unsettled. Moreover, she stared at him like she was afraid of him. Like he, too, had transformed into something malevolent in the dark.

"You came all this way because you seek the knowledge of how you will die," she'd whispered.

"Actually," he'd corrected, "I was seeking some food."

The woman didn't appear to have heard him. "We will speak of death today, but not of yours."

"Oh," he said. "Okay."

She leaned in, the light from the crystal refracting beneath her chin. "Listen closely and heed my warning. One day, a white rabbit will appear to you. For most, the hare is a symbol of blessing and renewal, but for you it is to be a harbinger of great misfortune. On the tail of the rabbit's arrival, you will meet a girl. Should you give chase, you will pursue her into the mouth of the wolf, and you will be consumed by the madness that follows."

Somewhere unseen, a window unit clicked on. The air went cold. It pebbled his skin. Across from him, the woman had gone silent, waiting.

"Cool," he said. "Thanks. I think?"

Still, she stared, unblinking and otherworldly. He pulled out his wallet, intending to give her the money she was due, but she recoiled from him as though he were a snake.

"Killer," she hissed. "Get out of my shop."

That was years ago. He was twenty-one now. Halfway through his senior year at McHale and drowning in coursework. A history major and a pre-law hopeful. He'd shaken much of his adolescence loose, the way people did, shedding themselves in years like layers. But he'd never been able to shake off that rainy day in New York.

It was his fault, really. He should have known better than to relay the words of the crazy old woman to his friends. They'd found the whole thing endlessly entertaining – that his fate might be inextricably tied to a white rabbit, like Alice in the looking glass. The ribbing he endured was endless. They stuffed pictures of rabbits in his locker. They gifted him a rabbit's foot for his birthday. Eventually, the nickname stuck. He wasn't Mason anymore, with the ninth most common name and a fairly ordinary reputation.

He was Bunny Bunsall, the white rabbit boy.

They didn't know how it haunted him. How could they? They hadn't seen the look on the old woman's face as he stumbled out of the smoky dark.

They hadn't heard her call him a killer.

To his friends, the fortune was little more than an inside joke and a running gag. A term of endearment to lob down the locker-hemmed hallways of their tiny high school: *Bunny, wait up!* It stuck to him through freshman formal on to baseball camp, to sophomore homecoming and junior playoffs. It was stitched on his jersey, graffitied on his textbooks, scribbled in his yearbook.

It followed him to college.

"Earth to Bunny," said David Liu, dropping a stack of books onto the table between them. The slam rattled his teeth. Or maybe it was only the six cups of coffee that rattled him. Maybe it was the lack of sleep. Across from him, his roommate pushed his glasses up on his nose. His blue ballcap sat askew on his head, black hair poking out from beneath. "I'm telling you this as a friend – your body odor smacked me in the face the second I stepped inside the library."

"Ha ha ha," Bunny said, with as much disdain as he could muster.

But David wasn't done. "I overheard the desk clerk talking about you. She says if you sit there any longer, you'll grow into the seat. When's the last time you left?"

Bunny sat back and scrubbed a hand over his face. The patchy, three-day-old scruff of a beard itched at his jaw. "Don't know," he admitted. "What time is it?"

"Nine," said David, dropping into the adjacent chair.

"P.M.?"

David's eyes narrowed and slid to the windows, where the black night pressed its face against the glass. "Yeah," he said. "P.M. You should head back to the apartment. Sleep for a bit. Eat. Consider a shower."

His apartment was the second story in a two-family home, all dormered rooms and windows too small for an air-unit. The furniture was sparse and secondhand. The lights were off. Only the soft burble of the fish tank greeted him. He kicked off his shoes and headed for the shower, scraping away layers like rime. He felt a thousand lifetimes old as he stood beneath the feeble spit of water until it turned to ice.

When he fell asleep that night, it was at his desk, the lamp still burning and his laptop on, his thesis half-finished. He dreamt of missing the deadline. He dreamt of showing up nude to his exams.

He dreamt of the scream of brakes, the bone-crunching bite of metal. And then, in the final dregs of sleep before dawn, he dreamt of a wolf. Fangs bared and eyes black, its hackles raised.

The same dream he'd had nearly every week since that rainy day in Coney Island.

When he awoke, it was to the sound of a howl. A blink, a yawn, and the lone baying dissolved into the wail of a far-off ambulance. The single spear of sunlight through his blinds set off sparks in his blood.

He was late.

And not just a little bit late.

If Bunny Bunsall hated anything, it was being late. Being late led to rushing, and rushing led to mistakes. The kind of mistakes you couldn't undo. A quick glance at the clock told him he could make it if he drove, but Bunny had never owned a car. Not after he'd driven his father's brand-new F-150 through a red light and t-boned the oncoming sedan. He'd been running late that day, too. Harried and overtired and missing pre-season practice, he'd been dreading the negging from his teammates and the verbal lashing from his coach. He'd woken in the hospital with several contusions and two broken ribs and a girl's death on his conscience.

Nora Hagel.

He'd never forget her name as long as he lived.

"You got off easy," his father told him, when they'd left court with a hefty fine and a license suspension. "If the judge had decided to rule it as a felony, you'd have done time."

He didn't get behind the wheel these days.

And he was never, ever late.

A quick search of the street outside showed him that David had already left for campus in his little green Fiat. Linus Fletch, their third roommate, was still asleep in his room. He didn't have a car, either, but Bunny wasn't against riding bitch on his moped if that's what it took. But when he tried to rouse Linus, he was met with a middle finger and an incoherent mumble, and he knew Linus well enough to know that was as far as he would get.

By the time he reached the bike rack out front, he was later than late – he was missing class. His bike was carbon fiber, light and fast and expensive. Meant for road races, not for slogging through the rain. It would be fine, he told himself. He'd corner slowly. He'd give himself time to stop. He'd make it with enough time to slip in the back and sign in before Professor Lobb caught sight of him.

Bunny was nearly to school when it happened. A white rabbit scampered out from beneath the brush and darted in front of his tire. He swerved, losing traction, and felt the twiggy snap of something brittle beneath his wheel. There followed a sickening lurch, the hard brace of an impact, and then he was sprawled out in the grass, wet and aching and clambering to his feet. A quick search showed him nothing. Fog gathered over the ground in thin blankets of mist, shrouding what little he could see in gray.

Beneath his chest, his heart rioted against his bones. He was so certain he'd hit it – that he'd find it lying in the road, its fur matted in blood and its chest heaving and the life slowly going out of its eyes.

Like Nora Hagel.

He blinked and blinked. The rabbit didn't appear. The whiplash ache of a fall bled into his bones. When at last he gave up and walked his bike to school, it was with a limp.

The following day was more of the same. Gray and wet. A sky like pea-soup. Cold that sucked the air from his lungs. This time, Bunny woke early enough to catch a ride with David. When his classes were through, he ate a quick dinner in the student center and limped across the quad to the library. He felt off-kilter, his world slipped off its axis. The thought of Nora Hagel sat in his stomach like a stone. The snap of bone beneath his tire played on a feedback loop in his head. He felt indefatigably tired, a headache blooming behind one eye, and he found himself looking forward to sliding back into the lamplit quiet of the reference room.

In the paltry warmth of the lobby, he drew up short.

There, in his usual seat, was a girl. Porcelain-pale and wildly pretty, with a shock of white hair to match, she looked less like a girl and more like a ghost. The sight of her struck him cold. He was here every day. He was here most nights. He was certain he'd never seen her before.

She didn't look up at him as he hovered there, his coat half-off and openly gaping. She was focused, instead, on jotting down notes with one hand, her other wrapped in a hard white cast. There were no names scribbled into the plaster. No doodled hearts from friends and no gel-pen well-wishes from family. Instead, someone had outlined a single white rabbit.

Two things happened then, and with astonishing quickness. First, his stomach flipped clean over in a sickening somersault.

Second, he laughed right out loud – tickled by the ridiculousness of it, that his mind instantly slipped to the Coney Island charlatan and her dollar store crystal.

Several heads picked up at the sound. He was met with at least three stares of disapproval, a single, disembodied *shh!* Tailed by his own echo, he approached the white-haired interloper at his table. When she didn't look up, he cleared his throat.

"You're in my seat."

Her focus remained lasered on her task. "I wasn't aware the library had assigned seats."

"They don't. But it's a small school, and I'm kind of a staple here."

She turned a page in her textbook. The sound rustled all through the whisper-quiet of the library. "Here, on campus?"

"No," Bunny said, "in this chair."

Her gaze flicked up at that and he was met, at once, with an arresting, two-toned stare. One eye blue as a midmorning sky and the other black as a new-moon midnight, they sat slightly too far apart on her face. It gave her a stark, fey appearance that set him inexplicably on edge.

"Uh." He felt, suddenly, like he'd swallowed a cupful of sand. "You can have the seat, though. It's no big deal. I'll see if I can track down a spot in the stacks."

The next day, she was there again. Seated in his chair like she'd always done it. Plucking up his courage, he pulled out the seat opposite her and sank down into it. The striking colors of her stare flicked up quickly before dropping back to her book.

"Giving up?"

"I'm playing the long game." Bunny set a pile of textbooks between them like a bulwark and added, "I'll get my seat back."

She examined the stacked spines in front of her. "Let me guess. Pre-law?"

"Unfortunately."

"Who guilted you into that?"

"I did." He tucked a pencil behind his ear and peered around the barricade. "I haven't seen you around campus before."

A twinkle sparked in her eyes. "Maybe you just didn't notice."

"I would definitely have noticed."

"Oh." Pinpricks of pink climbed into her cheeks. "I'm a recent transfer."

"Ah. Got it." He tipped the chair back on two legs, tugging himself into a stretch until his joints popped. For the first time in several days, he didn't think about Nora Hagel. "Last school didn't work out?"

Something funny crested and then sank in her stare. "No," she said, and nothing more.

"Well, welcome." He let his chair fall forward and drummed two fingers against the lip of the table. "It's nice to meet you, even if you did steal my seat. I'm—"

"Bunny," she finished for him, with another fleeting glance.

The first hint of unease licked through him. "Uh. Yeah, to some people."

"I don't mean to weird you out," she rushed to say, this time meeting his gaze and holding it. "I overheard you and your friend talking the other day. It's a pretty memorable nickname."

He winced. "It's unfortunate, is what it is."

"I like it. It goes with mine."

"Oh, does it?" If he hadn't been before, he was certain, now, that she was flirting. "And what's yours? *Rabbit?*"

"It's Arlen." She tucked a loose strand of white behind her ear, a smile catching at the corner of her mouth. "Which, ironically, comes from the phrase hare-land."

Thoughts of the rabbit slammed into him with a freight-train quickness. The streak of white. The crack of bone. The feel of his bike skidding out from under him. Across the table, the girl had fallen to fussing with her cast. It looked, he noted, fairly new.

"It's kind of a funny coincidence, isn't it," she said, just as the very same word scuttled through his skull. He stiffened, certain she'd plucked the thought clean out of his brain.

"What is?"

"That we met. Bunny and Arlen."

"Maybe." He swallowed around the lump in his throat. "Or maybe it's fate."

More color bled into her cheeks. Her gaze dropped back to the open sprawl of her notes. He felt he ought to say something more, but he was still thinking about the rabbit. About how certain he'd been that he'd clipped it with his tire.

After several seconds had slow-ticked past, he caved and asked, "What happened to your arm?"

"Oh." Arlen drew her wrist into her chest like a shot. Her gaze shuttered and she was suddenly closed off. "Nothing."

"Nothing?"

"It was stupid. A biking accident."

Another coincidence. Frowning over at her, he asked, "You bike?"

"No," she rushed to say. "I mean, I know how to ride a bike, yes, but I don't cycle. Like, I'm not one of those neon spandex, annual triathlon-types. But I was out for a walk, and I wasn't paying attention."

"Ah."

He didn't mention that he'd done a triathlon the previous year, or that he had a drawer in his apartment full of lime green jerseys. He was too busy thinking about the white rabbit. The crunch of bone and Coney Island, the haunting final warning of the medium. Across from him, Arlen had begun packing up her things. She seemed to be in a sudden rush, as though she'd remembered she had somewhere far more pressing to be. He hadn't even noticed the shift.

"Everything okay?"

"Fine." Her smile was fleeting. Her eyes were gilded in the soft glow of the overhead lights. In the broad bay windows at her back, the sun had just begun to sink back beneath the hill. "I don't like to be out after dark."

He rose to his feet after her. "I can walk you home, if you're worried."

"No." The answer came out whipcord quick. Her eyes darted to his and away. "Thank you, but I'm fine. See you around?"

"I hope so," he said.

And then she was gone, and Bunny was left alone.

That night, he didn't dream of Nora Hagel dying. He didn't dream at all. He lay awake, staring up at the stagnant ceiling fan in his little dormered room. Mattress on the floor. Lampshade askew. His head full of regrets. Outside in the common room, the television was on. The smell of weed drifted in on the liquid flicker of blue beneath the door.

The word *coincidence* danced through his head like sugarplums.

He didn't sleep.

The next morning was clear and blue. Glassy puddles mirrored the sky, steadily shrinking beneath a broad, yellow sun. He rode his bike past the close-pressed dual family homes and out into the looping maze of wooded roads, zipping steadily toward campus.

A half mile out, he saw it.

The rabbit.

White and wet, it huddled in the same place where he'd left it – shivering in the lingering dawn, its left leg drawn into its chest.

"Shit."

He skidded to a stop and lowered his kickstand, then approached the creature as slowly as he could without startling it. With each step, he readied himself for the inevitable bolt. Instead, the rabbit stared out from beneath the dew-dazzled green of a fern, wall-eyed and shivering.

"Hey," he said. "Hi, there. I'm really sorry. I didn't see you in time."

The rabbit's ears twitched in his direction. He was met with a beetle-black stare, the nervous thump of a restless hind leg.

"What if I get you some help, huh?"

He took another step, and the rabbit scampered back. In the sudden shift of light, he could clearly see that the rabbit's other eye was blue.

Pale blue.

Sky blue.

Arlen blue.

The thought zinged through him and he fell back with a start. Frightened, the rabbit took off into the underbrush, staggering at a limping pace, its left foot aloft. *Like Arlen's bandaged wrist*, trundled a voice through his head. The thought ripped holes in his chest. Panic bled through, cold and keening.

"No, wait," he called out, now on his hands and knees. "Wait!"

But the rabbit was gone.

By the time he got to school, Bunny was late, wet, and cold. Kneecaps muddied and hands scuffed, he got himself a hot coffee and staked out a corner booth in the crowded student center. He barely managed to choke down a first, scalding sip before his roommates found him.

"What the hell happened to you?" asked David, sliding into the adjacent seat. "Did you get into a fight or something?"

"Bunny? In a fight?" Linus landed next to David with a bounce, readjusting the maroon knit of his beanie as he did. Bleach-blond fuzz peeked out from beneath the brim. "With his kickstand, maybe. It looks like he bit dust. I hope you had a helmet on, Bun. Safety first, and all that."

"I didn't fall." He stared out at the crowd, unwilling to admit who he was looking for. White hair. One blue eye. One black. As an afterthought, he added, "I was trying to catch a rabbit."

A heavy pause followed his words. And then both of his roommates exploded into laughter.

"Sorry." David pried off his glasses to paw at his eyes. "You were following *a rabbit*?"

"Bunny followed a bunny," chortled Linus. "I like it. It's poetic. It's romantic."

"It's weird," David said. "You missed Dua's lecture on social stratification."

Something defensive webbed through him like spider's silk. "So?"

David's eyes boggled. "So, you've never missed a class as long as I've known you. You're an annoyingly good student. Once a week, I have to physically scrape you out of the library. You're early for every deadline. You don't not show up to class because you were chasing after small woodland mammals."

Heat crawled into his face, and he wished he'd said nothing at all. He didn't know how to explain the heaviness he carried in his chest, or the way he sometimes still saw Nora Hagel lying in the street when he closed his eyes. Seared like an afterimage on the back of his eyelids.

He didn't know how to say he wished he'd done everything differently.

When he spoke, his voice came out in a curt, "Excuse me."

He left his coffee unfinished, his conversation incomplete, shouldering his bag and shoving into the close press of students, a tension headache ramming spikes into his skull.

It was dusk when he found her again.

This time, she'd chosen a spot in the library's twisting warren of books. Something akin to relief slammed through him as he settled into the crook of her wooden carrel desk, striving for a nonchalance he didn't feel.

"I see you've relinquished my seat," he said. "Victory was easier than I expected."

A faint smile caught at the corners of her lips. The feel of it sharpened in his stomach. "I wouldn't be so quick to count it as a win," she said. "Maybe this is all part of my plan."

"Yeah? And what plan is that?"

"To get you to follow me."

The way she peered up at him through her lashes made him feel a thousand things at once and, for a moment, he forgot all about the rabbit in the wood. Swallowing thickly, he asked, "And where will you lead me?"

A strange light came into her eyes. A sun-flare sparkle and a starlight twinkle. Softly, she said, "You'll have to wait and see."

And there it was again, pervasive as a haunt – that shivering memory of the rabbit in the mist, its foot mangled and its eyes wide and fearful. A girl dying in the street, her mouth pooled with blood. Somewhere in the bowels of his consciousness, he heard the hinge of fangs snapping shut. Saw the blood-red muzzle of a wolf. He cleared his throat.

"So, I didn't see you around campus today."

That gleam hadn't left her eyes. "Were you looking?"

"No," he hurried to say. Then, because he'd already been caught, "Well, yes, but only because it's a relatively small campus. I figured we'd have bumped into one another."

"Hmm." Arlen tapped her eraser against the desk. "Maybe I'm a crepuscular being."

His head jerked up at that. "Sorry, you're what?"

"*Crepuscular*," she repeated. "Like, a creature that's only active at dawn and dusk."

He couldn't think of a response to that. Not a witty one, anyway. Instead, Bunny sputtered uselessly in her direction until color climbed into her cheeks and she laughed. It was a soft, musical sound that flooded the quiet between them.

"Kidding," she said. "It was a rabbit joke. Because of your nickname."

"And because rabbits are out at dusk," he said, as though catching on. He tried to smile, but it came out weak. A wan, watery version of what he might have done if his insides weren't busy turning themselves inside out. "I get it. You're funny."

"I try my best. Are you okay?"

He pawed at the back of his neck. "Fine," he lied. "It's been a weird couple of days. I didn't get much sleep."

"A lot on your mind?"

"You could say that."

"Want to talk about it?"

He balked at the question, his unease zippering into embarrassment. Should he tell her about the medium from Coney Island, and the way she'd looked at him as she called him a killer? About Nora Hagel, and how he'd left her bleeding out in a four-way intersection? Or how his father played golf with the judge, or how the survivor's guilt kept him lurching awake in the dead of night?

Should he tell her about the rabbit?

"I don't know," was where he landed, in the end. "Do you and I know each other well enough to share our deeply personal secrets?"

Her smile widened. It gave her a wicked, fey appearance that sent a frisson down his spine. Coyly, she said, "I'll tell you what keeps me up at night if you tell me what haunts you in the dark."

"Well, how can I resist that offer?" Bunny scrubbed a hand over the messy, brown crown of his head and waited for a lie to come to him. Panic threading his veins, he settled on, "I was stressing over a poly-sci paper."

She faked a shudder. "I don't think I could cut it in a non-liberal arts major."

He latched onto the change in subject, relieved. "You're studying – what? English? Theater?"

"Art," she replied. "Specifically, sculpture. Recently, I've been making figurines out of natural materials."

"Impressive."

"You haven't seen my sculptures. They might be terrible."

"Doesn't matter," he said. "I'm still impressed... What about you?"

"What about me?"

"What keeps you up at night?"

Arlen's nose crinkled as she peered up at him. In the dark of the library, her eyes were liquid-bright, one glittering like sapphire and one dark as an onyx. Her hair sat atop her head in a braided crown of white. He was reminded again of the rabbit in the brush. Its two-toned stare. Its broken foot.

"Wolves," she said at last, and the air was snatched from his lungs.

"Wolves," he echoed.

"Well, not wolves exactly," she corrected, "but the sounds they make. Have you ever heard them killing something?"

He faltered. "I haven't."

"It's awful." She suppressed a shudder. "I grew up in a really rural area. There were always wolves. Sometimes at night they'd sound like they were right outside my window. I could hear whatever they were killing, too. I used to have nightmares that it was me out there, trapped in the dark with the pack. I still do, sometimes, when I'm really stressed."

He stared, unsure what to say. In her purse, an alarm sounded. Both of them jumped at the noise. She drew out her phone and silenced it, cursing when she caught sight of the time. Gathering up her books, she rushed to shrug into her coat. At her back, night bled in through the glass in reams of violet-tinged dark.

"I'm late," she said.

"I get it." His stomach sat in a tight coil. "You have to get back to your burrow."

Her eyes flicked to his. She looked surprised, some of the color gone from her face. "What?"

"That's what a crepuscular being does, right? They spend the night in hiding?"

"Right." Arlen seemed to relax, her smile returning. "Another rabbit joke."

He cringed. "Maybe we should stop with those."

"Maybe," she said, and smiled. "It *is* pretty lame. See you tomorrow?"

"I'll be in my usual seat," he called after her, as she disappeared into the maze of shelving.

That night, he sat in the common room and ignored his looming deadlines, watching Linus cut down ogres on the PlayStation.

"Hey," Bunny said, when the game was paused, "remember that period of your life last year where you were weirdly obsessed with Norse mythology?"

"It's not weird, man," Linus said, taking a swallow of soda. "My great-grandma was Norwegian – that shit is interesting to me. Plus, it was for a grade. Remember? I was writing that paper on Loki for my course on Nordic literature. And I found out some fascinating stuff, if you two bothered to listen."

"It *was* weird," David said, without looking up from his phone. "You had that giant poster of Thor on your bedroom door all year."

"He's the Norse god of thunder, sky, and agriculture," Linus parried, as though this was explanation enough. "Ladies love him."

He'd begun gaming again, and the clash of swords flooded the sparse quiet of the hand-me-down living room. From his spot on the couch, Bunny fiddled with his ballcap, searching for an in that didn't leave him looking clinically insane.

"I want to hear more about what you found out," he said at last, hesitance lacing his delivery.

David glanced up, surprised. "You do?"

"Of course he does," Linus said, and threw down his controller. He took another swig of soda and slammed it onto the table hard enough to splash suds all over the peeling laminate. "What do you want to know, ye mortal?"

"Uh, well, Loki was a shapeshifter, right?"

"He sure was."

"Are there, uh, *other* shapeshifters in Nordic lore?"

"There sure are," Linus said again, with equal enthusiasm. Across the living room, David took off his glasses and pinched the bridge of his nose.

"What is happening right now?"

"Quiet, David," said Linus. "The grownups are speaking. And, Bun, since you asked, you should know, my great-grandma *was* a shapeshifter."

"For fuck's sake," David said, irate now. "No, she was not."

"She was, too," said Linus, folding his fist over a hiccup. "My grandfather told me. He said my great-grandmother was a Nordic witch who would shapeshift into animal form and get into all kinds of mischief, until one day my great-grandfather wised up to her tricks and set out a trap. He caught her and he married her."

"Bullshit." David tugged a pillow out from beneath him and chucked it in Linus's direction. "That didn't happen."

"Oh yeah?" Linus shoved the pillow back. "Were you around in 1936?"

"I didn't need to be," David said. "It's a made-up story."

"Shut up, both of you." Bunny scraped a palm over his brow. He was sweating in spite of the cold, and he wondered if he was coming down with something. "What did she shapeshift into?"

At that, David let out a groan. "Don't encourage him."

"For your *information*," Linus said, with a sideways look at David, "she transformed into a hare. It's an incredibly common bit of Nordic folklore, if either of you could be bothered to look it up."

Bunny's heart was a fist. It closed up tight enough to hurt.

"Excuse me," he stammered, shoving off the couch and fumbling for his room. From behind, David called out for him to wait, but he hardly heard over the snick of his door slamming shut, the rush of blood between his ears.

That night was another sleepless one. The dawn crawled, gray and cold, into his window and his eyes were like sand. Bunny blinked and blinked and couldn't clear away the grit of sleeplessness, the pinch of paranoia. It crept through his veins like a rot. It crawled into his skin.

He went through the day by rote – sitting in his classes without taking notes, staring at his coffee without drinking. It was nearly dinner, a crowd just beginning to congregate outside the student center, when he pushed his way across the wind-bitten quad and into the treacle-lit warmth of the library.

And there she was, curled up in his seat.

A white-haired girl with rabbit eyes and a rabbit name.

"Hi," he said, as he dropped into the chair opposite her.

"I was wondering when you'd arrive." She looked up with a smile, though it disappeared immediately at the sight of him. "Oh. You look terrible."

She was right. He did. There was no denying it. Bunny hadn't shaved in days, and his beard was growing in uneven patches of dark. His curls flopped into his face in an unwashed mop. He couldn't remember the last time he'd eaten.

"I was up late working on a term paper," he lied. In reality, he'd spent the night glued to his computer, scouring the school's digital repository for books on Nordic folklore. Ignoring the growing pile of overdue assignments on his desk. "Hey. Where'd you say you lived before this?"

Her 'brows drew together. "I didn't."

"But it was somewhere rural, right?" He was vaguely aware that he was blowing past all the stops. Ignoring the mating dance that came with meeting someone new. He could see the flicker of uncertainty in Arlen's eyes, but he couldn't stop himself from prying.

He was so tired. And there were too many coincidences.

"That's right." Hesitance crisped her reply. "My family is in Northern Wisconsin."

"Wisconsin, huh?" He let out a whistle. "America's dairy land. And have you lived there your whole life?"

She tucked a loose strand of white behind her ear and reclaimed her smile, though it glowed with a fainter light than before. "You're asking a lot of questions today."

He tipped a smile back at her. "I make it a point to know my enemies."

She blinked, startled. "*Enemies?*"

"Sure. You're occupying my seat, remember? That makes you the enemy."

The sound that slipped out of her was a barely-stifled laugh.

Even stunted, it sunk into him like tenterhooks. "We moved there a few years ago," she admitted. "After my sister died."

"Oh." A hard frost settled in his blood. And there, again, was Nora Hagel. Imprinted on the backs of his eyelids. Wedged in the space between his heartbeats. Gasping for air in the crack-riven road. His condolence came out graveled. "I'm so sorry."

"Don't be." She fluttered her fingers in a dismissal. "It's okay. My parents just didn't want to live in our old house anymore, with her things and her bedroom, so we packed up and moved. My uncle was already out in Wisconsin on his wife's family farm, and it made sense for us to end up there, too."

"Ah. I see."

Logic found him in that moment. Cold and bitter, like stepping into the Atlantic on a winter's day. Slapped awake by the sea of sensibility, he nearly laughed aloud.

He was cracking. He was unspooling like thread. He'd spent the night researching old wives' tales, and for what? There was nothing supernatural about Arlen. Nothing other or strange. She was just a girl. The way Linus's great-grandmother was just an old Nordic woman who'd married a man with a penchant for tall tales.

The way Bunny Bunsall was losing his goddamned mind.

Just like the psychic said you would, tiptoed a voice through his head. A wick of doubt lit in his chest and he rushed to smother it. He wouldn't do this – surrender to idle misgivings. Spend another midnight chasing delusions on shady internet forums. Miss another deadline, his grade point average circling the drain.

What he needed was a cold shower and decent night of sleep. A fresh start in the morning.

A quick glance at the window showed him the sun beginning to set. "It's almost dark," he said. "Can I walk you back to your dorm?"

Arlen pulled her bottom lip between her teeth. "I don't live on campus."

"Can I walk you to your car, then?"

She seemed to consider this, a crease deepening between her 'brows. Finally, she nodded. "I think that would be okay. As long as we don't hold hands."

He faked offense. "You don't want to hold my hand?"

She held her left arm between them, wrist encased in plaster. The outline of the rabbit was hard and dark against the white wrap. His heart tithed a beat, but only just – an echo of panic still reverberating in his chest.

Outside, the night was cold. The air slapped against them in a way that left their cheeks stinging, their shoulders kissing as they drew together for warmth. At the edge of the parking lot, she stopped. He'd spent the entire walk biting back the sort of laughter that encroached on becoming hysterical and now, flooded with the relief that he'd only gone temporarily mad, he felt overcome with courage.

"You know," he said, unprompted, "I read in a book once that crazy people always think they're perfectly sane, while sane people think they're going crazy."

Arlen paused in rooting through her bag for her keys, peering up at him. It had begun to sleet, and rain gathered in her lashes in little glass crystals. It gave her an ethereal glow beneath the streetlamps. This time, instead of thinking she was something fey, he thought she was something lovely.

"Oh." The tip of her nose had gone pink in the cold. "Are you saying you think you're going crazy?"

"Maybe." Bunny laughed right out loud then, his breath pluming in front of his face. Not a hysterical laugh, but a happy one. "I can't hold your hand," he hedged, "but no one said anything about a kiss."

Her eyes went big and wide. Sapphire and onyx and diamond.

"No," she admitted, "we didn't cover that."

When he leaned in to kiss her, she didn't protest. When she kissed him back, he felt as though the earth were sliding out from under his feet. Tilting on its axis, until the stars were both above and below and the night was a riot of color. And then – just as soon as it began – it was over, and she was backing away, tucking that single loose strand behind her ear.

"I thought we were enemies," she said.

"We are." He couldn't stop smiling like an idiot. When he spoke again, it was to lob her own words back at her. "Maybe this is all part of my plan."

The next day was Saturday. No classes. No alarm. Bunny woke, refreshed, from a night of dreamless sleep. He woke with a plan.

Grabbing a still-intact cardboard box from the towering pile of recyclables in the kitchen, he toed on his shoes and headed for his bike. The ride was empty and quiet, and he wheeled beneath a cotton candy sunrise, watching the clouds stretch across the horizon like spun sugar. A half mile from campus, he slowed.

This time, he spotted the rabbit from several yards away. It sat by the curve in the road as though it had been waiting all this time, gazing up at him through that two-toned stare. He would have burst into laughter at the ridiculousness of it all if it weren't for its little paw, still held at an odd angle. The wave of guilt that collided into his chest knocked the air from his lungs.

He skidded to a stop with plenty of space, quietly loosening the empty box he'd affixed to the back of the bike. When he approached the rabbit, it didn't run. When he scooped it into his arms, it didn't panic. It seemed too tired to do anything more than sit there in this crook of his elbow, its breathing labored and its paw curled inward.

"I really am sorry," he said quietly, as he eased it into the box. He felt it scamper into the sides in a panicked jostle. "I didn't mean to hurt you."

He blinked and saw Nora Hagel, her eyes big and frightened. Her mouth a red, red line. Her fingers reaching for him through the smoke. Pulling out his phone, he found the number for the nearest animal rehab. A woman answered on the fourth ring, sounding harried.

"Hi," he said, in response to her query. "I've got an injured rabbit here. I think it has a broken foot. Can I bring it in?"

"Sure," said the woman. "We're here until five."

He glanced down at the quietly shuffling box in his arms. The coroner's report said Nora Hagel had been pronounced dead on arrival. He hadn't stuck around long enough to see.

"What will you do with it?"

The woman blew out a breath. "Ah, well, let's see. We'll do an intake and assess the injury. If the leg is broken, we'll splint it and give the rabbit time to recover. When it's good and strong, we'll release it back into the wild."

"Okay," said Bunny. His breath crumpled in his chest. This time, he hadn't run.

It didn't erase the sting. It didn't evict the silver-filling dread from his stomach. The crunch of metal from his head.

But it felt like a start.

On Monday afternoon, he arrived at the library to find his chair empty. A strange cold stole through him at the sight. He'd been so sure he'd find Arlen there, waiting with that smile tucked up into the corner of her mouth. Her hair in a crown of braids, her eraser tapping against her open book.

Bunny took a seat in the chair opposite and went to work on a paper, now well past due. He watched the sun set through the windows. He ignored his growling stomach.

Arlen never arrived.

The next day was more of the same. He biked to school. He went to class. When the day was done, he headed to the library to find his chair unoccupied. This time, he set out in search of her, panic skating through his veins. But she wasn't in the stacks. She wasn't in the reference lab. She wasn't in the media room.

She wasn't there on Wednesday.

She wasn't there on Thursday.

She wasn't there on Friday.

By the time the weekend crawled around again, he'd gone back to sleeping in fits and starts. To falling into dreams and then wrenching awake, hounded by the snap of teeth and the crunch of metal. Each dawn, he sat awake, going over everything in his head. Every conversation. Every glance. The words of the seer. The coincidences and coincidences.

How strange, that the very day he'd scooped the rabbit out of the street, she'd disappeared.

He wanted to call Arlen, but he didn't have her number. He didn't even know her last name.

The following Monday, there she was. Seated in his chair like she'd never left, her hair loosely curled and her cast gone. Relief somersaulted through him as he shrugged out of his coat and hat. He wove through the clustered tables in a half run, careless of the heads that whipped around in his direction. When he pulled out the chair opposite her, she smiled.

"Miss me?"

"I thought I'd scared you away," he admitted. He didn't know how to explain that the sight of her had steadied the ground beneath him. Not without sounding like a lunatic.

Her laugh rebounded through the quiet of the library. "Your kissing wasn't *that* bad."

"I didn't say it was bad," he shot back, pretending to be offended. "I was just worried I came on too strong."

"Nope." She held up her wrist. "I flew home for a few days. Had to get my cast off. My mother wanted to personally see to it at the family physician's. She's been intense about that sort of thing ever since my sister passed."

"I get that." He sank slowly into his seat, still buoyant with relief. "How did she die, if you don't mind my asking?"

"It was an accident." The reply plunked onto the table between them. As though she realized she'd been blunt, she added, "Sorry, I don't like to talk about it."

"Understood." He leaned back and peered over at her. "It was pretty nice having my chair back for a couple of days."

"I bet it was." She looked mollified by the change of subject, her smile brightening. Reaching for her bag, she said, "I made you something."

"Did you?"

He watched as she parsed through the contents of her purse. From its inside, she withdrew a small, gray sculpture. A rabbit, he realized, hewn of heddle and wood, lashed together with bits of what appeared to be broom brush. When she held it out to him, he accepted it, though something in him screamed to keep it at arm's length. It looked like a totem – a poppet to pin with needles or set aflame.

"I love it," he said. "What is it?"

"It's a promise."

The hair rose along the back of his neck and he dragged his gaze to hers. The way she'd said it, soft and slow, had sounded very nearly like a threat. But when he met her eyes, it was to find her smiling.

"What sort of a promise?" he hedged.

She shook her head. "You'll have to wait and see."

He was a half mile from campus when he spotted it. The white rabbit. It stood shivering in the dark, peering out from the brush. Back in the wild, its splint gone and its leg recovered. Bunny slammed to a stop, a horrible sound rupturing out of him. In his hand, the wooden rabbit felt like a dead weight. Something heavy enough to drown him.

"No," he ground out, without meaning to. "Not you."

But the rabbit was gone, quick as a blink. Silent as a wraith.

By the time he crashed into his apartment, his heart was racing. He slammed on the light, his head full of neurosis, his stomach folding in on itself. Linus and David flew to their feet at once, David blinking like a vole in the overhead light and Linus reaching for the bat they kept propped by the balcony door.

"Oh," he said, setting down his weapon. "It's just you."

"Why the hell would you tear in here like that?" asked David, falling in behind Bunny as he stalked through the kitchen and headed for Linus's room.

"She's a witch," was all Bunny managed to say.

Linus joined David in the open door, looking intrigued. "Who's a witch?"

"Arlen." There was rugburn in his throat. Electricity in his lungs. He set to tearing through Linus's belongings, panic pinching his stomach. "Arlen is a witch. A shapeshifter."

"Sorry." David's intrigue had slipped into concern. "You think someone—"

"Not someone," he bit out. "*Arlen.*"

"Okay, Arlen. Who is Arlen?"

"A girl from school. I met her in the library. She gave me this."

He fished the rabbit statuette out of his pocket and tossed it through the air. Linus reached out and snatched the object before David could get ahold of it. "Sick," he said. "A milkhare."

The word burned up the ridge of Bunny's spine. "A what?"

"A milkhare," Linus repeated, as though he simply hadn't heard. "It's another piece of Nordic lore. Witches would make these as a symbol of their pact with the devil."

"I'm sorry," David said, "but with what, now?"

"She said she was an art student," Bunny murmured, unease flattening his delivery. "She said she made, uh, environmental sculptures."

"There's a bit of bone woven in here," said Linus, studying the figurine. "Hey, here's a question: What are we doing in my room?"

Bunny snatched the wooden rabbit back. The splinter-slick of the wood scraped at his skin. *A promise*, she'd called it. He assumed she'd meant it for him. But what if the promise had already been made, and to something insidious? A pact with the devil. An unholy covenant.

"The other day I was riding my bike to school," he said, the truth twisting from his lips. "I was going fast. It was wet. I hit a rabbit."

"*Dude*," said Linus.

"Linus, shut *up*," said David.

"I was pretty sure I broke its leg." Bunny's swallow felt like glass. "At school the next day, I met this girl with a cast on her arm. The *same* arm."

David's 'brows tightened. "That's called a coincidence."

"Sure," Bunny agreed. "Except this girl, right? She's got white hair."

In the door, his roommates stared over at him.

"It's a white rabbit," he said, insistence creeping into his voice.

"My great-grandmother had white hair," Linus said, in an effort to be helpful.

"You're not listening," Bunny spat. "That's *two* coincidences. And here's a third, ready? She has two different colored eyes. Blue on the left, black on the right."

"Let me guess." David looked as if he didn't know whether to be weary or worried. "So does the rabbit."

"Bingo." Bunny's voice cracked on the delivery. He felt riddled with hysteria, his sanity seconds away from coming all to pieces. "Anyway, I caught the rabbit and brought it to an animal rehab. I tried to do the right thing, you know? And the entire time – *the entire time* – it was there, Arlen didn't show up at campus once."

"Cool." Linus raised his hand. "I'm convinced. Let's go on a witch hunt."

"Put your hand down, stoner," snapped David. "Bunny, think about this logically. It's been a rough semester. You're not sleeping. I mean, listen to yourself. You think this girl, what? Sold herself to the devil? Come *on*, Bun. Think this through. Could it possibly be you're making connections that aren't there?"

"I'll show you," he insisted. He'd found what he was looking for – a gridded have-a-heart trap from when they'd discovered a mouse in their kitchen earlier in the semester. David had come home with standard mouse-traps and Linus, ever the pacifist, had gone out and bought something a touch more humane. In the morning, they'd found the mouse's body broken in David's snap trap, a piece of cheese in its petrified fist.

"You're going to catch the rabbit." David had gone pale as a ghost. "And then what?"

"I'll bring it back here." Determination razed through Bunny like wildfire. "I'll keep her here for a day or two, and then you'll see. She won't show up to school."

David's voice clipped warily out of him. "Because you think she'll be in our apartment."

"Exactly." He didn't care that David didn't believe him. He'd prove it.

"I'm in," said Linus, smothering a yawn. "I've got nothing else to do."

"You're both certifiable," snapped David, but he tugged his coat on when they did. He followed them out into the dark. They took his Fiat out to the curve in the bend where Bunny had last seen the rabbit, the radio off and none of them speaking. And there it was, waiting in the soft glow of moonlight, its stare obsidian in the dark. By the time they coaxed it into the cage, it had begun to rain. A soft, wet sprinkle that glazed the dark in a lamplit gold. In his lap, the rabbit sat dormant in its cage. In his pocket was the milkhare.

A devil's pact.

A witch's promise.

He'd see it undone.

The next evening, when Bunny and Linus went to the library, David reluctantly went with them.

"Admit it," Linus said, catching him in the side with an elbow, "you're curious."

"I'm concerned," said David. "Bunny, you do realize this is unhinged?"

But Bunny didn't answer. He was frozen in place in the lobby, the world slipping off its axis.

There, sitting in his seat, was Arlen; her legs tucked up under her and dutifully taking notes. As though she felt him looking, she glanced up. That secret smile caught at the corner of her mouth and she wriggled her fingers in a wave. His chest crumpled, all the air fleeing his lungs.

"That's her, isn't it," said David. "It is. Jesus Christ, Bunny. Of course, it is!"

At home, Bunny sat at his desk and watched the rabbit flail in its cage. Beating at the sides in an attempt to get free. Packed with more fight than he knew a beast of prey could possess. He wondered, dully, if Nora Hagel had fought like that, too, as she crawled across the pavement after him.

Help me, please!

His stomach felt sick. His head was all static.

"I'm sorry for everything I put you through," he said, his voice small. "I'll take you home. I'll set you free."

Outside in the common space, the kitchen and living room were empty, his roommates back on campus for their evening classes. He carried the cage downstairs and fastened it onto the back of his bike. He felt like a husk, scooped clean out of himself as he pedaled through the looping backroads, out to the curve in the road where he'd found the rabbit waiting for him day after day. Dropping the kickstand, he set down the cage and pried open the hatch.

The moment the rabbit darted out, wraith-white in the moonlight, he heard it.

The snap of a stick.

The padded gait of a predator.

A dark shape descended, its lips peeled back in an ivory snarl. He heard the rabbit's scream, uncanny as a human child's cry. Saw the red gush of blood, the crimson mat of a wolf's bloodied maw. And then the beast was off, surging into the looming wood and the ceaseless dark.

Terror clawed through him and he took off like a shot, branches tearing at his skin. His howl a lone wolf's cry against the dark. Scrabbling at the matted pine beneath him, his fingers closed around a stone. Winding up, he pitched it hard in the wolf's direction – step back, leg lift, release, extend. When that didn't work, he opted for a stick, lichen crusting off beneath his palms. He swung it like a bat, clipping the wolf hard on the hindquarters.

With a whine, the beast dropped the rabbit and drew back. Beneath the palest trickle of cloud-smothered moonlight, Bunny saw that it wasn't a wolf at all, but a Labrador retriever. A woven collar hung slack around its neck, an invisible fence indicator blinking red. A loose dog, acting on instinct. With a doleful glance in his direction, it took off between the trees, tail tucked between its legs.

Casting aside his stick, Bunny spun out, sick and disoriented – searching for the rabbit.

There, in the moonlight, he saw her. Not a rabbit at all, but a girl. Her hair was done in a crown of white braids, her eyes wide and lightless. Bold red gouts of blood poured down her throat as she reached out a crimson hand, grasping for him through the pale spills of silver.

"Arlen."

Her name choked out of him, the sound throttled and strange. The dark pressed close, the world blurring at its edges. Before he could think, he was through the trees and slamming to his knees in front of her, his hands sticky with sap. Only, there was a rabbit there where a girl had been. A frail little creature, dying in the dark.

"Arlen," he said, and shook it. "Arlen. *Arlen*."

He fumbled with the phone in his pocket, thumbs bloodying the blinding white of the screen. His throat was all bile. His hands shook and shook.

"9-1-1," he heard. "What's your emergency?"

"There's a girl here," he cried out. "A – a rabbit. She's been bitten. She's bleeding. It was a wolf. No, I think – I think it was a dog."

"Sir?" The dispatch officer was every bit his opposite. Calm, where he was wild. Steady, where he was panicked. "I need you to take a breath and try to explain where you are and what happened."

He was on his feet, the rabbit limp in his arms. His phone lay discarded in the dirt, the woman's voice chirping out of the speaker. The next few moments came to him in snatches: He was staggering through the woods. He was toppling into trees. Beyond the thick press of pine the lights of his campus winked awake in stipples of gold. Already, several students had caught sight of him emerging from the forest. They stood frozen on the path, their surprise pluming into the night in thick clouds of gray.

"Someone help me," he gasped out, his hands slick with blood. "I killed her. *I killed her.*"

The rabbit was dead by the time police arrived.

It lay limp in his arms, red where it had once been white as snow. Stiff, where it had once quivered and shaken. A crowd had gathered to watch, and in it he could just make out the maroon of Linus's beanie, the lamplit spark of David's glasses.

"Mason Bunsall?"

He couldn't remember the last time someone had called him that. Mason, not Bunny. He didn't look up at the officer in front of him. He didn't look at the crowd. He looked only at the little broken body in his arms, the words of the seer mocking him without end. *Killer. Killer.*

"You alright, kid?"

"No." He shook his head. "I killed her."

"Yeah?" The officer crossed his arms. His badge winked silver in the light. "You want to tell me who?"

He stared down at the rabbit. One black eye stared back. "I already told the other cop," he said. "Her name was Arlen."

"He means Arlen Hagel," said the officer he'd spoken to earlier, rejoining the scene. Her hair was slicked back in a bun and she peered down at him, unsmiling. "I've just had a word with the Dean. He says she's a student here at school. Just transferred at the start of the semester."

Hagel.

Hagel.

The name thrummed through him. That couldn't be right.

"Not Nora," he said, still clinging to the rabbit. Already, rigor mortis had begun to creep into her body. The blood on his wrists had dried to brown, rusting flakes. "Nora's been dead for years. I'm talking about Arlen. Her name is *Arlen*, and she's *right here*."

"Okay." The first officer depressed a button on his walkie. "We've got a 5150 here. We're bringing him in for an assessment."

Bunny lifted his head. He felt like he'd stepped outside himself. Like he was looking down on the scene from miles away. Dully, he asked, "Am I under arrest?"

The cop's eyes went wide. "For killing a rabbit? No. But we're going to get you in for a psych evaluation."

"But I killed her," he ground out as he was led to the car. Still clutching the rabbit, the crowd still gathered, the statue still in his pocket. "I saw her. I followed her. And I killed her."

"You can tell it to your psychiatrist, kid," said the policeman, pulling open the door to his car.

Across the street, Bunny saw a shadow step out of the darkness. Caught in the whirl of the lights, her face lit up red then blue then red again. Arlen Hagel, her two-toned eyes bright in the darkness, that secret smile on her face. His stomach bottomed out.

"That's her," he said, as her smile stretched wide. Fey and Other – a witch's grin. "*Over there*, that's her."

But the officer wasn't listening. He was prying the rabbit out of Bunny's hands, muttering about getting blood in his squad car.

"I didn't do anything," Bunny Bunsall cried, his voice scraping against the night. "She's right there. I can see her. Just *look*, would you?"

The door slammed shut

The sirens pealed through the dark. Arlen Hagel wriggled her fingers in a small, fleeting wave. And then she was gone, quick and quiet and a wraith. All that was left was Nora Hagel's name in his mouth and the milkhare in his pocket – a devil's pact and a sister's promise, the whispered words of a medium from Coney Island ringing and ringing in his head.

X HOUSE

J. T. Ellison

In the beginning, there was a simple bridge that led to the sea. A marsh of cattails and sea flowers spread beneath it. The edge of the lake licked the lower pylons when the rains were heavy, and the sea touched the railings when the storms were severe.

It was rare to have a lake so close to the ocean, but this land was different than most. It kept secrets. It's said that there was something about it that drove people mad. It made them do things they wouldn't normally do. It hypnotized. It seduced. The sea called, and the body answered, helpless against the pull of the tides.

There was a bog near the bridge, on the other side of the forest. The things that disappeared into that place… Animals. Trees. People.

Yes, it was beautiful, but it was dangerous. So many were lost over the years, women who vanished into the woods and never returned. Why someone would build a school in this desolate area was a forever unknown. The architecture was classic Gothic, severe verticals with arches and buttresses, harled stone two feet thick to keep out the worst of the winter nor'easters, turrets and mullioned windows and chimneys sticking up like fingers from the expansive roof – it looked like it belonged in the British countryside, perched in decaying solitude upon the moors. But the building was well maintained, inside and out. Each room had a fireplace and a view – facing south over the gardens, west over the lake, north over the marsh, and east over the sea. To the cliffs. To certain death.

So many felt that siren call to the sea. Others went into the forest and didn't return. Not enough that people didn't want to send their girls there. Just an adequate supply to stoke the rumors. The cooler months were especially amenable to the darkest of tales about the school's lost inhabitants, and the girls were happy to oblige with their own fanciful stories. They claimed graves of the children born to the women who studied here lined the kitchen wall, marked with tiny white crosses that only showed when the grass died. No one could ever find them, but they were there. A cemetery in consecrated ground offered a home to the bones of the people who first built the school; it was by the folly near the garden gate, and if you went there at midnight during the dark of the moon, you could talk to the founders of the school and hear their warnings. The third floor had a gray lady, and if she appeared, you were certain not to graduate. There were tunnels from the basement to the cliffs.

Isolation and cold breed a certain kind of madness that disguises itself well.

A consortium bought the school in the eighties, spiffed it up with a fresh coat of white limed paint and beautiful landscaping, and rebranded it as the Bridgend School. They established four houses within the confines of the building, sectioning them off so the individual members could build character together. They were named after the original builders: Bromley, Camden, Easton, and Xavier. The consortium did their best to dispel the rumors that plagued the institution, made a slick brochure, appealed to the wealthiest of the wealthy, and it worked. Bridgend was the destination school for the young ladies of the northeastern elites for quite a few years.

And then a student supposedly leaped from the cliffs, and all the old nasty rumors came out of the woodwork. Rumors, and stories, and secrets. This is one.

1. MIA

Mia's first impression of Xavier House is girls. They are everywhere, lounging, books covering faces, coltish legs thrown over the arms of cracked leather chairs, glossy hair past their shoulder blades hanging toward the rugs. This is a study hour, and they seem to be doing just that, suffering in silence, the pages of their books whispering truths into their young brains.

Tension flows through the room when they realize a stranger is in their midst. The pages stop turning, and all eyes follow as she walks by, led by the headmistress, a dour woman of indeterminate age named Elonia Tavish. Miss Tavish wears a thick gray-and-black tartan skirt and a white button-down under an oyster-gray cardigan. Sturdy, sensible brogues encase her surprisingly small feet. She is cadaverous in this bland school uniform, and Mia can only imagine how washed out she will appear in the same outfit. Somehow, the gray suits this woman, who seems encased in fog as she strides toward the dormitory.

A *tsk* of the headmistress's tongue startles Mia. She's stopped walking and is staring at the girls she will soon be teaching. She hurries to the headmistress's side, who clears her throat delicately. A gentle susurration moves through the room as the girls sit up, close books, and stand, arms at their sides, chins up, shoulders back.

"Ladies, this is Miss Savage. She is your new English Literature and Classics professor. She is stepping into the very big shoes of Miss McPhee, and I'm sure you will welcome her and help her learn our ways. Bridgend can be a shock to outsiders, and as the ladies of Xavier House, you are encouraged to set the example for Miss Savage. Now step forward and introduce yourselves."

Their names are familiar because Mia has already studied their files. Each girl takes a half step toward her, looks into the empty air over Mia's right shoulder, says their name, then steps back.

"Mary Davis."

"Lily Clarkson."

"Kathryn Blanton-Hughes."

"Amelia Bright."

"Virginia McKenzie. Call me Ginny."

"Tabitha Jacobson."

Mia gives them a warm smile when they're back in their tidy line. "It's a pleasure to meet all of you. I—"

Miss Tavish nods briskly and takes Mia's arm. "We'll do your full introduction during classes tomorrow. Now, we must allow the girls their study time."

"Oh. Of course," Mia says, and as they step out of the common space and into the drab hallway, she can swear Call Me Ginny stifles a giggle.

The floors to the dormitory are cracked and warped, covered in a thin runner that might have once been red, but is now the palest peach, bleached out from years of use and the meager but relentless light from the windows along the arched transom.

"You will find the girls of Xavier House models of decorum, intelligence, and decency. Each house at Bridgend School has its strengths, and you will be responsible for enhancing the natural inclinations of your girls. They are not sporty, nor flighty. They are quiet. Studious. Shy." She looks at Mia with narrowed eyes. "Much like you, I suspect."

Mia nods. Shy is a good descriptor of her nature. She's always preferred the company of a novel to a person. Bookish girls are a heavenly assignment. The dean continues her elocution.

"We only use surnames here. Too much individuality is discouraged, as is familiarity. I expect you to keep your distance from these girls. You are not their friend, you are their professor. You are their guiding light, not their confidante. You will address your girls as Miss, and they will address you as Professor. If you have any problems, seek me out. They are good girls, though. I've never had a complaint." She hesitates. "And they've been through so much."

Miss Tavish opens a door, and Mia steps inside her new world. It is surprisingly cozy: A fire in the grate crackles merrily, a thick, warm rug covers the wide plank floors, a sofa with a cushion that sags toward the left arm offers a welcoming embrace for evening reading and tea. A desk sits under the window with two rose-colored wingback chairs – one for her, one for a student or friend. There is a small kitchen, a bright copper kettle already on the stove, and a room beyond with a bed and bath that overlooks the garden. The sun is setting already; this far north the sun is fully gone by late afternoon during the colder months.

"The sunsets over Lake Indall are quite lovely. We have twenty-eight acres, with several walkable areas. If you venture out, keep to the paths. They are quite well marked. The gardens are equally tranquil. Stay away from the cliffs, though. They are off limits to all Bridgend staff and students." The headmistress looks around the small space, pitches her voice lower. "And of course, anything you need, I am always available."

"I won't hesitate to call on you."

"Good. I'm sure you will be happy here, Professor Savage, once you get used to the place."

"Call me Mia."

"Professor. You've earned the title, and you should be called by it." The headmistress seems anxious to leave, and Mia sets down her bag with a nod.

"I understand. Thank you, Miss Tavish. I'm sure I will."

Mia senses Tavish wants to say more, but what else is there to say? They both know Mia's role here. They aren't destined to be friends.

"I'll let you get settled. Dinner is at six p.m., sharp."

The door latches with a quiet *snick*, and Mia lets out her breath. The tension between them was palpable, but that's not unusual for her – Mia has never been a fan of authority figures. Utterly ironic, considering.

She doesn't have much to unpack. She puts her small portable safe in the bedside table drawer, hangs up her clothes, aligns her shoes, and washes her face. The closet already holds two uniform kilts, three white blouses, and a gray cardigan. Either her predecessor was the same size, or Miss Tavish asked for Mia's measurements. She shucks her cardigan and jeans and gets dressed in the school colors. Though the wool of the skirt is a bit scratchy, it's warm, and the cardigan is soft against her cheek.

She has thirty minutes to spare. The school's grounds are expansive, but it's dark, so she's not about to go exploring, even though she could use a walk. There's a forest on the edge of the kitchen garden, this she knows from studying the map of the school. And marshlands that lead to the lake. She will hoof it around the place when it's light out, get a better sense of the layout of the grounds and school firsthand.

She fills a glass with water – it smells a bit brackish, but they are on the edge of the sea here – and takes in the rest of the room. A wind has started outside; a storm is coming up the coast and will blanket the school in rain overnight. There is plenty of firewood, thick white candles, and blankets if it gets too chilly. The space will do.

On the small desk under the window is a folder. She flips it open and sees familiar faces, flips page after page. Mary. Lily. Kathryn. Amelia. Ginny. Tabitha.

And one more. Mia turns the last page to see a bland, broad face with wide-set blue eyes and a slightly receding chin, blonde hair pinned back from her face with a black headband. Cynthia. Dead Cynthia. The one who supposedly flung herself from the cliff's edge two weeks ago.

The remaining six girls who were in the common area are now her charges.

Six girls to teach.

Six girls to keep safe.

Six girls to keep alive for the rest of term.

Someone is trying to murder the young women of Xavier House, and Mia is here to stop them.

2. LILY

The whispers start at breakfast, building to a fever pitch before their food is served.

Rollie's replacement is coming today.

Lily buries her face in her porridge and tries not to hyperventilate.

Rollie's replacement – it could be anyone. How are they supposed to trust a newcomer after the semester they've already had?

Rosalind McPhee wasn't a bad professor. Most of the girls liked her, but some thought she was creepy. "Call me Rollie," she'd said the first time she met everyone, and shook hands, a wide smile on her horsey face. There were all kinds of rules about students and professors touching, not to mention that the students are supposed to be called by last names only, and her "Professor," only, but Rollie wasn't much for rules. That's probably why she was dead.

Cynthia, too. She hadn't liked Rollie. Cynthia was a rule follower, almost to the extreme. So much so that when she missed class that Tuesday, Rollie immediately went to Miss Tavish. A few hours later, when X House and then all of Bridgend proper had been searched, and there was no sign of Cynthia, Rollie was the first to call for the professionals.

When they finally found Cynthia, hours later, on the rocks at the base of the cliff, torn to pieces by the surf, she was almost unrecognizable. She was wearing the Bridgend uniform, though, and her candy-floss blonde hair that she always wore back with an Alice in Wonderland-style headband was undamaged except for a large chunk torn away over her right ear. Cynthia was a nervous mouse of a girl, and it was hard to imagine her standing on the cliffs and jumping into the sea. She wasn't the type. But there she was, twisted and broken, the gulls swooping and fighting for the choicest morsels from her body.

Cynthia was bad enough. A week later, Rollie was found in the gardens, her eyes bugging out of her head like she'd seen a ghost, or worse, though the autopsy said she'd had a stroke. The stress of Cynthia's death, most likely, the headmistress said. Lily knew women in their forties who were incredibly fit rarely had strokes, but who was she to argue with the officials? Having an answer so benign was a relief, really.

Losing a teacher and a student in the first month of term put Bridgend School in the papers, and Xavier House was regarded with a combination of horror and fascination by the rest of the girls at school. They avoided this end of campus, which was easy to do. Xavier – the quad of X House, as it was known on campus – was detached from the rest of Bridgend by a walking bridge over the westernmost edge of the lake. "X Stands Alone", that's the motto. It's incredibly accurate now. No one wants to hang with the X girls.

Lily likes the freedom it brings, this minor separation. She hasn't always been good at making friends, preferring long walks in the gardens and along the sea to the gossip sessions of the other girls. She isn't close to any of them but Cynthia, and now Cynthia is rotting in the ground.

When the new professor comes through the common room during study hours, the rest of the girls pretend not to notice her, but Lily watches closely. The new prof isn't old, maybe early thirties, dressed in jeans and a chunky oversized cardigan that are at least somewhat hip. She has green eyes and pale skin, and blushes pink as the headmistress's roses when Lily catches her staring. She has a tragic haircut, uneven and severe, almost like she's gotten gum caught in one side and chopped it all off herself. Lily is good with hair. She might offer to fix it, if it seems that suggestion would be welcome. Professor Savage is an unknown, so for now, Lily will keep her head down and try not to draw any attention to herself. It's how she usually approaches her days, when she can. Cynthia was Lily's roommate before her swan dive off the cliff. She'd even been Lily's friend for a while. Until the day she'd gone to Rollie and told her that Lily had stolen the key to the pantry and made a copy for Ginny so she could have access to the kitchens. Then, Cynthia was just the jerk she roomed with.

Dinner will be the second opportunity to lay eyes on their new prof.

It's been a long day of rumor and innuendo, and dinner tonight is her favorite, fried chicken and roasted green beans. She eats at the long trestle table with the rest of the girls from her class, present but apart, warily watching to see how the new prof will be treated. Lily is an anxious girl to start with; fear has been ingrained in her since she could walk. Cautiousness is next to godliness in her family. She doesn't think it fair. In another world, she would be totally normal, but her dad, who is a congressman, is alternately popular and hated, which makes her mom nervous as a thoroughbred. Her parents are in a constant state that something might happen to him, to her, to the children. So Lily is always on alert, too.

They'd tried to pull her out of school when Cynthia died, and again when Rollie kicked the bucket. But Lily stood firm. She loved Bridgend, she loved X House, and she wasn't going to leave. She'd surprised herself with her vehemence, considering she was sleeping with the lights on and tried never to go to the bathroom alone.

She feels a little sick thinking about Cynthia. That was a hard way to die.

A buzz is starting. The new prof, encased in gray tartan, enters the dining room. She looks as out of place as Lily often feels. She doesn't look like a teacher. She doesn't have that introspective arrogance. She seems more like a predator.

Especially when she meets Lily's eyes. It is like she's singled her out, like she knows something no one else does.

The hair stands up on the back of Lily's neck, and a small frisson of panic runs through her body. For a girl who's spent her life looking for threats, the new prof seems like a prime candidate for chaos.

How is she supposed to sit with this woman day in and day out? This is not good. And she can't touch base with her parents, either; they've taken her older sister to Colorado to a specialist to have a surgical procedure done. Fleur trashed her hip in a field hockey accident at her college in Vermont and had to have a replacement, something not many orthopedic surgeons were comfortable doing on a girl who was still growing. There is a specialist in Denver who has agreed to do the surgery, and they are stuck out there for a few weeks with her. Lily knows her parents – they might be nervous nellies, but they aren't going to leave Fleur's side and fly to Maine to pull Lily out of school because a teacher gives her an odd feeling.

As if she knows what Lily is thinking, Ginny kicks her under the table and shakes her head, then gives her a long slow smile, raises a 'brow, and shoves a chunk of green veg in her mouth.

Breathe. It's all okay. Tavish would never bring in a teacher she hadn't fully vetted, right? And Lily's own father had a security contingent, they would have to approve the new teacher, too. Do background checks and all that.

Damn, now the woman is staring openly at Lily, a small smile on her lips. Lily feels herself flush, and that makes the panic attack even worse.

"Gotta pee," she mumbles to the girl next to her, Kathryn Blanton-Hughes, and bolts, ignoring Ginny's peals of laughter ringing behind her.

There is a bathroom right outside the dining hall, but Lily runs past it and up the stairs to the dorm. It is the first time she's been totally alone since Cynthia died, and that doesn't hit her until she is locked in a stall and the motion sensors go out. She is plunged into darkness.

Oh, crap.

Her heart is thundering in her ears, her breath coming short. She is in the grip of the attack now, is practically blind with fear.

Breathe, breathe, breathe. It's a panic attack. You're going to be okay. You're going to be fine. You're safe.

Was she? Cynthia had thought herself safe, too.

The door squeaks, and the lights turn on.

A strange voice calls her name.

3. MIA

Mia sees the girl run from the dining room and is on her feet a moment later. Something is wrong, and her instinct is to help. She ignores Tavish's "Professor Savage!" and is out the door and up the dorm stairs on the girl's heels. She sees her disappear into the bathroom and slows to a walk. There isn't any way out of there except through the door.

Mia gives the girl a few minutes to collect herself, then opens the door.

"Lily?" she calls softly. "You okay? Are you sick?"

A sob comes from the last stall on the right.

"I'm your new professor, Mia Savage. I know you've had a rough go of it. You were Cynthia Andante's roommate. I've read your file. It must be so hard to lose a friend like this."

"Please go away."

"I wouldn't be much of a teacher if I left you here crying, now, would I? Why don't you come out and we can get a cup of tea? Have a chat."

"No!" The wail is accompanied by panting, then a heavy *slump*. An arm and part of a ponytail show under the stall door. The poor thing has fainted.

Mia pushes against the stall door experimentally, but it's locked. So she takes the girl's arm and slides her out gently. Mia puts her cardigan under the girl's head. She is already coming to, her lids fluttering, the heartbeat in her throat pulsing. Mia shushes her, patting her hand and stroking back her hair.

"It's okay, I've got you. You're fine. You just fainted. Panic attack? Or haven't you been eating?"

The girl closes her eyes and swallows. "Panic," she mumbles.

"I get them too sometimes. Or I used to. Now when I feel one coming on, I remind myself it's just a chemical reaction and breathe it out."

"Tried. Didn't work."

Lily is making motions like she wants to sit up, and Mia gently raises her to a seated position and lets her lean back against the wall.

"Whenever you want to get up off the floor, let me know. This is gross. All these girl germs…"

Lily stifles a giggle, which Mia takes as a good sign.

"What happened to your hair?"

Mia resists touching the choppy edges. "Um… I had an accident last year. It won't grow in right."

"You hit your head?"

"Kind of." Shit, this kid is way too observant. Not a huge surprise, considering. But Mia isn't about to lay bare her problems to a child, much less one she is assigned to.

"You freaked me out," the girl says, catching Mia's discomfort and changing the subject deftly. "You were watching me."

"You know why?"

"Because my roommate died. And people think I had something to do with it."

"Because your father sent me to keep an eye on you."

"What?" Now the girl looked genuinely alarmed. "Why? What did he say?"

Mia glances toward the door. This is a total breach of operational security, and exactly what she isn't supposed to do. But Lily has a look of sheer horror about her that makes Mia realize honesty is going to be the best policy. Sort of. There is no reason to alarm the girl more than necessary.

"He's been worried. With Cynthia's death, and Professor McPhee's so soon after, he just wanted to be sure you were safe."

"Safe. Right. Like that's ever possible." What bitterness from such a young girl.

"Don't think like that. You're at a lovely, though isolated, school that many young women would give their left arm to attend. This is meant to be the safest place for you. Your father told me you love it here."

"I did. Then everyone started dying around me."

"Well, you don't need to worry about that anymore. I'm here." Mia crosses her fingers behind her back in a very childish gesture as she tells the lie. She is worried. Very worried. From what she's seeing, this will be a security nightmare. "Though you need to keep that to yourself. As far as everyone else on the campus is concerned, I'm replacing Miss McPhee."

"Are you even a teacher? Or just a bodyguard?"

"I am a teacher. I have a degree in English Lit. I taught before I started this job. Met my now boss on campus. He was there on a protection detail for the daughter of a Saudi prince. We hit it off. Now. Can you stand? We should go back to the dining hall."

"Do I have to? The girls will look at me strange if we go in together."

At Mia's slightly raised 'brow, Lily ducks her head. "Fine. Let's go."

Downstairs, Lily looks over her shoulder before they enter the dining room. "Is your name really Savage?" she asks.

Mia smiles. "It is. I always wanted to be vicious and unapproachable to match the name. Didn't really work out."

"Vicious and unapproachable. I like it." Then she slips through the doors and is back in her seat before Mia can respond.

Miss Tavish is glaring, lips pursed in disapproval, but Mia smiles and gives a little wave of assurance. This job is going to be harder than she thought.

There is something off about Lily Clarkson.

4. LILY

After dinner, Lily is in the study room with the rest of her class, nose deep in a book, respecting the quiet time that is supposed to be sacred, when Ginny McKenzie plops down next to her, shoving Lily's feet to the floor to make room for her ample behind.

"So?"

Lily shoots her an annoyed glance and returns her feet to the sofa, though she is scrunched onto a single cushion now.

"So what?"

"How was she? The new prof?"

"She was fine. Nice."

"Nice? Rollie was nice, and look where that got her."

"Don't even think about it, Ginny. It's too soon. They'll figure it out."

Ginny is a buxom girl who would have been called handsome fifty years ago, with curly red hair and a killer hourglass figure that tends toward a bit of pudge, resulting from her many late-night sojourns with the frozen yogurt dispenser. She is tall, too, almost a foot taller than Lily. She takes up space in the world, as Lily's mother always encouraged. Lily does not. Maybe that's why she went along with it when Ginny, Kathryn, Amelia, and Tabitha decided Cynthia needed a bit of hazing.

Maybe she was afraid they'd pick her instead. Maybe she knew they would pick her, for sure, if she didn't play along.

"Don't go making friends again, Lily. These professors need to know their place in our world."

Lily sighs. Why hasn't she just told Miss Savage the truth about what is happening here? Hazing is terrible in private schools, especially among girls. Because they numbered so few in their class, they had to be even more cautious in their tortures. Mary, for instance, they hadn't even gotten to yet. Lily had the chance to say hey, these girls are insane, and they hurt Cynthia, and they hurt Rollie, and they'll hurt you, so let's get out of here.

But she hadn't.

Why?

Because she wants Ginny McKenzie to like her. She wants to be strong like Ginny and her shadows. She wants to take up space. She doesn't want to be an anxiety-ridden mouse who's afraid of the dark and doesn't like to be alone. She doesn't want to be overcome by panic attacks. If she has any chance of succeeding in this life, she has to be hard as nails. They are honing her; she is their knife. Their attentions hurt, but they also feel good. They make Lily feel special in ways she never has before. Being the daughter of a famous politician means she is often relegated to the back seat, and she isn't about to stay there. She has ambitions. She has plans. And the girls of X House are going to get her there.

"You did a good job getting her alone. What did you learn?"

Lily glows inside but plays it cool. "Thanks. She was all over me. She's been a teacher for five years. She's single. No boyfriend that I heard of. I pretended to faint and lifted her keys. I could only get into her room for a few minutes after dinner. She has a small safe in the bedside table. I made a copy of the key to go back another time. You'll need to distract her so I can get into it and do a more thorough search. We'll find whatever she is hiding."

Lily already knows what Miss Savage is hiding. But there is power in knowledge. She has to figure out how she will use what she knows.

"Give me the key."

It's pointless to say no. Ginny will just take it from her if she doesn't hand it over. Lily looks over her shoulder, then hands Ginny the key. She perfected the method at her old school – charring the edge of the main key with a lighter, laying it on a piece of clear tape, taping that to a piece of plastic (expired credit cards worked perfectly) cutting the key out of the plastic. It wasn't foolproof, but it usually worked.

"You distract her, and I'll get into the safe," Ginny commands.

"Shouldn't we wait a few days?"

Ginny's gaze grows cold, and Lily immediately moves on. "Wonder what it is? Money?"

"Could be."

"Jewelry, maybe."

"I hope it's money. Or grass. I could use some grass."

Ginny had tried marijuana over the summer, and now it's all she talks about.

"Whatever it is, it will be valuable. Good job, Clarkson. We'll make an X girl out of you yet."

It is stupid how much those words mean to her. She tries for insouciance, gives Ginny a Mona Lisa smile, and nods at her book. "I should—"

"Still such a good little girl." Ginny smiles wickedly. "But you have to be a bit naughty for me, so I can find out about Professor Savage."

"I'm open to suggestions."

"I'd say a stroll in the grounds will do. There's a big storm coming. You know where to go."

The familiar panic snakes through her stomach. Outside alone at night freaks her out badly. But if she is going to have Ginny on her side, she can't afford to show any kind of weakness.

"Okay. I'll knock on your door when I'm heading out. Now I really do need to get back to work."

"Hope it's something cool in that safe," Ginny says, not a little wistfully. That is the problem with their surroundings. As lovely as Bridgend is, as warm and inviting as X House can be, it still feels like they are visitors in a very old, very expensive building. It will never feel like theirs. Having some extra cash to buy little pieces of things that remind them of home goes a long way. The staff is excellent at accepting bribes, for the right price. They'll bring in most anything and leave it in the dresser drawers. Lovely folks.

Lily thinks she knows what's in that safe. She is a little thrilled at what the night ahead holds.

5. MIA

Mia does a final security check on X House before she goes to bed. On the surface, the place isn't hard to secure: one door in the front, one door in the back, one door to the garden – all alarmed.

The windows are a bit challenging, numbering well over fifty on each floor, but they, too, are alarmed. She has a list of everyone who has access, from people in the administration, cleaning staff, cooks, other teachers, and students themselves, though she assumes it isn't complete. The only sane thing to do is change the locks and control who gets a key going forward, which will blow her cover too quickly. She wants to maintain some secrecy about her mission for as long as possible if only to keep Lily safe.

She prowls through X House, getting to know its nooks and crannies. A draft on the third-floor corridor needs further investigation, but the door to the space it's coming from is locked. She'll have to get the keys from Miss Tavish. The hall doors between the different houses are blocked off with bookcases, keeping the girls in a cocoon within their house. They, too, are secure.

On the second floor, the dorm rooms are quiet and peaceful, full of the breathy kittenish noises of young women at rest. She pauses for a longer time outside Lily's door, listening, yet hears nothing but tiny snores. The girl is asleep. Good.

X House is quiet at night, and in the way of all grand old houses, the hall floors make a terrible racket, groaning and squeaking as she moves through the dark hallways. Good to know; she should be able to hear anyone walking around. They'd have to pass her room to get to the girls. It isn't a perfect setup, but considering their isolation, it should work.

Satisfied the house is secure, Mia retreats to her new space. The fire has been banked for the night, releasing a warm glow. She makes a note to find out who is servicing her room – her firm has already run deep and extensive background checks on all the school staff, focusing hard on the Xavier House servants, and everyone has come up clean. But someone on campus is a killer. Cynthia *might* have fallen off the cliff, and McPhee subsequently suffered a stroke, but Mia doesn't believe in coincidences. They don't have toxicology back on McPhee's body yet. There is more to learn.

Mia doesn't think she'll sleep easily, but the bed is surprisingly cozy, and she wakes just before dawn feeling more rested than she should after only four hours of sleep. The storm is upon them, lightning streaking through the silver skies, and she resists the urge to pull up the covers and wallow for another few minutes, instead taking advantage of the still quiet morning to stalk the halls one more time. Lightning illuminates things she hadn't noticed earlier, strange paintings and murals, a massive clock that, as she counts, booms five times.

As she had at the beginning of her rounds, she stops in front of Lily's door and listens carefully.

No snores. No movement.

A crack of lightning is followed by a clap of thunder so loud and close Mia jumps. A few small screams sound from behind the doors on the hall; there is no way anyone can sleep through nature's commotion.

Nothing from Lily's room.

Mia knocks lightly. When there is no answer, she tries the knob. It turns easily. She opens the door, heart suddenly in her throat.

The room is empty. Worse, the window is open. Rain slashes through the curtains; a puddle has formed under the sill.

Lily Clarkson is nowhere to be seen.

Mia is out the window onto a slippery black metal fire escape in a heartbeat. She hadn't noticed it on her earlier rounds, but it was dark outside, and she hasn't had a chance to see the whole house yet. Cursing Tavish under her breath – why would she put the one girl who needs to be the most secure in a room with such easy egress? – Mia climbs down. The rain obscures any tracks, but she sees a light bobbing in the distance.

"Lily!" she cries, her calls drowned by the storm.

The light is growing fainter. Mia has no choice. She follows, tripping and slipping, getting soaked to the bone and muddy to the knees. She isn't dressed for hiking, and holds an arm up to shelter her face from the worst of the rain.

"Lily!" she calls again, and this time, the light stops. "Thank God," Mia mutters, hurrying carefully toward the specter of her charge. Five minutes pass, and she can't remember being more miserable, wetter, colder. The rain is one thing; the sea causes a damp to settle in her joints, making her feel like she's walking through molasses.

Mia spots the girl at last, white as a ghost near the edge of the cliff, and runs to her, screaming. "Stop! Stop! Oh my God, Lily. What the hell are you doing?"

Before she gets to the edge, Mia runs into something that feels like a tree branch. Right into her stomach. She doubles over then goes down, hard on her back. She can't breathe, realizes she must have broken a rib. Bruised her sternum, too. Sips of air, little sips, her diaphragm tries to help her, and finally, she is able to inflate her chest, and with that comes water, mud, and tears.

Lily. Where is Lily? Mia will have to deal with her own injuries later. She needs to stop the girl from jumping.

Mia rolls over, bruised, and gets to her hands and knees, the rocks

sharp under her palms. Looks up into the round hole of the Glock
19 that was supposed to be in the safe in her bedside table drawer.

6. MIA

Mia tries to make sense of what she's seeing, but it is too
incongruous. She has come to save this girl, and now, is staring
at her own gun. But who is holding it? How did they get it?

She wipes rain from her face and looks past the metal eye to the
strangely blank face of Lily Clarkson. Seeing the recognition on
Mia's face, Lily smiles at her, teeth flashing in the darkness.

"Shouldn't have left this behind," she says.

"Lily. Give me that before you hurt yourself. I can help you. I can
make everything better. Just hand me the gun."

There is noise to Mia's right, and Lily is joined by Kathryn Blanton-
Hughes, Amelia Bright, Ginny McKenzie, and Tabitha Jacobson.
Ginny slings an arm across Lily's shoulder and brushes a lock of wet
hair from the girl's face. "Good job," she says, then turns to Mia.

"Hi, Professor. You really shouldn't be out wandering the grounds
by yourself. It's against school policy." Ginny *tsk*s, and it's the same
horrid noise Miss Tavish made when Mia stopped to admire these
girls flopped like kittens all over the X House furniture – God, was
it yesterday? Less than twenty-four hours, and she's lost control.
She's lost Lily to these monsters. She is going to die here, with the
leering faces of these girls, too young to survive alone in the world,
still growing, still becoming. Becoming world-class murderers,
that's for sure.

They disappear from her view, laughing and crowing, these lost girls of X House, leaving Lily facing her. The gun doesn't waver in her hand.

"Sorry, Miss Savage. It's you or me. I choose you."

"Lily. Lily, don't do this."

"Walk," Lily says, gesturing toward the cliff. Toward that roaring, a monstrous scream relentlessly rising and falling. It is hungry and demands a meal. It has no conscience, the sea. It takes what it wants and spits out the remains.

Mia isn't about to go along with this anymore. They may have been able to bully a child, and God knew what happened to Professor McPhee, but Mia will not allow this to continue. She reaches for the gun, snapping, "No. Give me that. You're making a huge mistake. I can protect you from them."

Lily laughs, and the shot is masked by thunder. The ground to Mia's right puffs in response to the bullet, dirt and pebbles and shells lashing her leg.

"Walk, Miss Savage."

Mia turns and walks, plotting. She has to get the gun away from Lily. She will have to tackle her, use the element of surprise, whip around—

Calls. "Yoo-hoo! Over here!" To her horror, Mia sees the girls of X House lined up by the cliff's edge, manic smiles on their drenched faces.

No. God, no.

Mia leaps toward Lily, trying to get the gun, trying anything. They grapple in the dirt and mud, spitting and clawing at one another.

It is all so clear now. Cynthia Andante, Rosalind McPhee. This pack of wolfish teenage girls murdered them both. They were all in this together. The ladies of X House aren't being terrorized from outside. They are the terrors.

Who knows, maybe Miss Tavish is in on it, too, sanctioning this bloodlust. Or they drug her, or bribe her somehow, to hide their true nature.

Mia has her hand on the weapon now, but she's been too focused on the fight with Lily to realize she's surrounded. She is taken down by the scrum of teenagers. Her face is mashed into the ground. She screams, but the wind carries her voice away like a piece of paper caught in the breeze. She can hear it dancing around the water, echoing down the cliff face. She sounds like a mountain lion, she realizes, that wild scream tearing from her throat as she calls for help again, then someone kicks her in the ribs, hard, and she has no more breath to give her voice.

They bombard her with kicks and punches. They are shockingly strong, but that's the adrenaline feeding them, the frenzy of the kill.

Mia manages to look up and sees Lily is back on her feet with the gun in her hand, still pointing it at the woman who was meant to keep her safe. She honestly has no idea what to do. She tries to rise, but a blow to her stomach knocks out her wind again. She is filled with horror instead of air. She is going to die here, in this Godforsaken place, this spit of cursed land by the sea, at the hands of a group of teenage maniacs, and she wants to give up, to lie in the dirt and cry, but she gives it one last go, blood streaming down her face mingling with the rain, blinding her. She struggles to her knees.

Another punch, another stomp. Then Lily's voice, stronger than Mia has ever heard it, with a tone of complete derision.

"Bye, Mia."

They pick her up, all those little hands, and pitch her off the cliff's edge.

The last thing Mia hears as she goes over is the chorus of shrieks chanting her name, "*Mi-a, Mi-a, Mi-a,*" like she is chugging a beer at a party. Their sweet voices drift away the farther she falls until the roar of the sea and the rocks rush to greet her, and she—

THE RAVAGES

Layne Fargo

When Renee saw her girlfriend kissing another woman, she wanted to scream.

But she couldn't, because they were in a library. The 19th Century section of the Women's Academy archive, in fact. While Natalia pressed her new paramour up against the shelves, raking her coffin nails through the young woman's upsettingly cool pixie cut, Renee peered around the edge of a bookcase several rows down and wanted to die.

But she couldn't do that either – she refused to give Natalia the satisfaction. Nat loved death. Her Bloomsbury flat was filled with vintage taxidermy, and she never took off her favorite necklace, a chunk of obsidian fused with a broken raven spine. Their first date was an afternoon stroll through the older, west side of Highgate Cemetery, where they had their first kiss next to the final resting place of Christina Rossetti.

A spurned lover tragically offing herself might be the best thing that ever happened to Natalia. Everyone would feel sorry for her, she could write endless poetry about it, and she'd finally have an excuse to break out her collection of Victorian mourning veils.

So Renee didn't scream or cry or slash her wrists with the nearest bookbinding awl. She ran away – through the towering stacks, past the hush of the reading room, down the limestone steps, and out into the misty mid-October afternoon.

The arched windows of the Women's Academy seemed to stare after her with the same stern expression her boss Dr. Winters would surely have if she knew Renee was cutting out on work early. But the Head Curator was attending some fancy high tea fundraiser at Kew Gardens for the rest of the day. She'd asked Renee to accompany her, but Renee always found excuses to get out of such public-facing events. "Being a curator requires advocacy, public speaking, cultivating the right connections," Dr. Winters was fond of telling her. "It's much more than hiding in the dark with dusty boxes of artifacts."

Renee knew the older woman was trying to help her advance in her career, to prepare her as a potential successor capable of taking over the Head Curator position one day. But Renee *liked* hiding in the dark with dusty boxes. She loved the orderly serenity of the archive, the smell of old paper and leather, the feeling of touching real history with her bare hands (or sometimes, pristine cotton gloves). She wasn't religious – not even in the vaguely witchy way Natalia purported to be – but since the first time she stepped inside the Women's Academy archive, it had felt like a sacred space to her. A sanctuary.

And now Natalia had defiled it.

The next morning, Renee showed up at work at five 'til eight like always, carrying a Thermos of home-brewed Earl Grey. When Natalia arrived thirty minutes later – relatively early for her – she greeted Renee like nothing whatsoever was wrong.

"You never texted me back, love," Natalia said. "Working late again?"

In recent weeks, Renee had been putting in extra hours processing a new collection of correspondence by the poet Viola Vance. Renee had spent twice as long as she should have on the Vance collection already, and she still wasn't even close to finished. She was usually disciplined and focused when it came to cataloging new materials and creating finding aids; Natalia was the one who got distracted by every detail, spinning dramatic stories about the lives and loves attached to the items.

Viola Vance's letters, though, were a rare exception. Rather than simply noting dates and recipients, Renee kept getting caught up in reading the correspondence – particularly the series of missives from the summer of 1899 that chronicled a scorched-earth falling out between Viola and her childhood friend (/rumored lover) Liane Palmer.

"Sorry," Renee said. "I had my phone switched off. Everything all right?"

"I just missed you, that's all."

Natalia kissed her on the cheek, leaving a smear of dark red. Natalia's signature lipstick left marks everywhere, making skin and shirt collars and teacup rims alike look ripe and bitten. The shade was called "Ravenous," and Natalia certainly was that. The first time she and Renee had slept together, it turned into an entire weekend of passion in Natalia's velvet-draped canopy bed, the stuffed falcon on her dresser getting quite the show. Renee had always set a hard limit, though, on fraternizing at work. Had Natalia intended to punish her, by bringing that other woman to the archive? Had she *wanted* Renee to see?

Before meeting Natalia, Renee had been with other women of course, but she'd never loved anyone like this. She thought Natalia felt the same. She thought they would be together forever, die in each other's arms and then haunt each other for all eternity like Cathy and Heathcliff on the moors.

Instead, they were turning out to be more like Viola and Liane. Scholars had argued over Viola's sexual orientation for years, but the Women's Academy's new acquisitions were sure to put that debate to rest. Renee didn't see how anyone could continue insisting that the two women were just gals being pals after reading those letters. You don't write stuff like *even after we are both in our graves, I hope the ravages of your betrayal torment your withered soul* to someone who's only a *friend*.

Renee felt so foolish. She should have known her relationship with Natalia was too good to be true. Natalia was like some sapphic fantasy Renee might've dreamed up back when she was a closeted teenager in rural Michigan – the perfect Sullen Witchy Nightmare Girl, with her pallid complexion, posh accent, and macabre taste in accessories.

For the rest of the day, Renee tried to concentrate on her work, but even the most torrid letters between Viola and Liane did little to take her mind off what she'd witnessed in the stacks. Natalia's fingers in that stranger's hair. Their slim hips pressed flush. Heavy breathing like the *shush* of turning pages. The woman had been Renee's physical opposite in every way: gamine where Renee was buxom, bright where she was dull, effortlessly pretty where Renee was plain. Renee couldn't decide if that made it better or worse, that Natalia had chosen someone so totally different from her to cheat with.

Regardless, she couldn't let Natalia get away with this. She had to confront her.

Not yet, though. Being an archivist took extreme perseverance, a willingness to attend to every detail no matter how long it might take. Unlike Natalia, Renee wasn't impulsive or impatient. She could wait. She could plan. She could bide her time until the moment was exactly right.

The first week of November, her opportunity finally arrived. Dr. Winters had to leave the country, to attend the funeral of an American colleague. She left Renee in charge during her absence, entrusting her with spare keys, security codes, everything.

Natalia was in great spirits that day, humming a Florence and the Machine song as she updated the Academy's Brontë Sisters collection guide to include a set of quill pens, ink pots, and various ephemera recently acquired in an estate sale. The absence of Dr. Winters always lifted her spirits; while Natalia was unfailingly polite to their boss's face, behind her back she referred to the curator only as *The Wintry Bint*.

The Women's Academy had few other staff members: besides Dr.

Winters' personal assistant and the specialists who came in on an as-needed basis to assess the preservation needs of their more delicate holdings, the only other people regularly in the building were a rotating mix of visiting scholars and archival fellows. After six p.m., Renee and Natalia would have the place entirely to themselves.

At five fifty-five, Renee perched on the edge of Natalia's desk. "Hey."

"Hey." Natalia looked up from her laptop. She had her dark hair in a braid today, and a few pieces had come loose to frame her exquisite face. She was so beautiful, Renee found herself having second thoughts. This could only end with an apology or a breakup, and Renee had never heard Natalia apologize for anything, not even a muttered *sorry* when she bumped into someone while moving through the narrow passageways between shelves.

But it had to be that night. Dr. Winters had booked a red-eye for after the funeral, so she would be back in the morning. Renee took a deep breath and dangled the bait.

"I was thinking… what if we finally tried that séance?"

Natalia squealed and clapped her hands together. "*Yes.* I knew you'd come around."

The archive building had started life as a church back in the eighteenth century, and Natalia was convinced the archive was absolutely *teeming* with ghosts. Ever since she'd been hired – even before they started dating – she'd been after Renee about attempting to make contact with the spirits.

Renee slid closer, so the toe of her sensible thrift store loafers brushed the heel of Natalia's Alexander McQueen ballet flats. "I even stopped by The Astrology Shop and got some supplies. Want to see?"

Natalia nodded eagerly. Renee retrieved the *Out Damn Spot* Royal Shakespeare Company tote bag full of mystical accoutrements from under her own desk and held it out for Natalia's inspection.

"So *that's* what I've been smelling all day," she said, drawing out a stick of Dragon's Blood incense. "I thought you were trying a new perfume or something." She looked up at Renee and smiled; her lipstick had started to flake so late in the day, leaving pale fissures in her wine-dark lips. "This is so sweet of you, baby."

Of course she would think this was a romantic gesture. To Natalia, nothing could be more romantic than a night of dark rituals and ghost-hunting. It was the perfect way to keep her on the premises so Renee could get what she required.

"We need candles," Natalia said.

Renee shook her head. "No candles."

"But it's a séance."

"And this is an archive, chock full of priceless and flammable objects."

Natalia pouted. "Fine. No candles."

They did a thorough sweep of the reading room to make sure no one was lingering after closing time. It was all too easy to lose track of the hour in the windowless space; Renee had seen a figure seated at one of the long worktables well after ten p.m. one night, and it'd given her such a fright, she spent a few heart-pounding seconds believing in Natalia's theories about restless spirits before realizing it was just a graduate student trying to finish up some transcribing.

Once they were sure they were alone in the building, Natalia headed toward the door to the lower level.

"Where are you going?" Renee asked.

"To the basement," she said. "The energies will be strongest down there."

Though it had been remodeled to allow for climate-controlled document storage, the building's underground level was originally a crypt. Some ghosts of the original structure, rib vaults and decorative molding, were still visible in the corners, and even a skeptic like Renee had to admit the space felt quite unsettling.

"How about we start up here? No need to dive into the deep end on our first try."

"Don't tell me you're scared. I know you don't think anything's going to happen."

Renee started to protest, but Natalia gave her a *really?* look.

"My adorable little skeptic." Natalia kissed her, smearing red over Renee's clear lip balm. "But fine, if you insist. Let's set up in the reading room."

They dimmed the space, leaving only one of the glass-shaded reading lamps illuminated, then arranged the crystals Renee had purchased in the center of the pool of light. The woman at the shop had recommended a chunk of quartz for clarity and a black tourmaline tower for grounding and protection, and Renee had tried not to wince when she saw just how expensive a couple of rocks could be.

Then they lit the incense with Natalia's black BIC – Renee holding her breath until the flame was out and only fragrant smoke remained – and Natalia made a slow circuit of the table, weaving a hazy wreath in the air.

"We need something for the spirits to communicate through," Natalia said.

"Like a Ouija board?"

Natalia rolled her eyes. "No. This isn't a primary school slumber party. Like a pendulum, or – wait, I know!"

She slipped off her raven spine necklace and hung it over the lamp so it dangled above the crystals.

"How's that supposed to work?" Renee asked. "The ghosts just… poke it?"

"We can ask questions, and the pendant will move one way if the answer is *yes*, the other way if it's *no*." Natalia gave her a playful elbow to the side. "And since it's hanging from the lamp, you'll know I'm not moving it myself."

They sat across from each other, knees touching under the table. "Take my hands," Natalia said. Renee did. Natalia closed her eyes, but Renee kept hers open.

"Greetings to the spirits who reside in these hallowed halls," Natalia intoned. Her usual plummy accent dropped into a deeper, smokier register, and Renee stifled the urge to laugh. "We are here bearing only light and good will, open to any messages you wish to share with us this evening."

The necklace stayed motionless. Natalia kept going, importuning the spirits repeatedly in English and then tossing in some of her Swiss boarding-school French and Italian for good measure.

"I don't think this is working." Renee leaned back, trying to tug her hands free.

"Don't break the circle!" Natalia gripped her tighter. "You have to give it time."

After ten more fruitless minutes, though, Natalia tired of the ritual too.

"I bet they're staying away because they can sense you're not a believer," she said. "I'm sure they'd speak to me if I was alone."

Renee was certainly sure that, were there no other witnesses to contradict her account, Natalia would *tell* people ghosts had spoken to her.

"Oh, well." Natalia let go of Renee's hands and stood up, crossing to the other side of the table. "We've still got this whole place to ourselves for the night, haven't we?"

She nudged Renee's legs apart with her knee and leaned down, her braid slithering over Renee's shoulder like a snake. They hadn't been together since before Renee saw Natalia kissing that other girl. Natalia had been all too willing, but Renee had kept demurring with excuses like exhaustion, headaches, basically every dissatisfied housewife cliché. She assumed she would feel disgusted, knowing Natalia had touched someone else.

But much to her dismay, she didn't feel disgusted at all. When Natalia pressed her lips to Renee's neck, it was all too easy to give in, to tilt her head back and moan low in her throat like she always did. Soon they were entangled on the antique rug, Natalia's hair tumbling free from her braid, Renee's leggings pushed down past the swell of her hips.

This was not the plan. This was the last thing she expected to happen tonight. But as the carpet scraped against her bare skin and Natalia's lipstick spread across her mouth like a bloodstain, all Renee could think about was the flutter of Natalia's clever fingers on her—

Crash.

The two women started, their lips separating – though their legs stayed intertwined.

"What was that?" Natalia asked.

The sound had been like a close clap of thunder, but it wasn't storming outside.

"I don't know," Renee said.

"I think it came from the stacks." Natalia stood up, readjusting her clothing. Renee felt the absence of her touch like a hundred bruises throbbing all over her body. "Come on."

Renee followed Natalia toward the maze of shelves. The motion-detecting overhead lights flicked on as they entered each section, then switched off again as they moved to the next one. The Renaissance playwrights were undisturbed, as were the Romantics. Natalia darted into the next row, her fingernails rasping against the spines, then stopped with a gasp.

"Renee. Bloody hell, look at this."

One bookcase, right in the center of the 19th Century section, was empty. All the books that should have been shelved there were on the floor. That would have explained the crash they heard – except the volumes weren't in a chaotic jumble, like they'd tumbled off.

They were stacked in neat rows, perfectly parallel to the base of the bookcase.

"It *did* work!" Natalia exclaimed. "It's the ghost, she's trying to tell us something!"

Renee would have asked why Natalia assumed their new spectral friend was female, but to be honest, she'd never seen a man arrange anything so precisely. The corner of every cover was at an exact right angle, the books layered by size for stability.

"What's she trying to tell us – that she thinks we should use Library of Congress classification instead of Dewey Decimal?"

"Don't be so *glib*, Renee, you'll scare her off." Natalia wandered farther down the aisle, calling out, "We're here, we're listening. What message do you have for us?"

Renee picked up one of the stacked books with a sigh. This would take at least an hour to put back to rights. She was never getting to sleep tonight.

Then she took a closer look at the top book on each stack.

"Natalia."

Natalia turned, what was left of her braid whipping over her shoulder.

Renee held up the book. "They're all Viola's."

"What?" Natalia looked for herself. Every stack had a volume of Viola Vance's poetry on top. Her eyes widened with excitement. "What if…"

"Don't be ridiculous."

"I didn't even say anything yet!"

Renee put the book back, lining up the corners again. "No, but I know what you're going to say. If the soul of Viola Vance has unfinished business on this mortal plane, I highly doubt it involves archival organization."

"Maybe she wants to thank you," Natalia said. "For what a great job you're doing cataloging her letters."

"Or maybe she wants to haunt my ass for reading her private correspondence without permission." Renee meant this as a sarcastic comment, but Natalia ran with it.

"What if her spirit was… attached to the letters somehow? And you released it by reading them? My ex's ex-girlfriend told me about this case in Glasgow, where…"

She trailed off, staring toward the far end of the row. "What?" Renee said.

"Do you hear that?" Natalia tilted her head, listening harder.

"No, I don't hear—"

But then she did: whispers, coming from somewhere in the dark. Not a single voice, but many, layered and unintelligible, high and low and everything in between.

And growing louder.

Renee backed away. Natalia advanced, until the lights for the next section turned on. She kept moving, but the pool of illumination didn't. As she reached the end of the row, darkness swallowed her. The whispers were so loud now, Renee wanted to cower and cover her ears.

"Natalia?" The whispers were so loud, she had to shout. She didn't believe in ghosts. She *didn't*. But this felt so real. "*Nat*. Say something."

The whispers cut out. And then, in the silence, Natalia screamed.

Renee didn't think. She ran toward her girlfriend's panicked voice. The lights responded to her, blazing bright as she rounded the row to find Natalia cowering on the floor, arms flung up to cover her face.

Renee knelt beside her. "Are you all right? What happened?"

"I felt something." She clutched at Renee's sleeve, trembling. "A presence. It brushed right past me, and I felt so cold, and – I smelled flowers."

"Flowers?"

Natalia nodded. "I don't smell it anymore, but it was like a whole bouquet, right under my nose. Like… gardenia, or maybe jasmine?"

"Or tuberose."

"Yes! Yes, I think that's what it was. How did you know?"

"Viola Vance's letters. She always wore tuberose perfume. Well, until…"

"Until what?"

"Until her falling out with Liane Palmer. Liane used to buy a bottle for Viola's birthday every year from a certain perfumery on Bond Street."

"Why did they break up? Maybe that's part of Viola's unfinished business."

"The letters don't say for sure," Renee said. "But it sounds like Liane betrayed her. Broke her heart." *Even after we are both in our graves, I hope the ravages of your betrayal torment your withered soul.*

She watched Natalia's face for any reaction, but she hardly seemed to be listening. Her eyes were still wide and frantic, darting around the shadows in search of phantasms.

"Let's get out of here," Renee said. "I think that's enough ghost-hunting for one night, don't you?"

Natalia let Renee help her up. As soon as she was on her feet, though, she stiffened and pointed, the blunted tip of her coffin nail indicating a pale shape in the darkness.

"What's that?"

"It's just a statue." Renee tried to steer her away. "That bust of the goddess Eris. It's always been there."

"I know it's a *statue*. I meant, what's that mark on its face?"

Renee squinted. There *was* something there – a small smear

across Eris's slanted marble cheekbone. Probably some graduate student had run into it and neglected to report the damage. Typical.

She walked closer, pulling Natalia along. The lights over the bust flared to life.

"Is that *blood*?" Natalia whispered.

The mark was red, but it didn't quite look like blood. Renee ran a fingertip over it. The texture was waxy, and the pigment stained her skin.

"It's lipstick." Renee turned toward Natalia. "Actually, it looks like *your* lipstick."

"Well, I didn't put it there."

Renee tried to wipe the red onto her black leggings. It didn't budge. Her hand looked like a crime scene. She didn't even want to think about what would be involved in safely cleaning the statue.

"Come on, Nat. This has gone far enough."

Natalia folded her arms. "Excuse me?"

"You got me, okay? You freaked me out. But damaging artifacts for some silly prank? That's way too far. Do you want Dr. Winters to fire us both?"

"I had nothing to do with this! I'm just as freaked out as you are!"

"Yeah, sure." Renee turned and started walking away. "I'm going home. You made this mess, you clean it up."

"Renee, you cannot be serious right now."

Renee kept walking. Natalia chased after her, catching up.

"Don't leave me alone in here!"

"You think the vengeful ghost of Viola Vance is going to get you? Give it up, Nat."

"Renee, please, I—"

They both felt it at the same time: a blast of cold air, like a window had been left open during a winter storm. And something underfoot too, wet and slippery.

Renee looked down. There were red marks on the floorboards – and this time, they very much *did* look like blood.

"What the hell." Natalia spoke in a shuddery whisper, barely audible. "*What* the—"

The marks weren't random smears. They were words, written in a messy, hasty scrawl. But Renee recognized them right away.

"Even after we are both in our graves…" Renee read aloud.

Natalia had started to hyperventilate. She wrung her hands together, long fingernails clacking like teeth. "This was all a mistake. It was a bad idea. I'm sorry, I never should have—"

A flicker of motion drew their eyes, like a hand passing over a candle flame. The door to the archive's lower level was open. And someone – or some*thing* – stood on the threshold.

Renee and Natalia froze. So did the figure in the doorway. Only its diffuse outline was visible against the darkness of the stairwell descending into the crypt.

"Please." Natalia clawed at Renee's wrist. "I'm sorry. I'm so sorry."

"What are you sorry for, Natalia?" Renee said. She was shocked at how steady her voice sounded. How cold.

The figure still hadn't stirred. It was vaguely feminine – and tall. *Too* tall, its face – assuming it had a face – hidden by the peaked doorframe.

Natalia was weeping now, black mascara streaking down her face. Renee watched, impassive. Seeing her girlfriend unraveling didn't feel the way she thought it would.

It felt so much better.

"Natalia," she said.

Shaking, Natalia turned her head. Renee leaned in, lips tracing Natalia's ear.

"I hope the ravages of your betrayal torment your withered soul," Renee whispered.

The apparition surged over the reading room threshold, a blur of diaphanous red, the billowing scent of tuberose and leather and Dragon's Blood smoke in its wake.

Natalia didn't even have time to scream.

"Renee? Are you there?"

Renee jolted awake, her shoulders twinging as she sat upright. She had been bent double over her desk, cheek pillowed on an empty file folder. Not the first time she'd fallen asleep there.

Dr. Winters appeared in the office doorway. Even after a transatlantic red-eye, she looked put together, her gray hair pinned into a smooth twist, not a wrinkle to be found on her olive pantsuit.

Renee stood, doing her best to brush the creases out of her own clothing. "Dr. Winters. You're back. How was your trip?"

"*Exhausting*," she said. "But if I sleep now, I'll be even more jet-lagged. Best to press on."

She cast an appraising look around Renee's cluttered workspace. "Still working on the Vance collection?" she asked. Renee nodded. "I certainly hope you didn't pull another all-nighter."

Renee gathered up some of the letters scattered across her desk, stacking them neatly. "I should be done in another day or so."

"Good," Dr. Winters said. "Because I'd like your eyes on some of these fellowship applications. We'll need to extend an offer within the next few weeks."

"Of course," Renee said. "I'd be happy to—"

"*What* is that dreadful sound?"

"What sound?"

"That horrible banging. You don't hear it?"

Renee did, though she thought it might be her own head, pounding from her uncomfortable sleeping position and tragic lack of caffeine.

"It sounds like it's coming from downstairs," Dr. Winters said.

As they made their way toward the basement door, the sound got louder – and more erratic, with longer pauses between each thud. Renee stood back, as Dr. Winters retrieved her own set of keys from her pocket and unlocked the door.

The door swung open, and Natalia was sprawled at their feet, staring up at them, wild-eyed. All her dark lipstick had worn away; Renee realized it was the first time she'd seen her entirely without it.

"Natalia?" Dr. Winters said. "What on *earth*…?"

"She's down there," Natalia said. "She's down there waiting in the dark and she's going to kill me. She's going to kill us all."

Dr. Winters peered dubiously through the open door. "Who's down there?"

"*Viola Vance.*" Natalia grabbed their boss by the shoulders. "She's angry, she's so angry, she won't stop *screaming*."

Dr. Winters shrugged away, brushing off the furrows Natalia's nails had made in her blazer. "Please get ahold of yourself. If this is a joke, I don't find it very humorous."

"It's not a joke!" Natalia spun toward Renee. "Tell her what we saw last night."

Renee looked into her girlfriend's tormented, pleading eyes. Then she turned to Dr. Winters. "I have no idea what she's talking about."

Natalia's face fell. "Renee. That's bollocks and you know it! Tell her about the books in the 19th Century section. Tell her about the damaged statue."

"A statue was damaged?" Dr. Winters said. "Which one?"

"I'll show you." Natalia took off toward the stacks. "The bust of Eris. There's a stain on the cheek, right—"

She stopped. The marble was flawless white, not a mark on it.

"It was right *there*," Natalia insisted. "This red mark. Like lipstick. It looked like red lipstick, right, Renee?"

Renee said nothing.

"Perhaps you've been working too hard, dear." Dr. Winters took a cautious step forward, like Natalia was a feral animal who might bite. "Why don't you go home, and—"

"No! I'm telling the truth." Natalia pointed at Renee. The nail on her index finger was broken, a crack cutting right down the center. "*She's* the one who's lying. What is this, some screwed up revenge plot?"

Renee tried her very hardest not to smile. Her face ached from the effort.

"You want me to apologize? Is that it?" Natalia was practically screaming, her usually polished voice corroded as a rusty blade. "Fine. I'm sorry I cheated on you. Can you blame me? If you weren't such a little *freak*, you would have just confronted me and Liv when you saw us hooking up in the stacks that day. But no, you have to make everything a whole *production*, and—"

"Excuse me."

Natalia stopped, what little color was left in her face draining out as she realized what she'd said.

"Am I to understand," Dr. Winters said, "that you engaged in *intimate activities* here, at the Academy? During *working hours*?"

"I can explain," Natalia said.

"I'm sure you can." Dr. Winters turned on her kitten heel. "My office, now. We can consider it your exit interview."

She strode away. Natalia slunk after her, shooting a look back at Renee.

Now Renee smiled. She gave her girlfriend – well, she should say *ex*-girlfriend, shouldn't she? – a little wave too. Why not, since it was possible they'd never see one another again.

Natalia's expression darkened, but she didn't say anything. What could she say, without making things even worse for herself?

Renee waited until she heard Dr. Winters' heavy office door slam shut. Then she descended the steps to the crypt.

"Liv?" she said, switching on the lights. "You can come out now."

Liv stuck her head out from behind a pile of acid-free file boxes. She was still wearing the gauzy red robes, but she'd removed her face-concealing veil, leaving her pixie cut artfully mussed. Her platform shoes had been discarded too; Renee had no idea how she'd managed to run in those things without snapping an ankle.

"So?" Liv said. "Did it work?"

Renee nodded. "Dr. Winters is sacking her as we speak."

"Brilliant." Liv grinned.

The day she'd seen Natalia and Liv in the stacks, Renee had fled. She'd tromped along the Thames, cold rain mixing with hot tears on her face. Then the drizzle gave way to a proper downpour, and she turned around and headed back to the archive.

Right as Liv waltzed out of the building's Gothic double doors.

Renee had hung back, hoping for a better look – and to make sure Natalia's lover didn't catch sight of her looking so bedraggled and pathetic, clutching her soaked cable-knit cardigan around her shivering frame. Liv was smiling, cheeks flushed and lips stained with dark red lipstick.

Liv had tugged a beanie over her cropped hair and flipped the collar of her battered leather moto jacket up against the wind. Renee had taken a step toward her. Then another. Liv didn't seem to notice.

So Renee had done something uncharacteristically impulsive: she kept following. First to Pret A Manger, where Liv ordered a large coffee to go, though it must have been well past five p.m. by that point. She continued on toward King's Cross, and Renee kept up her pursuit, staying a few paces behind.

At the intersection of Euston and Argyle, Liv turned her head, and Renee froze, pulse pounding – but a sick little thrill lighting up her nerves all the same. She wondered if this was how serial killers felt when they were hunting their prey.

Not that she planned to hurt anyone. She just wanted to know more about her competition. Simple curiosity, born out of stomach-churning jealousy.

The rain began to slacken, then ceased, though the evening was still gray. Finally, Liv stopped. Her destination was a nondescript storefront in Clerkenwell. The windows were covered with black drapes, and there was no sign above the door. Renee tucked herself into an alleyway across the street and watched as her rival dug a sizable keyring out of her jacket pocket and let herself into the mysterious building.

Despite its lack of distinguishing features, something about the place seemed familiar to Renee. Then the drapes parted, a red neon light in the shape of a dagger switched on, and Renee remembered.

The building was a theater – the home of the obscure new company Natalia had been going on about since the summer, when their latest production had gotten a lot of attention from the sort of underground arts publications whose opinion Natalia prized. The show was some avant-garde immersive affair, part theatrical production, part haunted house, part escape room – exactly the sort of thing Natalia adored, and Renee would rather cut her own heart out with a dull blade than participate in. Natalia had nagged her about going for weeks, before ultimately giving up and attending without her, one of the nights Renee stayed late at the archive to work on the Vance collection.

Natalia had called the show intense. Exhilarating. Life-changing. "When you're confined in a space with someone," she'd said, "then you find out who they really are."

That day, Renee had thought about going home. She'd thought about spending the evening slumped on her sad gray secondhand sofa, devouring a twelve-pack of Crème double chocolate cookies while deep-diving into Natalia's social media accounts for more evidence of her infidelity.

But while baked goods are one cure for heartbreak, revenge tastes so much sweeter. So Renee had gone into the theater and bought a ticket for the show that night.

She assumed she would hate it – all those people pressed together, actors in flowing ceremonial robes leaping out of the shadows to scare and seduce and sneak up behind audience members to whisper clues in their ears. But Natalia was right: it was a thrill, intense and inspiring. Renee wouldn't have gone so far as to call it "life-changing" – though the conversation she'd had afterward certainly was.

She'd waited in the lobby until Liv appeared from backstage, then introduced herself as a "friend of Natalia's." Over pints at the pub around the corner, Renee learned that Liv was a designer, the creative force behind all the show's eerie, enchanting special effects. And she had been under the impression she and Natalia were exclusive too.

They'd planned their payback together, though Liv kept many of the more theatrical elements secret, so Renee would be able to react naturally in the moment. Even knowing that the ghostly whispers were coming from a hidden Bluetooth speaker and there was a flesh and blood human being under that long red veil, the experience had been terrifying.

"I thought she was going to piss herself when she saw me in the doorway," Liv said. "Probably wrong to enjoy her suffering so much."

Renee smiled. "Probably. That cleaner you gave me worked a treat, by the way."

While Liv had been busy haunting Natalia in the pitch-black

basement, Renee had set everything in the stacks and the reading room back to rights – just in time to catch a quick nap before Dr. Winters returned.

"Yeah, that stuff'll get lipstick off anything," Liv said. "Came in handy when I was dating Nat."

Before Renee discovered them, Natalia and Liv had already been seeing each other for weeks. Neither Renee nor Liv had suspected a thing – which made Renee wonder how many more times Natalia had lied to them both.

Not that it mattered. Unlike Viola Vance, Renee had gotten revenge on the woman who betrayed her, and now she could move on. She'd found out who Natalia really was, and she wanted nothing more to do with her.

"I couldn't have done this without you," she told Liv.

Liv smiled. "My pleasure. Serves her right for letting a girl like you get away."

"For letting us *both* get away." Renee looped her arm around Liv's narrow waist. "And trust me: I won't make the same mistake."

FOUR FUNERALS

David Bell

Angie's levelheaded. She tells me not to go.

I ignore her.

She follows me to the car, sweater sleeves pushed to her elbows. A beautiful day. The sun bright, the leaves golden.

"It's not about you, Mike," she says. "Enough people blame you already. If you show up there, and people see you…"

I toss an overnight bag in the back seat, put my phone on the console. The map's called up. The route laid out. Four counties in two days, crisscrossing the state. I can do it if I stay focused, if nothing goes wrong.

Whether it's the right thing to do or not—

Maybe Angie's on to something.

"I'll keep in touch," I say. "Or you can track me."

"And what if someone hurts you. In one of these towns, at one of these funerals."

I lean in, kiss her on the mouth. Coffee breath, and a damp line of perspiration above her lip. "I'll lay low. I promise."

Angie steps back, gestures at the house. "And if they come here again?"

My eyes trail to the boarded-up window, the one the brick went through. The brick and the note: *There's blood on your hands, asshole. Watch it.*

"Go to your dad's," I say. "He has guns. He'll be happy to see you."

"He always thought you were too stubborn. That you didn't listen."

I slide into the driver's seat, click the seat belt. "That's one thing the old man's right about."

"You're running again. Just like when I lost the baby—"

"Please. Don't say that."

Angie shakes her head, looks at the ground.

"I'm not running away. I'm going toward something."

I close the door, wave, and as I drive off realize she's right. This sure feels like running away.

I make Tompkinsville just before one. Just as the service is about to start.

The First Presbyterian Church sits off the square and has seen better days. Its redbrick façade is in need of a cleaning. The town consists of a laundromat, a tattoo parlor, a pawn shop, a dollar store.

But Tompkinsville is overrun today. Cars everywhere. A few news vans from Louisville.

Better for me, as I blend in, join the line of mourners entering the church. I stand in the back, shoulder to shoulder with the others. The air is hot and close. Sweat trickles down my chest.

I loosen my tie, try to breathe more freely.

The pallbearers bring the coffin in. Six young guys, tall and muscular. Stone-faced. Randy Higgins played football in high school, even wanted to walk on at the university. He wrote stories about sports, about characters experiencing glory on high school athletic fields.

He didn't write that well, and he barely spoke in class.

But he laughed at my jokes. When he did speak, he offered encouragement to his classmates.

They found his body near the shooter's. Like he'd been trying to charge him, trying to save the others.

The coffin reaches the front of the church. A woman in a black dress, about my age, steps forward. Her wailing cry fills the church. She drapes her body over the coffin.

I feel bile rise in the back of my throat. I might be sick.

But I can't move. I don't know where the bathroom is, and I'm boxed in by mourners on either side of me. I shift my weight from one foot to the other, loosen my tie more and fan myself with the program.

"You alright, hoss?" It's the man next to me. He wears a bushy beard. His hands are rough and callused. "You getting hot?"

"I'm okay. I just…"

"It's a lot, isn't it? Young people dying that way."

"It is. I'm sorry. Thank you."

"No worries."

The minister comes down and helps Randy's mother to her seat. He whispers in her ear. She nods, listening to his words.

"You know who I don't feel sorry for?" the man next to me asks.

"Who?"

"That dumb son of a bitching professor, Buckley, the one who knew this shooting was going to go down and didn't do anything about it."

The sweat on my back turns cold. My hand shakes holding the program. "Oh…"

"Four kids killed, six injured. He doesn't have a scratch on him. Somebody's going to kill that bastard soon. Randy's my cousin, so it might just be me going to that campus to do it."

I reach Manchester by four. It's a graveside service for Cassandra James.

The cemetery sits adjacent to the town center. It's surrounded by a wrought-iron fence. The graves date back to the nineteenth century and encircle a marble obelisk dedicated to the county's veterans who died in foreign wars.

Cassie's coffin rests over a hole in the ground. A green tent provides shade to about twenty mourners who sit on folding chairs. When the wind kicks up, the flaps of the tent whip like sails.

I stay back. Way back. The minister reads from a worn Bible, the words unintelligible to me. I keep my body behind a thick oak. Its multi-colored leaves fall on me during the service.

I scuff my shoe in the dirt. It's peaceful here. Calm. But my heart thumps. I still feel sick. A headstone a few feet away from me tells the life story of a man named Patrick McGee who came to Manchester from Ireland in 1874. *Beloved Schoolmaster. Loving Husband.*

I look up. A woman walks past the cemetery wearing large sunglasses, a winter coat – too thick for the weather – pulled tight around her body. She glances inside at the service, slows her pace and almost stops. She reaches up, wipes at her face and then keeps going.

The mourners stand, start to exchange hugs.

It's over, so I need to go. I step gingerly over the graves, avoiding plots and gnarled tree roots. I can only imagine myself turning my ankle, ending up on the ground writhing in pain while Cassie's family comes over to investigate.

And recognizes me as the man who couldn't prevent their daughter from dying.

I make it out to the car, open the door. I need a hotel for the night, maybe something to eat.

"Mike."

I turn cold inside.

The voice sounds like a hiss, my name spoken sharply. A dagger thrust in my direction.

"Shit."

I get in, fumble for the ignition button.

"Mike. Stop."

A familiar figure comes toward me in a trench coat. Tall and gaunt. He's alone, the cluster of mourners still at the grave.

He reaches me, looms over me where I sit inside the car. I can't get away.

"Harold, I…" Harold Prescott. Dean of the College of Arts and Sciences. "I was just…"

"What are you doing here?" Harold asks. "Jesus, Mike."

"It's a funeral for one of my students. A very good student."

Harold makes a shooing gesture with his hand, his fingers long, the nails perfectly manicured. "Get in there. We need to talk."

Harold goes around the front of the car, folds his long body into the passenger seat. He slams the door, looks over at me.

"Well?" he asks. "Are you going to start it? Can we get out of here before Cassandra's entire family descends on us? There's a park just down the way."

For once I do what Harold tells me. I pull my door shut and follow his directions to the park.

When we get here, Harold pushes his door open. "Let's get out. It's a nice day."

He takes his coat off and throws it into the back seat. He's wearing a black suit and a red and white bowtie. University colors. He starts down a cinder running path, his dark shoes crunching. I catch up, while he reaches into the inside pocket of his jacket and brings out a pack of cigarettes. He lights one with a silver lighter and slides the pack into his pocket again.

"You didn't want one, did you?"

"No."

"Can you tell me what you're doing here?"

We walk side by side. *Crunch-crunch-crunch*.

"I told you – it's my student's funeral—"

"Did you go to Tompkinsville?"

I don't answer. I watch a group of kids throwing a football around. Two women jog by in the opposite direction.

"Damn you, Mike. You were told not to go, to keep a low profile."

"No one knew I was there."

"I saw you today. Hiding behind a tree like a weirdo. You're lucky Cassandra's family was too distraught to notice."

"Why are you here, then? Why aren't *you* keeping a low profile?"

Harold stops, picks a fleck of tobacco off his tongue. "I'm representing the university. The president is going to one of the funerals tomorrow. The provost is going to the other. I knew Cassandra a little. She served on the Dean's Council last year."

"Okay, I'm representing the English Department. Cassie was an English major."

Harold takes a last drag on the cigarette, tosses the butt away. "I know you feel responsible, Mike. You saw the story *he* – I refuse to say his name – *he* wrote about shooting up campus. I know you don't want to censor your writers, or act like we're running a daycare for college students. I know you're dedicated to your teaching. More than most faculty members."

"Thank you."

"But my feelings don't matter. A lot of people are blaming you. A lot of parents whose kids got shot in your classroom are blaming you. They think *you* – and the university – should have intervened with a heavier hand. Got that kid out of there before he could do anything violent."

I retied my tie after Randy's funeral, so I unknot it again, pull it all the way off and hold it in my hand. "If we removed every kid who wrote a violent story, I'd be sitting in class alone. They all write stories about murder and zombies and the end of the world."

"I know." Harold digs in his pocket for another cigarette. As he lights it, he says, "Do you realize I smoked for twenty years and quit? Cold turkey. I started again this week. Once the shooting happened."

"I'm sorry."

"I'm weak, I guess."

"You know, my first novel is about a woman being kidnapped and held in a basement. Another one is about a serial killer."

"And the media is poring over all your books, finding lots of juicy, violent passages."

"I should have known that would happen."

Harold puffs away, brow furrowed.

"What?" I ask.

"There's something else. We were going to have to deal with it after the funerals, but since we ran into each other this way…"

A shiver passes through me. My knees feel rubbery. "What else could there be?"

Harold clears his throat. "They've found some videos the shooter made. Apparently, he was recording his thoughts and posting them somewhere on the dark web, whatever that is. Anyway, they've surfaced."

My body grows colder, even as the sun hits the back of my neck.

"He says that he wrote that story for your class about the shooting as a way to plan the attack." Harold clears his throat again. "When you workshopped that story in class, he says you didn't think it was believable, that the shooter wouldn't be able to get a gun into the building the way he described it."

My chin quivers.

"He thanks you in the video. He says you suggested he have his character come in the back way of the English Department, to use the stairs off the faculty lot to avoid detection as long as possible. And that's exactly how he ended up doing it in real life, Mike. It's all over social media and the news now."

My mouth fills with saliva. My stomach twists.

I go past Harold and off the trail and into the bushes where I throw up the little I've eaten that day. And when that's out, my body heaves and heaves until I'm completely empty.

I drive Harold back to his car. The odor of his cigarettes doesn't help my nausea. I power the window down, let the breeze wash over my face.

When we get to the cemetery, all the mourners are gone. Two guys in denim coveralls are backfilling dirt over Cassie's coffin. I wish I hadn't seen that.

Harold stays in the passenger seat, his eyes staring off into the distance. "What does Angie think of this little expedition of yours?"

"She's opposed to it. Strongly."

"She's always been smarter than you."

"She is."

"I can't make you do anything. You're an adult, and these funerals aren't university events. But think about going home to your wife. Talk to her. Let her ease your burden. There's nothing to gain by going to these funerals. And tomorrow, the one for Alicia MacDonald… her father is making the most noise about your culpability. It's not a place you want to be."

"Thanks, Harold. I know you're trying to protect me."

"And you seem to want to flagellate yourself in some way." He gathers his coat, pats me on the knee. "It's a terrible thing, isn't it? Young people dying this way. Senseless." His eyes squint. He looks like he wants to say more. "Did I ever tell you I had a brother who died in an accident when he was two?"

"No, you didn't."

"I don't talk about it much. I was three, and – well, I don't really remember him. But it crushed my mother. She was never the same." He pats my knee again, pushes the door open. "See you back at the ranch."

After Harold drives off, I stay in the car. The gravediggers finish their work. They smooth down the mound of dirt on Cassie's grave, then cover it with bouquets of flowers. A giant wreath remains nearby on an easel.

I plan to stay in Manchester, find a motel. I can leave early for Corden, get there in time for Jamar Jansen's service. I reach for my phone.

Someone is walking past the cemetery, someone in a winter coat and sunglasses. The woman from earlier, the one who walked by during the service.

She comes to the spot where Cassie is buried and stops. She rests her hands on the wrought-iron bars, leans her head down like she's praying.

I don't think I know who she is. But if she's a member of Cassie's family, why didn't she stand with everyone during the service?

Is she just an interested stranger? An estranged relative?

Cassie talked about her parents. She was close to them, so it wouldn't be her mother. Is it an aunt? An old friend?

The woman stands there, head bowed for a good five minutes. Then she straightens up and starts walking away.

But she looks back once, and even though her eyes are obscured by the sunglasses, I know she's staring directly at me until she disappears out of sight.

The motel room smells musty.

Highway 32 runs right out front, and passing trucks rattle the windows and the light fixtures. I don't feel like eating, so I drink a lot of water and call Angie once I'm settled.

It takes her a long time to answer, and when she does, she asks me where I am.

"A motel. In Manchester."

She sighs as loud as the passing trucks. "So, you're sticking to your itinerary."

"I think so. Where are you?"

"Home. Why?"

"I thought maybe you'd go to your dad's like we said." The TV starts playing loudly in the room next door. "I saw this woman at the funeral today. She was hanging around the edge of the crowd. And then… she might have been following me. Or maybe she's a reporter. I'm not sure."

"Did she threaten you?"

"No, she didn't even speak to me."

"Well, there've been no more bricks. No more dog shit smeared on the car. And I disconnected the landline so no one can call and threaten us. Maybe you're projecting guilt onto this person. Maybe you think you deserve to be stalked and attacked."

"I saw Harold here." I don't tell Angie what Harold told me. About the stairs. About my suggestion aiding the shooter with his plan. "For what it's worth, he's on your side."

"I always liked Harold. For an administrator he's not so bad."

"Yeah, you're right." A sipping noise comes through the line. Angie's having wine. I can't blame her for that. "I'm sorry for what I said about your running away. And the baby. I know – I know things are more complicated than that."

"It's okay. You're not entirely wrong."

The TV gets even louder. The walls must be made of cardboard. Then it happens – *bang bang bang*.

I yelp. And jump.

The phone flies out of my hand and hits the thin carpet with a thud.

I'm three steps across the room and almost to the door when I figure it out.

The gunshots. Next door. The TV. Not real shots, just on TV.

I'm heaving again, trying to catch my breath. Every cell in my body shakes.

Angie's voice comes through the phone, tinny and distant. "Mike? Mike?"

"Fuck."

I go over and bend down. Pick up the phone.

"Mike? What the hell happened?"

"I'm okay. It's just— I heard a noise. Several noises. Through the wall."

"Did something happen? Are you safe?"

"No, it's…" I go over, slam the side of my fist against the wall. "Turn it down, asshole. Turn it down!"

"Mike?"

The volume doesn't change, but the shooting stops. I slump to the edge of the bed, bounce on the sagging mattress.

"Mike?"

"I'm okay. The TV's so loud next door. Some movie where everybody is trying to kill everybody else. Bullshit like that."

"Mike, take some deep breaths."

I do. I gulp more water, empty the shitty glass. My thundering heartbeat starts to slow. I can breathe a little.

"Mike, you've had a trauma too. You were in that room. You almost got killed. This is PTSD. Come home and call Dr. Franklin again."

"I didn't almost get killed. I didn't."

"You did."

"He didn't shoot at me. He shot at his classmates, but he didn't aim at me. I was in the front of the room, right in the center. If he wanted me dead, I'd be dead. He spared me for some reason."

"He didn't *spare* you. He's a maniac. He just missed you. He sprayed bullets all over that room, and he missed some of those other kids as well. Thank God. Just come home and talk to someone. You're not feeling well. And you're creating some scenario where you encouraged this student, so he liked you and didn't shoot at you. And that's just more of your guilt. Survivor's guilt, I'd say. It's a normal response."

"None of this feels normal."

"I know." Her voice lowers. It sounds like home and safety – if such a thing is possible anymore. "Come back here, and we can take care of it. Okay?"

"I will. I promise. I'll be home tomorrow night. After these funerals."

Angie sighs again. Not as loud as before. More resigned, almost defeated. "Okay, then. Okay. If that's what you need to do, I'll be here when you get back."

"Thank you. I know I'm acting strange but thank you."

We talk a few more minutes about trivial things. Things that have always been trivial but seem more so now. The leak under our sink in the kitchen. The weather.

We hang up and say goodnight, and I remain on the edge of the bed, staring at a cigarette burn in the carpet.

The fictional shooting starts again next door, even louder than before.

I flop down on the mattress, pull one and then two pillows over my head, trying desperately to block out the sound.

By the time I arrive in Corden, Jamar Jansen's service is underway. I slept poorly, waking every hour or so imagining someone was trying to get into my room. I eventually wedged a chair under the doorknob. It helped marginally, but I'm still worn out. My eyes feel dry and raw. My head hurts.

I try to do the same thing I did at Randy's funeral – slip in the back and keep out of the way. But Jamar's service is in a massive church, full of friendly and considerate people. Someone slides over and waves at me, urging me to sit rather than stand. So I do.

My clothes feel tighter and stiffer than ever. I've been to three religious services in two days. I haven't been to church three times total in the last twenty years.

Harold told me the president of the university would speak at one of the funerals – and this is it. The cynical part of my brain attributes her appearance to the size of the town – it's the largest where one of the funerals is taking place – and to the importance of the parents – Jamar's mother is an award-winning researcher with three patents. His father's a neurosurgeon. We're also close to the border between Kentucky and Tennessee. This coverage might make the Nashville evening news.

Elaine Martens wears a black skirt and jacket with a white shirt. Her hair is pulled back. Her posture is erect, dignified. She looks like she could be the president of the United States instead of a mid-sized public university in Kentucky.

Elaine speaks eloquently, addressing her comments to Jamal's parents. She talks about being a parent herself and how heartbreaking it would be to lose a child, especially in such a violent and tragic way.

Everyone around me is in tears. I feel emotion rise through my chest and into my throat, a floating bubble. I bite down on my lower lip.

Elaine's tone shifts. Her voice becomes sharper, more like a politician on the campaign trail.

"We take the safety of our students – your children – very seriously. It's of the utmost importance to us. To *me*. That's why I've ordered the creation of a commission made up of faculty members and community leaders to investigate this tragedy. They are to examine every aspect of what happened, and we will reevaluate our pedagogical procedures. Trust me when I say I take this very seriously, and I will hold anyone and everyone accountable for their actions."

Heat flashes across my face. I know I'm red.

I imagine every eye in the church has turned my way. They see me – they know who I am.

I'm the guy who needs to be held accountable.

In reality, no one looks at me. They watch Elaine. They focus their energy on Jamal's parents. As they should.

But my face burns like a skillet.

As the service winds down, I slip out of my seat and find a side exit. I want to get out before anyone recognizes me or talks to me – especially Elaine. And I have a three-hour drive to the last funeral.

I'm pulling the car door open when I hear my name.

"Dr. Buckley?"

Shit.

I keep going, pretending I didn't hear. I slide into the seat, start the ignition.

"Dr. Buckley?" Louder.

A woman comes down the sidewalk, waving her hand in the air. She's still wearing the sunglasses and winter coat she wore yesterday.

No, no. I don't need this. Whoever she is – I don't need it. Reporter, pissed off parent. I'm out of here.

I slam the door and reverse. I go too far, and my bumper kisses the car behind me.

"Shit."

I crank the wheel to the left as far as it will go. She's getting closer and closer, still waving her hand.

I shake my head. I accelerate, miss the bumper of the car in front of me by centimeters.

I take off down the street, leaving Corden and the woman in the sunglasses far behind. Running away again and again.

I eat half of a fast-food hamburger on the drive to Deep Creek. It tastes like rubber and sits in my stomach like a rock. I yawn a lot, turn the music up loud and open the window to stay awake. Why wasn't I this sleepy last night when I kept thinking someone was shooting at me from the next room?

The church in Deep Creek is modern – it's round with lots of glass and a parking lot that covers acres and acres and runs up against a fence where two horses swish their tails on the other side.

I park way back here. People file in, mostly at the front. A lot of words ring in my ears. Elaine's. Harold's.

Angie's, of course.

I should listen to them and just go home. I'm tired, and I'm not doing any good.

But I've come so far. And this funeral is for Alicia MacDonald, the best student in the class. Maybe the best student I've ever taught. I was supposed to direct her honors thesis this year, and she planned on applying to the Peace Corps. If I don't make an appearance here of all places…

There's a door on the side of the church no one is using. I can go in there, stick my head inside and see the service for just a moment. Then I'll get out and head home, face the music that awaits back on campus.

I may not have a job if Elaine's commission finds fault with me. It's okay. I'm not sure I deserve to keep it. I'm not sure anything should ever be the same.

I start across the parking lot. The wind picks up, and a cloud moves across the sun. I look back once, and one of the horses – a spotted gray – shakes its head, as if it knows something I don't.

But I keep going.

I reach the door and slowly pull it open. I step inside, my shoes landing on soft carpet. It's a short hallway at the rear of the church with three doors on either side. Church offices, I suppose. The walls are painted off-white and decorated with religious art. Pictures of saints and the Crucifixion.

I'm halfway down when a man steps out of a door on my left. We almost run into each other. I take a step back, then realize who it is. I met him once before, at a department awards ceremony the year before. I've seen him on the news, denouncing the university's security measures to anyone who would listen.

Alicia's father, Bill.

His body fills the hallway. Broad shoulders and thick hands. Alicia's the first in her family to go to college. I don't remember what Bill does for a living, but I'm pretty sure it involves smashing things with his hands.

His face flushes a deep red and purple, like his air's been cut off.

He says one word: "You."

I backpedal but not fast enough.

Then he's swinging, his hands flying at me in the narrow hallway like two cinder blocks. He connects a couple of times, once on each side of my head. My ears ring like somebody smacked me with a tuning fork.

Bill has me by the shirt, my feet leave the ground. He's driving me backward. I hit the door, and we go flailing out into the parking lot. Bill lands on top of me, forcing all the air out of my lungs. The cinder block fists resume their swinging, landing with greater and greater frequency and force.

My mind disconnects from my body. I'm floating above us, watching it happen. I know the man on the ground getting pummelled deserves it. He had it coming. Maybe that's the only reason he went to these four funerals.

Then other people are here. They're pulling Bill off the man on the ground. Bill's fists flail at thin air, his face even redder than before. His head might explode.

"I'll kill you. I will. I'll kill you."

"Bill, easy, easy."

"Shhh, this is a church."

"Come on, Bill, let's get inside. Nicole needs you."

Somewhere in there, I stop floating. My spirit and body reconnect. I'm on my back, the parking lot grit poking me through my clothes. I'm staring at the sky, a giant dark cloud filling my vision. I can finally sleep.

I close my eyes, and the lights go out.

"Hey, hey."

Someone slaps my face. One cheek and then the other. Gently, then with more force.

I'm back in that classroom. Blood smeared on the walls and floor. Screams.

Vomit and feces and screams and shots—

Pop-pop-pop

"Hey, come on."

My eyelids flutter. The sky is still gray. Light rain spits down on me.

My chest heaves.

"Can you get up? I don't think I can lift you."

I keep blinking. It's a woman's voice, one I don't recognize.

But before I turn my head and look, I know who it belongs to. She's crouched down next to me. The sunglasses perch on top of her head, revealing eyes red from crying. She's about my age, but the lines around her eyes and mouth look freshly etched, like she's aged rapidly in the last few days.

"Who are you?" I ask. "What do you want from me?"

"I think we need to go. You were out for about ten minutes, and I don't know how long Mr. MacDonald is going to be held back. Even if they're in the middle of his daughter's funeral mass. It's not safe for either of us."

"Who are you?"

"You don't know?"

"No."

"If I tell you, will you get up?"

"If I can."

She lets out a deep breath, like she's preparing to tell me really bad news. When she does that, I can guess what she's about to say. She says it anyway.

"I'm his mother. *His.*"

"Oh, shit."

"Right. Wendy Timmons." She looks back to the church. "Will you get up now? I've been wanting to talk to you."

Despite saying she couldn't help me up, her arms slide under mine, and with what feels like minimal effort on my part, I'm on my feet. I wobble. My head hurts. I reach up and find a dab of blood on my fingers.

"You okay?" she asks.

"I think so. How bad does it look?"

She examines me. "You have a cut by your lip. A bruise starting on your cheek. I thought you'd look worse." She waves her hand. "Come on. I'm parked near you."

"You've been following me."

"Yes and no. I think we both had the same idea. To attend all the funerals."

I wobble again. My mouth is parched. "Whoa."

"You sure you're okay?"

"No. But I agree I shouldn't stay here. I should have listened to – well, to everyone."

"Let's go." She places her hand on my arm, and we start to move across the lot.

As we go, I feel better, more steady. My head still thumps but not as bad. We get halfway to the car, and I stop.

"What is it? Are you going to fall?"

"No." I turn to face her. "I'm sorry. I am. About Tyler. I'm sorry for your loss."

Her eyes fill with tears, but they don't spill. "Thank you for saying that. I'm sorry too. Deeply sorry for what happened to everyone else." She applies gentle pressure to my arm. "Let's get in the car. I want to ask you something."

I'm in the passenger seat of her RAV4. The windshield's dirty and spattered with bugs. Wendy reads my mind and reaches into the back seat, hands me a water bottle. "I stocked up for the trip. I've eaten and slept in the car, trying to stay out of everyone's way."

The water tastes great. I guzzle half the bottle. Everything is quiet at the church, which means the service is still going on. And Bill is staying inside.

"You wanted to ask me something," I say. "I'll tell you anything you want to know if you answer *my* question first."

Wendy shakes her head. "I can try, but I'm not sure I know anything. That's the one thing I've become certain of over the last week – I don't know anything."

"Yeah." I start to form the words then stop. "You know what – it doesn't matter. It's – it's not important."

"I don't mind. Ask. My whole life has been turned upside down the last week. Ask away."

"It's stupid but… my wife and I, well, I think Tyler didn't want to shoot me. I think – I think he liked me. And he let me live… for some reason, I guess. Maybe only a reason he knew. I mean, I was right there in the center of the room, sitting at my desk. I was the first person he'd see walking into the class. What do you think?"

Wendy takes out her own water and swallows, her throat bobbing. Her lips are cracked, the skin on her cheeks raw. "You've heard about the videos, the ones the cops keep finding?"

"Someone told me about them."

"Have you watched them?"

I shake my head.

"That's *all* I've done. Over and over. Like I'm trying to punish myself. Or figure out something that doesn't make sense." She swallows a big gulp of water again. "He talks about you in one of them."

"He does?"

She nods. The air in the car starts to feel close, humid. I want to open a window, but the car is off. "He says you're his favorite professor. You encouraged him and supported him when other people didn't."

"I shouldn't have asked."

"He also said he wanted to kill you last. After all his classmates were dead. He planned to shoot you at your desk so you could see his whole story play out. The investigators think Randy Higgins slowed him down enough that the police got to the door. Then Tyler... you know... to himself..."

Wendy starts to cry. Silently. Tears run down her cheeks.

I don't know what to do. Her information really doesn't make me feel better or worse. Just numb. He didn't spare me, not at all. I was just lucky.

"I'm sorry, Wendy." I reach over, place my hand on top of hers.

She wipes her face. "This service might be over soon. We should get out of here."

"You didn't ask me your question. I assume you want to know – you know, about Tyler's last moments. What it was like in that room. I can try—"

Wendy's shaking her head. "No, not that. The cops keep telling me about that. Even when I don't want to know. They seem to think I need to hear, and maybe they're right. No, it's not that."

"What can I tell you, then?"

"I don't want you to *tell* me anything." She places her water bottle in the cup holder and adjusts her body. She reaches into the back seat. My eyes follow her arm. She said she'd been sleeping in the car. Her hand reaches for a blanket. She flips the blanket back, revealing a small, lacquered box. "That's him. What's left of him. Tyler."

"Oh."

"I want you to go with me while I, you know, scatter him. Someplace quiet and peaceful."

The side door of the church swings open. A few people trickle out. More people emerge at the front. "Looks like this service is wrapping up," I say.

"All the more reason for us to get out of here."

My head really starts to thump again. The adrenaline has slowed, and the pain from Bill MacDonald's cinder block fists starts to rise all over my upper body.

My car sits twenty feet to the left. A two-hour drive home. Back to Angie. We can go to her dad's, ride the storm out. Even if I get fired, we'll be okay. Angie works remotely and makes more money than I do. We can live anywhere. I can change my name, start all over in a different state.

Leave all of this behind. Focus on what works.

What matters.

Run!

"I don't see why you'd want me around," I say. "I should have stopped him. I allowed all of this to happen. I encouraged his violent writing."

Wendy wipes her eyes, nods. "Sure, I get it. You have a life too."

Up ahead, Bill MacDonald steps out of the side door of the church. He doesn't look our way, but he stands with a few other men. One of them places his hand on Bill's shoulder.

I reach for the door, turn the handle. "Drive safe."

"It's just – I don't have anybody else. Tyler's dad's never been in the picture. My parents can't deal with this at all. My friends... no one knows what to say to me... And I'm driving around with my son's..."

Bill MacDonald and his friends walk in the opposite direction from us, out to the front of the church where the rest of the mourners wait. I can easily get in my car and go.

But should I?

I push the door open, then pull it shut again.

"Okay," I say. "Where do you want to go?"

Wendy drives west on Highway 112. We're quiet.

The tires hum against the pavement. The clouds part a little, and the sun leaks through. I have no idea where we are or where we're going. I'm not familiar with this part of the state, but Wendy seems to have a plan in her head. The car scatters the fallen leaves on the side of the road.

After thirty minutes, Wendy slows. I'm not sure what she's doing, but she turns the car, and for a moment, it looks like we're just going off the highway. I grip the door handle.

Then I see – an opening in the trees. A gravel road, narrow and shaded. The RAV4 bounces in a pothole, jarring my teeth together. But she keeps going, the tires crunching over the small rocks and stones, a plume of dust rising behind us.

"Where are we going?" I ask.

"There's a little spot ahead. I grew up in this county. My dad used to bring us here. Tyler too when he was little…"

A mile down the road a small pond comes into view. Tall grasses grow around its perimeter. A flock of black birds rises and scatters as the car stops. Wendy cuts the engine, and we sit. The sun is dropping in the sky, the horizon turning orange and red.

"I don't want people to know where he's buried," she says. "I don't want people, you know, doing things. Turning it – his grave – *him* – into some weird shrine or whatever."

"I get it."

We climb out, and Wendy reaches into the back seat and picks up the box. She carries it under her right arm, like a football. She starts for the water, and I follow until we reach the edge. The water smells like rotten eggs. A fish rises to the surface in the middle, striking at an insect, sending ripples all the way to the edges of the pond.

I wait, hands stuffed in my pockets.

"He was a happy kid, you know. It was only when he got older that he got… moodier, I guess. After his dad left. When he started high school. Still, I never thought anything like this would happen."

"Sure."

"Do you think it's okay that I remember him as a young boy, when he was happy, and not like he was the last few years?"

"You should remember him however you want."

"Do you want to say anything?" Wendy asks. "You're a writer after all."

Her question stumps me. My mind scrambles for something profound – a line of poetry, a verse from the Bible.

There's nothing there to draw on.

So, I keep it simple. "Rest in peace, Tyler."

Wendy nods. She takes the lid off the box and turns it over. A cloud of ashes comes out, gets caught by the breeze. Most of them fly into the pond, but some come back, land at our feet and on our shoes. Wendy shakes the box, makes sure everything that can come out does.

Our little ceremony ends quickly.

Wendy's hands shake as she fits the lid back on the box. The sun drops farther, and the air cools. Crickets start to chirp in the tall grass.

"What do you think is going to happen next?" Wendy asks. "To me, or to you?"

"I don't know."

Wendy remains in place as the sky grows darker. A night bird squawks in the distance.

I don't move either. I'll stay with her as long as I have to.

THE UNKNOWABLE PLEASURES

Susie Yang

Elliot Wilson's seminar, *The History and Philosophies of Eastern Religion*, was one of the most popular classes on campus and it wasn't until the fall of her senior year that Sophie won the lotto and snagged one of the twenty spots. Rumors about Professor Wilson, concerning both his teaching methods and his personal life, abounded around the school: He never prepared his lectures in advance nor gave the same lecture twice, he spoke about the meaning of dreams, of prophecies, he had memorized every passage of the *I Ching*, he ate a fruitarian diet like Steve Jobs, he was friends with Steve Jobs, he led the class in hour-long mushroom-fueled meditations, he was a Communist, he had an ongoing feud with the dean, he had a wife and a young male Greek lover and all parties knew about this arrangement. Those who admired him spoke of him like some kind of spiritual genius; those who disapproved of him spoke of him like a heretic outlaw. Either way, there was awe in their eyes, and admiration.

When Sophie entered the lecture hall on the first day of class, she didn't see the appeal. He could have been any liberal arts professor in his late thirties, with sandy-blond hair and alert brown eyes, wearing an oversized blazer over a black T-shirt. He was tall and thin, almost gangly, and he walked across the stage with his hands clasped behind his back like an old man. The only signs of his bohemian nature were a bracelet woven of red thread that he wore on his left wrist, and the fact that under his buttery suede loafers he wasn't wearing any socks. He carried a small notebook that he laid down on the podium (later, they found out it was a diary, which he took with him everywhere and pulled out at random times to jot down – what? They longed to know) and then his stern face broke out into a wide, sunny smile. "Call me Elliot," he said, after the introductions.

In the coming weeks, Sophie came to like Elliot Wilson. Underneath the larger-than-life persona, he had, she discovered, the heart of a mischievous boy: a Tom Sawyerish figure she imagined growing up on some midwestern farm, reading adventure books and butchering chickens, pulling the braids of milkmaids, before discovering God and literature and leaving his hometown to travel the world; a more devout and sober Hemingway, in search of deeper meaning, but never losing sight of where he came from. In class, he loved to say provocative things to see who would rise to the bait. He loved it when the class broke out into heated debate, loved it when people said, "But that's just crazy, Elliot." He did not speak to them like a professor, or even an adult, but as one of them, always sitting in the same dilapidated swivel chair that he set in the middle of the stage, fingertips pressed together under his chin, using his long legs to push himself around and around in circles so that their discussions were always punctuated by the continuous squeak of plastic wheels over laminate.

He was irreverent about faith, but he could be somber and reflective too, about the unknowable miracles of the universe. "Some people think that the pursuit of beauty and the pursuit of God are incompatible," he said, "but to me, they are one and the same. *Beauty is truth, truth beauty – that is all. Ye know on earth, and all ye need to know.* Keats." He seemed to know as many poems as he knew Bible passages.

Sophie found herself wondering about his wife (she'd heard he'd left her back in his hometown to run her family's General Goods store) and his Greek lover (how had they met? What language did they converse in?) and other aspects about his unorthodox life as she sat in her room, trying to study but really just doodling in the margins of her binder, or turning over a phrase of his as she gathered her shampoo and soap bar into her caddy, or smiling over her eggs and toast in the dining hall, remembering a witty remark Elliot had made in class. "What are you smiling about?" her boyfriend, Alan, asked. She told him the rumor about the *ménage à trois* but he didn't seem to find it amusing.

Sometimes she even wondered if she was developing a crush on her professor. Surely, she was spending an inordinate amount of time thinking about him, talking about him. But then she'd perform the "kiss test" that, since hitting puberty, had never failed to reveal to herself her true feelings about a boy: she imagined herself leaning in toward Elliot's face, closer, closer, close enough to see the amber flecks in his eyes and the stubble on his chin and – and nothing. She only felt a mild disinterest, not quite repulsion but definitely not desire. I do not like Elliot Wilson, she thought, with relief and disappointment.

Not all her classmates enjoyed the class as much as Sophie did, however. There was one boy, Lawrence Tao, who seemed to positively despise their professor. Lawrence was pale and slim, almost delicate-looking, with dark, wavy hair and full, expressive lips. He came from a family of pastors and ministers in whose holy, unblemished footsteps he was determined to follow. Lawrence was the president of the Theology Club, led Bible study groups every Wednesday in his off-campus apartment, and was first violinist for the St. Andrews Symphony, which was nationally renowned; they'd even been invited to Buckingham Palace once to play for the Queen. During Sophie's freshman year, she and Alan had attended the winter concert and she'd literally gasped out loud when Lawrence had stood up for his solo under the warm honeyed light of that mahogany stage, the velvety tux hugging the lines of his slim body like a possessive lover. His eyes had remained closed for the entirety of his solo, his body trembling like a dewdrop to the tune of Bach's Sonata no.1 in G minor. Overnight there had sprung up legions of Lawrence Tao fan girls devoted to stalking him around campus. Yet he had no friends. He never smiled. He was frightfully intelligent.

Most of the time, Lawrence didn't partake in discussions during Elliot's seminar, but he had a natural gravitas that made other, more insecure, students glance in his direction after flailing in their own poorly-formed arguments and ask nervously, "What do you think, Lawrence?" Then, with a few sharp and succinct sentences,

Lawrence would lay out his opinion, which would usually be the opposite of whatever Elliot was saying, and then the gaze of the entire room would ping-pong between Elliot and Lawrence as they sparred like lawyers in court, unaware of anyone else in the room, one flushed and always in motion, swiveling in his squeaky chair or pacing across the stage, the other pale and still, growing ever more pale and still with each word.

It seemed that Lawrence tried to avoid speaking or even looking at Elliot, but Elliot loved to pick on Lawrence. "Why don't you grace us with your opinion, Mr. Tao?" he'd say in a sing-song voice with an undeniable ring of mockery. He never called Lawrence by his first name. There was none of the chummy nicknames he used with the rest of them: Jilly or Big Ben or Soph. With Lawrence, it was always: Mr. Tao. Lawrence would try to keep his composure but, eventually, he'd be goaded into losing his temper. Once, in retaliation to Elliot's accusation that he didn't have the logical wherewithal to see his own contradictions, Lawrence finally lost his cold yet polite composure: "There are no *contradictions* in my argument, you fool, you're being deliberately pedantic to rile me up!" The Cheshire Cat smile Elliot wore for the rest of the class was like a trophy, even though he was the one who'd been called a fool.

"Why'd Lawrence even enroll in the seminar if he hates Elliot so much?" Alan asked as she filled him in on the latest drama. It was an early evening in October; they were walking to the gym for a game of racquetball. She hated sports but Alan had been complaining about gaining the "senior fifteen" recently, and she'd said, "That's not a thing, Alan." The Japanese maple trees lining the quad were in full autumnal bloom and their unnatural blood-red hues filled her with a piercing, melancholic joy. She wished she were heading to a toasty armchair with a book instead of the bright, atmosphere-less stink of the gymnasium.

"I mean, it's not too late for add-drop," Alan went on. "He can take something else, it's not like he needs the credits."

"You know, I think he enjoys it," said Sophie. She hadn't realized this truth until now, but in retrospect, maybe she'd always known. Yes, Lawrence enjoyed his verbal sparring with Elliot. He enjoyed the challenge of an intelligent mind who could keep up with his own. Elliot probably felt the same way, which was why he didn't treat Lawrence the way he treated everyone else, with kindness and patience, like the way you treated children, instead of with mockery and spirited assaults, the way you treated a worthy adversary. When the two of them spoke, even if they were addressing other people, it was like they were speaking for the other to hear. No, the thing that crackled so ferociously between them could not be called hatred. It was something else altogether.

One morning, a week later, Elliot decided to have class outside. It was eighty degrees and balmy, autumn's gloomy chill temporarily driven back by one of summer's last pine-scented breezes. Squirrels chased each other up and down the oak tree with acorns stuffed in distended cheeks. "In a past life," said Elliot fondly, "I think I must have been a squirrel. I am so *partial* towards them there's no other explanation." That day, he had them meditate for forty minutes to practice the Tao concept of *wu wei*: non-action, or inexertion. It was incredibly boring and difficult to hold still in one position for so long. When they opened their eyes at the end of the session, all of them were slumped over to various degrees; only Elliot and

Lawrence still retained their perfect postures, hands on knees, back erect. That day, the two of them were wearing similar outfits: a blue button-down shirt, jeans, white sneakers. Elliot looked rakish and young; Lawrence was radiantly handsome. "Stand up slowly," Elliot instructed them. "You may feel a bit dizzy at first." Lawrence placed his hands on the ground to hoist himself up, then let out a little hiss. He looked down at his hand. A second later, Elliot was by his side. "What is it?" There was a long, almost two-inch piece of glass sticking out of Lawrence's palm, near the fleshy part of the thumb. "Don't move," said Elliot, a tiny crease between his 'brows. He cradled Lawrence's palm in his own, and with his other hand, pulled out the glass. Blood immediately began to gush out. Elliot took off his shirt – underneath he wore his usual black T-shirt – and made a tourniquet to wrap Elliot's hand. "Come on, I'll walk you to the infirmary. It doesn't look like it'll need stitches."

Lawrence snatched his hand away. "I'll go on my own." He grabbed his backpack and walked away, cradling his hand in his other arm like a wounded bird. Elliot watched him leave with an unreadable expression. "Alright, Soph?" he said, catching her gaze.

Sophie's skin felt both hot and cold and tingly, like the time she rubbed mint-infused aloe over a bad sunburn. She was embarrassed. She felt she'd seen something she shouldn't have, something private and vulnerable and potentially dangerous. But perhaps that was an overreaction. No one else was acting weird. But maybe no one else had seen what happened. Elliot was still smiling at her in a relaxed and careless way, but she couldn't help feeling that the relaxation was affected, to demonstrate that he had nothing to hide, or perhaps to insinuate the attitude that she, too, was supposed to adopt about the entire situation. She nodded and babbled on about how much she'd enjoyed the meditation.

"Wonderful. You look a bit dazed. Need me to walk you to your next class?"

"No, I'm fine." She tried to form her most relaxed smile but probably failed because she couldn't even meet his eyes.

Elliot was sick the following week and they spent the class watching a documentary about seventeenth-century bookbinding during which the class fell into a listless stupor, interrupted by fits of coughing that would catch from person to person until the entire room was coughing and sniffling and honking into tissues. A few days later, on her way to pick up coffee, she ran into Lawrence in the Student Center; he, too, looked listless and peaky, though it was hard to tell with Lawrence since he was so pale and fragile-looking by nature. He was buying a bag of cough drops and some NyQuil. "I guess it got you too," she said, meaning the bug that was going around. He nodded at her, then went up to pay, throwing in a bag of clementines at the very last minute.

When Elliot returned the following week, he looked thinner and somehow more refined; small, dark veins coloring the thin skin under his clear brown eyes. The skin of his hands was practically translucent in the gray morning light. He coughed throughout the lecture, a wet phlegmy cough that made her own throat ache. He was in a bad mood. Not as eloquent as usual, his scathing remarks about the missionaries from 1800s Portugal who'd gone over to Manchuria to butcher the yellow-faced heathens who refused to convert to Christianity had the ring of personal bitterness, not historical tragedy.

"That cough sounds pretty bad," she said after class, lingering by the podium on her way out. Elliot was jotting something down in his diary, one ankle crossed over a knee.

"Nothing a glass of whiskey won't cure," he said with a tired smile. "Don't take your youth for granted, Soph. Once you're an old man like me, every ache and pain keeps you up at night."

She was about to leave but then a flicker of bright orange caught her eye. Elliot's messenger bag, one of those floppy canvas ones that couldn't stay upright on its own, was on the floor, unzipped. Inside she saw a bag of clementines.

"Do you like clementines?"

Alan yawned and looked up from his book. "Sure. Those little oranges, right?"

"They're not oranges, Alan."

"Close enough."

"Did you know that the Student Center sells them?"

"No."

"Have you ever bought a bag to eat?"

"My mom buys them sometimes."

"But have *you* ever bought them?"

"No. Hey – you think they're good for digestion? I feel like I've been blocked up recently, *down there*, if you know what I mean."

"Do you have any friends who buy them? Like, is that a normal thing for a guy to buy for himself?"

"I don't know. Why this sudden anthropological interest in clementines?"

She hesitated, then laughed at her own hesitation. She told him what she'd seen – Lawrence at the Student Center, the bag of clementines in Elliot's bag.

"So you think Lawrence bought the clementines for Elliot?" said Alan.

"I thought I saw him go up to talk to Elliot when I first came in. He must have given them to him, then."

"So what?"

"Don't you think that's really sweet?"

"I guess." Alan gave her a strange smile. "Or your teacher could have bought them for himself."

"But why would he bring them to class, then? The bag barely fit inside his bag. I'm sure it was Lawrence."

"Okay. That's nice." Alan paused. "Wait – is this one of your hints for, like, things you wished I did for you that you don't actually want to explicitly tell me? Because it wouldn't be romantic if you *told* me to do it, so you want me to think of it myself?"

"No, Alan." She sighed and looked out through the tall windows of the library. It was gray and drizzling; the branches of the Japanese maples were bare now. A pasty couple in shapeless winter coats were making out in front of the chapel with broad, simpering smiles on their blurry faces. Why did love always have to look so idiotic? "I don't like citrus fruits, remember?" she said. "Let's just get back to studying."

Sophie sensed a shift occurring in Lawrence and Elliot's relationship. Elliot didn't pick on Lawrence so much in class; Lawrence didn't look like he was smelling something foul every time Elliot opened his mouth. They hardly spoke at all and by all superficial observations, they appeared to have gone from mortal enemies to indifferent strangers. Yet Sophie sensed a more meaningful game being played under the missed glances and purposeful evasions that went beyond coincidence.

She thought often about that scene outside by the oak tree: the gold glint of Elliot's hair as it fell over his face when he bent over Lawrence's small hand, cradled in his much larger hand. The two of them in their crisp button-down shirts with the top button undone to reveal long, creamy necks. This tableau was so striking it made her wistful and sad, like that one time when she was very young and had seen, at a distant aunt's wedding in England, two flower girls dancing around a water fountain with silk ribbons trailing behind them in the petal-strewn grass.

December arrived; wet, cold, barren. The sun set at half-past four and everything smelled like frozen dirt. Walking to pick up a muffin and coffee for breakfast at the Market Café before church, Sophie had the thought that her blood was made of ice; she could never get warm. This early on a Sunday morning, there were few people on campus. A bicyclist whizzed by, splattering her skirt with mud. A woman with frizzy hair and a long, pleated skirt hurried into the Science building with her head down, her pumps leaving little indents in the shallow sprinkling of snow. There was only one other person sitting inside Market Café, at a table by the window, and Sophie almost walked by Elliot Wilson without recognizing him.

Only when he shifted in his seat and turned a page of his book did she identify those long and fluttering fingers and that particular rangy way of moving.

"Professor Wilson?"

The man looked up. It *was* Elliot, unshaven and gaunt, wearing a black beanie, wire-frame glasses, and a faded flannel shirt. He looked like a tired, sleep-deprived graduate student, and this threw her into a state of nervous confusion like when you run into a celebrity you stalk on social media but have no idea how much their public persona overlaps with their real selves. What tone should she adopt? It struck her that this man was a stranger; he had never given any indication of having a wife, let alone a young male lover.

"Sophie!" he said heartily. "Haven't been called Professor Wilson in a while. What are you doing up so early?" She told him about the morning sermon. "You may be the only person under sixty attending that session," he said. "Why not just go to the ten o'clock one like the rest of the heathens?"

She laughed. "I don't know. I'm a morning person, I guess."

"That's a superpower, that." They paused. He saw her glancing at his book, a dog-eared paperback copy of *Brideshead Revisited*. "Have you read this?" When she shook her head, he said, "It's supposed to be a Catholic book but so far I'm not convinced. The only divinity I sense is the divine suffering of these poor boys who love each other but are driven apart by a slew of interfering moppets." Moppet was the term Elliot used for anyone he considered close-minded, idiotic, inconsequential. She laughed uncertainly. He laid his book down on the table, spine up. "I'm going to get another coffee, can

I get you something?" But before she could answer, his eyes slid behind her, and his face broke out into a serene smile.

Sophie turned; Lawrence was at the entrance of the café, brushing snow off the lapels of his dove-gray peacoat. The tip of his nose was pink from cold. Seeing her and Elliot at the table, he walked over without a break in stride. "Hi, Sophie," he said noncommittally. He did not greet Elliot at all, which she found awkward and rude and immediately tried to cover up by talking a lot, in an overly exuberant kind of way. She asked Lawrence about the concert he had coming up but soon the conversation came to a halt, as all conversations with Lawrence were wont to do. Failing to come up with another topic of conversation, she looked toward Elliot for help, expecting to see the erudite face of her professor ready to steer the ship of discourse toward more stimulating grounds. Instead, she saw that Elliot – and Lawrence – were gazing at her with polite inquiry, as if asking if there was anything else she needed, and it dawned on Sophie that this was not at all a random encounter. They were not surprised to see each other. In fact, the opposite was true: they had a prior engagement to meet here. She was the one who was making everything awkward. She was the intruder. Even as Elliot was pulling up another chair for Lawrence, she sensed his blustering heartiness was in fact compensation to hide that he wished she would excuse herself, that they wanted to be alone.

She stammered out that Lawrence should take her seat, she couldn't stay, she was supposed to meet her boyfriend before church. They were still looking at her politely as she pushed the door open, like a host couple waiting for the last guest to leave before sinking into their armchairs with happy groans of relief.

Lawrence was still standing; he had one hand on the back of Elliot's chair.

"Where's my coffee?" said Alan, as she slid into the pew.

"Oh goodness. I completely forgot." She must have looked so crestfallen that Alan's irritation dissipated and he gave her shoulder a little squeeze.

"It's alright, I think I still have a packet of Nestlé in my room."

But after the service, she didn't want to go back to Alan's room, like they usually did on Sundays after church, to watch movies on his laptop, eat gloppy pizza and icy salad for lunch in the dining hall, perhaps meet up with some friends at the gym for a game of racquetball. She felt constricted and unsettled and wrong in her body, what her mother used to call "the fuzzies," whenever Sophie flew into one of her tantrums ("She had the most crazed and insoluble terrible-twos," Sophie's mother still liked to tell relatives). "Let's *do* something today," she said.

Alan looked at her quizzically. "Like what?"

"I don't know." She struggled to come up with the most romantic thing she could improvise in the moment. "Let's go into town. We can do some Christmas shopping and have sushi at Riki's for dinner." Walking hand in hand in the cold, brushing snow off each other's mufflers, ducking inside to some wood-paneled bar for a glass of wine by the fireplace – wasn't that idyllic?

Alan said, "I think it's supposed to sleet later." He checked his phone. "Actually I think it'll be okay. It's not supposed to start until nine."

And so they changed out of their church clothes into their knit sweaters, jeans, scarves, and heaviest boots. Sophie took a long time doing her makeup and curling her hair, even spraying some perfume – Chanel No. 5, her mother's birthday gift – onto her wrists. It lifted their moods that the bus into town, which came every forty-five minutes, pulled up precisely as they arrived at the bus stop. "I timed it right," Alan explained triumphantly. She kissed him with extra warmth. She was happy he was happy.

The shops on Main Street were all decked out with beautiful Christmas decorations. They took their time examining all the various tree ornaments, the ribboned gift baskets of yarn and popcorn and candy canes, thick hand-knit socks in sunset colors. Alan bought a cat mug for his mother. Sophie kept her arm tucked into Alan's. She laughed a lot and expressed delight over everything. At every window-front, she glanced at her reflection, hers and Alan's, and felt a kind of detached pleasure at the attractive couple they made. "I'm so happy," she said, standing on tiptoes to nuzzle her cold face into Alan's neck. He kissed her on the forehead, pleased. She liked that, being kissed on the forehead. It made her feel like some small vulnerable creature in need of protection. At Riki's, an expensive restaurant where Alan had taken her for their anniversary last year, she wanted to intensify the romantic, heady mood and suggested ordering a bottle of hot sake to share. But Alan frowned and said it was kind of overpriced, $36 for a small bottle, and besides it was Sunday and he had to get up early for crew. She ordered a cup of green tea, and Alan said he was fine with water. He did not want to order appetizers since they'd had a lot of snacks that afternoon. They ate their sushi rolls in less than ten minutes, and Alan asked for the check. He pulled out his wallet, smiling at her sweetly. "Do you want to split it on two cards, or do you have cash on you?" She said she had cash.

Back in his room, just the two of them (Alan's roommate always went home on weekends to visit his parents), she tried to salvage her mood by putting on some music when Alan was in the shower. Arranging herself comfortably on his bed in a silk negligee she'd packed into her purse especially for tonight, she flipped through pictures on her phone of the two of them. Alan was all-American handsome like a firefighter. He was photogenic too, especially in one photo she'd taken last summer at the beach, of him staring out into the water. She examined his long lashes, his symmetrical and clean-shaven features. If she squinted a little, she could almost imagine Alan as a stranger, some Calvin Klein underwear model or the lead singer of a boy band. But when the real Alan returned from his shower in his flannel pajamas smelling of Head & Shoulders shampoo for his wintertime dandruff, the fantasy of Alan as an unknown stranger was impossible to hold on to. She still found the blood-and-flesh Alan cute and wonderful, yes, even in his thick wire-framed glasses and retainer, yet the sheer physical reality of him – of his precise, mathematical mind, his gym-sculpted body – failed to incite any emotion in her other than admiration, the kind you feel for a good-looking horse or dog, without any personal stakes.

She scooted over so Alan could squeeze in beside her on the tiny bed. Cuddling was their Sunday nighttime routine, sometimes, though less frequently now, followed by sex. Alan was smoothing her hair with one hand, reading a book with the other. Idly, she let her fingers trail down the buttons of his shirt, toying with the frayed drawstrings of his elastic waistband, tied in a loose knot. He turned a page. She pulled the knot loose. He smiled down at her. "You know what's weird? My stomach kind of hurts from the sushi, did you have any funny business going to the bathroom?" She said she hadn't. "Well, the fish isn't sitting right with me. Oops, sorry." He waved away the stink in the air, a remnant of his indigestion. "Do you want to order a pizza? I think the carbs will help settle my stomach."

She felt a quiver of disgust. She smiled back. "Sure. Extra pepperoni, please." They rolled apart so he could go get his laptop.

Now that she knew about Lawrence and Elliot's relationship, Sophie couldn't believe that it wasn't obvious to everyone in the entire class. It didn't even appear like the two of them were trying to hide it. She spotted them everywhere together: talking before and after class, walking side by side across the lawn toward the Student Center, elbows knocking into each other, or Elliot's arm thrown casually over Lawrence's shoulder; one time she saw Lawrence getting out of Elliot's car in the faculty parking lot. Elliot was sliding a pair of Ray-Bans over his eyes while Lawrence was leaning over the passenger's seat saying something in Elliot's ear over the hum of the engine. One morning Lawrence came in and she spotted on his wrist the same red woven bracelet that Elliot wore. She couldn't stop staring at it. He'd even rolled up his sleeves as if to better display this unofficial declaration of their coupledom. Yet as Sophie looked around the classroom trying to detect in the faces of her classmates a common sense of knowing, veiled smiles or discreet glances and wry gossipy whispers, she saw nothing more than the usual preoccupation with their own silly lives. The latest rumor surrounding Elliot was whether he was Rupert Murdoch's illegitimate son. Lawrence's fan club of squealing underclassmen still followed him around hoping to get noticed by their prince.

Sophie sometimes wondered if she were crazy. Making up an illicit affair where none existed. So one day, she presented all her evidence to Alan because he was the most rational person she knew, and could help validate her observations as truthful. She spilled everything: the time outside by the oak tree when Elliot cradled Lawrence's hand, the morning rendezvous at Market Café, the matching red woven bracelets, and reiterated all the other clues she'd observed in the last four months.

"And you think this means Lawrence and Elliot are both gay and in some kind of secret relationship now?" said Alan, not at all as impressed with her sleuthing as she'd expected, but weirdly slack-faced, not even giving her his full attention as he usually did.

"I don't know if they're gay, but I think they like each other *specifically*, if that makes sense."

"That doesn't sound very plausible. And Lawrence has had a girlfriend before. That foreign exchange student from Amsterdam – Julia?"

"You're not listening to me. That doesn't mean he can't have developed feelings for Elliot."

"But… why?" Alan was speaking more and more slowly; Sophie felt her voice rise with frustration. Was Alan purposely being dense? Or homophobic? "You were just saying how much they butted heads last month."

"But that was before they got to know each other," she said. "They're polar opposites but that's why they're drawn to each other. I'm telling you, Alan, if you just *saw* the way they looked at each other, you'd believe me." She was practically shouting. Alan looked at her levelly.

"Okay."

Pause.

"Okay what?"

"I don't know them, Sophie. Maybe? Or they could just be friends."

"*Friends* don't act like that, Alan. Seriously, you should come to my seminar next time. They hold their eye contact and exchange secret smiles. It's like they're in their own world."

Again, that irritating, "Okay."

"You think I'm exaggerating," she said bitterly.

"No."

"But then why don't you think I'm right?"

"I have no idea if you're right or not," said Alan, finally losing his faux calm demeanor, his voice tight. "And honestly, who cares? I think you're getting overly invested in your teacher's personal life. You're becoming a little – obsessive." He said this with a slight stammer, as if he'd exchanged the word he really wanted to use with this more tactful *obsessive*.

She felt furious, foolish, and betrayed. She wasn't obsessive, she was only curious, and yes, *interested* in the nature of Elliot and Lawrence's relationship, but only the normal way everyone was interested in everyone else's hook-ups and relationship gossip, especially the illicit ones. And if she appeared more invested than usual, it was because she liked both Elliot and Lawrence, she wanted to support them, to protect them from harm.

On Friday morning, Alan patted her head in lieu of a good-bye kiss – and they went back home to their respective small towns for Christmas, him to Texas, her to Ohio. She spent the entire break re-reading her favorite stories on the website Ao3: *Stay or Go*, *Because I Knew You Before the Edge of Time*, and her all-time favorite: *Abyss of the Orphan*, set in nineteenth-century England, about the love between a ship-builder and the street urchin he saves who eventually becomes the head of the Anglican church. She often wondered if she'd been born in the wrong century. People seemed to live so differently in the past, with real purpose and romance – true romance – born of suffering and sacrifice and courage, not this modern-day idea of romance made up of cheap words, alcohol, and trivial gestures. Perhaps the problem with her and Alan's relationship was that they had never done anything to earn their love, like survive a war or fight through insurmountable obstacles (disapproving parents, societal judgment, physical separation) to be together. Yet she also knew this was a stupid desire, a product of her peaceful, privileged life that romanticized suffering as a way to feel something deep and meaningful.

When Sophie walked into class in January, Lawrence wasn't at his usual seat. He'd never before missed a single lecture. She thought he might be sick, or returning late from a family holiday, but when he didn't show up for the following two lectures, Sophie waited after class to ask Elliot if everything was okay.

"With Mr. Tao?" Elliot said with a cool flick of his head that could have meant anything: disdain, anger, a mask for his concern. "He asked for personal leave these next few weeks."

"I'm sorry to hear that," said Sophie. "Is everything alright?"

"I really can't say. You know how Lawrence is. You can ask him yourself."

You know how Lawrence is. With those words, Sophie felt a warm heady gush of gratitude toward Elliot. Such a simple phrase yet it seemed to encompass everything she hadn't known she'd been longing for until this moment: acknowledgment of her familiarity, gratitude for her concern, understanding of her intentions as a friend and ally.

When the elation faded, she was able to grasp that Elliot's implied meaning was, indeed, that something had gone awry with Lawrence, something he was too proud to share with others and so Sophie would have to sleuth out the truth herself. She fretted for a few days, unable to finish her Childhood Lit paper ("Is something wrong?" said Alan. "You seem out of it these days." She shook her head. No, nothing. She wasn't going be called "obsessive" again), yet just when she had convinced herself that Lawrence was dealing with some kind of dire emergency, perhaps health related, she spotted him in the dining hall, perfectly healthy-looking in a moss green sweater, twirling a strand of spaghetti onto his fork.

"Look, it's Lawrence!" Sophie said, tugging at Alan's arm.

"So?"

Too late, she remembered she hadn't updated him on Lawrence's absence from seminar. "Oh, it's just that I haven't seen him in class for a few weeks. I think he's been sick – I'm going to go over and see if he's feeling better." The look Alan gave her said he knew her intentions perfectly but he wasn't going to start a fight right here in the dining hall.

Yet when she found herself standing beside Lawrence asking him if everything was okay, she felt foolish and intrusive, her mouth forming crude shapes, her arms damp and unwieldy by her sides.

"I'm fine now," he said.

"Elliot's been worried about you. He told me to ask after you."

She sensed, under his icy expression, an undercurrent of pain at the sound of Elliot's name. "That's kind of him. Thanks for letting me know, Sophie." No further explanation as to why he'd been absent. He got up and bussed his tray, leaving most of his spaghetti cold and uneaten.

Lawrence, despite his reassurance that he was fine now, did not return to seminar. Every time Sophie saw Elliot, he appeared a bit more diminished, a bit rangier. His sandy hair looked limp and unwashed; once he came to class, looked around tiredly, and said he didn't feel like lecturing that day, maybe they could all just spend the hour reading *The Bhagavad*. She could see the sharp bone of his Adam's apple protruding from his sinewy neck. Her heart welled with sympathy, imagining his sorrow.

One Thursday morning, she went to class but no one was there. She pulled out her phone and saw that she'd missed an email from Elliot notifying them that class was canceled that day. Sophie was worried, but what could she do? She had no idea where Elliot lived. She supposed she could linger by the faculty parking lot to see if Elliot's car was there. She'd gone to Market Café for the last four Sundays, hoping to run into them again, but the two of them were never there again.

There were still another two hours before her next class. Despondent, she wandered into an empty hallway where she heard the echoes of other seminars being taught, life carrying on as usual. She felt flat and listless. She pushed open the door to the stairwell, unable to stand the idea of being trapped in the elevator – just in time to hear Lawrence's unmistakable ringing voice saying, "It's not right. I won't go along with it."

A light, pleasant laugh. "So what are you going to do about it? Don't be silly."

Lawrence, again: "I mean it, Elliot. I won't." A long pause. "I'll come with you."

Then a low: "*Don't*. Lawrence—"

"Hold on – I think someone's coming down."

They looked up at her, frozen at the top of the stairs.

"Sophie!" Elliot said in surprise. "Did you not get my email that class was canceled?"

"I didn't check it this morning," she said. "Sorry, I was just on my way out." Even though they were standing by the exit sign, she raced back upstairs to take the elevator.

That night, she went over to Alan's and even before he had a chance to lock the door, she'd flung her shirt onto the floor. She felt an awareness of his body in a way she never had before, and this awareness was almost desire. She had never before desired a man's body, never desired to see Alan naked, to see the full bulk of his manhood under his boxers that she'd fondled and touched and jerked because she knew this was pleasurable to Alan and it was part of her duty as his girlfriend to provide these stimulations. But tonight, these administrations were pleasurable because she could imagine that this was how Lawrence and Elliot touched each other, and it made her feel a part of them. Afterward, Alan, moved by her passion, went down on her. Sophie pictured again Lawrence and Elliot standing in that stairwell, probably holding hands or embracing before they jumped apart upon seeing her. She heard Elliot's voice saying *Lawrence*. It was *Mr. Tao* in public, but when it was just the two of them, a low and loving and yearning *Lawrence. Lawrence. Lawrence. I mean it, Elliot. Lawrence!* And when she came, her first orgasm in her twenty-two years of life, it was Elliot's voice she heard in her ears calling out for his Lawrence.

"So you should come over around 10:30 tomorrow morning," Alan said lovingly into her ears, "so we can get there by 11:15."

"Get where?" said Sophie.

"What do you mean? I told you a few weeks ago that I needed you to drive me home tomorrow from my doctor's appointment."

She tried to look as if this wasn't the first time she'd heard such a thing. "Why did you need me to come again?" she said casually.

"I'm getting a colonoscopy, remember? They said I might still feel woozy from the anesthesia. I'm worried I have Celiacs – my mom has it – or IBS or something. Colon cancer runs in my family, on my dad's side too."

"Right, right." She did her best to look sympathetic. Alan, despite his aura of Olympian vitality, was a terrible hypochondriac.

"You forgot, didn't you?"

She said, "Well you told me weeks ago."

"I mentioned it again yesterday."

She couldn't even deny this because Alan remembered everything everyone said ever.

She wondered if things felt this way between Elliot and Lawrence when they fought, like wading through a dark and murky swamp, your eyesight dimming, your legs sinking deeper with every step. Wasn't anger supposed to be a normal part of every relationship? A sign of passion, even? But she was pretty sure that what she felt when she and Alan argued had nothing to do with passion, but a deep sandpit of anxiety that had no beginning or end.

"You're thinking about them again," said Alan.

"Who?"

"I can see it on your face."

"See what?"

"It's bizarre, Sophie, you *do* realize that, right? It's messed up. You've gone and concocted an entire fantasy in your head. No wonder our relationship just doesn't do it for you anymore. It's just not *exciting* or *forbidden* enough, is it?"

She heard herself saying weakly, "What are you talking about?" but her tone lacked conviction; she couldn't even muster up the indignation to defend herself.

Alan pulled the covers over his shoulders and turned to face the wall. She took that as her cue to get dressed and go home.

When she woke the next morning, at a quarter to ten, she saw a text from an unsaved number, sent the night before, at 3:48 a.m. *This is Lawrence. I was wondering if you're free tomorrow at noon to meet for lunch?*

In a second, every cell in her body was buzzing, as if she'd been shot with a bolt of electricity. What did this mean? How did Lawrence get her phone number? It was so strange of him to ask her out to lunch, and to make the request in the middle of the night. *Something must have happened with Elliot.* Perhaps they were finally going to – what? Announce their relationship? Elope? She was so worried that her response might not reach him in time she considered simply phoning back. But that might make her appear desperate. *Yes, of course I can meet you for lunch,* she wrote. *Where?* He texted back immediately: *Market Café.*

Sophie felt a second of pure, unadulterated elation. Then she remembered Alan. She remembered their fight. She sent a text: *Sorry, Alan, I woke up this morning feeling terrible. I think I have a fever. Do you mind just taking a cab today to your doctor's appointment? Let me know how things go. Good luck! I love you.*

He texted back: *Oh man, that sucks. I wonder if it was the sushi. I'll pick up some meds for you on my way back.*

She sent him a heart emoji (he did not appear to be angry with her anymore), then forced herself to stare at her thesis for the next few hours, rewriting and deleting the same paragraph over and over again. When she finally allowed herself to look up at the clock, she was thrilled to see that it was almost noon and she would be late if she didn't hurry. She haphazardly ran a comb through her hair, checked her purse for her keys and wallet, and fast-walked across campus.

Even before she entered the café, she spotted Lawrence sitting at a round table in the back corner by the window. But he wasn't alone. Across from him sat Elliot, in a plaid shirt with his long fingers pressed in front of his face. Lawrence was wearing a wheat-colored sweater that made him look very wan and vaguely Irish. He was looking out of the window, not toward the direction she was coming from but the opposite, toward the belltower. There was nothing about either of their postures or expressions that revealed any clues to their moods or intentions or even the nature of their relationship. They could have been friends, roommates, advisor and student having office hours, strangers sharing a table on a crowded Wednesday at lunchtime. She watched as Elliot picked up his cup, took a small sip, placed it back on its saucer. Were his lips moving or was that just a trick of the sunlight filtering through the trees? Lawrence shifted in his chair; he crossed his arms. Someone had once told her that crossing your arms meant you were feeling defensive or vulnerable – she'd found the pronouncement obvious and reductive – but that didn't mean it wasn't true. *Was* Lawrence feeling defensive and vulnerable? Why hadn't he told her in his text that Elliot would be at lunch as well? Were the two of them still fighting, or was this their conciliatory lunch, a celebratory affair that they had invited her to so they could make a joke of their old grievances ("You know that day you ran into us in the stairs? Funny story, we were having a fight about a silly misunderstanding."). Or was the purpose of this lunch something altogether more serious – perhaps they wanted her to mediate, or listen to their various confessions?

In just a few minutes, she would go inside and get the answers, yet somehow she found herself walking slower and slower. It was puzzling, even to herself. Wasn't this the very thing she had been hoping for? To see the two of them together, to become an intimate part of their lives, to finally *know* the truth? She imagined the three of them in the future, chatting in Elliot's office, drinking wine in Lawrence's apartment, perhaps inviting Alan along for a double date – the theater, dinner at Riki's. She could say, carelessly, over a cup of sake, "So when did this thing start between you two?" She could say, "Where were you planning on going together anyway?" Under the warm bonds of their new friendship, she could ask any question freely, see them whenever she wanted: up-close, unshaven, distraught, happy, tired, nervous; all mysteries would dissipate like the flames of a candle extinguished by the cold light of day. The idea appalled her.

Maybe Alan had been right all along. Maybe all these were just delusional fantasies. Seeing Elliot and Lawrence at the café surrounded by the bustle of ordinary campus life, it felt absurd, risky, and impossible to imagine them even brushing hands, let alone doing all the things she'd been imagining. It seemed more and more likely they just wanted to talk about Eastern Religions and what her and Lawrence's plans were after graduation. Who knew what was real?

Before she knew what she was doing, she had turned around and was pushing past the throng of people to get back to her apartment.

The sun was very bright and burned her eyelids, which felt very inadequate. Her heart was racing. She felt young and tender and wildly free, like someone who'd just narrowly avoided a terrible traffic accident.

Alan was surprised to see her waiting for him at reception after he came out of his appointment.

"I thought you had a fever?"

"It went down," she said, wrapping her arms around his waist. She asked him how his colonoscopy went; he said it would be a few days before the results came back but the doctor checked his lymph nodes and thought they might be inflamed. She was genuinely worried when he told her this, and her obviously sincere concern softened all the lines on his face. They did not address their argument last night.

On the drive back to campus, her phone buzzed with a text. *Sophie? Are you still coming?*

"Who is it?" said Alan.

"No one," she said, and silenced her phone.

WEEKEND AT BERTIE'S

M. L. Rio

Lou closed the basement door behind her, dazed after the darkness by the sticky summer sunlight oozing down the hall, pooling like honey in each whorl of the hardwood. Every floorboard creaked and she stepped lightly until she found more solid footing on the cold kitchen tile. Tiny espresso cups crowded along the windowsill above the sink, holding flakes of sea salt, pink peppercorns, a forgotten bulb of garlic shriveled and brown as a lump of cancerous lung. Lou looked down the hill to the belt of trees that hid the big house from any prying eyes on the winding road from town. She gathered her hair at the nape of her neck and vomited into the sink.

After four or five heaves nothing came up. She opened a cabinet at random, filled a crystal water goblet from the tap, and gulped it dry before remembering where the vodka was. Bertie liked it cold but refused to water it down, so there was always a bottle of Belvedere wedged in the freezer between slabs of meat and tubs of gelato. Lou filled the goblet to the brim and put the bottle back. After a few bracing swallows, her hands were still shaking. She pulled her phone out of her pocket, too distracted to feel the Siamese cat insinuate itself between her ankles. She tripped over him as she turned and crashed against the cabinets, landing in a froglike squat. Gershwin yowled around her knees, tail flicking as he paced in agitated figure eights. She pushed him away and held her breath until her stomach stopped trying to climb up her throat. The phone seemed small and distant in her hand, her thumb obscenely enormous over the EMERGENCY icon. Before she could tap it, an alert from her banking app dropped down with a cheerful *ding* to announce that her account was overdrawn.

She was still squatting there like a gargoyle, holding her phone at arm's length, when Daniel Hahn, of all fucking people, came around the corner. She hadn't heard him come in, and he seemed equally startled to stumble on her. His step hitched in the archway between the kitchen and the great room and he froze there, framed like an icon in a church alcove. *A niche*, her father would have corrected her. He was a pedant first and an architect second.

"Lou. What are you doing here?"

"Dropping off some books for Bertie." She gripped the edge of the counter and pulled herself up. "Same question to you."

"She said she'd be gone for the weekend, but maybe she got the date wrong." He glanced down at Gershwin's indignant meow. "Wouldn't be the first time. Where is she?"

"In the basement."

"In the basement?"

Lou nodded and reached for the goblet. The glass had frosted over and she nearly dropped it, but Daniel's back was turned. She heard the floorboards creak, then the shrill complaint of the basement door. The house dilated around her in the subsequent silence, the black maw of the fireplace and the huge mirror over the mantel tunneling into the wall while the windows bulged outward, grotesquely agog. She waited. Wondering, still, what he was doing there, what she was doing there, what the hell they were supposed to do now. Everything shrank back into place as the basement door squealed on its hinge, the floorboards squeaked, and the cat meowed behind his lips again.

Daniel stopped exactly where he'd stopped before, suspended between the two rooms. His expression hadn't changed, but a spot of pink burned high on each cheek – too dark to be called blushing, but mottled like a fever, blotchy as a bruise.

"What happened?" He hadn't set his bag down and clutched the strap tightly in the middle of his chest.

Lou blinked. "What, like I murdered her? She was like that when I got here." When she arrived, when she knocked, the door swung open on its own. Bertie often left it unlocked when she was expecting Lou, who was expected to deliver books and mail and proofs and papers directly to her desk in the study on the second floor. But Bertie wasn't there when Lou went up to look, didn't answer when she called.

"Which was when?" Daniel retreated into the great room. The cat followed Daniel, and Lou followed him.

"Dunno – maybe fifteen, twenty minutes ago. What are you doing?"

He was groping around the roots of a gigantic potted plant

hunkered down beside the piano. "Soil's dry." He straightened up, silhouetted against the bay windows that looked out over the garden. "She's been down there a few days, at least."

Lou squeezed the goblet, just to feel the ridges in the crystal prick her skin. "Very clever, Dupin, but if that were true wouldn't she *smell*, by now?"

"Didn't say she's been dead a few days. If—"

"Thanks, I get it." Lou sank down on the couch, old Life Alert ads she dimly recalled from her insomniac childhood stuttering through her head. *"Help, I've fallen and I can't get up......"*

"Fifteen, twenty minutes— Why haven't you called the police?"

"Because it's a big house and the basement wasn't the first place I looked for her, Jesus." She'd wandered around upstairs for a while, and then a while longer, unable to resist the temptation to snoop but completely unprepared for what she found. "I didn't even know there *was* a basement until I tried the door – it's always closed."

"To keep the cat out." Daniel clambered out of the underbrush. The messenger bag swung around and crashed against his knees, knocking him into the nearest chair. "He knows his food's down there."

Lou raised her eyebrows. "So, you got the housesitting gig." He frowned, just barely. "Saw it on the listserv," she lied. Bertie needed a sitter every summer but had never asked Lou, despite her dropping none-too-subtle hints about second jobs and rising rent every June. She had a sneaking suspicion Bertie didn't trust her. She realized she was glaring at Daniel. "You don't have a car."

"I have a bike."

"You bike all the way here?" The house languished in the shade of red oak trees and shortleaf pines, ten miles from the college, most of them uphill. There were a few neighbors, but not many, and they seemed farther distant than they really were – kept out of sight and mind behind a staggering zigzag of evergreen.

Daniel disentangled himself from the bag and set it down. "Sometimes I stay the night. *Not* like that," he added, when the eyebrows went up again.

Lou shrugged. "She's been alone up here a long time." Bertie rarely came to campus anymore. That was what research assistants were for. "A woman's got needs."

"She doesn't like to leave it empty if she's going to be away. Gershwin gets restless and tears up the furniture. But whether I stay is mostly up to Rosie."

"Of course it is." Lou's amusement sputtered off like a bad faucet and left her impatient – to get out of the house and out of his presence and nailed to a barstool somewhere she could blur the memory of Bertie's crumpled body at the bottom of the stairs. "Why don't you call the cops, since you've got all the answers?" She thrust her phone at him but snatched it back when the screen lit up. Not fast enough for him not to see the notice from the bank. She smacked it down on the glass-topped coffee table. Gershwin peered up at her from underneath, with his sooty little face and uncanny blue eyes.

Daniel cleared his throat, fingers laced, looking at the floor. "Aren't— Weren't you Bertie's RA?"

She laughed. "Did you think that was lucrative?" A goblet of vodka on a very empty stomach was bound to make her mean.

"I haven't been solvent since Rosie left me with no subletter and six months left on the lease to go move in with you."

He nodded, head bobbing automatically. Gershwin leapt into his lap and headbutted him in the chest until he lifted one hand to stroke him in the same automatic manner. He did nothing else for so long that Lou thought she'd have to make the call after all, but suddenly he stood, dumping the cat on the carpet. He started down the hall again, with Gershwin close behind.

"Where are you going?" She took her phone, took the goblet, took another gulp as she passed the basement door. The hall disgorged them into a soaring foyer, where stained-glass sidelights made motley tessellations on the marble floor. Lou tiptoed from a square of ochre to a rose-red diamond, then followed the cat up the stairs at the front of the house. They were carpeted in threadbare bottle green and mercifully softspoken compared to the bare basement steps and the whining hardwood in the hall. It was an old house, built in a quasi-Italianate style and lucky to survive the Civil War. It had been in Bertie's husband's family for a long time but would go to the college when she died, since their students were the closest thing they ever had to children. Nevertheless, *Never was much for mothering*, was the first thing she said to her advisees, before she left them to their own devices – unless they were particularly promising or absolutely hopeless. Lou, to Bertie's enormous annoyance, was both.

Books had spilled out of the study and were stacked against the walls along the second-floor corridor – each pile rising to a height of about six feet (which must, Lou assumed, be as high as Bertie could reach) before a new pile began. She didn't know who to pity more – Bertie or the floorboards, aching under the weight of all the words she'd never have time to read. She'd built these little pillars halfway down the hall on either side, leaving a path between barely wide enough for one person, and only if they were willing to do an undignified Electric Slide. Gershwin moved more easily, tail whispering out of sight around the doorjamb.

Inside the study, journal proofs and reams of chapters Lou had scanned and stapled threatened to topple off every edge of the desk – a hideous claw-footed thing disfigured by coffee rings and flecks of red wine frozen in time, dripping down one leg like blood. Floor-to-ceiling shelves on every wall made the room feel smaller than it was, and hundreds more books piled crazily on the floor shrank the square footage to about four by four. *There's a fine line between cozy and claustrophobic*, was one of her mother's many interior decorating axioms. Bertie had barreled across that line and never looked back.

"Gonna tell me what the hell we're doing?"

Daniel was interfering with another houseplant – this time a tentacular monstrosity creeping along the top of a bookcase. *Devil's ivy*. Her mother's voice again. It had taken on a tinny quality, probably because Lou had only spoken to her over the phone since two Christmases ago.

"Looking for Eddie." Daniel pushed a tumble of marbled leaves aside and a human skull grinned down at her from the gap in the foliage. It was missing a tooth, which gave it an oddly piratical appearance.

"Is that real?"

Daniel climbed down from the stepladder he'd liberated from

underneath a stack of nineteenth-century pharmaceutical journals. The top issue loudly advertised seltzers, cyanide, and other "mercurial preparations."

"She bought him at an antique store in West Virginia for $99," he said. "Or so she told me."

"It must be so nice to have tenure."

Daniel smirked – or she thought he did. She'd never seen him smile that she could remember, not that they'd spent that much time together. They bumped into each other on campus and at conferences and, for a few months before Rosie moved out, in the cramped galley kitchen of the apartment Lou still lived in but could no longer afford. He rose early, drank tea instead of coffee, and had often washed every dish in the sink by the time she shuffled in with unbrushed teeth, eyes still smeared with last night's liner, highlighters stuck in her hair. "Might make you six figures a year," he said now, with that ambiguous glimmer of a grin, "but it might loosen your screws, too." He found whatever else he was looking for on the bottom shelf, nestled against the fraying spines of an old *Edinburgh Encyclopaedia*.

"Is that a hearth cricket?" Another term she'd learned from her mother, who sent them to everyone they knew who bought a new house, whether there was a hearth to put it on or not.

"Gold-bug." He held it out to her – a burnished scarab beetle with black blotches on its back in a decidedly cranial arrangement. "What's it look like?"

"Eddie."

"Exactly."

She stared at him, feeling very stupid. She felt very stupid very often for someone who had been in school for twenty years and would be paying off student loans for the next eighty, if she lived that long. "Exactly what?"

"You know, the Poe story, 'The Gold-bug.'"

"No, I don't know. I'm not a Poe scholar, but you can't write about house and home and gothic tropes in American lit and not do a chapter on 'Usher.'" Which was how Bertie wound up on her committee, how she became Bertie's Girl Friday. How they'd become anything more than that was more of a mystery. A few afternoons had faded to evening and work was abandoned in favor of whiskey and cigarettes and shit-talking colleagues. But they were too much alike to like each other much – the resemblance was unflattering.

"I'm not a Poe scholar either," Daniel said, "but I read 'Gold-bug' about a thousand times for the Digital Poe project because we couldn't get the cipher rendered right." He worked in the digital humanities, but Lou couldn't recall the particulars of his research. Something about the public domain and literature in translation online. "In the story, you find Captain Kidd's buried treasure by dropping a gold beetle through the eye socket of a skull nailed to a tree branch. In here, you find Bertie's stash of petty cash on whichever shelf the bug is on, directly under Eddie... so it makes about the same amount of sense." He reached for the second fat volume of the encyclopaedia: *Comparative Anatomy to Astronomy.* He riffled through the book until a gaping hole opened in the middle, as if someone had cut the pages out with an X-Acto knife. It looked uncannily like an open grave, but where the tiny coffin would have lain there were two fat stacks of fifty-dollar bills.

"This is *petty* cash? That's five grand if it's five bucks."

"Never counted," Daniel said. "Never would have known it was here if we hadn't run out of cat food last time she left town. I had to bring it back from the store on my bike, but she told me to buy myself a pizza for my trouble." He dumped the money out, some of it still bound in tidy little bundles with paper sleeves like napkin rings. Lou had underestimated – it wasn't five grand, but ten at least, probably more. "Anyway, she won't miss it."

Lou understood, with a sudden flush of embarrassment, what they were doing up there. He pushed half the fifties into her hand. She twitched when the steel band of his old Timex T80 brushed her skin. "What did she want this much cash for?" she asked, just for something to say, something to take the edge off the heavy silence of the house. "Was she in witness protection or something?"

He might have been grinning again; she still wasn't sure. "She just didn't trust technology. It was a nightmare with Digital Poe, she changed the passwords constantly but could never remember what they were and had to keep them written down." Gershwin demanded Daniel's attention with an insistent meow. As he crouched down to placate him, Lou stuffed the money into her waistband. The old desk didn't lock, so she started pulling drawers open at random. Spooked by the scrape of the casters, Gershwin hissed and darted out of the room.

It was Daniel's turn to ask, "What are you doing?" When he was on his feet again, *Anatomy to Astronomy* had been replaced and the rest of the cash had disappeared, but she didn't see where.

"Following a hunch." Most of the drawers had devolved into junk drawers, overflowing with unbound papers and loose paperclips which together constituted so many lost opportunities. Only the shallow middle drawer showed any signs of regular use, loosely compartmentalized to accommodate pens, Post-its, address labels, and an unmarked notebook bound in black leather. Lou grabbed it and glanced through the first five pages. "There it is, Digital Poe… no wonder she couldn't remember the passwords, look at this gibberish." There were three columns for each entry: name, date, and a string of wingdings which were surely the result of Bertie trying to satisfy the requirements of so many different security keys anew every few weeks. *Password must be between 8 and 12 characters, contain at least one uppercase letter, one special symbol, and the phase of the moon at the moment of your nativity.*

"Wait," Daniel said. "Wait." But he didn't elaborate, just stood there as she jiggled the mouse. The monitor crackled to life and abruptly displayed Bertie's last email, saved as a draft and never sent – something about submissions to the *Poe Review*. Lou opened a new tab, struck one key and was gratified to see the address bar autocomplete the URL for Bertie's online banking portal. "Wait," Daniel said again, louder. "Cash is one thing, but—"

"But what? Aren't you curious?" She scanned the notebook for the most recent password listed under Chase Bank. When she hit *Enter*, a red exclamation mark popped up. Mismatch. The notification from her own banking app flashed through her mind. She brushed it away like a bothersome fly and tried again. No dice. She forgot Daniel was there until the floorboards wheezed underneath her as he leaned on the arm of the chair. He peered over her shoulder at the notebook and made a soft, glottal noise that sounded like disbelief.

"Bertie, you crazy old bat."

"What now?" Lou asked, annoyed by his powers of deduction and annoyed at herself for being so much less perceptive.

"It's a cipher. All the passwords— Hold on." He nudged her aside with one elbow and pulled up the Digital Poe landing page. A dropdown menu brought them to the interactive cipher tool. As he clicked around, characters lit up and whirred like the reels of a slot machine until something new clicked into place. "See?"

"See what, you showing off?"

Those pink patches glowed on his cheekbones again, so bright she thought she might feel the heat if she pressed her finger to his cheek. "It's just a good model," he said. "The most common letter in English is *e*. Then *a*, *o*, and so on. Bertie had so many passwords to keep track of I doubt she'd use random letters and numbers, so there must be some linguistic logic here. If we find the most used characters—"

"We can puzzle it out from there."

"Right." He was already tallying letters with faint pencil marks in the margins – so absorbed in the puzzle so immediately she wondered whether he remembered why they were cracking ciphers in the first place. She said nothing, afraid to break the spell, unsure whose heartbeat was thumping in her ears – hers or his or the house itself. Daniel made another small, triumphant noise and decided, "That has to be it." He reached across Lou to type the password and tapped the *Enter* key with a flourish. The browser went blank for a split second before Bertie's bank accounts materialized. They both leaned in closer, and the floorboards moaned.

"Whoa." Whatever Lou expected, it was more. "What about savings?"

Daniel scrolled down to the savings and retirement accounts. Froze. Muttered faintly, "Quoth the raven, *what the fuck*."

"Why go to the trouble of making a cipher that easy to crack?" Lou asked.

Daniel snapped out of his trance, took his hand off the keyboard. "I doubt she expected her own advisees to hack her home computer posthumously. I mean, she trusted me – with the house and everything."

"Okay, but consider it: What does she need a retirement for? She's as retired as she's ever going to get."

"You can't just empty an IRA like that."

"So pick an account, any account. We could take a life-changing amount without making a dent."

"Life-changing in the sense that we'd spend the next decade in prison, unless you have a convenient orangutan to frame."

"What if I did?" That stopped him – he didn't have a ready objection and she pressed her advantage. "Just think, if we *could* pull it off, who would it hurt? She doesn't have any descendants or dependents, except Gershwin. It's a victimless crime."

He was very quiet – leaning forward on the balls of his feet, like he was afraid to set his heels down and disturb the floorboards, rouse the house. She didn't interrupt, sensing he was perched on the edge of something and might be blown over one way or the other by the slightest wisp of interference.

"This… orangutan," he said, speaking with a sticky sort of difficulty, as if his jaw were wired shut. "Explain."

"Not an orangutan." She fought back a nonsensical smile. "Just a good old-fashioned phishing scam. Bertie was a documented Luddite, right? Nobody would think twice if she fell for one, if anybody even bothered to investigate." She chewed her lip, puzzling through the particulars. "It would have to come from her, from here, and we'd have to lay some breadcrumbs first, and cover our tracks afterward…"

He rolled his eyes. "Don't tell me how."

"I know a gal."

He folded his arms, shook his head. Looked sidelong back at Lou. "No bullshit?"

"No bullshit."

"You trust her?"

"I trust her to cover her ass and I've got dirt on her I've just been waiting to use."

His eyes narrowed. "Who?"

"My sister, Merel. She's hacked in every color hat you can imagine, but she specializes in social engineering because she's a bloodsucking sociopath."

"Runs in the family, huh?"

"Survival of the most unscrupulous. I'm not sorry."

"How nice for you."

"Remorse defeats the purpose, Montresor. Do you want me to call her or not?"

He returned the beetle to the bookcase and paused with his back to her, fingertips clinging to the edge of the shelf. "I want you to walk out of the room and do whatever you're going to do where I don't have to hear it… and I couldn't possibly stop you."

She was on her feet before he had time to change his mind. The smile flashed across her face in the safety of the shadowed hall. Her sneakers scuffed sparks from the carpet, and she marveled for a moment that the books hadn't caught fire by now. The hallway seemed to cave in around her as the passage probed deeper into the heart of the house – where the bedrooms must be, if there was any logic to the layout. Lou pulled her phone from her pocket and swiped the overdraft notice out of sight. She dialed Merel's number and listened to it ring four, five, six times. The call went to voicemail, but she expected it to. She tried the last door on her left and was pleased to have her architectural instincts vindicated. *Runs in the family*, Daniel had said, and so it did. So what? She let herself into the bedroom.

The coverlet was white matelassé gone yellow with age. A silk kimono blushing with cherry blossoms dripped from the bedpost, but the belt had come loose and spooled on the floor underneath. Something about serpents and innocent flowers flitted at the edges of her subconscious, but she couldn't quite grasp it before her phone buzzed in her hand, for the second time that day.

Unknown number. She answered on the second ring. "Hi, honey, how are you?"

"I told you not to call me on that line."

"Got you to call me back though, didn't I?" Lou wandered over to the dressing table – intrigued by the first picture frames she'd found in the house. She picked up a small silver one that must have been from Bertie's wedding, but the doe-eyed sylph in the white dress bore little resemblance to the craggy, hawk-browed harridan she'd known.

"What fucking *for*?"

"Oh, just to reminisce about old times." She set the frame down and reached for another – one of a dark-haired man she thought might be Bertie's husband, when he was younger. With a weird, queasy feeling she recognized the whey-faced likeness of Poe. "Specifically, Christmas in St. Louis and an odd call *I* got from the Tri-County Water Authority." There were a few other photos. No family.

Merel's voice dropped an octave. "What do you want?"

Lou tried to summon that wicked grin again, but her reflection in the vanity only looked uneasy. "I thought you'd never ask."

It was one of those wet and steamy southern summers where it stormed every day in the late afternoon. Squalls unfurled out of nowhere, clouds white as wildfire smoke – blistered and bloodless and boiling. Humidity pressed in on the house from all sides like a malevolent force.

Daniel sweated in the kitchen, relishing the precision of a gas range. His English basement apartment, too small by half even before Rosie moved in, had two electric burners built into the counter. The only oven was convection. He'd lived there so long he'd learned to hate cooking, but Bertie's kitchen was a minor paradise – not least because Lou's interest in it ended with the wine rack.

"Amontillado," she said, blithely uncorking a bottle and pouring the first of two generous glasses. "How original." When he refused the second, she said, "Suit yourself," and disappeared into the great room with both. He heard nothing for a while but the syncopation of the rain on the roof and the patio out back, the occasional snarl of thunder overhead. But she must have grown bored, because the tumble and creep of piano keys soon filled the staccato silences of the storm. The music sawed on his nerves, not because she played poorly but because she was so carelessly, artlessly *good*. She had instinct more than technique and a fittingly promiscuous repertoire, leaping across styles and centuries with offhand abandon. Beethoven's "Appassionata" metamorphosized into a passable rendition of "Papa Don't Preach." He listened without wanting to listen until she got sloppy – intoxication catching up with her, he assumed, until she said, "Gershwin. Gershwin, you asshole, *get down*." After a clang of wrong notes, he heard the cat hit the floor on all fours.

The domestic mundanity of the scene disturbed him. Until Merel planted the evidence and gave the green light to make the transfer they couldn't go anywhere – but what the hell were they doing playing house while Bertie lay unburied beneath their feet? He stabbed at the skillet with a scarred wooden spatula. At least the kitchen tile didn't sigh and groan like the floorboards in the hall. So many hard surfaces. Even the couch was uncomfortable – a stiff cream cabriole with batting bulging through the gashes in the satin stretched over each arm, as if the miserable thing had tried to slit its wrists. It was a beautiful house, or must have been once, but it didn't make much of a home.

His phone buzzed three times in quick succession, but the rattle of the case against the countertop was lost in the drumming of the rain, the ripple and glissando of the piano. He could almost pretend he hadn't heard it. He took the saucepot off the fire and poured pasta through a colander waiting in the sink. Steam rose like a mushroom cloud and mingled with the sheen of sweat at his temples. He turned to the second burner, where fresh tomatoes sizzled and burst and slipped out of their skins. Bertie had never cooked for herself and rarely ate meals, subsisting instead on hors d'oeuvres and desserts spooned straight from the jar or the can or the carton. The only fresh produce he'd ever seen her eat was a bunch of grapes plucked off a buffet table at one of those depressing academic events where the only incentive to attend was free food.

Despite her overbearing attention to the houseplants, she gave him free run of the garden, which was more like a jungle when he first took the job – fecund and feral and wildly overgrown. After two weeks yanking weeds, he unearthed a fishpond scummed over with algae but still supporting a dozen calico koi fish who gulped greedily at the surface when the water was disturbed. He fed them greens and chunks of melon ripened in the soft black soil, learned to recognize the Rorschach patterns on their backs. His grandmother always warned not to feed fish before a storm, but he never knew whether that was wisdom or some half-cracked superstition. On the off chance it was wisdom he refrained that afternoon, ducking outside just long enough to cut back the basil plant running riot under the kitchen window. He washed the best leaves and stirred them into the ripe red swirl of capellini. He shrugged off the disquiet. They hadn't eaten all day and they both had valid reasons to leave fingerprints all over the place. Starving wouldn't solve anything.

The phone buzzed again, but his hands were full. He left it behind and carried two bowls into the great room. Lou looked up from the keys, face bookended by the wineglasses standing at either end of the music shelf. One was empty, the other half full. Gershwin had curled up beside her, fluffy tail wrapped around him like a scarf. He opened his eyes when she withdrew from the music, tensed and flattened his ears as she swung one leg over the bench. Daniel handed her a bowl and they sat on the sofa and slurped in silence for a while, no conversation necessary with the rain and wind lashing at the house. He couldn't bike home in this monsoon, even if he wanted to. Not that he preferred being stuck there with Bertie and Lou. All the windows had fogged over, walling them in from the outside. Glass glazed and milky as a drunk man's eyes. The reflection of the room blurred to an impressionistic watercolor – inflexible furniture and decorative accoutrements bleeding together in a wash of bronze lamplight and viscous black shadows.

"Any word from Merel?"

Lou licked a smear of sauce from the edge of her spoon – a snakelike dart of her tongue, purpled by the wine. "Patience. She needs to set up a couple of dummy accounts to bury the scent."

"And then?"

"We do the transfer, she reroutes it through some third-party payment service, and we take it to our graves. Be cool, okay?"

He nodded, pushing his pasta around without enthusiasm. Lou opened her mouth again and a thunderclap came out – or so it seemed. With a deafening *boom*, the full fury of the storm broke right over the house. Every hair on the back of Daniel's neck stood on end, goosebumps erupting up his arms. The thunder died away, but something wailed in reply somewhere in the walls, a beam or a joist exhausted with propping the roof up for so long. Spooked by the sound, Gershwin dropped off the piano bench and slunk out of sight. Daniel reached for the bag he'd abandoned on the floor what felt like weeks ago. "You were saying?"

"Just wondering about earlier." Lou set her bowl aside. "What made you change your mind?"

He rummaged around in the bag, searching for an excuse as much as anything else, but he came up empty – intellectually overtaxed, perhaps, by the demands of that strange, catoptric day. What did it matter what she knew? They already shared their dire misdeed. The line was thin, he realized now, between conspiracy and mutually assured destruction.

"Rosie's pregnant," he said, with a preposterous swoop of relief. He'd known for two weeks but told no one else, maybe because that would make it more real than he could stand – or maybe because nobody else knew Rosie quite like Lou.

Her eyebrows rose again, in that expression of extravagant surprise. "Don't think I have to ask if that was planned."

"She's on the pill, but—"

"You have to take it every day."

He knew, she knew. And he should have known better – Rosie was consistent only in her inconsistency. She tried ten different outfits before leaving the house, tweaked her order in a restaurant until the waiter took the menus away, changed her dissertation topic so many times she still hadn't finished her first chapter even though she was starting her last funded year in the fall. If she even got that far, because by then she'd be how far along? He knew nothing about maternity, and neither did she.

"She wants to keep it." He looked up from his own ghoulish reflection, slanting across the coffee table. "Lou, I don't have a car. Where am I going to put a baby, in a basket on the handlebars? I can bike ten miles here and back because I couldn't keep the lights on last year without the extra cash from DoorDash." He hadn't even told Rosie that. The humiliation was too acute; he tried to hide how tired he was, how hard he'd worked for how long and how little he had to show for it. He flinched away from the memory of his parents' perennial complaint, *We didn't mean* that *kind of doctor.* "I ride my bike all fucking day, and I don't mind biking out here because I can always do more pickups on the way." As if that were the only reason. Cycling sedated his hypertrophic brain as nothing else did – but he had a few fail-safes, in case of rain. He'd gotten his rolling kit out of the bag without thinking.

"Have you… told her?" Lou asked. "I mean, that's life-changing on a whole other level. I think I'd rather go to prison." She watched his fingers work with inebriated intensity – gratified, perhaps, to learn he had his vices, too.

"I've told her. But it's not my body, is it?" Not his body carrying the thing – he couldn't call it that out loud, but it wasn't a baby, not yet, just a bundle of cells stuck together by bad judgment and biology. But it would be his body on the bike, his body bent over a desk, his body sweating and straining to make a buck to feed a family he didn't want or plan for. Rosie had never had a real job and approached her degree with all the impractical idealism of the costume dramas she devoured when she should have been writing. "You care if I smoke?"

Just one eyebrow this time. "Only if you don't share."

He inhaled as the thunder crescendoed and crested and dopplered off into the distance. The rain came in waves, slithered off the roof and dripped from the eaves, like the whole house was melting. He blew smoke at the ceiling, watched it unwind between the teardrop prisms of the brass chandelier. "She can't be logical about it at all." Weed made him unusually talkative. He offered the joint in Lou's general direction and felt her pinch it from his fingertips. "It's like she's possessed."

"Well, she sort of *is*," Lou said. "*This house has a high incidence of unpleasant happenings…*"

He wanted to laugh for one idiot moment before he remembered what they were talking about and groaned instead, the noise not unlike the self-pitying sighs of the floorboards, the rafters, the staircase. "God," he said, leaning back against the overstuffed cushions, trying to rub the exhaustion from his eyes. "What would you do?"

"Me, or God? Pretty sure those answers would be pretty different."

"You. *I was brought up a Catholic… now, I don't know.*"

She tapped the joint into a lotus-patterned cloisonné ashtray that was almost certainly intended to be decorative. "She's going to do what she wants to do, so I'd give her a good reason not to want to have a baby with you."

He squinted down the couch at her. "Like what?"

She sat forward, leaned toward him – slowly but suddenly, if such a thing were possible, some strange obliquity in the architecture bending time and space into sublime, phantasmatic shapes. He'd never looked at her so close before, eyes drawn in half a dozen directions at once – the tiny gap between her front teeth, the treacherous crevice between her breasts, the black widow inked behind her left ear in lines so precise it looked real. He could almost taste the wine, warm and metallic like blood on her tongue as she said, "Something's bound to… come to you." He couldn't move, transfixed by the smoke that spilled from her lips, entwined in her black-coffee curls. The brush of her hand inside his thigh stung him like an electric shock and he abruptly threw her off.

Her head hit the arm of the couch with a sound like a stone dropped on the hardwood floor. Sweat broke out on his brow again as the walls closed in, crushed the air out of the room. Lou squeezed her eyes shut with a laugh, then a small, startled gasp. Her fingers tangled in her hair as she groped at the back of her head. *"Ow."* It was so incongruously childlike he thought she might cry – or he might. His vision swam as he lurched off the couch, took her wineglass without asking and retreated to the kitchen. He dumped what was left in the sink, then grabbed the bottle by the neck and poured it out, watching it swirl away down the drain, the sound subsumed by the unrelenting rain. He turned the water on to rinse the basin and stood there gripping the lip of the sink, waiting for the dizziness to pass.

He didn't hear his phone at first, deaf to everything but the uproar inside his head. *Zzt zzt.* It spasmed off the counter and clattered onto the floor. He crouched down, turned it over gingerly, as if it were a piece of dead wood harboring grubs and worms and other creeping, crawling things beneath. Seven new texts, all from Rosie.

ROSIE But you said you'd be home by…

ROSIE Can't you come back before…

ROSIE We were supposed to…

ROSIE Earth to Daniel. Are you…

ROSIE There's nothing left over…

ROSIE I didn't have time today…

ROSIE Can you stop on your way…

He didn't need to read the rest of each message; his mind autocompleted as well as the keyboard. He realized he'd left the water running. The rush of the tap and the rain pulled him one way and then the other, with the sinister persuasion of a strong undertow. He was still for a moment, then dropped the phone in the sink and went back into the great room.

Daniel woke too early, stretched out as much as the cabriole allowed, the ceiling coming slowly into focus. In the weak light the chandelier was freckled with tarnish, and a long, osseous crack branched out from the canopy in a web of reticulated tributaries – the contour map of some imaginary river system. The rain had stopped sometime in the night, and the morning was eerily silent, except for the intermittent grumbling of Gershwin. The cat's claws pricked through his shirt and snagged his skin, rudely displacing the drowsy weight of some malformed, abortive dream. He sat up halfway and Gershwin meowed loudly in his face before leaping off his chest and stalking across the room. He made a tight little circle around one leg of the piano and meowed again, hackles raised. Daniel squinted toward the windows, sky hazy and pale as an egg white outside. Gershwin came back toward him, then darted away, repeated the maneuver with a strange, skittish insistence.

"What's with you?" He held one hand out, but the cat kept his distance, hissed faintly, then shot across the room and out the back door. "Shit!" Daniel bolted off the couch, jammed his feet into his shoes and stumbled outside.

The patio was dangerously slick, the garden swathed with mist, the humidity gone cold as old sweat on the stones and the leaves and the dark, dripping bark of the trees bowed over the house. Daniel ran clumsily, slipping on his shoelaces and the soft, splashy earth. Lou loomed so suddenly out of the brume that he almost crashed into her, nearly knocked her into the fishpond.

"Grab him! He's not an outdoor cat—" But Gershwin had already streaked past her, vanishing into a dense clump of roses, burgundy blossoms blown and soaked and shriveled as spent tissue paper.

"Relax." She looked absolutely unbothered, with a halo of riotous bedhead, sipping coffee from a chipped brown Delamere teacup. "If he knows his food is in the basement, he'll be back."

Daniel wanted to shake her for being so blasé about Gershwin, about Bertie, about the whole fucking thing, but he was no better, he knew that – in some ways probably worse. He stared into the flat black pond – his reflection and hers stretched almost as tall as the trees behind them. The highest gable of the house made a sharp, shadowed peak against the sickly sky.

"Heard from Merel?" he asked, prickling with impatience to be done with it.

She shook her head. "She's on California time, and the wire won't go through before business hours anyway."

He glanced at his watch – wondering how long she'd been up, whether she'd even slept. Maybe nothing sat as easy on her soul as he imagined.

"Some storm, huh?" Steam rose from the teacup, mingled with the thin, ghostly vapor in the air. "I'd drive you home, but—"

"Better if you don't." His phone was still in the sink. He had no idea what he'd be going home to, but going home with Lou would make it worse.

"No, I know." She slurped her coffee and said nothing else. They stood in roaring silence, louder than the loudest thunderclap the night before. Stalling. Waiting for a call that wouldn't come for another few hours. Now he was out of the ruinous old house, he didn't think he could go back in, gripped by the irrational conviction that its malignant influence was working on them both.

"Do you—"

A hollow *crack* interrupted the question. He watched in the glassy surface of the pond as a skeletal black bough broke off the trunk of the tree that bore it and fell heavily onto the roof. An acorn cap bounced into the water like a wrecking ball, smashing through the heart of the inverted mirror-house. Daniel and Lou turned to look. He thought he heard the wind again but realized – too late and too soon – that the sound had come from the structure itself: a low, laborious groan. He felt Lou's fingers close on his sleeve, heard her swallow a scream as the steep pointed gable buckled under the weight of the branch. The whole roof caved in with a grisly, earsplitting *crash* – walls shearing apart, ceilings collapsing into the rooms below in a tumult of splintered wood and pulverized plaster.

They stood side by side in mute paralysis until a dog began to bark, not too far distant.

Lou let go, turned toward him slowly. "Daniel, my dear, I'm thinking we should get the hell out of here."

"Right behind you." The neighbors might be out of sight, but they weren't out of earshot.

"Get your bag. I'll get your bike." She threw back what was left of her coffee and pitched the empty cup into the pond. He hadn't moved, and she gave him a shove. "Go or I'm going without you!"

He didn't need to be told again. The back door hung open at a strange, dangling angle and he ducked inside. The house was cracked wide open under the livid sky. The weight of Bertie's unfinished business must have been too much to support anymore – the study had pulled the roof down, countless books ripped from their bindings and strewn around the ruins of the great room. Loose pages fluttered around him like wisps of ash. The mirror over the mantel had cracked in half when it came loose and struck the marble, throwing shards of silver fifteen feet across the room. The chandelier had shattered the coffee table, precious prisms crushed into the carpet with the grit of common glass. Daniel's ears rang with the echo of the crash, fragments of his pale reflection watching him from every corner, every treacherous edge and angle. He dragged his bag from underneath the couch, fished his phone out of the sink, doubled back to snatch his wallet off a side table that was somehow still standing. A car horn blared in the drive. He took one last, dumbfounded glance, then left the house behind.

When he rounded the corner, Lou was slamming his bike in the back of her blue CR-V. "Get in!"

He clambered in as she rammed the key in the ignition. The radio came on with the engine and Sonic Youth screamed through the speakers – *Shoot, shoot shoot!* Lou hooked one hand behind his headrest and craned her neck to see over her shoulder. He fumbled for the seatbelt, watching one wheel of his bike spin dizzily as they boomeranged backward down the narrow gravel drive between the trees.

Lou was a natural-born getaway driver – they burst out onto the paved road and she yanked the gearshift back. They stared at the shell of the house at the top of the hill, then spoke at the same time.

"What now?"

"This never happened."

The dog still barked in the still morning air as they tore away toward town.

The next time Lou saw Daniel, Bertie had been dead for three weeks. A handful of students showed up to the memorial service and decamped to the nearest bar afterward. They settled around a high-top for ten in their exequial blacks, like a murder of crows. Lou came in late, leaving her car parked a few blocks away, counting on the stumble back to sober up before she got behind the wheel again. She'd never been very careful with her life; life had never been very careful with her. She slid onto a stool with a glass of sweet smoky bourbon, worth sipping slowly, and eavesdropped on the talk around the table.

"How old was she, anyway?"

"Not old enough."

"What a horrible way to go. Out there, all alone."

"I used to say my dissertation might kill me, but literally? Crushed under your own books? No thanks."

"I heard she was already dead—"

"But she was such a fucking recluse nobody thought to go looking until the house fell down."

"Daniel was there."

Lou looked up, surprised to find herself looking right at Rosie. Pale but wearing her usual pout, face framed by a dark little bob that would have looked severe on anybody with a stronger jaw. Black diminished her somehow. Daniel sat beside her but with just enough distance between them that anybody who didn't know better might have mistaken them for strangers.

"Daniel was there," she said again, to her glass – which could have been a mixed drink or diet Coke disguised as something stronger. "In the house, after she died."

Lou thought she saw a streak of irritation cross his face. He avoided her eyes but must have felt them, hers and everyone else's. He shifted, tugged at his tie. The old T80 peeked out of his sleeve, but the suit looked new. Unlike Rosie, he wore black well. "Just to feed the cat. No idea she was even there," he added, before anybody could ask. "She told me she wouldn't be home."

A shiver made the rounds, passing from one warm body to another until it reached Lou and the trail went cold. She sipped her whiskey. Licked her lips.

"That's so scary," someone said.

"I think I'd have nightmares," someone else declared.

"Fuck man, I'm sorry."

"Did you talk to the police?"

"Not much I could tell them. They told me."

Unlike Lou, who simply bided her time until she heard the story through the departmental grapevine. By then it was so misshapen by speculation and conjecture that she almost laughed. But nobody came near the truth, stranger than their wildest fictions.

She lost interest after that, carried by the currents of other people's conversation, the harmless noise of drunk adjuncts and graduate students cutting loose for one more night before the fall semester started in the morning. When her glass was almost empty, she made her way back to the bar. She was surprised to find Daniel there, waiting on the bartender to slide him a receipt.

"Fancy meeting you here."

"Couldn't miss the funeral party of the year." He signed the check without looking up, intent on the pen as he tallied the total. "*When I get a little money, I pay my rent... If any is left, I pay my respects.*"

Lou leaned back on the bar on both elbows – amused at the willful misquotation of Erasmus, which was probably misattributed to begin with. She risked a slipshod grin. Maybe he tried to return it. Maybe she'd never be sure. "Bertie would have loved this," she said, and he followed her eyes back toward the table, where the gossiping continued unabated. "Leaving so many little mysteries behind."

"You think so?"

"You don't?"

"I don't know what to think. Still a mystery to me." He dropped the pen and looked up at Lou. Inscrutable smile. Inscrutable shrug. "But I guess I barely knew her."

"My condolences."

She watched him disappear into the crowd, suddenly tired of drinking in public and keen to be drinking at home. She tilted her glass until one copper drop splashed down on the bar. One last libation for the crazy old bat.

"Another?" the bartender asked.

"Next time," she told him. "Close me out?"

"Your friend paid your tab. Said he owed you a drink, anyway."

She rolled the pen between her fingers. Shook her head and chewed her lip. Left a hefty tip and let herself out without saying goodbye to anyone.

After the feverish press of the bar, the dark felt fresh and weightless. The first whiff of autumn was in the air, or perhaps that was wishful thinking. She always felt that primordial itch to howl at the moon, to warm her blood over a bonfire, to lay last year's regrets to rest in soft hibernal earth. But what was put to rest sometimes came back to light and she wondered, would she blush to see her sins reanimated? The dozy indolence of the whiskey wore off faster than she wanted. She caught herself ruminating – asking, as always, whether she did shitty things because she was a shitty person, or if she was a shitty person because she did so many shitty things.

A breeze swept up the street and hastily made havoc with her hair. She pushed it back and brushed against the memory of a bruise. Some nights she wandered in and out of dreams, up and down the halls of the crumbling house, reaching around every dark corner in search of remorse, but could never find it, never grasp it, never hold it fast. Sometimes, to tame her restless hands, she ran her fingers through her tangled curls and savored the tenderness there.

The Professor
of Ontography

Helen Grant

"Don't come in," said Phoebe suddenly as the battered Morris Minor pulled in to the side of the road.

"But Phoebe…" said her mother reproachfully, her hands still on the steering wheel. She glanced up at the grey stone wall looming over them. "You know I'd love to see inside."

Phoebe did know. She imagined her mother wandering everywhere, poking into everything, saying "This is lovely" at the top of her voice. Or perhaps running a finger along a ledge or windowsill and saying "You'd think with all this money…" She felt guilty thinking this, but she was equally determined that it was not going to happen.

"I'd rather you saw it when I've got myself settled," Phoebe said. She paused. "Really, Mum."

Her mother was silent for a few moments. Then she said,

"But your trunk! It weighs a tonne. You can't possibly carry it to wherever your room is by yourself."

"I won't have to do that," said Phoebe confidently. "I'll ask the porters to help."

In actual fact she couldn't imagine asking the porters to do any such thing; they were far too grand. But she thought she could probably enlist someone else to help, or even drag the thing herself, heavy as it was.

"Phoebe…"

"I love you, Mum," she said, leaning over and kissing her mother's cheek. "But don't come in. Next time, okay?"

Her mother was still touching her face where her daughter's kiss had landed as Phoebe got out of the passenger seat and closed the door. She went around and opened the boot. The trunk sat end on; they'd had to put the back seat down to fit it in. It was absolutely brand new, with gleaming brass fittings, and as ominous as a sarcophagus; she couldn't imagine how she was going to move it herself. However, she gamely wrapped her fingers around the handle at the end and heaved.

The trunk barely moved, and she could feel the muscles in her back straining. Phoebe saw her mother turning in her seat, and knew it wouldn't be long before she was out on the pavement, trying to help. Worse, she might go into the porters' lodge and ask *them* to do it. She cringed with all the self-consciousness of her eighteen years, and pulled again, desperately.

Then, miraculously, help appeared.

"Need a hand?" said a male voice, and she glanced up into a rather good-looking face under a mop of blond hair.

"Yes please," she said gratefully. "It's really heavy." She stood back as he slid the trunk out of the back of the car and deposited it, end on, onto the road.

"Oof," he said. "I see what you mean."

He turned and scanned the street. "Oi! Toby! Come and help move this."

While he was doing this, Phoebe shot an anxious look at her mother, wondering whether she would get out of the car and interfere. But the older woman, eyeing the proceedings in the rear-view mirror, had evidently decided that she could best serve her daughter's interests by staying out of it. Phoebe sent up a silent *thank you*.

The two young men hoisted the trunk between them.

"Where to?" asked the one called Toby, and she had to fumble out the piece of paper with the staircase and room number on it. Then they set off, because it wasn't sensible to stand about holding such a weight between them.

Phoebe knocked on the driver's side window. When her mother wound it down she said, "Bye, Mum. I'll phone you at the weekend, alright?" Then she hurried after the trunk.

When Phoebe saw the staircase she knew she could never have dragged the thing up it by herself. Her room was on the second floor and when she got there, the two young men were standing outside it. The trunk was on its end again and she wondered about her books and shoes and bottles of shampoo all jumbled up together.

"Key?" said the one with blond hair.

"Oh. I forgot it," she said, and she could feel herself blushing.

He grinned. "Go and get the lady's key, Toby."

"You don't have to—" she began, but Toby had already started down the stone stairs.

She looked at the blond one. He was leaning against the door frame, looking comfortable. Then he put out a hand.

"I'm Charlie, by the way."

She stared at the hand for a moment and then she put out her own and shook it.

"Phoebe."

It was 1982, and she had just met the love of her life.

Charlie was reading Engineering, she discovered, the college having a particular tradition of favouring the sciences. Phoebe was going to read Classics, which the university called *Literae Humaniores*, and that was another thing about which she was rather self-conscious; the college had only recently begun to admit women, and she felt she ought to have chosen something robustly scientific and traditionally male, just to show them all. She couldn't help what she liked though, nor what she was good at.

The college was large and sprawling and although it was popularly known as "Old's" it was not simply "Old College"; it actually took its name from the fourteenth-century founder, whose name was Henry Oldys. Charlie's room was in a different building to Phoebe's. She traced and retraced paths between her room and his, the lecture hall, the library, the dining room and the buttery, with increasing confidence. After a couple of weeks she no longer lost her way trying to find particular rooms, and then she began to explore. There was a charming little chapel done out like a Wedgwood vase in blue with white plaster moulding, a tiny quadrangle with a handful of fruit trees, and a forgotten alcove housing an oil painting of the college founder. This last item was very dingy and it was hard to make out much of Henry Oldys beyond the yellow gleam of a bald head. However, underneath the painting there was a little gilded notice inscribed with the words *Henry Oldys, Master of ye College.* Phoebe had to screw up her eyes to read it.

She studied the painting for quite a while, but couldn't really pick out much in the murk. A pale patch, like the glimpse of a fish belly in dark water, was a hand resting on something. It seemed a little disrespectful that the founder's portrait should be in such a poor state, and tucked away like this, and Phoebe wondered whether there was spite in it. It was one of the many peculiarities of the college that the incumbent head of Old's was always known as the *Deputy Master*, due to a condition laid down by the founder that there should never be any *Master* other than himself, even after he was long departed. A good deal of wealth rested upon that condition, but Phoebe could imagine that holders of the post found it irritating. She thought it was quaint; that and the various other eccentric traditions and superstitions of the college were excellent material for her weekly telephone conversations with her mother. It wasn't as though she could tell her what she had been doing with her time between lectures and tutorials, since a lot of it had been spent in bed with Charlie.

By the end of the first term, Phoebe thought she knew her way around the college pretty well. It was a surprise, therefore, when one dark and blustery morning in January she found herself lost again. The room for a particular tutorial had been changed because a pipe had burst, causing water damage, and the new one was in an unfamiliar part of the college.

Phoebe went through a doorway she didn't remember having seen before; there was a worn red velvet curtain drawn to one side of it, and she had the impression it had always been drawn across before. Beyond it lay a long stone corridor, one side of which was studded with narrow windows like horizontal slits, too high up to see out of. She walked down it rather briskly, because she was in danger of being late. There was nothing on any of the walls – no pictures, no sconce lights – and the sound of her shoes rang out on bare stone flags. At the end she stopped, confronted by a heavy oak door set into a pointed stone arch.

Above the door in faded black lettering were painted the words: DEPARTMENT OF ONTOGRAPHY.

Phoebe stared. Ontography? She had absolutely no idea what that was. It seemed improbable that this was the way to the room she wanted, but she tried the door anyway, grasping the iron handle, which was black with age.

The door didn't budge. It was clearly locked. There was a keyhole, and on impulse she tucked her dark hair behind her ear, stooped and tried to peer through it. It was blocked; the key had been inserted from the other side.

Odd, thought Phoebe. She wondered why someone would lock themselves in, but without knowing what the discipline was, it was hard to guess why that would be necessary. She decided to look it up later. In the meantime, she thought she had better retrace her steps and try to find the proper room.

Much later, lying next to Charlie in his untidy room, she said: "What's ontography?"

"What?" said Charlie drowsily.

"Ontography."

"I don't know. Aren't you the languages buff?"

"I thought maybe it was a science," said Phoebe.

"Don't think so."

"Hmmm."

"Why do you want to know?" asked Charlie.

"Because I came across the Department of Ontography today and I wondered what it was."

"Rings a bell, but I can't tell you. Why don't you look it up?" He gestured vaguely. "There's a dictionary on the desk. It's Toby's – I borrowed it for that bloody essay."

Then he sat up and stared as she got out of bed and padded over to the desk.

"You really want to know, don't you?"

"Mmm," said Phoebe. She leafed through the dictionary. "It's not in here."

"Well, who cares?"

"I do. It's kind of… odd. A whole department and it's so obscure." She looked at him. "Don't you think?"

"I think," said Charlie, "that if you keep bending over that desk I'm going to get out of bed and come over there."

She put down the dictionary. "You have a one-track mind, you know that?"

"I like to think of it as intellectual focus. Come back to bed."

"Alright," said Phoebe. "As long as you promise to help me find out what it is."

"Anything," promised Charlie.

He tried to keep his word. The next day when they were having lunch in the buttery he said, "I looked for ontography in the big dictionary in the library, and it wasn't in there either. But without joking, you *are* the linguist. Can't you work it out?"

Phoebe considered. "Well, the *graphy* bit is easy – it means writing about something, or maybe describing it. *Onto* is a bit more difficult. It's the present participle of the Greek verb *to be*. So I suppose ontography might be the study of beings, or actually being."

"That's vague," said Charlie. He thought for a moment. "Perhaps it used to mean something, and doesn't anymore. There were a load of things that used to be considered sciences, like phrenology. And alchemy. When Henry Oldys was around, that was actually a science – I mean, he studied it. So it could be something like that, only..."

"Only?"

"I went to the porters' lodge to have a look on the board – you know, the one with the list of names, and the hooks for spare keys. And it's on that."

"The department?"

"Well, not the department. It says *Professor of Ontography*."

"Was there a name?"

Charlie shook his head. "No, just that."

"Doesn't mean there still is one. It might be old."

"I don't think so – I mean, they redid the lodge a year or two back. Wouldn't they have taken that out, if there wasn't one anymore?"

They looked at each other.

At last, Charlie said, "Why don't we just go down to wherever this Department of Ontography is, and have a look? We can ask them what Ontography is."

"Isn't that a bit…" Phoebe's voice trailed off. She couldn't think of quite the right word.

"They ought to be pleased we're expanding our minds," said Charlie.

"I suppose," said Phoebe. "Alright, then."

But when they found their way back to the spot where the corridor to the Department of Ontography was, the red velvet curtain was drawn across it, and behind the curtain the door was locked tight. Phoebe tried it twice, rattling the handle, but it wouldn't budge.

"Damn," she said.

"You've really got a bee in your bonnet about this, haven't you, Pheebs?" said Charlie.

She was a little shamefaced. "I suppose you think I'm nuts."

He grinned. "Not at all. Well, a bit." He put his head on one side. "I've got an idea."

The Dean's office was on the other side of the college, quite some distance from the Department of Ontography, and as they trotted across campus Phoebe began to entertain second thoughts.

"Maybe we should think about this," she said, glancing uneasily at Charlie.

"We're not chickening out now," he said firmly. "Anyway, why shouldn't we ask about it? Intellectual curiosity and all that."

He was increasing his pace, as though he thought he'd better get there before she changed her mind altogether. Phoebe opened her mouth to say something, but then they were hurrying up the stone steps, and the next moment the door was swinging shut behind them and the Dean's office lay directly ahead.

With enviable confidence, Charlie rapped on the door with his knuckles and went straight in, Phoebe following him.

The first thing they saw was an enormous polished desk, at which a middle-aged woman with half-moon spectacles and a gorgon-like expression was installed. The Dean's office lay beyond her, behind a further door which currently stood ajar.

"Yes?" said the gorgon peremptorily.

"I'm thinking of changing course," said Charlie.

"In the first instance," came the severe reply, "you should speak to your moral tutor. It is not—"

"To Ontography," he said, cutting across her.

There was a pause, and then the gorgon said, "*As* I was saying, in the first instance you should speak to your moral tutor. However, I can tell you that it is completely impossible to change to Ontography. There are currently no courses running in Ontography." She reached for a binder and began to leaf through it. "No. Nothing at all this year."

"Next year, then," suggested Charlie, but she was shaking her head.

"There are no courses in Ontography scheduled for next year, either."

"Well, can I speak to the Professor of Ontography, then?" Charlie did his very best to look appealing. "Honestly, I'm really keen. It's like a calling."

Phoebe bit her lip very hard to stop herself laughing, although she found Charlie's audacity almost terrifying.

"Who wishes to know about Ontography?" enquired a deep voice, and the corpulent form of the Dean appeared in the doorway behind the desk.

"I do," said Charlie.

The Dean emerged right out into the room, a ponderous figure in a dark academic gown.

"Tell me, young man, what is it that attracts you to Ontography?"

The Dean's bushy eyebrows rose as he waited for Charlie to reply.

"Um…" For a moment, inspiration failed Charlie. Then he said, "Well, everything really. It's… er… the intellectual challenge."

There was a silence.

"And what, pray, are you reading at present?" enquired the Dean at last.

"Engineering," said Charlie, with some relief at being asked a question to which he could easily reply.

"And how do you see Engineering as a preparation for Ontography?" asked the Dean. "What particular aspects would you say these two have in common?"

"Well… just… I suppose any two disciplines, there's the… intellectual…"

"Challenge," supplied the Dean dryly.

"Um… yes."

"And how would you, exactly, define the discipline of Ontography?"

"I…" Charlie shot Phoebe a despairing glance.

"It's the… um… study of *being*," said Phoebe nervously.

The Dean swivelled towards her with alarming speed.

"It is, is it? And do you also wish to change course to Ontography, Miss…?"

"Long."

"Miss Long?"

"I… I don't know," stammered Phoebe.

"You don't know. And your *friend* here doesn't seem to know what Ontography is. I submit that neither of you has a serious intention of studying Ontography, and that you are motivated by simple, and if I may say so, idle curiosity." The Dean's mouth pursed. "Or perhaps this is one of your idiotic undergraduate dares?"

Phoebe shook her head, not trusting herself to speak. To her amazement, however, Charlie made one last attempt.

"It's really not. If we could contact the Professor of Ontography, maybe we could just discuss it?"

"You may not," said the Dean. "The Professor of Ontography does not currently see students."

"His name, though…"

"… is none of your business." The Dean frowned. "I advise you to drop the topic, Mr…?"

"Stanford."

"Stanford, Engineering. Noted. As I say, I advise you to drop the topic if you wish to make a success of your time here at Old's. Levity, and may I say, unnecessary curiosity, are not appreciated. The same applies to you, Miss Long. And now, if you will excuse me…"

He opened his arms and shepherded them out into the corridor.

When they were outside the building, down the steps and out of earshot, Charlie said: "I don't believe there even is one."

"Why would they make up a professor?" asked Phoebe.

Charlie was silent for a moment.

Then he said: "That's what I'd like to know."

For some time, the matter rested. Charlie now seemed, if anything, more interested than Phoebe was; she became deeply embroiled in her studies, and her spare time was occupied with Charlie himself. And the Dean's warning bothered her more than it did Charlie, who found it easy to laugh such things off.

One lunchtime in the spring term, he dragged her to a quiet reading room at the far end of the college library and made her look out of the window.

"Here," he said, holding her by the shoulders. "Press yourself against the wall a bit."

"What am I looking at?" asked Phoebe, baffled. All she could see was a vista of uninspiring architectural features: a corner of flat roof, some ill-advised corbie-steps out of keeping with the other buildings, a row of disused chimneys. It was an overcast morning and the light was flat and grey, reducing contrast so that everything blended into everything else.

"Look," said Charlie in her ear, standing close. "Between the end of those step things and that bit of roof. The patch of green. Can you see it?"

"Ye-e-e-s," said Phoebe. "What's so special about that?"

"I think it's the roof of the Ontography department," declared Charlie. He was peering over her shoulder. "But I can't work out what the green is."

Phoebe glanced at him. "A metal roof?"

"Maybe," he said. "Could be copper. But it could be glass, too."

"I don't know," said Phoebe.

Charlie wasn't listening. "I came up here last week with Toby's binoculars and had a look," he said. "But I still couldn't tell."

"We're probably never going to know," said Phoebe.

"I really want to, though."

Phoebe heard the earnestness in his voice; she saw his brow furrow as he peered out of the window. It was very quiet in the reading room; there was nobody else here at present. She felt a surge of love for him – for his confidence, his determination, his funny little obsession with this obscure department, and yes, for his blond good looks. She turned and put her arms around him, and then she pressed her lips to his and did her best to make him forget about the Department of Ontography for a while.

In May there was a ball, and Charlie asked Phoebe to go. Since they were both students, Phoebe would have to pay her half of the ticket money, which was an even more colossal amount once she realised the price was – bizarrely – in guineas, and not in pounds.

She foresaw weeks of living on hot buttered toast and tea if she went. On the other hand, the thought of seeing Charlie in evening clothes, and posing as *jeunesse dorée* for an evening, was irresistible. She agreed, hoping her mother would advance her some birthday money towards the expense.

Afterwards, she remembered Charlie knocking on her door while she was putting her earrings in; she opened it, the second earring still in her curled fist, and there he was, looking as gorgeous as she'd ever seen him, and very slightly self-conscious in his evening wear. She saw his eyes widen as he took her in. She was wearing a taffeta dress in a deep shade of green and she'd had her dark hair put up and fastened with little gold pins.

Phoebe dropped him a curtsey. "Mr Stanford."

"Miss Long." He offered her his arm.

Phoebe put the missing earring in, took his arm, and off they went.

The ball was taking place in a huge marquee that had been erected in the quadrangle. There was rather loud music and a great deal of free alcohol – or at any rate, you didn't have to pay for it on the spot; Phoebe supposed the phenomenally expensive tickets covered it. Both she and Charlie drank more than they were accustomed to. The fancifully named cocktails were so sweet and sticky that it was hard to take them seriously, and after a few of them it was difficult not to become reckless and keep taking more.

They ate a lot of canapés that did not really soak up the cocktails, and danced to the thunderous music until there was a sheen on Charlie's skin and Phoebe's hair was coming down in places. It was becoming uncomfortably hot inside the marquee, and people were growing raucous. Eventually Charlie took Phoebe's hand and they went outside for some air.

Charlie was very drunk, drunker than Phoebe, and he was an opinionated drunk, whereas Phoebe was beginning to concentrate her attention on not being sick.

"Come on, Pheebs," he slurred, pulling her along by one hand while she tried not to stumble over the hem of her dress.

"Where're we going?"

He stopped and looked at her. He was swaying very slightly on his feet.

"Department of *Ontography*."

Phoebe stared back, open-mouthed.

"Never get in."

"Oh yes, we will. Over the wall," insisted Charlie. He began pulling her along again.

"But Charlie…"

It was useless; she couldn't seem to formulate a proper objection. She staggered along, doing her best to keep her balance on her high heels, which were beginning to hurt her feet. Outside the marquee, the night air was rather cold. She wished Charlie would slow down.

By the time they came to the outer wall of the building in question, the lights and music of the ball had faded in the distance, and Phoebe was limping.

She pulled her hand out of Charlie's and bent over, catching her breath.

"Go back," she suggested.

Charlie didn't reply. He was standing at the bottom of the wall, looking up at the slit-like windows. He tried a jump, his hands grabbing for the nearest windowsill, but it was too high; he had no hope of getting a purchase. He dropped, staggered back and looked up again.

"Charlie," she said.

His head was turning, looking for a way to get up. To the left there was a drainpipe bolted to the wall, an old-fashioned cast-iron one with heavy brackets that offered a solid toehold. Already his hands were on it, testing it.

"*Charlie.*"

It was no use. He was off the ground, moving clumsily but with energy. It made her feel giddy to watch him.

When he was most of the way up, he looked down.

"C'mon, Pheebs."

She knew it was hopeless before she started. She didn't think she could have climbed the drainpipe stone cold sober and in trainers; drunk, and dressed in a floor-length taffeta dress and heels, it was absolutely impossible. After several attempts she had simply scraped one of her arms and torn a six-inch-long hole in the hem of her gown.

Charlie kept going. He passed the windows and reached the top of the wall. He had some little trouble getting over the parapet, and Phoebe's heart was in her mouth as she watched him swaying. Then he heaved himself over it, and vanished.

Phoebe stood below on the paving stones and waited for him to stick his head over the top and tell her what he could see.

Perhaps a minute passed, and then another. There was no sign of movement from the top of the wall. Phoebe found herself shivering in the cold air.

"Charlie?"

She wondered what was happening up there. Had he moved away across the roof? Had he somehow managed to find a skylight or roof hatch that he was trying to pry up? Or was he just lying there, catching his breath as the alcohol fizzed through his body and the stars seemed to whirl above him?

"Charlie?"

She kept calling his name, but there was no reply. Then she thought she would try climbing again, but it was just as impossible as the first time, and she fell back with an impact that jarred unpleasantly through her left ankle. Her head was thumping and she felt hideously nauseous. How long had it been now? She wasn't sure. She began screaming for Charlie.

Her distress began to attract attention. A couple in evening wear appeared around the corner, and the girl seemed on the point of speaking to her when the robust and reassuring figure of one of the college porters came striding across the lawn towards them.

"Alright," he said to the couple. "I'll deal with this."

To Phoebe he said, "What seems to be the matter? It's Miss… Long, isn't it?"

Phoebe nodded. She was swallowing now, trying to force back panic and nausea.

"It's Charlie," she said, and then she was violently sick, all over the porter's shoes.

The following morning Phoebe awoke face-down on her bed, still in the torn ball gown. Her head, her whole body, seemed to pulse with the hangover. With infinite care, desperate not to provoke any more sickness, she rolled onto her side and sat up. Then she put her head in her hands.

Charlie, she thought. She remembered telling the porter something, and she had a vague memory also of someone bringing her back to her room – the girl from the couple who had nearly spoken to her, she thought. The porter had seemed angry. Where had Charlie been at that point?

Eventually she managed to get up and take off the taffeta dress. She pulled the remaining gold pins out of her hair. Then she grabbed her dressing gown and went to the bathrooms, where she stood under a hot shower for a long time. After the shower, she forced herself to drink a large glass of water and eat a piece of dry toast. Then, clad now in jeans and a sweatshirt, she went to find Charlie.

There was no answer when she knocked on his door, although she tried for a long time. There was a little semi-circular window above the door, so eventually she went and borrowed a chair from Charlie's next-door neighbour, and stood on it, so she could look through the glass. The room was empty.

Phoebe returned the chair. There was a strange cold feeling in the pit of her stomach. She went to the buttery and looked, but Charlie was not there. She thought he must be at least as hungover as she was, so it was unlikely he had gone off to the library or the lab. He wasn't the sort to try and run off a hangover either. She went back to her room, in case he had gone there, looking for her, but he hadn't.

Little bits and pieces were coming back to her. She went downstairs and outside, back to the spot where Charlie had climbed the wall.

There was a curl of party streamer on the ground, carried there on someone's shoe, perhaps hers or Charlie's. She looked up at the high windows, at the iron drainpipe, at the parapet. Then she looked down, at the drain under the pipe, and saw something winking in the morning sunshine. Bending, she saw that it was a cufflink. One of Charlie's cufflinks. Phoebe looked up again, biting her lip.

She knew that she and Charlie would be in trouble if she reported what he had done to anyone. Phoebe remembered the Dean saying that he advised them to drop the topic of Ontography if they wanted to make a success of their time at Old's. What if Charlie had gone off somewhere, somewhere perfectly reasonable that she simply hadn't thought of? He might come back and discover that Phoebe had landed them both in hot water.

She thought all of this over, looking down at Charlie's gold cufflink in her hand. Then she went to find the porter.

The night porter had gone off duty, but he had evidently described the events of the previous evening to the day porter. The man listened to what Phoebe had to say and then remarked, "So you must be the girl who…"

She wanted to sink through the floor, but she persisted. A horrible image was taking shape in her head, of Charlie lying unconscious on the roof of the Ontography department, a prey to injury or exposure. She explained again what he had done, and where, and begged for help.

The porter looked at her and then picked up the phone and called someone, holding the telephone in one hand and turning away to exclude Phoebe from the conversation. He spoke at some length in a low voice. When he had hung up, he turned to Phoebe.

"We'll have someone check the building in question."

He seemed to be waiting for her to go. Phoebe hesitated. She was not as confident as Charlie and yet she could not bear to leave the matter with the porter in such a desultory way. She assailed him with questions.

Could she go with the person who checked the building? —No.

Could she at least go and wait outside? —No.

Could she stay *here* and wait to see what they said? —No.

"Look, Miss," said the porter in the end, "if we find anything, someone will come up and let you know, alright?"

She had to be content with that. She went upstairs and tried to read something, her eyes on the clock. Unable to settle, she went over to Charlie's room again. There was still no reply to her knock. She wandered through the quadrangle where an army of cleaners were sweeping up splintered plastic glasses and party poppers; no Charlie. She tried Toby, and Toby came to the door of his room looking very much the worse for wear, but unable to tell her anything of Charlie's whereabouts.

Later, she went back to the lodge and they told her they had searched the building where the Ontography department was and found no trace of him.

"Are you sure, Miss," asked the porter meaningfully, "that he isn't spending time with someone else?"

"Of course I'm sure!" snapped Phoebe. Her head was beginning to throb again.

It took her several days to persuade the college authorities that something was genuinely wrong. Charlie missed a lecture, and then a class, but it was not unknown for students to do that, and if he *had* gone off with someone else, then of course he wouldn't have been in his own room…

At last someone was induced to contact Charlie's parents, in case he had taken it into his head to go home suddenly. He hadn't. The college spoke to the police in a low-key sort of way; a constable spoke to Phoebe but she felt that her account of events was not being taken seriously – she had been drunk on the night of Charlie's disappearance, after all. Who knew what she had *actually* seen?

Phoebe could feel herself descending into something she couldn't name, a morass of terrible emotions. At last she went to the place where the red curtain hung across the door and tore it back, and beat on the door, shrieking for Charlie, until they came and dragged her away.

Afterwards, through the fruitless investigation and all the weeks and months of her recovery, she could never be quite sure that she hadn't heard her name floating back through the locked door in a voice that was faint and anguished, but still recognisably Charlie's.

Love eluded Phoebe from then on. She thought sometimes that it was because Charlie had vanished; she never found out what had happened to him, and that meant that he could, in theory, reappear at any time. There was no line to be drawn under the affair. When she imagined him reappearing, even many years later, he was always exactly the same as he was in 1982: fair-haired, blue-eyed, unwrinkled. With him varnished into her memory she couldn't give all of herself to anyone else.

After the breakdown, she left education altogether for a while, and when she went back, it wasn't to Old's. But she decided academia was where she belonged, even if occasionally she had the uncomfortable feeling she wasn't moving on. In her thirties she tried marriage with a friend, but it wasn't sufficient, at least for him, so she found herself alone again, with a new name, and nothing to throw herself into but work. She moved up, and up, shining like a solitary star with no gravitational pull to anything else. Eventually, when she was in her fifties, a post came up which was absolutely perfect for her – and which happened to be at Old's.

Even as late as the night before she moved back, Phoebe wondered whether she was doing the right thing. Would simply being there reawaken the desolate eighteen-year-old walled up inside herself? People spoke about closure, but she didn't think it would offer her that, either. Whatever had happened to Charlie that night remained a question mark. If a body had later been discovered in a loft space or wedged into a disused chimney, she was pretty certain she'd have heard about it; someone would in kindness have sought her out and let her know. But no word had ever come.

That night as she prepared for bed, she studied herself in the bathroom mirror and thought: *You can cope with it. You're a grown-up now.*

And that was true – the grown-up part, anyway. Phoebe looked good for her age, but she was no longer young. There were thick streaks of white in her dark hair, and subtle lines all over her face. She had left Charlie, eternally twenty years old, far behind her.

She looked down, spat toothpaste into the sink, and then turned out the light and went to bed.

—

For the first few days at Old's, Phoebe never went anywhere near the scene of Charlie's disappearance. She had no reason to; her tutorials and lectures were to be given in another part of the college, and all the other things such as the dining hall and the library were at a distance too. And then there were a great many meetings to be scheduled, and altogether there was no time available to explore the college again. She was not consciously aware of avoiding the building that had housed the Department of Ontography back in 1982. She was somehow aware of its location in relation to herself as she went about her business, and knew that it was a thing she would have to face in the end. But not yet – no, not yet. She supposed that by now, forty years later, it would have been cleared out, changed, remodelled. It might have gone altogether and been replaced by some sleek modern creation in metal and glass, drenched in bright light and full of the sound of hurrying feet. As for the curiously inactive professor, he could not possibly still be at Old's after all this time, and she hardly thought the college would have installed a successor.

After ten days, however, she had to go over to that side of the college for an afternoon meeting. She rounded a corner and there was the stretch of wall with its curious narrow horizontal windows set too high up to see through. In the autumn sunshine it looked nondescript, even a little dowdy. All the same, Phoebe felt her heart thudding. She stood there for a moment, her arms around the files she was carrying, and stared at it.

It will be different inside, she said to herself. *After all this time.*

She went unwillingly towards the wall. The same iron drainpipe was still there, the brackets a little rustier than before. Phoebe went over to it and looked up; then she looked down, at the drain, as though she expected to see a gold cufflink winking there.

Of course there was nothing, except a handful of flame-coloured autumn leaves.

She went to the designated meeting room and found a note taped to the door, saying that the meeting had had to be cancelled at short notice because someone was suddenly unavailable. Phoebe stood there indecisively. There was time to go to the buttery and get herself a coffee before her next meeting in an hour's time – it made perfect sense to do that; it wasn't as though she felt at all nervous at the prospect of looking for the Department of Ontography. Then she knew she had to *prove* to herself that it didn't make her nervous.

Even after all this time, she found her way there unerringly. Several turns of the corridor, and there was the red velvet curtain, looking even more disreputable than it had in 1982. Only in such a place as Old's would a thing so tatty go unreplaced. It was half drawn back, the door behind it partly visible.

Phoebe went over, juggling the files, and stretched out a hand. She assumed it would be locked, but the handle moved under her fingers, and the door opened. She stepped inside, into the stone corridor. Though she had only ever been here once before, it was dreadfully familiar. There were no decorations on the walls, and the light slanted down from those long high windows. She made her way towards the door at the far end, her footsteps resounding smartly on the flagstones. Even before she got there, she could read the words DEPARTMENT OF ONTOGRAPHY in faded black paint.

Phoebe went right up to the oak door. She tried the handle of this one too, but it didn't budge; the door was locked fast, as it had been before. She stood there for a moment, and then on impulse she laid her cheek against the panel, pressing her right ear to the wood.

After, as she almost *ran* back down the corridor and drew the door shut behind her, yanking at the curtain with a hand that trembled, as she hurried away to the fresh air and the open sky and the little knots of students standing about the quad, she told herself that she had *not*, definitely *not*, heard her name uttered faintly and hoarsely on the other side of the door.

That night it was formal hall in Old's, the first Phoebe had attended since her return to the college. She had an instinctive feeling that the presence of so many people, the murmur of conversation, the clinking of cutlery, the light reflected from the glasses and the gilded frames of the portraits on the walls, would be reassuring. It would remind her why she had allowed herself to be lured back to Old's; it was a grand, ancient, traditional place. Its history stretched far further back than her own melancholy experience. She took a little wine with her meal, feeling its warmth spreading through her, and tried to feel part of something bigger than herself.

It didn't work. Phoebe felt subtly excluded. Conversation ebbed and flowed about her but she never seemed able to dive into it; instead she found herself silent, thinking of another time that only she remembered, another set of fresh young faces, long since faded. There was a hard, brittle edge to the clash of cutlery and glasses that hurt her ears. Even the wine lay sour on her stomach. She pushed the food around her plate listlessly.

Did I do the right thing, coming back? she asked herself again.

When the coffee arrived at the end of dinner Phoebe exerted herself, feeling that the meal was fast becoming a familiar instance of her failing to engage with others. She turned to the man on her left, a lean and rather hunched individual in a tweedy suit, who had shovelled his food into his mouth with great alacrity throughout the meal, saying little.

"The food was very good, wasn't it?" she said, for lack of another opener, and he looked at her, startled. He was older than she had thought – older than she was – with a long upper lip and pouches under his eyes.

"Yes," he said, and then, "well." After that he stopped, and Phoebe wondered whether he had been going to qualify the "yes" and thought better of it.

"I suppose you know everyone," she said, and he nodded.

"Yes."

"I'm new," she said, hoping to enlist sympathy, but all he said was "Yes" again.

There was little to invite further conversation, but she found herself persevering.

"I was here a long time ago," she said. "As an undergraduate. I suppose everyone will have changed – the older people will have left, I mean, and new people arrived." She hesitated, and then it came out in a rush. "I was wondering… Is there still a Professor of Ontography?"

"Ontography?"

"Yes."

A few moments drifted past.

"I daresay," the man remarked in the end, "that you would be hard put to define *Ontography*."

"Well," said Phoebe, "I suppose…" She paused. "But is there? A Professor of Ontography, I mean?"

"I couldn't say," came the laconic reply. The man addressed himself to his coffee cup and Phoebe gave up the attempt. They did not exchange another word.

After formal hall had ended, Phoebe dropped by the porters' lodge on the pretext of checking for a non-existent delivery. Rather against her expectations, the board with the staff names and the hooks was still there and while the porter was checking for her parcel she leaned over the counter and studied it. At the very bottom she read: *Professor of Ontography*. Her eyes widened.

"Looking for someone in particular?" said the porter, and she realised he had turned back to her.

"Um… no. Not really."

"No parcel yet, I'm afraid," he said, looking at her with a quizzical expression. "Try again tomorrow."

Phoebe gave him a wan smile. She went outside, into the dark, thinking that she should go back to her lodgings and look at some papers for the following day. Instead, she found herself irresistibly drawn across the college campus to the building with the curious high windows. There were lamps lit, and she found her way perfectly easily, but the air was damp, even a little foggy; in the large quadrangle the edges of everything looked a little blurred. The sound of her footsteps had an odd, flat quality.

When Phoebe came to the stretch of wall she stopped and looked up at the long windows. They were dark, as one might have expected;

it was well after working hours. Feeling self-conscious, she stepped close to the wall, and listened. It was a still night; she picked up feet on flagstones some distance away and a burst of excited voices, and then silence which stretched out for minutes.

Nothing, she said to herself. *Or at any rate, nothing that isn't from inside my own head.*

Phoebe could believe it, that she would imagine Charlie calling for her. In a way he still did – psychologically. Somehow she had failed, not knowing what had become of him. She leaned against the wall, putting her hands over her face. At last, when she began to shiver with the cold, she went home, her head bowed.

Later, as she lay alone in bed, she said to herself: *I will put it behind me; I will forget.* But when at last she fell asleep, she dreamed of the Gothic spires and corbie-steps of the college, of stone corridors and unlit windows, and over them all drifted a thin, hoarse voice calling *Phoebe, Phoebe...*

The next evening, as she huddled in her sitting room over a large glass of malt, she realised she was going to have to get into the Department of Ontography. She knew now: the wound was still fresh; she had to look. The question was, how to manage it? The outer door was sometimes open, but the inner one seemed to be kept locked.

There might, she supposed, be a spare key in the porters' lodge, but she could not think of a plausible excuse to ask for it, and the place was never left unattended, so she couldn't simply take it. She had an instinctive feeling too, that letting anyone else know what she was up to would lead to trouble.

She sipped the malt, and put her head back to stare at the ceiling, and eventually an idea came to her.

Phoebe had grown up in a ramshackle Edwardian house, which had quite as many draughts coming in around the edges of the windows and under the doors as Old's did. Once she had shut herself up in the dining room in a fit of mischief, and turned the key on the inside. Her mother would be quite unable to get in, she had judged gleefully. In this she had been mistaken. Her mother had slid a large piece of paper under the door, and then she had taken a knitting needle and poked the key from the outside, pushing it right out of the lock. It had fallen onto the sheet of paper, which she had then drawn under the ill-fitting door. A second later she had had the key in her hand; she had opened the door and Phoebe had been rewarded for her misdemeanour with a resounding slap on the leg.

She thought she would try this same technique with the door to the Department of Ontography.

Phoebe did not possess any knitting needles, but in her kitchen drawer she found something that would do just as well: a long slender metal skewer. It had a wickedly sharp point, so she stuck a cork onto the end and then she put it at the bottom of her bag so that she could carry it about with her, along with a folded sheet of paper. She did not expect to find the door behind the curtain open the next time she tried it, nor did she. For three and a half weeks, whenever she dropped past and tried it, the door was always locked.

At last, late one Sunday afternoon, when the college was at its drowsiest, she found the door unlocked. It was very quiet, and the sound of the outer door closing behind her was crisp and loud. Phoebe walked down the corridor doing her best to tread softly, and feeling in her handbag for the skewer.

When she got to the second door, with the legend painted above it, she stooped and peered through the keyhole. Sure enough, the key was on the other side. Then she knelt and examined the bottom of the door. As she had hoped, there was a gap between wood and stone. She took out the sheet of paper, smoothed it out as best she could, and slid it under the door. Then she inserted the sharp end of the skewer into the lock and pushed. If the bit had been turned to one side, she supposed it would be impossible to push the key out of the lock, but it hadn't been; with a little clatter that made her freeze, the key fell out of the other side of the door. She grasped the edge of the paper and pulled it very gently towards her. The key came with it.

Phoebe stood up, the key in her hand, a queasy kind of triumph in her heart. She inserted this into the lock, and it turned fairly easily. She began to push the door open, hardly aware that she was still grasping the skewer in her left hand.

At first she could make out nothing at all; ahead of her was simply darkness. She put out her right hand and felt some kind of heavy material. It was something like a blackout curtain. She grasped it, disliking the coarse feel of it and the mouldy odour it exuded, and pulled it aside.

The area beyond was very dimly lit; there was another of those high-up, slit-like windows, but it was partly hidden behind a towering glass and wooden case that filled most of the wall. Of the contents of this case she could make out very little, but against the opposite wall stood its twin, and the meagre light fell directly on the upper part of that. Phoebe saw that it was crowded with glass jars and bottles, seemingly extremely old and of a very evil appearance – the seals were blackened with age and the liquid inside was brownish and murky. Some contained animals – cycloptic rabbits, two-headed lambs – and others that appeared to be human body parts. Phoebe saw a puffy white hand pressed up against grimy glass as though it had been stuffed with some force into the jar, and next to it several ears nestling on a bed of gritty sediment. Her gorge rose and she tried to tell herself that this must be some kind of store room for antique samples; certainly she could not imagine them in any modern display.

Every sense was on red alert now. Her nostrils flared, taking in the odours of preserving fluids and something else – something burnt. Her eyes strained in the dim light, picking out other and more repellent shapes within the jars. Her ears detected something too – a light pattering, as though something were running about underfoot close by. Rats? She could not have said why, but she thought it was something bigger than that – a cat, perhaps, or a very small dog. And then, like a distant sigh seeping through the air, she thought she heard her name.

"Phoebe…"

She pressed her hands to her ears, the skewer sticking out of her fist like a dagger. She did not want to hear – she *refused* to hear.

Turn, she thought. *Run*. But she knew she wouldn't. Even as the dead weight of dread settled on her, she knew she had to know.

At the end of the room there was another oaken door, a little ajar. Phoebe went up to it, and pushed it right open.

Inside, the space was larger than she had expected, although so cluttered that it was hard to gauge its full extent. Looking up, she saw that the roof was of green glass, but so filthy that the light only penetrated through the clear spots here and there, and patched in one place with a rusty sheet of metal. A fire was burning quietly behind a glass screen. There was a great wooden table in the centre, but not such a table as anyone would eat from; the surface was pitted and scarred as though things had been hacked and sawn up on it. There were more of the cases crowded with glass jars, and in one of them, a very large one, Phoebe saw a human head. She didn't think, even for an instant, that it could be Charlie – it was nestling on a great bed of tangled reddish hair and was very clearly female. But she was so horrified and incredulous that she couldn't stop looking at it. As she drew closer, nausea roiling in her stomach, she saw it *move*. The mass of hair trembled; the lips parted.

Phoebe stumbled back, her eyes wide, and clattered into something, which fell to the floor. Once again she heard something skittering about behind the furniture. Then it fell silent. She held her breath, staring at the jar.

You imagined it, she thought. She shifted the skewer to her right hand, tightening her grip.

Phoebe knew that this was all wrong. It was more than a repository for old biological samples. Someone had been working here. She looked at the gouges on the surface of the table, at the dark stains on it and underneath it. She looked at the crania that grinned from high shelves, at the crocodile suspended from the ceiling ribs on wires, at something that looked like sheets of vellum, but with *hair* at one end.

That pattering came again – a little hesitantly, a little closer than before.

Phoebe wondered if she had taken leave of her senses. Did the college authorities *know* about this place, these things? They must know; it was impossible that anything like this could exist within the college walls without them knowing. But how could they tolerate it?

She heard a creak then, so tiny and stealthy that it was barely audible, and Phoebe turned. In the far corner, she now saw, there was a large high-backed chair with carved arms, and from it someone was rising. He was clad all in black – the bombazine of academia; all that clearly showed were his pallid hands and the great white egg of his skull, looming up out of the deepest shadow.

Phoebe knew him at once: Henry Oldys, the Master of Old's. Paralysed with terror, speechless, she watched him approach, moving stiffly at first but with increasing vigour as he closed in on her, hawk-like, his dusty robe outspread like wings. She could *smell* him, the disgusting off-meat stink of him. Nearer he came, and nearer, and then as he reached for her she broke; with her back to a glass case she couldn't run so she stabbed with the meat skewer, more and more wildly, until suddenly the point of it slid home in an eye socket. She let go of the end and slipped to the side, out of his failing grasp, her ears full of his dreadful keening. She crawled away, under the bench upon which he had conducted his experiments into being, and crouched there, shivering, until the terrible sound had stopped. Then she raised her head, listening. Her hands were wet.

"Phoebe…"

She knew now that she had passed over some frontier; she was hearing things she could not possibly be hearing. First her name, and then that pattering again as something ran about the floor, circling her. She put her arms around her knees and huddled there, looking, listening.

Directly in front of her there was a patch of open floor illuminated by a slender shaft of light from one of the windows. She focused on that, on that small spotlight in the middle of the dark and grime.

After a while, something came. She heard the little footsteps again, the skittering. They slowed, and then it stepped into the patch of light.

It was Charlie's head. The blond hair was matted, and his skin was grimy, but she'd have known him anywhere. Below the head were a great many legs with bulbous little joints; those were what Phoebe had heard running about. In the middle of the legs hung a shrivelled bladder, designed to provide just enough air for speech. His face contorted with strain and slowly, painfully, the bag inflated.

"Phoebe," said Charlie, in that thin, hoarse voice. "Phoebe, help me. Help me, Phoebe."

And Phoebe screamed.

ꟼHOBOS

Tori Bovalino

On the evening of the penultimate ritual, once the scavenger hunt was finished and won, the neophytes were ordered to meet at the House when the clock struck midnight and the darkness was thick and black. Mila Orlicker made her way down Fifth with her hands deep in the pockets of her trench coat. She chewed on her own annoyance like a hearty meal, waiting for a reluctant end to the frustration that wouldn't come. She should've won the hunt, should've put the pieces together faster than Kurt Proctor and Hannah Locke. Not that it mattered – speed was not the goal; only completion. But she hated the sinking in her stomach when she'd charged into the cavernous halls of the Cathedral of Learning, up the stairs, and into the Austrian Room to find Proctor and Locke sitting at the table with Ian Gamble. She'd beaten Patrick Carmichael and Julia Riker, but that wasn't enough. She wanted to be first. She wanted to be the *best*.

But that was no matter now. Initiation into the Order of

Prometheus called for the completion of nine challenges scattered across the fall semester, and she'd been close to the top rankings in five of the eight they'd finished. She tried to cling to that thought, the memory of watching Proctor's smile fall time and time again instead of his smug grin from earlier that evening.

It would not do to be upset. That was not the behavior of someone in Prometheus – at least, she didn't think so. She took a deep breath on the sidewalk in front of Elbrus House. The House was an old, sprawling Victorian, settled deeper into the lawn than its neighbors. In her opinion, it was the jewel of the Shadyside neighborhood it lived on, so heart-achingly beautiful that she sometimes felt her breath catch just looking at it.

And to think, she wasn't just a watcher anymore, an observer on the street. Mila kept her head up as she walked down the long path to the front door and typed her code – her very own code – on the PIN pad. The door chirped happily; the lock clicked. Every time she did this, her heart fluttered, expecting the keypad to glow red, for the quick buzz to sound that meant she was denied entry – but never did. This was her house, her place, and soon enough, it would be permanent.

One more trial.

She stepped into the warm parlor of Elbrus House. Straight ahead, the mahogany-banistered stair wound up four floors, through the floor of study rooms and offices and the lush rooms where upperclassmen in Prometheus lived. She hung her coat and scarf on the great wooden coatrack, carved to look like hands reaching up to bring down God.

Ian waited in the foyer. One of the brothers had lit the fire before they arrived and laid out the cut crystal glasses on the low table, decanted the bourbon. Mila nodded to Ian and retrieved a great round ice cube from the insulated container on the table. She made Gamble his bourbon, neat, then poured the amber liquid over the ice in her own glass.

"You did well today," he said to her, but his eyes had none of their regular spark. If anything – Mila hesitated, halfway to the wingback chair next to the fire, the one she and Proctor always silently battled over – if anything, Ian Gamble looked inexplicably scared.

She kept a keen eye on his face as she leaned back in her chair. Gamble had dark, expressive eyes and a mouth that made secret-keeping impossible – they did not pass his lips, but she could read every quirk of those small muscles, every unsaid word, every half-smile or pursed lip. He was the kind of boy she could've fallen in love with, Mila thought every time she looked at his bitter-coffee eyes. New England stock, hair the color of freshly turned earth, handsome in the way of those who never *really* had to worry. She hated herself for it, all the posturing of growing up with*out*, but she trusted him implicitly.

"You okay?" Mila asked, the briefest break in propriety. Gamble was their mentor, their leader into the secrets of the Order – he did not need their help, nor their support, and he reminded them of this constantly. He was superior in every way.

But Mila was his favorite. And Gamble's mouth thinned to a line, the revelation of *you're going to hate this, I'm going to hate this* written so clearly between chin and philtrum that it was almost worse than him speaking the words to her out loud.

"Mila," Gamble said. The others, he called by their last names:

Proctor and Locke, Riker and Carmichael, in the way of former private school boys around their kin. But when they were alone, she was always Mila, sweet and soft in his muted baritone. And when they weren't alone, he barely addressed her at all.

"Ian," she replied, holding his gaze. She wondered, sometimes, when she was a full member of Prometheus, when they didn't need all this posturing... what could *happen* between them.

His eyes flicked to the doorway. The others would need to come in the same way as Mila – they'd hear the moment the door opened. Gamble sipped his drink, set it on the low table, and aimed his knees at her. His gaze was low, urgent.

"I need you to know. This is the last thing, the final sacrifice, that the Order will ask of you. Just do it, and it's all over. You're done."

His eyes were too intense – Mila looked away at the fire, but it was too bright, so quickly glanced down at her bourbon glass. She hated bourbon, truth be told, but it was one of those small Prometheus quirks, one of those concessions she made to prove herself to them. She took a sip of it, cold as ice, burning all the way down her throat.

"Is that a warning?" she asked. "Have I not proven that I can do anything you ask of me?"

"It's different, this time," Ian said.

The door opened and with it, the sound of raucous laughter echoed on the stone floor of the foyer. It was Carmichael and Proctor, both in trench coats and leather gloves that they didn't bother to leave on the coatrack. Carmichael discarded his coat on the piano bench, revealing a checked suit over a starched white shirt, open at the throat. The pin on his lapel was probably worth Mila's entire yearly scholarship. Proctor was still laughing as he tossed his cap on top of Carmichael's coat – it looked like it belonged to somebody's grandfather.

In her skirt and sweater, she felt horribly underdressed. There was no way to guess the code for these meetings – once Proctor had appeared in a full tux, straight from some sort of alumni dinner, while Carmichael wore gray sweatpants and an old rowing hoodie. The girls were just as hard to read, and even less likely to inform her. Riker and Locke came through the door Proctor had left open, shucking their coats to reveal jeans and T-shirts.

"Chair stealer," Proctor grumbled with a glare in her direction, settling himself on the sofa next to Locke. He was never creative in his insults. In her finer moments, in his weaker moments, she felt quite like Cyrano, schooling him in the methods of language his slippery STEM education hadn't managed to impart.

Since they were all assembled, Ian rose from his chair and went to stand in front of the fireplace. He gazed across them, looking at each in turn in a way that made Mila's skin itch. She didn't mind being looked at, but she hated being *seen*.

"Neophytes," Gamble said. He had the perfect voice for rituals, clear and solemn. "Nine of you were invited to the Order. Only five have stood the trials, strong enough to stand before me now. And yet, your greatest task still awaits."

He turned around and retrieved a stack of envelopes from the mantel. Mila was closest to his bourbon hand – she saw the way his fingers were tight on the cut crystal glass, knuckles white. Proctor took the opportunity of silence to whisper something to Locke.

She blushed red and covered her mouth – plans for later, possibly. Mila was pretty sure they were sleeping together.

"I must warn you," Ian said, hesitating. "The final gauntlet – you *must* complete it. Speak now and leave if you feel you are not up to the challenge. You know what the Order asks of you, what we've always asked of you."

She did know: On the night where they'd been blindfolded, dragged into the woods, and lined up in front of Ian Gamble with their hands tied behind their backs, he'd asked for all of them. Everything they had.

In return, they'd get everything they wanted.

Mila gritted her teeth. If she was going to leave, she would've done it a while ago.

Gamble let the beat of silence swell, then nodded. He set his glass down on the mantel where the envelopes had been and distributed them to the five: creamy white, heavy paper sealed with wax, embossed with the seal of the Order. Though she didn't admit it to anyone, the envelopes always reminded Mila of a British panel show her freshman-year roommate loved.

Mila's hands shook as she broke the seal. Next to her chair, on the sofa, Julia Riker sucked in a breath.

The words on the paper didn't make sense to her. Mila looked up, ready to ask for guidance, but Gamble had turned his face. He had his hands braced on the mantel, looking away from all of them, staring straight into the fire – *Don't ask me what I've done*, that mouth said.

Carmichael was the first to break. To *laugh*. "Okay, Gamble. Game's up. Give us the real task."

Mila watched the lines of Ian's back, the tension in his shoulders. He didn't brag about his workout regime like Proctor did, but she'd seen him at the campus gym more often than was totally comfortable.

"This isn't funny," Julia said. She'd crossed her arms over her chest, the task clenched tight in one fist.

"Gamble?" Mila said before she could hold back that one word.

This was what got him. Ian straightened robotically, squared his shoulders. Turned back to them. "Carmichael. Riker. Proctor. Locke. Orlicker." He stared straight ahead, face blank – he'd never been so difficult to read, and that made the whole thing worse. Mila's heart raced in her chest. "All of the information you need has been provided. Do the task, and the Order will take care of the rest."

Mila stared back down at the task, written, as always, in unassuming Times New Roman. She could picture one of the brothers upstairs with his laptop, typing the words, sizing up the font, printing it on the tasteful cream Prometheus letterhead. Maybe Gamble himself wrote it, easy as any term paper.

Kill a lesser scholar.

"But what does that even *mean*?" Proctor was asking.

"The information is there," Gamble repeated tersely.

"But…" Locke was staring at the far wall, at the spines of the dozens of leather-bound first edition books. She was sweating, her face covered in a sheen like she'd taken ill.

"What about the bodies?" Proctor asked, all smooth efficiency.

"You're taking it *literally*?" Riker asked, distraught. "Surely there must be some trick, some—"

"Of course it's literal," Proctor snapped. He leaned back, running a hand through his auburn hair. "Goddamn, Julia, it's like you can't fucking read sometimes."

All of this was too much – but Proctor had a point. They'd never been asked to do something for the Order figuratively. She looked back up at Ian, stone-faced and silent.

"Gamble?" she asked, one last time. Now, he did look at her – and his eyes were haunted.

I did it too, he didn't say.

"The Order will dispose of anything that needs disposing of," he said flatly. "The Order will erase the consequences in any way possible. The only request is that you use your brains: Do the task. Remain discreet. And it will all be over. You have one week." Gamble turned away, threw back the rest of the bourbon. Mila hated every muscle in his long, lovely neck. "You're dismissed."

It had to be a philosophical question. That was what she decided as she stalked away from Elbrus House, into the chill. She gritted her teeth against the fall air, feeling all too presently the absence of her lower left first molar – for their second task, the one that had driven off at least three of the other initiates, they'd been tasked with removing them with a pair of pliers, for no other reason that Mila could discern other than to show that they would.

"Orlicker!"

The call came from behind her. Mila hesitated, glancing over her shoulder. Carmichael, Riker, Proctor, and Locke stood in a loose circle, illuminated in yellow by a streetlight. Riker was still crying – she'd started at some point inside the house, silent tears rolling down her cheeks, and that's when Mila knew she had to get out of there.

"What?" Mila felt the differences between them like an all-too-literal chasm. They were wealthy; she wasn't. They went to Carnegie Mellon; she went to Pitt. They were juniors; she was a sophomore. They were so tightly knit, growing into one another, always intertwined; she was apart.

"Come back to Morewood," Proctor said, stepping between her and the others. He was in some frat at CMU – she'd been there once for a party with her roommates but the guys were all a little too touchy and she had no desire to spend more time with Proctor than she had to. "Let's talk this over."

She bunched her hands in her coat, crumpling that beautiful cream paper – but what was the point in staying away? Mila inclined her head, just enough, and walked back to the group.

They made their way to the frat house in a silent huddle. Up to the third floor, to the big room Proctor had to himself. Mila took it in: the futon, the scattered beer cans, the gigantic American flag that took up one wall. Proctor was Texas rich, oil rich, the kind of rich that Mila couldn't begin to understand. But he was smart too – and that's what made him dangerous.

"Right," Proctor started, pacing, making himself their unofficial leader in Gamble's absence. He always did this, and Mila hated it. She leaned against the wall, arms crossed over her chest, as Hannah sat on the edge of the bed and Julia and Patrick perched on the futon. She made herself think of them as their first names, made herself shake off the trappings of Prometheus and Elbrus House.

Except for Proctor. Proctor could fuck himself.

"Pat, you pull up the top-ranked universities in the country.

Hannah, get the rankings for the city. And Jules… please, just stop fucking crying."

She sniffled in response, wiping snot on her sleeve with one hand. Her brown skin was unusually pale.

"Why are you looking at rankings?" Mila asked.

Proctor met her gaze, unflinching. Proctor and Ian Gamble showed the full spectrum of the beauty of brown eyes: Ian's were gorgeous, deep, soulful. In contrast, Proctor's quite closely resembled a cow's.

"The instructions are clear: kill a lesser scholar. So we might as well… find a lesser scholar."

Realization hit like a kick to Mila's gut. Proctor, sadistic, elitist prick that he was, thought a lesser scholar meant one that went to a university that wasn't Carnegie Mellon, one that didn't strike a faint eyebrow raise, a note of *that's impressive* from anyone who asked where he went to school. The type of education that couldn't be bought with sweat and blood, or lots and lots and *lots* of money.

"That's… awful," Mila said. "You're taking it too literally."

Proctor laughed, low and terrible. The others only looked between them. Hannah fisted her hand in Proctor's awful navy bedspread – it was probably gross, Mila thought, considering the whole room smelled faintly of sweat and alcohol.

"You want to stand up for the little guy, Orlicker?" Proctor asked, moving closer. "You read it too. You know the rules. You know what Prometheus stands for. This task is about winnowing the chaff. Eliminating the people who half-ass things. The ones who go to shit universities for a piece of paper, then get shit jobs. Pretend to be like us. They don't care about rigor; they don't think like we do. We're above them. *That's* what Prometheus is about."

"Kurt—" Patrick started.

"Just give me the rankings," Proctor snapped, turning to the whiteboard.

"I don't think you have this right," Mila said, her throat thick and tight. But hadn't she thought something similar? Her, a first-generation college student, hopelessly disappointed when the Ivys turned her down, raking through arbitrary numbers and scales and ratings. CMU and NYU accepted her, but they were too expensive, even with scholarships – and didn't she *hate* it when the others in Prometheus looked at her and said, *Oh, you're the one at the state school*, as if that changed anything. Prometheus chapters were not tied to individual universities, but to cities. She'd earned her spot just as thoroughly as the others had.

Proctor raised a 'brow. "Maybe we should just kill *you*," he said.

Mila snapped her jaw shut. Clenched her fists. She wasn't going to convince them – and above that, exhaustion aside, she did not actually think she could kill someone.

"Forget the rankings for a second," Hannah said. "How are we doing this?"

"Prometheus will clean up after us," Patrick said. "Ian promised."

"I'm not *shooting* somebody," Julia hissed. The tears had mostly abated, but not by much.

And Proctor rolled his eyes. "Shoot 'em. Stab 'em. Syringe of air. Overdose. Poison. Strangulation. Doesn't matter as long as you kill them dead."

What Mila wanted to say was, *You're enjoying this*. Instead: "And if we don't?"

Proctor looked at her again, that awful hatred in his stare. He really would kill her, if he thought she was the best option – she was certain of it. "Then we don't join the Order," he said.

They'd come to her in the library on the first day of sophomore year, two girls in tweed suddenly standing over her while she was working on an English paper in Hillman.

"Mila Orlicker?" the shorter, red-headed one said.

Mila looked up, then around. "Uh, sorry, this is a quiet floor—"

But the taller brunette had only held out an envelope and said, "You're invited." And then the two of them walked away.

Mila opened the paper – it was what she now recognized to be that rich cream letterhead bearing the seal of the Order of Prometheus – to find an address and a time. Too curious to avoid it, she'd gone, for better or worse, and found herself in front of one of CMU's buildings off the main quad.

There, in the shadows, stood Ian Gamble. "I have an opportunity for you," he'd told her.

Mila had grown up in a two-bed apartment with a single mother just outside of Cleveland, Ohio. She hated Ohio: the flatness of it, the tornado warnings, the feeling that she could scream and scream and no one would hear her. As early as she could remember, she was escaping into books, falling into stories, cloaking herself from the great summer storms with silken words. By high school, she knew she wanted to be an English professor, and nothing in the world would stop her.

"I can get you into any program you want," Gamble had said

to her, eyes serious, as they sat facing each other across the table at the front of the lecture hall he led her into. It felt like a hostage negotiation, with her future on the line in the middle of the table. "If you make it through the trials, join the Order of Prometheus – the world is open to you, Mila. There are chapters in every major city. Brothers at every university worth its salt. A massive, esteemed alumni network. Want to work for the government? Done. Grad school at Oxford? Sorted. A position at Brown? You're in."

Her mouth was dry, her hands clasped together so tight that she'd leave shallow half-moon fingernail cuts in her palms.

"And it's not a scam?" Mila asked, thinking, inexplicably, of Mormons.

Gamble laughed, and it was probably that exact moment that Mila thought for the first time, *I could love him, if I tried.*

"Not a scam," he said, hands open, palms facing the ceiling. "Not a game. I'm offering this to you, Mila, because we think you have a great mind. And that's all we want: the best scholars, the best minds."

At that time, she hadn't known the best minds included the likes of Kurt fucking Proctor, but it didn't matter. The relief was like a balloon inside her chest: What if she didn't have to worry about a scholarship for grad school? What if she could just focus on doing really, really well? What if she never had to go back to Ohio again in all her life?

"I'll do it," she'd said. And then Gamble had taken her to Elbrus House, and her fate had been sealed.

The evening after they received their final task, Mila did not go to Elbrus House, even though she preferred to study there. Nor did she go the night after, even though the brothers usually brought the good alcohol out on Fridays, and even let the neophytes join in. Instead, she put on a very skimpy shirt and bold eyeliner and went to Hems with her roommate Yas.

They sidled in with fake IDs, compliments of the Order – it had been one of the first things she'd asked Ian for, and though he'd rolled his eyes, he'd obliged and passed them to her in a too-big manila envelope the following week, saying only "They scan, be safe" – and sat in the corner with sugary-sweet shot pitchers. Mila dug the gummy bears out of the ice with her fingers, not caring who watched.

"Not feeling the frat thing tonight?" Yas asked, sipping her second pitcher, looking at Mila through her eyelashes. That's how Mila had explained away Prometheus: a frat thing. After all, she was getting the shit hazed out of her. It wasn't too far of a stretch.

They want me to kill someone. And I think I might do it. Mila pursed her lips. "Just needed a night off."

"No worries," Yas said, scrolling through people's Instagram stories. "Looks like there's a party on Ditheridge, if you want even more distraction. And free-er alcohol."

Mila winced. "Maybe," she said, but she didn't want to go to a party on Ditheridge. She wanted to go to Elbrus House, to sit in one of the mahogany-paneled study rooms, at her favorite desk in the corner with a green glass lamp and a window that looked out to Fifth. She wanted to gaze across the room and catch Gamble looking at her, both of them pretending.

She wanted Prometheus – but if she wanted that… well. Mila took the straw between her teeth, drank deeply, as if the sugary mix of gin and grape soda could burn away all touches of Ian Gamble and his good bourbon.

"Let's go," Yas whined, laying a hand on Mila's arm. Her fingers were painted cornflower blue. "We haven't been out out in ages."

"We're out out *now*," Mila pointed out. But she drained her pitcher to the dregs, dug out the rest of the gummy bears, and slid into her coat. It would be a good distraction, locking eyes with some unknown person across the room, sidling over with a smile, her body pressed to a sweaty basement wall. Unfamiliar hands on her hips, in her hair, her tongue in someone else's mouth. She wasn't usually into hookups, but there was a time and place for everything.

Yas led the way back through the bar, which was filling up. They were almost to the door when Mila heard the voice over her left shoulder, saying, "Well, well, well, if it isn't our very own little Phobos."

Her teeth clamped together. Fists clenched. Proctor stood against the bar, plastic cup of beer looking out of place against his sleek button-down. He'd pushed his hair back with gel, but in the bar lighting, it only managed to look greasy.

"I don't have time for your shit today," Mila said, conscious of the fact her veneer was slipping; that gilding she'd pulled over herself was fading, chipped away by the same Order who promised to polish her.

He raised an eyebrow, tipped his beer towards her. And then, slippery as ever, his eyes slid over her and settled on Yas.

"And what's *your* GPA?" Proctor simpered.

Mila rolled her eyes and wrapped an arm around Yas – who, terribly, did *not* look disinterested. "Fuck off, Proctor."

She got them out of there and only half listened to Yas's unofficial rankings of the best party houses in South O. She couldn't kill someone – they couldn't *ask her* to *kill someone* – but Proctor was certainly going to, and if Proctor did, then the others would soon follow. And – then what? Was she implicated? Was she just as bad as he was, since she had not made an effort to tell the appropriate authorities, because she had no desire to betray the Order even though she knew what membership cost?

Yas talked them through the door and Mila followed, ditching her coat on the pile in one of the bedrooms. It was muscle memory to slip past the sweaty bodies, smile at the girl who she'd had Comp with last year, pour a cup of the toxic-red punch from a suspicious-looking plastic tub. She clutched the solo cup against her chest and admired the scene playing out in front of her, the grime and the sweat, the vitality of it all.

When her eyes locked with the boy across the room, the one with a crooked smile and brown hair, the one who she – if she closed her eyes – could pretend was Ian Gamble, well, it was a foregone conclusion. She gave in to the sweaty dances, the laughter, one cup of horrible punch after another and a thumbs up angled at Yas when she let the boy take her hand and lead her out of the party.

He lived in one of the dorms in North O, uncomfortably overlapped with CMU to the point where she felt she had to look over her shoulder every minute to make sure fucking Proctor wasn't following her. The boy pushed her up against the wall as soon as the door was closed behind them, his mouth wet and insistent on her neck in a way that reminded her of a gaping fish. She hissed a breath, her fingers digging into his shoulders as his hands slipped under her shirt, as he pawed at her chest.

But could she kill someone?

"Hold on," Mila said, breathless. Then, again: "Hold on."

"Don't worry," he said against her collarbone. "I have condoms."

She groaned – that wasn't the worry. Mila pushed him away but he wouldn't go, and in that moment – maybe she *could* do it. If it meant Ian. If it meant the end of this, the fumbling, the emptiness, the unknowingness of it all.

She gripped his chin, lifted it up, this unnamed boy who might be enough to die for her. He had a round face, thin lips, eyes dulled by hunger and softened with want. His stubble bit into her fingers.

"I have to pee," she said quickly, then pulled away. Stumbled through the dark common room, through the kitchen, to the bathroom. She splashed her face with water and stared at her reflection in the mirror. Her sharp eyeliner was all smudged, streaking black down one cheek. She wiped the makeup off, streaking the boy's cheap hand towel now with black marks.

She watched her reflection, the twitch in her jaw, the lines of her face. A stranger stared back. A stranger who was, quite possibly, capable of murder.

Prometheus had promised her everything. She just needed to be strong enough to work for it.

On her way back through the kitchen, she grabbed the knife. A foregone conclusion.

He was on his bed, stripped to his underwear, waiting for her.

Mila toed into the room, turned the lights off, kept the knife behind her back. His eyes were dim in the darkness, following her every move.

"What's your major?" she asked, not sure what else to say, hanging back by the door. What even *made* a lesser scholar? She wasn't ready to accept Proctor's definition.

He rolled up onto one elbow, expression clouding. "Uh, communications? You?"

"And how's that going?" Mila asked.

"Uhhhh…"

This was *ridiculous*. She felt the blood creeping over her collarbones, up her cheeks, the red-hot shame of it all. Mila sucked in a breath. This wasn't who she was – she had no idea what she was doing, why she was going through with it. She turned around and fled, left the knife on the kitchen counter on the way out.

She'd forgotten her coat at the party and it was *frigid* outside, but it was only a five-minute walk to Elbrus House, only another minute to punch in her keycode and stumble down the hall and begin up the stairs, a minute to push up the stairs and pound her fist on Ian Gamble's door.

She didn't even know if he was home – but of course he was. He opened the door, his hair tousled, unkempt in a way he never was otherwise. His eyes were heavy with sleep.

"I can't do it," she said.

Gamble looked at her silently. She stared back. *Tell me you didn't*, she wanted to shout at him, but she knew the truth: it was written in every muscle of his mouth, drawn into a tight line.

She wanted to knot her hands in his worn T-shirt, pull him

close, draw his face down and shout against him until he caved. She wanted to take all of the Order in her hands, push and push until it molded itself into something kinder, something that wasn't so sharp-edged and cutting against her. She wanted so badly to be soft. Wanted so badly for the Order to cave against her, to become a pillow to fall into instead of a shackle to rage against.

"I can't help you with the task," Gamble said, but he was caving. He ran a hand through his hair, sighing. "But we can talk about it. Just don't tell the others."

He stepped aside and let her in.

Though Mila knew where Gamble's room was, she'd never been in it for longer than a second, fetching a book he needed or bringing his laptop down. It was the complete opposite of Proctor's stale room at the frat house – a huge bed dominated the space, covered in sheets of quite possibly the highest thread count she'd ever seen. His laptop was the only thing on his heavy desk besides a bottle of amber bourbon, more befitting of a CEO than a college student. Besides that, the room was sparse: armoire closed, no pictures, no decorations. It was all so bare, so empty, so opposed to the layers of curiosities she'd seen in the man himself.

He took the desk chair, and since there was no other place to sit, she perched on the edge of his bed. He looked at her, evaluating. He wore navy basketball shorts with his rugby T-shirt and he looked so much like a regular boy that it made her chest ache.

But he wasn't regular. He was Ian, the keeper of all the things she'd ever wanted, her warden and her teacher. Once, she had thought she'd do anything he could ask of her – and now, she still wasn't sure. She'd looked up at him on that night, ages ago, blood thick in her mouth after she'd pulled out her own tooth, amazed at her capacity to let him unmake her. And then – then he'd lowered himself onto his knees, level with her, and wiped the blood away from her lip with one beautiful thumb. It was as if he'd confirmed every misplaced feeling she'd had.

"Have you been drinking?" he asked now.

She raised an eyebrow, brain fuzzy. "Do you disapprove?"

"No. I'm wondering if I should catch up."

She was probably too drunk for this conversation, still buzzed on adrenaline and the toxic punch. But she held his gaze as she got up, went around him, her thigh touching his knee as she grabbed the bourbon from his desk. His eyes didn't leave hers as she pulled the cork cap out with a *plink!* too loud for the dark room.

"Then catch up," she said. "And tell me what to do."

His lips parted. Ian's hand seemed to move without him telling it to, fingers fanning over her hip as she lifted the heavy bottle to his lips, tipped the bourbon in – probably too generous a shot, but whatever. She watched his Adam's apple as he swallowed, watched his tongue trace over his lower lip as she put the bottle down. His hand tightened on her hip. She wanted him to carve his fingerprints into her skin.

A door opened downstairs. Slammed shut. Feet thudding on the stairs. A commotion.

Then: "*Gamble!*"

He was up before she could even think, before she could catch her breath – up and pushing past her, stumbling over himself to get down the stairs. There was a high keening sound coming from somewhere, a sound Mila couldn't quite place.

Mila froze at the top of the stairs.

The keening, the commotion – it was three brothers, standing around Hannah Locke. She was hyperventilating in the foyer, working to a scream, and covered in blood.

Not her own, Mila surmised.

Ian rushed past her again, on his way to get towels. "Mila, you should go—" he started, but she grabbed his arm. Felt the flex of his muscle against her palm.

"I can't do this," Mila said. Without another thought, another word, she ran.

On the last day of term before Christmas break, Mila collected all of her items related to the Order. She gathered notes about brothers, tasks on heavy parchment, endless lists of reading recommendations from Ian, plans for where she would go and how she would get there and which brothers would be most useful. She put all of it in a big cardboard box and dragged it to Panther Hollow in the dead of night, where no one would come looking. There, then, she lit the match and dropped it, stood in the icy cold until it smoldered to ashes.

When she got back to her dorm, fingers numb, there was someone sitting on the steps up to her floor. She hesitated as the door shut behind her and Ian Gamble looked up to meet her gaze.

Mila sucked a breath through her teeth. The skin under his eyes was bruise-dark – she hadn't seen him in nearly four days, not since the night Hannah Locke finished her murder and Ian and the Order covered for her, and it looked like he hadn't slept since.

"I told you I was done," Mila said, conscious of the fact it was the middle of the night.

"I know. I came to talk."

Numbly, she nodded. He followed her up the rest of the stairs. Yas was already gone, on an overnight bus home to New York. The dorm they shared was too quiet without her. Mila flicked on the lights and led Ian to the tiny slice of kitchen. He leaned against the back of the sofa, watching her as she filled a glass of water and drank it deeply.

"I'm sorry we asked too much of you," Ian said. She remembered the look on his face the night he gave them their last task, the agony there. He'd hated it too, hated that this was necessary for them to prove themselves.

Mila set the glass in the sink, leaned against the counter, crossed her arms over her chest. "Did the others…?"

She wasn't sure what to say. Were the others murderers? Did they do the things she couldn't? Were they full members of Prometheus, privy to its secrets, when she'd be nothing more than a memory, forever a neophyte?

Ian looked away. Inclined his head ever so slightly and grimaced. It was enough – his mouth never lied to her.

She remembered that night, when they'd called her name. The four of them under the lamppost, the chasm between them.

They were all members of the Order; she wasn't.

"I couldn't do it," she said, her voice raw. She'd cried over it for the last few days, uncertain she made the right choice, sure there was no other choice she could've made. "Why would I kill someone else? How could that be expected of me?"

For a second, Ian looked like he'd actually answer her. But then he shook his head. "We all burn ourselves up," he said. "We consume ourselves, constantly. And for what? I'm no better a scholar than you are. Proctor – *fuck* Proctor – is probably no better than the poor freshman he killed. It doesn't matter. None of it's good, none of it's right."

"Then why did you do it?" Mila asked, unable to stop the tears from escaping. She scrubbed at her eyes angrily, forced it away. "Isn't Prometheus just… it doesn't *make* a better scholar, a better researcher, to have those connections. You don't have to work for anything. The Order is there to catch you. You don't have to push, don't have to reach, because the Order is there. It's the step under your feet, lifting you higher. The hand pushing the rest of us down. You let everyone do the hard work for you, and just keep climbing up on their backs. You're a coward. You, and everyone else in the goddamn Order." She scrubbed away the errant tears, forcing herself to stop. If she kept going, kept voicing the thoughts that had plagued her since the night she'd left Elbrus House for the last time, she'd go mad.

To her surprise, Ian only nodded. "You're right," he said.

Before she could recover, he pushed off the sofa and crossed the space between them in four easy steps. She couldn't recover before his hands were on her hips, her waist, before his mouth was crushing against hers.

Mila faltered – inhaled his breath, pulled her hands away from being crushed between them. She didn't know what to do with her hands – she didn't know what to do with anything. She could only grip his back as he lifted her bodily to sit on the counter, pushing the knife block aside, as he stepped in the space between her knees.

Kissing Ian Gamble was the best of all the worst thoughts she'd ever had. His shoulders were just as strong against her hands as she'd imagined. His lips were just as pleading, just as beseeching, as she'd desired. And when his hands came up from her hips, when he cupped her face, it was only like the tenderness she'd always imagined – until they slipped down, and his calloused hands closed around her neck.

Her eyes flew wide but there was no time for anything, no time for a reaction, for any breath. Tears leaked from his eyes. His face was twisted in a mask of anger, maybe pity, but she couldn't focus, couldn't do anything other than scrape uselessly at his chest as black spots crowded her vision. She gripped the counter, tried to kick, but it was no use.

He was going to kill her.

As if he couldn't help himself, Ian leaned in, pressed his lips to hers once more, trapping her panicked mouth. In that moment, Mila's scrabbling hand felt the knife block. Her fingers wrapped around a handle.

She didn't think. She didn't have the air to think, nothing left for her brain to do – there was only *lift*, only *stab*, only *defend*.

For protection, she thought later, her brain stopped recording. She came back to herself standing over his body, blood soaking the bottoms of her shoes, mingling with the ash that was all she had left of Prometheus. She stared at him, watching as the light left his eyes, as the blood trickled from his mouth. She did not call the police, nor the ambulance. There was no saving him.

When it was over, when her hands stopped shaking, she opened her phone. Called Carmichael.

"Mila?" he said, confused.

"Are you at Elbrus House?" she asked. She didn't recognize her own voice.

"Yeah."

She gritted her teeth. Mila crouched down and raised Gamble's cold hand to her lips, kissed his knuckles, and laid it over his chest to cover the worst of the wounds. She couldn't fathom the amount of blood seeping over the floor, soaking her shoes, her clothes, Ian's body.

"Call the brothers," Mila said, straightening and shifting the phone to the crook of her neck to free her hands. She turned away from Gamble, to the sink. Mila turned on the tap and washed her hands, watching the water run red. "I need to get rid of a body."

℗LAYING

Phoebe Wynne

Grace slid along the organ bench and moved her music to the side. She couldn't look at it if she was going to listen to the men talking in the chapel beneath her – the swirling notes against the yellowing paper were too distracting. She had a tendency to follow music with her eyes and it would trumpet out through her mind and fill her up with colours, so many that she might spill them out of her every pore. Sometimes when she played the organ deeply enough she felt her whole body shudder with song.

Grace felt privileged to be a channel for it – she believed that music was the best thing ever to exist in the world.

She glanced into the little mirror beside the organ keyboard, that pointed down to the pews where the choir and director of music usually stood. She could just about see the tops of the men's heads. Yes, it was the chaplain, and two more, one shorter than the other, and all three were discussing the funeral, their voices loud in the echoing throat of the chapel. Grace caught her own face in the mirror, pale and patchy without make-up, her fingers stuffed into her mouth as she bit at her nails, which were dirty and slightly bloodied from where she'd picked at her cuticles, or pummelled too hard on the organ keys. She pulled her fingers from her mouth and tugged her velvet jacket sleeve over her wrists, just catching the plush turn of the fabric in the light.

Grace tried to make out what the men were saying. It was curious, this was the third death in the local parish in as many months. Three in one term – they really ought to alert the university.

"And are you sure she wanted those hymns?"

The chaplain nodded. "I believe so."

"Isn't that the same programme as last month?" The shorter man's head jiggled about; Grace could tell he was irritated – he was often irritated, and resentful, being the vicar of the local church where nobody turned up to worship, preferring the glory of the university chapel instead. Grace wanted to roll her eyes, of course it was the same musical programme, none of them had any idea of how busy she'd been. They couldn't possibly expect her to learn even more new music on top of her scholarship, her weekly studies, and everything else.

"The family," the third man chimed in, "is very grateful that the university has allowed the funeral to take place here. It certainly is a wonderful space."

Ah, Grace realised, the unknown man was family and not a policeman, as she'd hoped. She felt a thrill of urgency. Nobody was asking the right questions! For the last few weeks she'd long wanted to shout her viewpoint to the authorities, cry out to them to pay attention, and perhaps even give them the chaplain's name. Oh yes – she'd seen his hard face, his continued fury at the governors, his frustration with the university and the local community, as he somehow served both while only employed by one. Why would anyone settle for crumbling old St Jude's and its boring vicar when they could come to this magnificent chapel and its high, painted ceiling, its decorative altar, its stained-glass windows, and of course – its exceptional organ.

Grace smiled at the instrument bursting out in front of her. She thought she might have chosen the organ for its great stature – how it enveloped her from when she was small and her grandfather sat her on the bench that seemed so high her feet couldn't touch the pedals. She was almost entirely grown up now, and tall enough that she had to bend over to bury herself in the heart of this metal and wooden musical flower. Here she was at her best – up in the loft, unseen and above everyone, close to the chapel ceiling and uniquely positioned to turn and shout over at them from her balcony if she needed to. Grace wondered if she should do so now.

"Of course we're happy to hold the funeral here," answered the chaplain, "Mrs Marney loved this place, she was here every week."

"Yes, so many of them are," said the vicar unhappily.

Grace nodded at that, Mrs Marney was always first to arrive at the concerts, choosing to sit in the front row, with her little gloved hands twisted over her handbag. Though she wasn't very generous after the Christmas concert last year, even after she won two of the top prizes at the raffle.

"We shall miss her," the chaplain added, rather unconvincingly. Grace eyed him carefully.

"It's the choir they like, isn't it?" the vicar attempted. "Especially at this time of year, all those carols."

"Yes, I think so."

Grace didn't like to hear that. Everyone raved about the choir, but they'd be nothing without her backing, her support, her rich chords to lead them on their way. She sniffed and caught a heavy whiff of wood polish – just catching herself, since she didn't want them to know she was listening. She held her breath.

The chaplain nodded with finality. "If you'll excuse me, I've lots to be getting on with."

Grace glowered down at the man, seeing his weariness, his discomfort. It was no good, he wasn't going to give anything away as the small group broke apart. She ought to phone the authorities herself and give them some information. Or the governors at least, if they would deign to see her. Tell them what she thought she knew, before the term was out and the year ended. Yes, she might have to do something about all this.

Grace's thoughts darted about as she slid her tray along the canteen railing. She was still panting from her cold, dark dash across the quad. She'd looked up as she always did at the great monster of the university building, peeping at the lit-up windows scattered like stars around the stacks of steeples stark against the night sky. There it was – her square of light, her own, her room. The only place of hers in this royal mess, there and the organ loft, her two favourite spots in this great, ancient block of building. They were like two points on a map, and she darted along the string from one spot to the other.

In the dining hall she sat alone at the only spare table. It had been mostly cleared away but the plastic tablecloth still lay sticky and flaked with grubby morsels of food. There was one remaining tray, messy with paper napkins that dragged from a bowl of gungy-looking soup. As Grace hooked her legs over the bench, the occupants of the table opposite her turned to sneer, before turning away again. Grace didn't mind too much, she was used to it from the other students – as if her presence, her very scent might pervade them. It wasn't her scent, she wanted to protest, it was the hot and oily air coming through from the canteen space, trailing after her, as if someone had poured the soup over her aura. That wasn't Grace – she had a magical scent, of sheet music and brilliance and perhaps the odour of the inside of her shoes. Those people just smelled ordinary. They *were* ordinary, all of them. The sullen boys and their hunched, muscly shoulders, the girls casually but expertly passing their hands through their flaxen-blonde hair – they smelled of the rugby game they'd just played, or the cheerleading session they'd just powered through, or the missionary sex they'd just had.

No, Grace was clean – well, her hair was greasy and falling across her face, but she was pure, and untouched. Grace knew what was important, she didn't need some hefty rugby player to embrace her and make her feel some version of valuable. Her music already made her feel that way, and her grandfather had made sure of that before he died. Grace's path was clear now, and it wasn't anywhere near those people on the opposite table that thought they were better than her. She'd leave here in just over a year with a First in Bachelor of Music and slot herself into some lofty cathedral and praise God and be praised for the rest of her life.

Her fingers fiddled with the tray as she ate, and she wondered whether she should get some music out to distract herself. Some Christmas carols the director of music had chosen perhaps, the new and "fun" arrangement she'd have to learn. She longed for the musical notes as she made her way through her pasta, somewhere to put her eyes instead of those blonde heads lit like halos in front of her.

But Grace was too distracted to get out her sheet music, her other thoughts were needling their way in through her mind. Each death among the local folk lined themselves up like those rows of students in the dining hall. One, then another, then all the other possibilities among that Sunday congregation so devoted to the chapel and the chaplain. Mrs Jennings, Mr Webster, Mrs Marney. It was growing into a list, growing with such urgency that Grace couldn't believe the police hadn't taken an interest. So what if each one had been a fall, a shock, or a quiet passing in sleep? Three old people couldn't possibly be so accident-prone, so close together. What was the connection? The local village, the chaplain. Yes, Grace thought, the blame could only lie with the chaplain.

Perhaps it would stop there. Three was a pretty number, three notes made a simple chord. A cadence, perhaps. Yes, that's what they were – a falling cadence of elderly dead people. Grace felt a sweep of guilt at that – she liked the old people, they were kind to her. Kinder than anyone in the dining hall, or the bar downstairs, or even the other girls in her bedroom corridor. She appreciated the old people and their neatly tailored clothes, their twinsets and pearls, their brushed hair, their tidy smiles. They looked at her straight in the eyes, they complimented her playing, and made cringeworthy but adorable references to Classic FM, imagining that they knew about classical music when they didn't.

The dining hall yawned tall with the evening as the long windows grew cold. It was December next week, and chillier than ever, so much so that Grace wondered if the glass might crack with the frost. She scraped her fork around her plate, frowning into her food and considering bringing out her music again, but she didn't want to stain the paper with the dirty table. But then she could just buy another copy; her favourite music shop in Windsor had an excellent version of the Saint-Saëns that she would love to have an excuse to buy.

A laugh came from the table ahead of her, accompanied by a flick of the head, so Grace dropped her fork decisively, and lifted her tray.

Later that evening, Grace propped her laptop on her knees and lay in bed as she watched Netflix. It was a documentary about a serial killer – she was particularly enjoying the overdramatic American accents and the spiky way it had been edited, which only added to the intrigue, and the nonsense. Marks on a torso! Traces under a fingernail! Smells left behind! The smells interested her, the talk of the smell of death, and how the killers covered it up – one old lady simply laid down a thicker carpet over the dried sludge of blood and whatever else. She hadn't had many visitors to her home, apparently, so she didn't have to worry, and probably just got used to the smell before she got caught. It was amazing what you could get used to, Grace thought as she sucked on a sweet from a paper bag.

Three sweets she was allowed, three she had allocated for herself. Rhubarb and custard tonight. She turned them around in her mouth with her tongue, and just at the right moment, she'd crunch down her teeth. Suck and crack and pull at the sweet, to make sure that she got all of it, that none of that sparkling sugar was left behind – since she certainly wasn't going out to the bathroom now that the corridor was so busy with the other girls. Grace had the best room on the floor on account of her music scholarship, and very early on in the term she'd set her bed in the circular turret space, which was raised above the rest of the room, and separated it with a velvet curtain. The square windows had a splendid view of the roofs and mirroring white turrets, and of course – if she stood at the right angle – the chapel. Sometimes Grace wished she could fly through the air, like those pigeons that darted and ducked past her window, and swoop into her organ loft, without having to venture downstairs, or even tread a single step outside her room, or meet any other ugly face of her peers. At this angle she could almost see that linking string like a magic tightrope to dance along and into her organ loft.

But she probably wouldn't go there tonight.

The sugary zing of the sweet should carry her all the way to breakfast, she thought. She touched the paper bag again, counting how many remained without looking, to see if she could trick herself into allowing a secret fourth. She needed to ration before her trip to Windsor next week, to that tucked-away sweet shop and its kindly lady before the hallowed Evensong at St George's Chapel. Sweet shop, music shop, Windsor Castle – her favourite routine. It was getting colder, she must remember to wrap up, since she'd almost caught a chill last week hanging around outside St George's waiting for the Advent carol service.

Grace clutched at the bag and rolled it up in an effort not to tear it. Fudge next week, she thought – clotted cream, or salted caramel. Let it melt on her tongue, sit and dissolve, rich and delicious. She couldn't wait.

On the chair beside her bed was a new embroidered waistcoat she'd just received, still wrapped in its soft tissue packaging, since Grace hadn't yet allowed herself to fully pull it out and admire it. She'd torn open the box when it had arrived, but then stopped herself to savour every thrilling moment of opening something new. The embroidered pattern had reminded her of her grandfather, even more in person than on the screen. And now the waistcoat was here, she wanted more. She'd already returned to the website and selected the suit she wanted to order next, a thick tailored set with the same lining as the waistcoat. She knew she'd look wonderful in it, and she knew she deserved it. She just needed a little bit more to pay for it – another big gig next month, perhaps, after the funeral tomorrow and before the end of term. She'd counted the money in the little wooden chest under her bed; she didn't yet have enough.

Perhaps Grace could wear the waistcoat for the funeral, to chivvy her along a bit. She liked to think that it would match the music, the same rich layers of fabrics and finery. The Widor *Toccata* definitely needed such a flourish. Was the piece ready? Was she entirely ready?

She'd fudged some of the bits last time, the parts in the higher register, it was greater than her at the moment. Grace loved that feeling more than anything, the moment where she climbed the mountain of a musical piece, not quite on top of it, but then, when she reached the summit with perseverance and good practice, when all the various parts suddenly slotted into her brain, her fingers, her soul – it was bliss, and she could slide down the mountain and enjoy the piece as it should be. She hadn't quite reached that point with the Widor *Toccata*.

The documentary was boring her now. Grace glanced over at the piano set straight and strict near the door. The stacks of music were getting so high that the piano seemed to be bowing underneath them, the thick wood curved with its burden. The truth was Grace didn't care for that piano, it came with the room and her organ scholar requirements, but it was a dreadful tinny thing; short, flat, and out of tune. It was almost an insult to her glorious organ.

And anyway, if she lifted off the music now, she'd look too much at it, and it would sing through her heart so much that she would collapse probably, and with the music splayed all over the floor, like a wilted flower with its blown-off petals.

Was she ready for the funeral tomorrow? Grace wondered whether she would go out to the chapel. The unachieved mastery of the Widor *Toccata* seemed to mock her, she couldn't stop thinking of the last section when it broke forth into peals of triumph and honour. She'd marked the moments where she so often went wrong – fudging her fingers, her feet moving too fast on the pedals as her heart beat quicker than the rhythm.

Grace sucked in her breath as it caught with the sugar of the sweet. How wonderful it would be to practise and perform the Widor tonight in the night's darkness, with no light on – perhaps she didn't need to look at the music, perhaps her fingers, her feet, would find a way. Grace didn't often practise at night, but tonight felt fortuitous.

One thing stopped her – Grace didn't want to bump into the chaplain; he might rush forward and shout that she was being "inappropriate", something that Grace hated to be called. That word had chased her through school, alongside "awkward", "strange", and "creepy". Grace wasn't any of those things, she was herself. She would answer the chaplain that, and drown out his protesting with her continuous playing. But what if he went further, and tried to push her over the bench, over the balcony and down onto the chapel floor? He might do to her what she thought he'd done to those old people – what those serial killers were doing in that documentary. Grace shook her head at the thought. When she played she knew she was stronger than anything, and it would be the other way around. Her arms, her legs could swing round along the organ bench and push him over the edge of the loft. It was a good three metres to the floor of the chapel below, and at that angle, yes, his back would crack and the mystery would be solved.

Grace let out a chuckle. She closed her laptop and pushed her bag of sweets aside.

Grace shot across the quad as the underground bar thrust out its night music. The shock of the cold thrilled her nerves and she moved faster, her hair falling behind her as she went.

She had to concentrate not to walk within the beat of the song. She couldn't even call it music, it was secular and modern, as if someone had cut out the percussion section of an orchestra and had them perform without the rest. There was the hissing of the tambourine, and the muffled blow of the drum. No melody, and nothing of merit underneath that heavy, electronic mess of noise.

Three skinny girls had slipped out of the bar doors and were shivering together in the winter cold. One of them was gesticulating wildly, her phone in her hand, lit up and casting a ghastly shadow across her and her two friends. Grace grimaced at them, before laughing to herself. The blast of the organ from across the quad would outdo all of this noise no problem, if Grace pulled out the longest, deepest stops she could. Perhaps she could play so loud that all of the partygoers at the bar would spill out as if summoned by her great instrument, gesticulating even more wildly and casting the light of their phones towards the chapel, to record the extraordinary sounds Grace and her organ were making. And then, only then, would they finally recognise her greatness and bow down as they should.

The monster was calling to her and she was ready to answer. Grace was already there – she skipped with anticipation, pulling open the little door beside the chapel entrance, dashing up the stone spiral staircase, rushing through the doorway, drinking in the queer darkness, and always knowing her way forward.

The organ loft met her warmly with that familiar smell of dried-out damp and wood polish. Grace lit the small lamp and pulled at the curtain by the window; she wanted to keep it discreet, but loud. She kicked off her shoes and slid along the bench.

Tonight she would play barefoot, barehanded and barefaced, as close to herself as she could get inside the music.

The chapel gaped behind her, its great throat alive and resounding with the organ's sound. The instrument blasted loud as every hair on Grace's body sparkled with joy and horror, as if she were being electrocuted by the music itself, or caught in the very middle, like the blue flame calm in among its dangerous surrounding heat. She played the Widor more fluently than she ever had.

Three names came to her as she played. Mrs Jennings, Mr Webster, Mrs Marney. One after the other, struck down. If that were to happen to Grace, if she were to die like one of those pensioners now, Grace would fall forward onto the keys, and with her whole body make a horrendous noise, long lasting and only to be eased when someone clawed her away, stiff and dead, from her favourite instrument. That had been the death of celebrated Louis Vierne in Notre-Dame de Paris, when a heart attack forced him forward, and the blast of noise from the organ made everyone storm out of the building. Yes, that would do well here, at the university, Grace thought. That would be a happy end.

The empty cold pushed at the windows and still she fought on, burying herself in the notes, pushing at the hardest passages, urging out the music, as if she were carving out the finest piece of marble she could from heavy stone, perfecting and refining at every moment.

Yes, Grace would like to die with her music, when it was time. But it was not time yet, she had so much more to achieve before then. It was not time to bleed into the keys, here, or at Westminster

Abbey, or Notre-Dame de Paris, or whichever organ waited for her in her great future

Grace played on.

Grace had woken up anxious. She hadn't remembered how she'd got back to her room – perhaps the staves of music had transported her through the air to her window, dancing along the icicles in the air, with the wind whipping up her feet, just as she'd always hoped. No, she would have remembered that. She had vague memories of slumping along the corridor, up the stairs, exhausted and worn out. She might have even fallen down, and forced herself back up. There might have been a dog at one point, which made no sense. Had the chaplain been there too? The music must have drugged her – Grace simply couldn't remember.

Her lecture was gruelling, as if her mind were being squashed and her ears hollowed out. It was over-warm in the hall, and she blinked at the lecturer until he became a blot in front of her eyes, picking at the paper cup of hot chocolate she'd bought from the coffee machine on the way, pulling at it distractedly with her bitten fingers until the girl next to her threw her a glower. She thought perhaps she could draw out some lines on her notepad in front of her, two octaves on a paper makeshift keyboard, and practise her fingerings – but her head was splitting and she didn't want to draw any more snooping smirks than she usually received from the students around her.

Grace hadn't felt like this last time, and she didn't like it. It was a relief when the lecture drew to a slow end, and she could depart to her room. She considered the organ loft too – like hair of the dog, an alcoholic that needed more booze, a musician who only felt alive seated in front of her instrument, whose heartbeat was directly connected to the pipe system. No, Grace wouldn't go there. She'd have to be there later this afternoon, for the funeral. She didn't want to overdo it.

But as the students packed up, the lecturer announced a group project, which drained the colour from Grace's cheeks.

"Find your group," he boomed out. "I'm giving you all a bit of independence, you'll have to slot yourselves into non-designated groups of four. Good luck!"

Grace stood still as the students moved around her. She wanted to protest – she couldn't do that, she worked alone, she wasn't an orchestra. She wasn't even a string quartet, nor a duettist. She certainly wasn't a conductor, which worried her sometimes, since it often came hand in hand with organ jobs in a cathedral. No, she was purely an organist. Face into the keyboard, playing in that elevated position above and away from everyone else. Leading hymns, leading songs, underneath, above, everywhere. Like God – kneeling at the feet of what was greater than her. Because the truth was – the organ *was* the orchestra: the glittering strings, the booming brass, the steady wind, the thrusting percussion – it was the king of all instruments.

She sifted out of the lecture hall after everyone else, telling herself that they'd spot the numbers, one group would be short, and someone would approach her to join them. Just not today, she thought, not today.

In a short flash of memory she saw the little dog again, puppy eyes looking at her. She blinked them away and pressed on, pushing out of the doors and into the cold, bitter, welcome air.

Grace was annoyed now, more than distressed – she had in mind to refuse the group work. She was cleverer than all of her peers, and hated sharing her energy; wasting it, rather. Perhaps she could talk to the professor, persuade him otherwise. She was quite sure he liked her, and had once recommended a book on composers' deaths, which made her hesitate, but then bloom with gladness, that he might recognise and accept that she liked the more morbid side of things. In a way the professor reminded her of her grandfather, the better parts. There had been a glint in his eye, so slight but so much there that she darted away, embarrassed, even though part of her was hoping he'd invite her over to his room and pass on musical anecdotes over a cup of tea, a glass of brandy, or even a sweet thing he might have set aside for special occasions. She'd heard he did that with the older students, and she wanted the same, or better – she wanted preference. Not sexual or anything – Grace wasn't switched on like that – what she really wanted was to drink in all the intellect and pick as many brains as she could while at university.

She'd go to the library, then, to look up the book. She'd take small refuge in the towering shelves, the falling stacks, the short tabled alcoves to tuck into, her favourite being the one at the furthest end away from the scattered and overcurious students. She could find that book and sit with it for an hour, or two, bury herself and come up again. Yes, all of that should clear her eyes and clear her head.

And then, the funeral. Grace would take her time to prepare, in the ritual she usually followed. She'd wash, scrub at her face, rinse her hair through, rub herself down, and change. Change into a smart shirt and her new embroidered waistcoat. Ready for the Widor, ready for the crowd. The anticipation beat at her, she wanted her performance to be good. She needed it to be great.

The Widor went brilliantly. The watching eyes of the congregation lifted in admiration and the crowd stayed to listen long after the coffin processed out, apparently forgetting why they were there. Grace brimmed with smiles as she played her glittering piece to its wonderful end.

She couldn't tell if she was thrilled by the music or by the news of another death the night before.

Several minutes later, Grace trod across the flagstones under the archways and directly through the open doors into the picture gallery. The long hall-like room, a mirror image in shape to the chapel, was now bursting with well-wishers and their chirpy talk. Grace wanted to attribute their good spirits to her excellent playing, but even she had to begrudge that Francesca Marney must have been very popular within the old people's community. She'd never seen so many of them all together – indeed the chapel had been packed.

Grace glanced over their heads. The brightly lit gallery was bedecked with enormous landscapes and portraits; her eyes caught on a painting of a row of exotic-looking women waiting to be sold at a slave market, then a frame of two polar bears roaring at each other over a ship's wreckage, and then the very famous portrait of the two young princes in the dark waiting to be taken to the tower.

All of them rather sinister, Grace thought, as they seemed to drive hard at her eye. The long frame-heavy walls were rimmed with cordons while at the far end a long table stood bearing food and drinks. Grace frowned; the trays were already being pilfered by the guests, she wanted her fair share.

She wouldn't normally stay for the reception after a funeral, but the news had drawn her there. Grace couldn't believe there had been another death among these dear old pensioners, it almost made her want to chuckle. It was so bold, to do them so close together – so ridiculously obvious. Surely now the authorities would come running? Four now, the notes in an arpeggio. Perhaps the number might even grow to eight, an octave.

The guests were buzzing with it, appalled, curious, and surprised. Grace had decided to observe the chaplain from a safe distance to see if he was behaving any differently, if he met her hard stare. She needed more information, and she was going to get it. Grace couldn't help but scoff as she made her way through the crowd towards the food table – she'd already spied a delicious-looking cake slice.

"Grace?" An old man with rheumy eyes stopped her as she reached for a plate. "What a piece – just a stunning addition to your repertoire."

"Oh, thank you… Mr Rose, isn't it?" Grace answered, beaming.

"Yes it is. You quite outshone dear Francesca. Did you know there's a lord here? He wants to speak to you about a performance or other in his local church, I believe."

Grace raised her eyebrows with surprise, and delight. "Well, it'll depend on the quality of the organ."

The old man's face creased in hilarity and Grace smiled too, even though she wasn't joking.

"We are so lucky to be surrounded by such talent," Mr Rose carried on. "It's lovely to be near the university and pop over for concerts. And lovely now that we're getting into Christmas music."

"Yes it's a lovely time of year. I love the choir," squeaked an elderly woman at his elbow, who Grace didn't quite recognise, "they were particularly good this summer, I thought. I just adored the Mozart's *Requiem*."

Grace continued smiling.

"Yes, they are good," gave Mr Rose as he turned to the woman. "Do you know Grace, Florence? She's the organist, she's darling, and the only one who talks to us fuddy-duddies. Grace, this is my wife Florence."

"Oh!" Grace smirked. "No, aha. Good to meet you, Mrs Rose."

"When's your next recital? I shall put it in the diary."

"It's not arranged yet." Grace tilted her head with a wince. "I need to fill out my repertoire otherwise it'll be much of the same."

"We don't mind that, do we, Roger?" said the old woman with a nudge at her husband.

"Grace works terribly hard," Mr Rose said kindly. "Aren't you doing your ARCO training? How is that going?"

"It's all right, thank you. I need to work on the theory side of things."

The conversation was starting to bore her, and Grace couldn't help glancing beyond the shoulders of the couple at the chaplain, who was staring at her in the same way she'd like to stare at him. No doubt he was wondering what she was saying about him, what ripe pieces of information she could expose to bring his treachery to light. Her shoe bag knocked against her thigh, and she steadied herself. Grace had to admit that the chaplain made her nervous.

"So sad about poor Mr Clifford, isn't it?" Grace blurted out to the pair.

The Roses looked at each other a little regretfully, so Grace took the opportunity to scoop up a slice of carrot cake and cram it into her mouth. The crumbs fell down her chest as her fingers clung to the icing. She didn't have a napkin.

"Terribly sad business," Mr Rose finally said, turning back to Grace. "Poor old Harold. I don't know what to make of it. We're dropping like flies."

"Not just that, he's got no family," Mrs Rose added sadly. "What on earth will come of his things? He made no plans, apparently. And his poor dog."

"Wretched dog," Mr Rose declared.

Grace considered as she chewed. She knew Harold Clifford's house – she knew where all of them lived, seeing them so often. Yes, she knew the dog too, she'd noticed the little walks Mr Clifford had taken across the campus grounds, alone with his pet. Grace wondered whether she should offer to take the dog, but couldn't possibly keep it in her turret room – and he might eat all her sweets. She frowned at the old couple as she swallowed.

A voice came up behind Grace and she started forward, almost dropping what remained of her cake. "Terribly sad business, yes – and it's all very dodgy, if you ask me. Why would he suddenly fall? Never fell once in his life, or his old age."

Grace swung her face around to meet a greying old man,

pushing on a walking stick, leaning too far forward, and gazing into her face.

"They say it might have been the dog, Gerard," Mrs Rose offered weakly.

"Gerard," Mr Rose intervened, "let me introduce you to Grace, she's our organist here at the university. Be civil now."

"I'm sure I shall be. Yes, I recognise you, wot?" The man screwed up his face at Grace. "How long have we got you then?"

"*Got* me?" Grace asked darkly. She didn't recognise the man, and she didn't like him at all. His accent and his silk pocket square placed him as very grand, too grand for their little community.

"How long until you graduate?" the old fellow demanded.

"Another year after this one."

"You look remarkably well-kept. Your scholarship must be generous?"

"I get by," Grace answered, her voice heating up with irritation. She threw the kindly Mr Rose a glance.

He responded by saying, "Yes, Grace works very hard. She's hoping for the Royal Academy, or a cathedral job."

"Yes, perpetually up there in the organ loft." The other old man stomped his foot as he spoke. "Looking down on us all, wot?"

"Not really," Grace answered simply, "I'm just doing my best."

"Ye-es… must be nice pocket money, all this," Gerard said, wiggling his walking stick as Grace grimaced at him, "for the average student. All these funerals…" He leaned forward. "We keep seeing each other, you must be raking it in."

Grace looked at the man, this Gerard, his round eyes narrowed but bright with his pushing questions. Too many questions. Perhaps he was just bored, or had watched too many Miss Marples – you never knew with these old folk. The answer was always more obvious than you expected, Grace knew that. But he had that stare too, identical to that of the chaplain, who still gazed at her from the other side of the room. What was worse – this Gerard, and the turn of his mouth, reminded her of her grandfather. The bad parts.

"Do you live nearby then?" Grace asked.

"Oh, wouldn't you like to know?" Gerard answered with a dry laugh.

Grace didn't like it. In the next moment she forced out a smile, before bowing her head minutely at Mr and Mrs Rose. And with another scoop of cake, she made to leave.

Grace closed the door, relieved. Her room greeted her warmly; the light was coming through the windows, and for a moment Grace thought it was no longer winter. She added the money – the handsome funeral payment – to the rest in her small wooden chest, bending to pull at it from under her bed. Beside the chest were her second pair of organ shoes, still in their box, and the two fabric suits she'd already got, resting quietly in their packaging. The third suit that matched her embroidered waistcoat would be a wonderful addition. She'd wait until January, a Christmas present to herself.

It was time to celebrate, even if her heart was hammering. Grace knew how to cheer herself up – she unearthed her paper bag stash of sugar sweets, and pulled at the topmost one, but her hands were still shaking.

The little dog's face appeared in her mind again, and she closed her eyes to be rid of it. She didn't like the way the animal had looked at her last night as she'd pushed Mr Clifford down the stairs, how it had whined and nudged at his master crumpled on the floor, wanting and urging him to get up. Grace must make sure that next time there weren't any pets – she'd been foolish to forget. There had been something awful about stepping over Mr Clifford's body and letting herself out while the little dog trailed after her, as if wanting some explanation. She couldn't very well kill the dog too – then it certainly wouldn't have seemed like an accident. And in some irony, it seemed that the dog might now be taking the blame. It was strange how things worked out in Grace's favour. After all, she was only playing.

Fancy that man, Gerard, asking her those questions. Perhaps he could be next. Yes, she'd appreciate the payout for his funeral, serve him right for throwing his bonkers accusations at her. She'd very much enjoy using his obvious wealth to purchase another item to adorn herself with, to love herself, to cherish and celebrate her skills and musical power. But if she was following a pattern, shouldn't it be a woman? Grace wasn't sure. Gerard, or not Gerard?

Another thought had been growing carefully in her mind – the others, the blonde-haloed girls, the disapproving student beside her in the lecture hall. If it were to be them, would their funerals be held here? Not likely, Grace thought, she should stick to what she knew.

Grace took another sweet, making a mental note to buy those rhubarb and custard ones again. Of course she realised that she should be saving for her future funding besides the organ scholarship, for the postgrad course at the Royal Academy, for any job at a cathedral further down the line.

But Grace couldn't help it, she liked treating herself. She liked playing. It was amazing what you could get used to, she thought, how automatic terrible things can become.

ABOUT THE AUTHORS

KATE WEINBERG's debut novel *The Truants* was named a *New York Times* Top 10 crime novel of 2020. It was also Book of the Year in *USA Today*, *The Observer*, a Top 10 Golden Age Detective novel in *The Guardian*, and an *Irish Times* Debut of the Year. It is currently being adapted for TV. She has written widely for national newspapers, as well as *Electric Lit* and CrimeReads, presented a radio show for BBC Radio 4, and produced her own podcast of author interviews, *Shelf Help*. Her latest novel, *There's Nothing Wrong with Her* was published in August 2024.

OLIVIE BLAKE is the *New York Times* bestselling author of *The Atlas Six* and *Alone with You in the Ether*. As Alexene Farol Follmuth, she is also the author of the young adult rom-com *My Mechanical Romance*. She lives in Los Angeles with her husband, goblin prince/toddler, and rescue pit bull.

JAMES TATE HILL is the author of a memoir, *Blind Man's Bluff*, a *New York Times* Editors' Choice and a Washington Independent Review of Books Favorite Book of 2021. His fiction debut, *Academy Gothic*, won the Nilsen Literary Prize for a First Novel. He serves as fiction editor for *Monkeybicycle* and contributing editor at Literary Hub, where he writes an audiobooks column.

KELLY ANDREW lives outside of Boston with her husband, two daughters, and a pernickety Boston Terrier. She has a Bachelor's in Social Work, but received her Master's in English & Creative Writing. When she's not writing she enjoys obsessing over a good book, soaking up family time, warming herself in various toasty lodges while her husband skis, and getting intentionally lost in the woods.

J. T. ELLISON is the *New York Times* and *USA Today* bestselling author of more than twenty-five novels, and the EMMY®-award winning co-host of the literary TV show *A Word on Words*. She also writes urban fantasy under the pen name Joss Walker. With millions of books in print, her work has won critical acclaim and prestigious awards. Her titles have been optioned for television and published in twenty-eight countries. J. T. lives with her husband and twin kittens in Nashville, where she is hard at work on her next novel. Visit jtellison.com for more information or follow her @thrillerchick.

LAYNE FARGO is the author of the novels *They Never Learn* and *Temper*, and co-author of the bestselling Audible Original series

Young Rich Widows. She lives in Chicago with a rescue pit bull and cat who are best friends, and the only man she never wants to murder (well, almost never). When she's not plotting twisted stories, she enjoys long walks in the local cemetery, binging trashy TV shows, and spending all her money at independent bookstores.

DAVID BELL is the *New York Times* bestselling author of sixteen novels, including his most recent books *Try Not to Breathe* and *She's Gone.* He is a professor of Creative Writing at Western Kentucky University in Bowling Green, KY, where he lives with his wife, YA author M. Hendrix. David can be reached through his website davidbellnovels.com.

SUSIE YANG was born in Chongqing, China and came to the United States as a child. After receiving her Doctorate of Pharmacy from Rutgers, she launched a startup in San Francisco to teach people how to code. Her debut novel, *White Ivy*, was an instant *New York Times* bestseller. She has lived across the United States, Europe, and Asia, and now resides in Seattle.

M. L. RIO is a recovering actor turned academic. She holds an MA in Shakespeare Studies from King's College London and Shakespeare's Globe. She is a PhD candidate at the University of Maryland and lives in Washington, DC.

HELEN GRANT has a passion for the Gothic and for ghost stories; Joyce Carol Oates has described her as "a brilliant chronicler of the uncanny as only those who dwell in places of dripping, graylit beauty can be". Her eighth novel *Too Near the Dead* won the Dracula Society's Children of the Night Award 2021. She lives in Perthshire, Scotland with her family, and when not writing, she likes to explore abandoned country houses and swim in freezing lochs.

TORI BOVALINO is the author of *The Devil Makes Three*, *Not Good for Maidens*, and edited the Indie-bestselling anthology, *The Gathering Dark*. She is originally from Pittsburgh, Pennsylvania and now lives in the UK with her partner and their very loud cat. Tori loves scary stories, obscure academic book facts, and impractical, oversized sweaters.

PHOEBE WYNNE is the author of *Madam* and *The Ruins*. She worked in education for nearly a decade and taught Classics in the UK and English Language and Literature in Paris. She left the classroom to focus on her writing, and went on to hone her craft in the writing rooms of Los Angeles and London. She is British and French, and currently splits her time between France and England.

ABOUT THE EDITORS

MARIE O'REGAN is a British Fantasy Award and Shirley Jackson Award-nominated author and editor, based in Derbyshire. She was awarded the British Fantasy Society Legends of FantasyCon Award in 2022. Her first collection, *Mirror Mere*, was published in 2006 by Rainfall Books; her second, *In Times of Want*, came out in September 2016 from Hersham Horror Books. Her third, *The Last Ghost and Other Stories*, was published by Luna Press early in 2019. Her short fiction has appeared in a number of genre magazines and anthologies in the UK, US, Canada, Italy, and Germany, including *Best British Horror 2014*, *Great British Horror: Dark Satanic Mills* (2017), and *The Mammoth Book of Halloween Stories*. Her novella, *Bury Them Deep*, was published by Hersham Horror Books in September 2017. She was shortlisted for the British Fantasy Society Award for Best Short Story in 2006, Best Anthology in 2010 (*Hellbound Hearts*) and 2012 (*The Mammoth Book of Ghost Stories by Women*). She was also shortlisted for the Shirley Jackson Award for Best Anthology in 2020 (*Wonderland*). Her genre journalism has appeared in magazines like *The Dark Side, Rue Morgue,* and *Fortean Times*, and her interview book with prominent figures from the horror genre, *Voices in the Dark*, was released in 2011. An essay on "The Changeling" was published in PS Publishing's *Cinema Macabre*, edited by Mark Morris. She is co-editor of the bestselling *Hellbound Hearts, The Mammoth Book of Body Horror, A Carnivàle of Horror: Dark Tales from the Fairground, Exit Wounds, Wonderland,* and *Cursed*, as well as the charity anthology *Trickster's Treats #3*, plus editor of the bestselling anthologies *The Mammoth Book of Ghost Stories by Women* and *Phantoms*. Her first novel, the internationally bestselling *Celeste*, was published in February 2022. Marie was Chair of the British Fantasy Society from 2004 to 2008, and Co-chair of the UK chapter of the Horror Writers Association from 2015 to 2022. She was also Co-chair of ChillerCon UK in 2022. Visit her website at marieoregan.net. She can be found on Twitter @Marie_O_Regan and Instagram @marieoregan8101.

PAUL KANE is the award-winning (including the British Fantasy Society's Legends of FantasyCon Award 2022), bestselling author and editor of over a hundred books – such as the Arrowhead trilogy (gathered together in the sellout *Hooded Man* omnibus, revolving around a post-apocalyptic version of Robin Hood), *The Butterfly Man and Other Stories, Hellbound Hearts, Wonderland* (a Shirley Jackson Award finalist), and *Pain Cages* (an Amazon #1 Bestseller). His non-fiction books include *The Hellraiser Films and Their Legacy* and *Voices in the Dark*, and his genre journalism has appeared in the likes of *SFX, Rue Morgue,* and *DeathRay*. He has been a Guest at Alt.Fiction five times, was a Guest at the first SFX Weekender, at Thought Bubble in 2011, Derbyshire Literary Festival and Off the Shelf in 2012, Monster Mash and Event Horizon in 2013, Edge-Lit in 2014 and 2018, HorrorCon, HorrorFest, and Grimm Up North in 2015, The Dublin Ghost Story Festival and Sledge-Lit in 2016, IMATS Olympia and Celluloid Screams in 2017, Black Library Live and the UK Ghost Story Festival in 2019, plus the WordCrafter virtual event in 2021 – where he delivered the keynote speech – as well as being a panellist at FantasyCon and the World Fantasy Convention, and a fiction judge at the Sci-Fi-London festival. A former British Fantasy Society Special Publications Editor, he has also served as Co-chair for the UK chapter of the Horror Writers Association and co-chaired ChillerCon UK in May 2022.

His work has been optioned and adapted for the big and small screen, including for US network primetime television, and his novelette "Men of the Cloth" has just been turned into a feature by Loose Canon/Hydra Films, starring Barbara Crampton (*Re-Animator, You're Next*), *Sacrifice*, released by Epic Pictures/101 Films. His audio work includes the full cast drama adaptation of *The Hellbound Heart* for Bafflegab, starring Tom Meeten (*The Ghoul*), Neve McIntosh (*Doctor Who*), and Alice Lowe (*Prevenge*), and the *Robin of Sherwood* adventure, *The Red Lord*, for Spiteful Puppet/ITV, narrated by Ian Ogilvy (*Return of the Saint*). He has also contributed to the Warhammer 40,000 universe for Games Workshop. Paul's latest novels are *Lunar* (set to be turned into a feature film), the YA story *The Rainbow Man* (as P. B. Kane), the sequels to *RED* – *Blood RED* and *Deep RED* – the award-winning hit *Sherlock Holmes and the Servants of Hell*, *Before* (an Amazon

Top 5 dark fantasy bestseller), *Arcana*, and *The Storm*. In addition he writes thrillers for HQ/HarperCollins as P. L. Kane, the first of which, *Her Last Secret* and *Her Husband's Grave* (a sellout on both Amazon and Waterstones.com), came out in 2020, with *The Family Lie* released the following year. Paul lives in Derbyshire, UK, with his wife Marie O'Regan. Find out more at his site shadow-writer. co.uk which has featured Guest Writers such as Stephen King, Neil Gaiman, Charlaine Harris, Robert Kirkman, Dean Koontz, and Guillermo del Toro. He can also be found @PaulKaneShadow on Twitter, and paul.kane.376 on Instagram.

ACKNOWLEDGEMENTS

And now for the important bit – our opportunity to say thank you. Firstly to all the authors for their contributions, to Sophie Robinson, Louise Pearce and all of the team at Titan Books for their support and tireless efforts on our behalf, as always. Finally, thanks to our respective families, without whom etc.

For more fantastic fiction, author events,
exclusive excerpts, competitions, limited editions and more

VISIT OUR WEBSITE
titanbooks.com

LIKE US ON FACEBOOK
facebook.com/titanbooks

FOLLOW US ON TWITTER AND INSTAGRAM
@TitanBooks

EMAIL US
readerfeedback@titanemail.com